Dedication

To Spock and Sherlock Holmes, who said, "When you have eliminated the impossible, whatever remains, however improbable, must be the truth." – Sir Arthur Conan Doyle, The Sign of the Four

Acknowledgements

Thank you to Judith Pittman and BWL Publishing Inc. for publishing this fourth book of my Paula Savard mystery series and to my editors Nancy Bell, Erin Celovsky, Victoria Chatham, and Rachel Small for understanding my story and making it better.

Thanks to Will Arnold, Maryann Breukelman, Allan Coates, Deborah Donnelly, Jean Humphreys, and Bernice Pyke, who generously read my novel-in-progress and offered advice and support. To Detective Dave Sweet, for giving me a tour of Calgary Police Service Headquarters – Westwinds and answering my numerous questions about police work. Any errors are mine.

The following books provided insight into my novel's subject matter: *Death in Mud Lick* by Eric Eyre (Scribner, 2020), *Overdose: Heartbreak and Hope in Canada's Opioid Crisis* by Benjamin Perrin (Viking, Penguin Canada, 2022), and *The Age of Fentanyl: Ending the Opioid Epidemic* by Brodie Ramin, M.D. (Dundurn Press, 2020).

I thank my good fortune to have the love and encouragement of a wonderful family: Will, Dan, Matt, Anne, and Vivienne.

Finally, thanks to *Spring Into Danger's* four narrators: Paula, Mike, Isabelle, and Novak. I couldn't write this series without you.

Chapter One

Paula Savard missed her colleagues. She wished she and her boss hadn't been forced to let one go, but their insurance adjusting business was drying up. Her remaining two colleagues had opted to work from home when Calgary shut down over five weeks ago to curb the spread of the COVID-19 virus. If the pandemic dragged into summer, Paula doubted their company would survive.

A message appeared in her email inbox, subject line *New Claim.* There'd been a break and enter at a bicycle store, discovered this morning. *Detective Mike Vincelli recommended we assign you the claim*, the insurance agent wrote. *Interested?*

That explained Mike's phone call and request to drop by her office on his way home from police headquarters. He'd arrive in about twenty minutes.

Paula opened the attached police report. Thieves had broken into Cycle Life after it closed the previous night. They'd made off with two electric bicycles and numerous bike accessories. No injuries noted, no staff on the premises at the time. The owner's attached statement confirmed the police details.

Why was Homicide involved? More importantly, why would Mike involve her? She'd told him she was finished with suspicious death cases. Mike had said he understood.

Paula left her cubicle and crossed the reception area to the kitchenette to make a fresh carafe of coffee. Even though she'd washed her hands when she arrived at work and hadn't come close to another human since then, Paula gave her fingers and palms a thorough scrub, humming "Happy Birthday" twice, which her mother had nagged her do when she was a child.

Happy birthday to you.

Paula's fifty-sixth birthday was next Tuesday, and she was supposed to be in Germany with her partner, staying in a castle hotel and touring fairy-tale-esque German towns. She'd also planned to spend two weeks in Hamburg, where Sam had moved for work, to see if she would like living there part of the year. He'd started his new job with a European architecture firm weeks before the virus shut down the world. Now they were stuck an ocean and two half-continents apart.

Paula dried her hands and then exchanged the towel for a clean one for Mike. The ever-changing health protocols bugged her sometimes. According to the current rules, they shouldn't be meeting inside since Mike wasn't in her "household bubble." Less than two months ago, she hadn't known what that term meant.

She set the coffee machine to brew. As she passed the reception desk on her way back to her cubicle, she heard the entrance doorbell ring. Mike's voice came through the intercom, his words garbled by static. She buzzed him in and went to the outer hallway to greet him. Footsteps sounded on the lower staircase. This was Mike's first visit to her company's office in Inglewood. He'd only been to their former premises, in Calgary's East Village. That boxy, 1960s building had been torn down and replaced by a retail-and-condo complex with lots of glass.

Mike's head appeared above the staircase railing. He reached the landing, passed the doors of the real estate and optometry offices, and stopped more than the requisite two metres from her. Thirty-six years old and six foot four, Mike was dressed in a blue suit—his detective clothes. Paula hadn't seen him since February, when they were unaware of COVID-19's impact. Now, his dark hair grew shaggily over his ears, thanks to the barbershop closures.

He glanced at the outer door to her office. On it was a plaque that read Nils van der Vliet Insurance Adjusters Inc. "How do you like your new location?"

"We've been here almost three years." She followed his gaze up to the scalloped mouldings that underlined the twelve-foot ceilings. "It's got more character than our old place."

"The date on this building says it was constructed in 1911." He stepped a half metre closer. "Is that a new scarf you're wearing?"

Paula looked down at the silk scarf loosely knotted around her neck. "My mother gave it to me for Christmas." Odd. Mike had never commented on her clothing before.

He squinted at the scarf. "Are those butterflies?"

She lifted a silk tail and peered at the orange, yellow, and green designs. "Flowers, with some butterflies flitting around. Why do you ask?"

He turned toward the door. "How about we start with the grand tour?"

Typical of Mike to hold off on explanations until he was ready. She ushered him inside and stopped at the reception desk, which had been stripped clean aside from the intercom system.

"You didn't meet Connor, our office administrator," she said, conscious of the sadness in her voice. "We hired him after the move. Great at his job, but we couldn't keep him on after COVID hit, even with the help of government programs."

"Not enough car crashes?" Mike's lip twitched into an almost-smile. "I got here faster than I expected with the minimal traffic."

She grimaced. "Morbidly, whiplash claims are our bread and butter. Since the shutdown, the insurance companies can handle them all in-house. The bike theft is the first new claim we've had all week." She stared up at him. "Why did you recommend me?"

Mike started. "You know about that?"

"The agent emailed me."

His lips tightened. "I told him to wait until after I'd talked with you."

"He didn't." She drummed the desk with her fingers. "The reports didn't mention a death, suspicious or not."

"There isn't one."

"Then why is it a homicide case?"

"It's not, yet. What's next on the tour?" He looked over her shoulder.

She'd learned it was futile to press Mike. "The closer cubicle is mine." She gestured in its direction. "Nils has the farther one. In our old place, I could close my office door, but I got used to tuning the sounds out. Now I don't have to with Nils, Isabelle, and Connor gone." She explained they'd chosen an open plan to let light into the reception area. Their only windows faced north, behind the cubicles. Today was especially gloomy with the clouds outside. She pointed out Isabelle's desk, behind Connor's. "Isabelle's taken over administration in addition to her telephone adjusting, which has become video adjusting from her home."

"The world moves on," Mike said.

She led him past the portable room dividers beside Isabelle's desk to the mahogany table and chairs. "Nils calls this our board room, but we mainly use it for lunch. All winter, when business was booming, I nagged him to hire an intermediate adjuster to relieve our workload. The plan was to push the board room toward the file cabinet wall to make space for a new desk. For once, Nils's procrastination paid off. The adjuster would be another person to let go."

Rather than dwell on that dreary thought, she continued to the kitchenette and told Mike to fill his own mug. "Seems my mum was right all along about sanitation. Kind of annoying."

He met her smile. "How is your mother?"

"Good, and I want to keep it that way."

His face sobered. Paula sensed he'd caught her meaning—she would no longer welcome claims that put her family, friends, and colleagues at risk.

Their mugs filled, she suggested they sit in the "board room." Mike took the chair with a view to the outer door. She sat across the table, facing the wall of filing cabinets. The wall behind the table's head chair featured the office's sole piece of art, a sketch of Lloyd's Coffee House circa 1688, where modern insurance began.

Mike took a sip of coffee and set his mug on the table. "This morning I got a call from a man who'd read a news report about the break and enter. He had a premonition."

Startled, Paula spewed a few drops of coffee, but Mike's expression was serious. "What report? I scrolled through the news around noon and didn't see this."

"A small item, online. I found it after he called." Mike stroked his mug handle. "Gabriel phones me every few months or so about some case that's in the news. This one's different, not being a homicide."

She tried not to smirk. "Gabriel, like the angel?"

"I doubt it's his real name. I looked him up but couldn't find him on social media."

"You do get your share of crank and kook calls."

Mike nodded. "That's probably what he is, but I always listen."

"Why?"

Mike picked up his mug. "You never know what strange rock will turn up the key that cracks open a case." His face darkened. Paula chalked it up to the waning daylight.

"Have any of Gabriel's 'premonitions' panned out in the past?"

Mike squinted, as though reflecting. "Some have come close, or his details were inspired guesses." He hesitated. "This time his premonition points to you. At least, I think it does. It also involves the future more than the present and past."

"How does this relate to the bike store break and enter?"

He sipped again. "Gabriel had a vision of a woman he sensed I worked with, possibly a police civilian employee. She had blue eyes, wavy dark brown hair, was in her fifties."

Paula touched her hair. "Lots of women have my colouring."

"None your approximate age who work in Major Crimes, including support staff."

"You actually checked?" she said. "I can't believe you went to this effort."

His jaw quivered, presumably at her implied criticism. "There were too many civilian staff to check. But Gabriel said the woman wore a scarf with a butterfly design."

Paula fingered the scarf on her chest. "That's why you noticed the butterflies." She lifted the tail for a view. "There really are more flowers."

"His vision came with an urgency. He said I must work with this woman to prevent a death."

Paula's arms prickled despite her belief that this was nonsense. If they paused to get more coffee, she'd grab her sweater from her cubicle. She'd told the building owner to turn off the heat, since she was the only person working in the old building that had trouble getting the temperature right in spring. "Whose death?"

"I gather Gabriel's vision stopped there." Mike glanced at her neck. "I can't say I consciously recalled you wearing that particular scarf, but it struck me that you wore them."

"Most women do, Mike. And floral designs are common."

"But butterflies."

"They tend to hang around flowers. Gabriel came up with generic details that were bound to describe a few women among the hundreds who work with the police. The scarf was a lucky guess."

"Probably."

She shook her head. She'd never seen this side of Mike. "I can't believe you're this superstitious."

He shrugged. "I was raised Catholic. Is this less credible than water into wine? People raised from the dead? Parting of the seas?"

"All with scientific explanations."

He wrapped his hands around his mug and leaned forward. "Paula, I completely respect your decision to steer clear of cases that might endanger your loved ones."

Paula looked at Isabelle's vacated desk. In January, three months ago, she'd put her junior adjuster and her own brother at risk when she pursued a suspicious death case. And Paula's actions on a claim almost three years ago had endangered her daughter. Now, her mother was living with her and could become collateral damage if a killer tracked Paula to her home. "But there's no death in this break and enter case," she said.

"None we know of, so far."

"The only reason to think there might be is this premonition by Gabriel, a self-described psychic?"

Mike stroked his mug. "You said yourself business is slow. This is work."

She studied his deadpan expression. "Are you using the vision to manipulate me into this?"

"Not intentionally," he said. "I wanted to give you the choice to say yes or no. You like to help others."

"You mean by preventing an unlikely death?"

Mike's brow knit. "I don't believe this, necessarily. Call it a hunch, if you prefer. In addition to the future aspect, there was something different about Gabriel's call this time. I can't put my finger on it."

Paula had always trusted Mike's hunches, which meant she should turn down the claim—there would likely be risk involved. But this time, it would feel like giving in to superstition. "I'll think about it."

"Fair enough," he said. "Since this isn't a homicide case—it will be handled by the district office—your decision suits me either way."

"I'll let the agent know before I go home."

"On that note, I should get going." He drained his coffee mug.

"If nothing else, Gabriel gave you the excuse to drop by." Paula smiled. Losing contact with Mike had been one of her regrets after she had decided to give up dangerous claims. She'd come to think of him as a friend, but they'd always met in connection with work.

Once he'd left, she washed the dishes and pondered the situation for a few minutes. Really, there was no logical reason to turn down easy work.

Decision made, she emailed the agent, copying Mike, and scrolled through the reports to find the store's phone number. Since it was probably closed, she'd have to leave a message. To her surprise, someone answered.

Paula explained who she was and offered to set up a video meeting with the man who'd introduced himself as Josh. "Are you familiar with RingCentral? It's similar to Zoom and Skype."

"Or you can come to the store," Josh said. "It's not too hectic first thing in the morning."

"Are you open?"

"Sure. We fixed the broken window and were back in business by noon."

"I meant, isn't your store closed for the pandemic?"

"Bikes are considered essential. We're transportation," he said. "Would nine a.m. work for you?"

In person was always better for assessing damages and claimants. While Paula had to take care not to pass the virus on to her eighty-two-year-old mother, the claimant's upbeat tone made the prospect of human contact appealing. Mike's visit had perhaps whetted her interest in seeing people again. She agreed to the time and hung up.

Next, she called Isabelle on RingCentral to have her set up a file for the new claim. Isabelle had switched on her favourite backdrop, which made it look as if she sat in a downtown-tower corner office, the snow-covered Rocky Mountains glowing in the distance through the virtual window behind her. Her blonde hair kept merging into the backdrop.

"Awesome," Isabelle said. "It's a sign work is picking up."

Paula decided not to tell her the claim had arrived via psychic vision. The explanation would take time, and she didn't want to be late for dinner. As she outlined the basics of the case, Isabelle disappeared momentarily when she shifted on her chair, reminding Paula of the ghost rumoured to inhabit their office building. Isabelle was both fascinated and frightened by another tenant's stories of spectral beings and unexplained creaks and groans.

Old buildings always creaked and groaned. Since Paula had started working here alone, she'd noticed the sounds that the whirr of office machinery and her colleagues' conversations had masked before.

She wrapped up the call with Isabelle, tidied her desk, and stuffed the business' mail in her briefcase. Nils had requested that she deliver the mail and some supplies to his house after work.

Something thumped in the hallway. Had a tenant come in to pick up items needed for work at home? The building's owner had asked Paula to keep an eye on the premises. She went out to the landing. No one there. She leaned over the railing and looked down the curved staircase to the ground level, and then up to the third and fourth floors. No person that she could see, no old plaster or light fixture had fallen to the stairs. She listened. No creaks or groans. Silence.

* * *

In her home office, Isabelle Lansing typed the details of the bike store break and enter into the company forms. Before COVID, Paula would have assigned this claim to her, but Paula said Isabelle was busy enough now doing Connor's old work on top of her own. Actually, she wasn't, Isabelle realized now. She started to email Paula to say she could easily handle the claim, when she got a call on Skype.

Isabelle answered, and Connor's head filled the screen against a background of the Colosseum. He wore his black-frame glasses. Her friend's beard had grown from patchy to bushy since she'd talked to him a few days ago.

"What's up?" he said.

"Isn't it the middle of the night in Rome?"

"I'm still messed up from the jet lag."

"After almost three weeks?"

"It takes time."

His transition lenses had darkened slightly. His rental apartment must have a bright light. During their previous calls, Isabelle had caught occasional glimpses of a kitchen when he switched backgrounds. What could she say to interest her former co-worker?

"We got a new claim," she said.

He sat upright. "That's great. What's it about? Are you handling it?"

"Paula is. A simple break and enter. If we get more, they might be able to hire you back."

"Even if I wanted to leave Rome, there's no planes." Despite the grounding of most international travel, Connor had managed to find a complicated route to Rome. His trip from Calgary had taken a couple of days. Isabelle supposed it was no wonder he was still jet-lagged. "What did the break and enter involve?" he asked.

She waved off his question, wanting to hear about Rome. "Have you been to the Colosseum?"

He shook his head. "It's closed, but I went to the Vatican Museums today. Usually they're packed, but I had the place almost to myself with the tourists gone. A guy snuck in a skateboard and zoomed down the corridor with Raphael paintings. His girlfriend videoed him."

"Cool."

A cat leaped in front of Connor, covering his face, then it turned and stared at Isabelle.

"Finnegan," Isabelle blurted.

Connor shoved the cat aside. "She's home in Calgary. This is a stray I let in."

Isabelle squinted at the screen. "It looks exactly like Finnegan." Connor's neighbour was looking after Finnegan while he was away.

"They're both a calico-tabby mix. That's why I felt sorry for this one when she howled outside my apartment. Rome has tons of feral cats. They miss the scraps these days, with no tourists and everyone else staying home."

The cat with orange-white-and-black fur nudged Connor's cheek. With its head turned sideways, Isabelle couldn't tell if this cat had Finnegan's characteristic tabby *M* on its forehead. Connor and his brother, Gabe, had rescued Finnegan from the cold this winter.

"Any news about Gabe?" Isabelle asked.

Connor shook his head. "I should have stayed home until he got back."

Two days before Connor was due to leave, his brother had stormed out of their apartment. Connor had been hassling him about his drug use. Gabe didn't answer any of Connor's phone calls after that. When Connor debated cancelling the trip, Isabelle reminded him that Gabe had disappeared for a few days at a time before. Connor suspected Gabe dealt drugs to support his addiction.

The feral cat hissed at the screen and clawed the air.

"You should report Gabe missing," Isabelle said.

"No."

The cat hissed again, seeming to support Connor's conviction. Isabelle was almost sure she saw an M shape in the cat's forehead fur.

Connor tried to shove the cat off his lap. "What if he's hiding from his drug bosses and the cops give him away? Obviously, Gabe doesn't want to be found. My neighbour promised to let me know if there's the least sign he's been to the apartment." Connor yawned. "I gotta go crash. It's after two in the morning."

After they'd hung up, Isabelle finished setting up the new claim file, her mind often drifting to Connor's more interesting endeavours. A dude skateboarding through a classy, empty museum would be so cool to see. His girlfriend had likely posted the video. It might have gone viral by now. Isabelle Googled "Vatican Museums." The first entry said they had closed on March 9. Of course, COVID had hit Italy right after China. She checked another entry. *Closed until further notice.* She searched Videos and found none of a skateboarder in the museums.

Maybe the girlfriend hadn't posted it yet? Or Connor had heard about this happening before the museum closed and told Isabelle he'd seen it to impress her? She'd noticed him wanting to impress Paula, but Isabelle had thought she and Connor were good enough friends to be real with each other. Had he lied about going to the museum because he didn't want her to think he was depressed and doing nothing but hanging around the apartment with a feral cat?

A cat who looked exactly likely Finnegan. Isabelle had met her a few times on Skype. She'd also hissed and pawed the air. Was this "Roman" cat Finnegan? Isabelle would bet ten dollars on it. Since he'd arrived in Rome, Connor had always Skyped with a backdrop of a tourist site, which would conceal his apartment.

Connor wasn't in Rome. He was in Calgary.

Chapter Two

Paula arrived home to the aroma of shepherd's pie cooking in the oven. She set her briefcase by the coat closet and entered the kitchen that extended the length of the house. Fabric littered the dining table, and the ironing board was set up by the front window. At the side wall, her mother, Theda, sat at the sewing machine cabinet, her back to Paula. The motor whirred. When it stopped, her mother turned around on her stool.

Theda started. "Paula, I didn't hear you come in." She held up a rectangle of striped material. "How does this look?"

"That depends." Paula moved closer, between the table and ironing board. "What is it?"

"A mask, once I add the elastics for the ears. We'll all be wearing them this summer."

At grocery stores, Paula had noticed a few people wearing masks. Many experts said they didn't protect the wearer and limited the virus spread minimally, although Alberta's chief medical officer recommended wearing them when physical distancing was difficult.

Her mother rose. "My sewing group spent an hour on Zoom discussing patterns. We decided this will be our new project."

"That's good." Anything that occupied her mother during the day would reduce Paula's guilt over leaving her alone. Almost three years ago, her mother decided to move from Montreal to Calgary to be closer to her granddaughters and Paula. Since then, Theda had lived with Paula's daughter Erin, Isabelle, and their ever-changing assortment of student housemates. Her mother claimed the young people boosted her spirits. But Theda's high blood pressure and elevated blood sugar levels, along with her age, put her at high risk for complications from COVID-19, which she might catch from her youthful housemates. She and Paula agreed she'd be safer in Paula's home.

COVID-19 had also cost her mother a boyfriend due to their opposing views on how to deal with the virus—assuming David, Sam's father, was in fact more than a friend. Paula and Sam had never figured that out. And they were fine with staying in the dark.

"It's fortunate I prepared dinner before our Zoom. Since then, I've been distracted with cutting and sewing." Her mother shuffled to the table. "I'll clean up while you change."

"I'm pretty much changed now." After a week of not meeting a soul in the office, Paula now wore comfortable clothing to work instead of her usual skirts or dress pants. This morning, she'd put on jeans, a fitted T-shirt, and a cardigan. She'd added the scarf at the last minute to dress up the outfit.

She helped her mother move material, thread, and scissors to one end of the table, to make space for eating.

"These aren't the most suitable fabrics," her mother said. "I'll order more online."

Paula smiled. After eighty-two years of barely touching a computer, her mother had been thrust into the digital age by pandemic restrictions. She Skyped with Paula's brother and his children in Montreal and Zoomed with her social groups from the seniors' centre and church.

"Can you stop at a store tomorrow to buy twist ties?" her mother asked. "They're key to the masks' tight fit, until I order flexible wire."

"Sure."

Theda left the table to get the place mats and cutlery, her movements lighter than they'd been this morning. While her mother filled their glasses with water, Paula set the salad and casserole dishes on the table. She removed her scarf to avoid spills on the flowers and butterflies. "Where did you buy this scarf, Mum?"

As her mother carried the glasses to the table, Paula repeated the question. Since Theda had moved in, Paula had noticed a loss in her hearing. They'd get it checked when clinics reopened.

"At a Christmas craft fair," her mother said. "Why?"

"Mike Vincelli stopped by the office today. The scarf caught his interest."

"Mike?" Her mother's blue eyes brightened behind her glasses. She and the detective had met several times over the years and had a soft spot for each other. "How is he handling the pandemic?"

"Okay. He needs a haircut."

Her mother peered at her. "You and I could use a trim too. I've ordered a hair-cutting kit online. I'll cut Walter's hair as well, and you can do mine. It will pay for itself in a week."

Paula scanned her mother's grey curls, which were looser than usual with more length to them. "You'll need a hippie headband soon."

"Walter could use one already. He joked he'll soon be tying his hair back in a ponytail."

Her mother had also connected with Paula's next-door neighbour. Theda and Walter both benefited from daily walks together. Walter's wife was in a long-term care residence, which was under lockdown. When Walter visited his wife now, he stood outside and looked at her through the window as they talked on the phone. Paula was grateful for her mother's good health, and on the whole, she enjoyed her mother's company, especially with Sam away. She glanced at the microwave clock. It was 2:48 a.m. in Hamburg. Sam would be asleep.

Her mother sat at the table, facing the entrance hall. Paula took her usual place at the end. Sam's seat, to her right, was vacant. They scooped shepherd's pie and salad onto their plates.

"I've been thinking, Paula," her mother said. "Would Sam mind my using his studio for making masks? We'd need help moving my sewing machine up there, but it would keep my work out of your dining room."

Paula glanced over her shoulder, in the direction of the backyard and Sam's studio, which was above the garage. Paula had considered making it her home office when she turned the main floor den into a bedroom for her mother, but the studio was Sam's space. Her working there would be a reminder that their forced separation could be long. Plus, she preferred keeping her work and home life separate, and to be honest, she liked the break from her mother's presence for five or six hours each weekday. Her office building was only a ten-minute walk away, so she could come home for lunch. The walk was a rare bonus of this business shutdown. Before, she'd had to drive the short distance because she was always heading out to meet claimants or check out damage sites. Now she did most of this work online, although tomorrow, she'd need to drive to the bicycle store.

Her mother swallowed a bite of pie. "I realize Sam is protective of his studio."

A studio workplace would involve a lot of stair-climbs for her mother, but Sam had designed the room with large windows for natural lighting. It might do her mother good.

"I'll email Sam," Paula said. "I think he'll be happy to see his studio put to good use. We'll return it to its former state before he comes home."

"They predict it will be months before travel resumes."

Paula speared a tomato, fearing that "they" were right.

"So why did Mike come by your office?" her mother asked. "I thought you'd given up the dangerous work you were doing for him."

"I have. This was about a routine break and enter claim."

"People get killed in them."

"Break and enter means no threat to a person."

While they ate, Paula related the details of the break and enter, which were public knowledge. She considered leaving out the "psychic's" premonition but then went ahead and told Theda, figuring her mother would find it entertaining and wouldn't be alarmed. She often scoffed at a friend in her sewing group who planned her life around her horoscope and tarot-card readings.

But Theda paused as she listened to the story, her fork in her salad. "Did I tell you about my experience with your father's screwdriver?" she said, when Paula had finished.

If Sam had said this, Paula would've gone for a double-entendre joke. "Only that he had eighty-seven of them in his workshop garage. You counted."

Her mother rested the fork on her plate. "When he died, clearing out his workshop was overwhelming."

Paula nodded, remembering her mother's daily phone calls. Paula had told her to take her time, that there was no rush to get rid of the stuff. They hadn't parked a car in the garage for thirty years. But her mother wouldn't slow down.

"I told your father's woodworking buddies, as he called them, to take anything they wished, but they all had their own collections of tools and scrap woods they thought might come in handy one day. Between the buddies, my garage sale, and putting the true junk out on garbage day, I finally disposed of everything."

Paula had heard all this before. She'd wondered if her mother clung to the irksome task to postpone dealing with her grief. Paula's father had died fifteen years ago this spring, of a heart attack. She still missed him.

"Finally, I had time for myself," her mother continued. "I opened my sewing box and there, staring up at me from among the spools of thread, was a screwdriver. A small hex. I'd learned their names from his buddies." She paused. "After all my work, the sight of one tiny screwdriver was too much. I collapsed on the bed and cried."

This information was new to Paula. She drank some water to wash down a clump of potatoes in her throat.

Her mother stared at her, her blue eyes damp. "How did it get there?"

"Obviously you'd put in your sewing box, in the midst of all the confusion."

"Why would I do that?"

"Mum, you were exhausted. Maybe you took out some thread to sew something, had the screwdriver in your hand, and absent-mindedly placed it in the box."

Moisture spotted her mother's glasses. "I was convinced your father put it there."

"Before he died?"

"It was the kind of thing he'd do, to tease me. But he wouldn't have done it ahead of time. He didn't know he was going to die."

"His doctor said he might have had symptoms he didn't tell us about."

"He'd still believe he'd live forever, in his optimistic way." Her mother reached for a rectangle of fabric. She removed her glasses and cleaned them with the cotton cloth.

"So you're saying he put the screwdriver there afterwards, as a ghost?"

"It was his type of humour."

Paula leaned back in her chair. She'd assumed those closest to her shared her realistic view of the world. But her mother's face was solemn, as Mike's had been when he told her about Gabriel's premonition.

Her mother put her glasses back on. The lenses were smudgy. "I sensed it was your father's way of saying goodbye. After I pulled myself up from the bed, I was more at peace with his passing."

Paula placed her hand on her mother's gnarled fingers. "I understand, Mum. Believing his spirit was there helped release your grief."

"His farewell to me was a joke. Typical of him." Her mother picked up her fork.

This conversation was heading down a weird path. Paula steered to different subject. "What would you say to having the kids over for dinner on the weekend?"

Her mother's eyebrows rose above her glasses. "Drs. Tam and Hinshaw advise us to stay in our household bubbles. No indoor gatherings."

Paula had expected that response. Canada's and Alberta's chief medical officers, Dr. Tam and Dr. Hinshaw, respectively, had become her mother's heroes. Unfortunately, the weather forecast called for cool temperatures through the weekend. "We haven't seen the girls in two weeks, though."

"I miss them, but their boyfriends work on the front line." Grocery store workers, they were at constant risk of catching COVID-19 from customers, suppliers, and each other.

Leah, Paula's oldest daughter, was unemployed. "I talked to Leah this morning," Paula said. "She doesn't seem to be doing much aside from moping in her apartment."

"We could invite her alone. Leah's lifestyle is safe."

Sadly so, Paula thought. COVID had ruined Leah's plan to open a wine and tapas bar and led to her breakup with her boyfriend cum business partner. The end of that romance was probably inevitable, but the bar had been ready to go this spring and even Paula, who'd initially been dubious about the venture, had thought its chances good. Leah had gotten out of the financial tangles, but Paula hated COVID most of all for quashing her daughter's dream. An evening with bubbly Isabelle and Erin might lift Leah's sprits.

"How about we invite just the girls," Paula said. "We'll keep our distance indoors, and wear masks you make for us."

Her mother frowned. "I don't know."

They finished the last of their dinner. Paula got up to wash grapes for dessert and returned to the table. It would be wrong to push her mother into a social activity that was a genuine threat to her health.

"All right," her mother said. "If we all promise to be careful and no hugs."

"Of course." Paula would miss those hugs.

Her mother tore a grape from its stem. "On the subject of visiting, could you drive me to David's?"

Paula winced. "Why? I'd thought your friendship was over."

"I owe him the benefit of the doubt." Her mother chewed on the grape; her expression grim.

"You won't convince him that COVID conspiracies aren't real."

"I might have misunderstood him on that matter."

Paula crossed her arms. "He called you a sheep for following the party line."

"I wonder now if he was teasing me, like your father."

"David doesn't joke." Paula and Sam had speculated that her mother's minimal sense of humour made it hard for her to tell the difference between nastiness and sardonic comments. David was Sam's father and Paula hadn't seen him in over a month. "I suppose I could take you this weekend."

"There's no hurry."

Perhaps her mother would rethink the idea over the next couple of days.

After they'd loaded the dishwasher, her mother settled in the living room to watch a recording of *Coronation Street* and Paula drove to her boss' home in Chinook Park. The deserted roads got her there in ten minutes. Under an indigo sky, she carried the bin of office mail and supplies to the backyard, set it under the covered patio, and texted Nils to say she'd arrived. The glass door opened and Nils flicked on the outside light, which illuminated his face. He looked older than his seventy-one years and had developed a stoop since withdrawing from the office last month. She made sure to stand more than the requisite two metres back to protect his lungs, weakened from over fifty years of smoking.

His wife appeared beside him. Helen came up to his shoulder. Grey roots flowed into her overgrown pageboy cut. Whenever Paula had met her socially, Helen had talked about her Dutch church. Now, her church activities had stopped, and she wasn't into Zooming. She told Paula now that she and Nils hadn't seen anyone indoors in over a month and only left the property for daily walks. They had their groceries delivered and scrubbed all the surfaces with alcohol wipes before taking them in.

"Any urgent mail?" Nils asked.

"Bills, notices, follow-up reports," Paula said. "Nothing that can't wait."

Helen said they'd leave the bin outside for a few days before touching it. "Nils has plenty to do combing government websites for programs to keep the business afloat."

"Band-Aid solutions." He scowled.

Helen gazed up at him. "I told Nils the universe is conspiring to finally get him to retire."

"And force him onto the internet," Paula teased. The business was Nils's prime interest. He'd founded the company when he was in his thirties.

"It hasn't forced me," Helen said. "I miss my friends."

"I wouldn't mind so much for myself, but I feel bad for young Connor," Nils said. "Isabelle will be next, and then you, Paula."

"I'll manage," she said, to cheer him up. "We got a new claim today. I could give it to Isabelle but will deal with it myself."

Helen looked at her. "Nils told me about your last murder case. I'm sorry for what happened. It must have been traumatic to see someone die violently."

Paula looked away. Shadows flickered on the outside wall of their home. She hadn't told Nils or anyone else about her flashbacks. During the past two months, they'd diminished to rare and less-disturbing appearances, although one last week had blurred to an image of her friend Callie lying twisted on the river pathway—an image Paula hadn't seen in real life. Callie's death had led Paula to Mike and two more murder cases. The one this winter had gone sideways. "I've learned from that experience."

"If you encounter trouble again, you'll handle it better," Helen said.

"No." Paula shook her head. "From now on, I stick with what I know I can handle."

Helen looked from Paula to her husband. "I tell Nils we can't know or control what comes next, but we need to have faith in ourselves and the world."

"My faith is hanging by a thread," Nils said. "I wouldn't bet on where we'll all be next spring."

Neither would Paula. Her work; her future with Sam; her daughters' well-being; the health of her mother, of Nils, and of other vulnerable seniors—Paula wouldn't bet on any of it thriving.

* * *

Mike Vincelli looked in on his nephew, asleep under his covers. Eli was six, in first grade, but at this moment he could be an innocent toddler. Mike had lived with him since he was born, but soon that would end. Lucy, Mike's sister, had fallen in love. Great guy, Kyle—great for both Lucy and Eli, who was growing increasingly attached to him. Kyle was a natural, relaxed with kids and life. Mike was stodgy in comparison.

The plan was for Kyle to move in, to keep Eli's homelife stable. Lucy and Kyle both insisted they wanted Mike to stay. He could have the basement bedroom and sitting area to himself, almost a separate bachelor suite. Mike was sure their urgings were sincere, but he refused to be a fourth wheel on their new family tricycle. Lucy talked of having a baby with Kyle before she turned forty. They all needed to move on, with Uncle Mike on the periphery.

On the way back to the living room, Mike stopped at the kitchen for two cans of Coke. One beer a night was enough for his friend and former mentor, Brian Novak, who was living with them temporarily. Novak's doctor had recommended he give up drinking—alcohol was a depressant and might affect his medication—but Novak said if he had to stop completely, he'd rather be dead. Mike doubted that was a joke.

Tonight, they'd almost finished their bottles when Novak's neighbour in southern Alberta phoned. Novak had hired the neighbour to look after his ranch in his absence and sounded confused by whatever the neighbour was saying about cattle and horses. No question, Novak's cognitive facilities were off, due to his depression or medication. Or both. If things didn't improve, Mike would suggest Novak ask his doctor to change his meds.

Mike carried the cans to the living room, plunked one on the coffee table in front of Novak, and resumed his spot in the armchair. When Novak finished his call, they could turn on the TV. Novak wasn't the greatest conversationalist these days. Lucy managed to draw him out a little, but this wasn't Mike's forte. Still on the phone, Novak asked his neighbour to repeat something.

Novak and his wife had bought the ranch after Novak retired from Calgary Police Service, and they had enjoyed two years of rural life until her cancer diagnosis. She'd died within days of her doctor's predicted six months. Novak had been her rock during her final days. And he'd crashed after the funeral this winter. His daughter had called Mike, his last Homicide partner, with a desperate plea for help.

"Would CPS hire Dad back part-time?" she'd asked. "I don't trust him alone at the ranch."

In his police work, Mike had met his share of suicide risks, including the one in his last case with Paula. He'd submitted the daughter's request to his staff sergeant, not expecting him to come through. But Travers said he'd been thinking of ramping up the cold-case team. A former Homicide detective working three days a week would suit their budget. Rather than share his doubts about Novak handling the job, Mike had hoped the return to his former routine would bring back the old Novak.

Finally, Novak said goodbye to his neighbour. He placed his phone on the sofa cushion beside him. His naturally ruddy complexion was flushed, likely due to the frustration of grasping the details about purchasing livestock. Novak's business model was to buy cattle in the spring, graze the herd through the summer, and slaughter the animals in the fall.

Novak raked his fingers through his thinning grey-blond hair, spiking the threads in all directions, and looked at Mike. "Where were we?"

"I was telling you about getting Paula on the break and enter case."

"Right. Your psychic friend had a vision of her."

"I wouldn't call him a friend."

"Aren't psychics usually female?"

"We shouldn't be sexist," Mike said. "Anyway, why can't psychic visions be clear and direct, like 'Get Paula on the case'?"

Novak picked up his Coke can, popped the tab, and set the can down. "I need to call my daughter." He grabbed his phone.

"You talked to her an hour ago."

"I forgot something." Novak tapped her number and spoke into the phone. "Hi, honey. How are the kids?" He stood and carried the phone to the hall, for privacy or to settle his agitation, a side effect of the meds or the illness, Mike wasn't clear which. He sensed Novak hated people hovering, treating him like a child. Mike would hate it too. It was one reason Novak hadn't wanted to move in with his overly protective daughter. Another was her home crowded with three children, two dogs, and a cat. Mike and Lucy had welcomed him into their basement guest room. Companionship and police routine had lifted Novak to functional. Then COVID-19 hit. Novak got into panics that the virus would take him, as cancer had done to his wife. New medication helped. Travers had ordered the cold-case team to work from home, to reduce the number of people at police headquarters. Mike had convinced him to let Novak stay, arguing that social contact was key for a widower getting back on his feet. Mike wondered if Novak accomplished any real work in there, but how much harm could he do on cases that probably wouldn't be solved anyway?

Novak returned and walked to the sofa with his trace limp from a horseback-riding accident years ago. "I thought my doctor's appointment phone call was tomorrow. My daughter says not for a couple of weeks."

Mike could have told him that.

"Where were we?" Novak said again. "Right. Paula. Glad to hear she's back in the saddle."

Mike shook his head. "She's still determined to stay off our Homicide horse, for reasons we can both understand."

"I don't. She was a sharp one in that case with her friend. A step ahead of you and me all the way to the finish line."

"Yes, but policing isn't her job."

Novak picked up his empty beer bottle. "That case was my last big one before I retired."

"And my first major homicide case."

Novak stared at the empty bottle, his brow knit. "It connects the three of us in some mysterious way. A triangle. You, me, Paula."

Psychics and people with certain mental illnesses tended to see connections where none existed. Mike rose to get the remote control from the coffee table.

"What do you want to watch?" he asked, knowing Novak didn't care. Comedies worked best. They both liked *Schitt's Creek*.

As they watched, Novak stared at the TV and managed the odd laugh, but Mike's gaze kept drifting to Eli's play corner on the far side of the sofa. A table and easel for his artwork. Shelves crammed with books, plastic trucks and cars, and dolls. Bins of LEGO bricks. A kiddie piano Eli loved banging on. He'd grow out of all this soon but had a few years of childhood left. Mike and Lucy's birth father had split when she was Eli's age. Mike, two years younger, didn't remember him and hadn't seen him since. Their mother married Ray Vincelli when Mike was five and then bought this house. Ray had become Mike's father in every sense, but Mike still felt responsible for them all. His mother said he was born old. He didn't need a shrink to figure out that he'd latched on to Eli to fuel his need for responsibility and make up for his lost fun in childhood. He dreaded letting that go.

A shrink would also note that, like Paula, Mike had been shaken by their case this winter. His fault for screwing up. He'd misread the situation and put her at risk. Now he might do it again, if Gabriel's vision came true. If Mike's action today turned out to be the wrong one and propelled Paula into danger, he'd quit Homicide.

He startled. The thought hadn't crossed his mind until this moment. Once you thought of leaving, did that mean you were on your way out? It took complete conviction to do the job. Four years in the Homicide unit was average for burnout. Mike would hit that milestone in four months.

"In my day," Novak said, jolting him from his thoughts, "there was this psychic who'd call now and then. I'd barely pay attention to what she said, my mind on real work. You're smart to listen."

"Paula thinks it's foolish."

"She's smart, too." Novak tried to sip from his empty bottle then set it on the coffee table. "Why don't you send me the break and enter report? It might jibe with a cold case."

"Why would it?"

"Connections."

Mike drank some Coke. Since all of Novak's work was likely a waste of time, the only problem might be Novak bringing some fanciful connection to Travers, who wasn't known for thinking outside the box. "Okay. If you find anything of interest, you can run it by me."

Novak cocked his head. "I'm too over the hill to deal with it?" His tone wasn't defensive, but there was a bite to the words.

Mike glanced at the corner full of toys. He too didn't like becoming obsolete.

Chapter Three

Paula arrived at the bicycle store in the city's northeast fifteen minutes early. She still hadn't adapted to the speed of getting around Calgary with less than half of its usual amount of traffic. Cycle Life was the middle store in the one-storey building in Mountainview Industrial Park. Paula parked in front of Cycle Life, facing the building. An outlet selling kitchen countertops was to her left, one selling furniture to her right. The building's location near the large commercial zone centred on Marlborough Mall would be convenient for customers shopping for specialty items.

She got out of her car and scanned the empty lot. The morning air was chilly despite the sun, which was rising behind the hot-tub outlet across the street. The police report noted that the three neighbouring stores—Xanadu Tubs & Spas, Furniture Sellers, and CounterTops—were all closed due to the pandemic. There'd been no witnesses to the Cycle Life break and enter, which occurred between six-thirty Wednesday evening and nine yesterday morning.

The Open sign on Cycle Life's door was unlit. Through the storefront window, Paula could make out bicycle shapes in the dark. She rang the doorbell. When no one answered, she took out her phone to check her messages while waiting for the co-owner and manager, Joshua Chapman.

An email from Connor—the first one he'd sent her since landing in Rome. *Museums closed. No tourists. Wandering alone past ancient buildings and monuments feels post-apocalyptic.*

She shivered with guilt even though he'd insisted his layoff was the kick in the pants he'd needed to pursue his dream of travelling and painting.

A cyclist rounded the corner, steered into the parking lot, and drew to a stop in front of her. "Are you the insurance adjuster?"

"Paula Savard."

He dismounted the bike and extended his hand. Paula withdrew hers.

"I keep forgetting." He laughed. "I'm Josh."

Josh was close to six feet tall and wore a light jacket and jeans. Paula guessed he was in his mid-forties, although his age was hard to determine with the bike helmet brim shading his face. His ski-jump nose crooked to the side

He slotted his bike into the rack on the weedy strip of gravel in front of the store window and locked the bike in place. "Can't be too careful these days. Theft must be booming with all the closed stores ripe for the picking."

"Actually, it's down, according to police statistics," Paula said. "Could be less random theft with fewer people on the streets."

"This one struck me as random."

"Why do you say that?"

"I'll show you." He punched the entry code into the pad on the front door. "I'm usually the one who opens up. First thing I noticed yesterday was the alarm wasn't set." Inside, he pressed the keypad to deactivate the security system. The door's Open sign lit up. "Obviously, they rode the bikes out this way and closed the door behind them."

"Are you certain you set the security system Wednesday night?"

"Absolutely," he said. "Wednesday is Herb's day off, and Kelsey always leaves before us." He turned on the light. "I'll leave the store closed until Herb arrives to deal with customers." He pressed a keypad button, and the Open sign went dark.

"Do you have other employees?"

"Nope. Kelsey's only part-time during the school year. She's in university. She starts full days next week, when she's done exams. We better get going before my ex appears. I'll show you how they got in."

Paula was intrigued by the comment about his ex, but that wasn't her business here. She followed him to the service counter, which was about ten metres straight ahead of the front door. Behind the counter was a partition wall. Josh draped his jacket and helmet on wall hooks and mussed his flattened sandy hair. His eyes were shadowed, perhaps from lack of sleep or stress regarding the break and enter? A tight T-shirt with capped sleeves highlighted his muscular chest and upper arms. Paula found the room cool enough to leave her jacket on.

The showroom extended from the door to a rear wall past the counter. She estimated it contained about one hundred bikes. Bicycle tires hung from the high ceiling. The service counter faced a few children's bikes and wall racks filled with bike accessories. The rear wall had two closed doors, one with restroom icons. Josh took a ring of keys from a counter drawer and led her down an aisle past the restroom to the store's workshop.

"I told Herb he was paranoid to keep it locked," Josh said. "Not anymore. We might upgrade our security system, even spring for cameras."

The motion detectors hadn't sent a notification to the security company. If Josh had been careless about activating the system, he probably wouldn't admit it.

Josh opened the door to the workshop. A fat-tire bike lay upside down on a platform in the middle of the room. Bicycle parts and tools crammed the shelves lining three walls. The rear window was boarded up. "They broke it and opened the door from inside."

"So what made you think it was an impulse theft?"

"They stole average-priced bikes that were easy to access. Sure, e-bikes are hot, but pros would have taken top-of-the-line. Same with the accessories they grabbed and, honestly, pros could have driven a truck out front and spent an hour loading—who'd have seen?" He opened the back door. "We'll upgrade the deadbolt lock and get bars for the new window."

The rear deck looked out on a T-shaped loading area. Two buildings ran along the T's stem, behind CounterTops and Furniture Sellers. Paula had an angled view of the buildings' loading docks, which meant anyone working there could see her on Cycle Life's deck. She saw no people or vehicles there now. The police report stated the district police had canvassed all the businesses, including the craft brewery at the end of the T's stem and across a street. All were closed during the time of the break and enter.

Paula looked over the railing. "Do you get your deliveries back here?"

"Out front," Josh said. "We don't have basement space."

A half-flight of stairs led down to the loading area, which sloped downward to the furniture store's rear entrance.

"Herb's the only one of us who comes out here, to smoke or eat lunch," Josh said. "I pitch in with bike repairs, but the workshop's Herb's space. He took care of boarding up the window while I dealt with the cops yesterday. That reminds me, I haven't had time to read our insurance policy. Is the window covered?"

She nodded. "Your commercial crime insurance covers specified perils, which include break and enter, theft, and related damage. You'll need to provide receipts."

"They're in the office."

They returned by the same back aisle, which Paula guessed was largely used by staff. No sign of Herb or the ex Josh had mentioned.

At the service counter, Josh pointed to two racing bikes across an aisle that continued through the showroom. "The bikes they took were there."

"Electric bikes?"

He nodded. "About three thousand each, retail. I'm almost out of e-bikes already. Everyone's thinking, 'What can I do now with stores and restaurants closed? I know—I'll take up biking.'"

"Or walking." Paula's neighbourhood streets and pathways were packed with people, especially on weekends. She glanced at the room full of bikes. Hard to see that the store was selling out. "You said you were meeting someone else here soon."

"Yes, my ex. Zabrina phoned this morning—woke me up—asking me to take Olivia, our daughter, today. Zabrina's parents have looked after her homeschooling since the schools closed, but they've taken off to their cottage." He motioned toward the floor-to-ceiling racks of bike accessories on two walls. "The dudes grabbed helmets plus, it seems, whatever would fit in the baskets and saddlebags we'd put on the bikes. They also ripped off a few racks in their haste, but we fixed those no cost."

Paula agreed it seemed a situation of two people happening by and stealing what they could easily and quickly carry. Or targeting the store because midrange e-bikes and accessories were worth a lot for personal use or black-market sale.

"I understand they left behind no clues?"

"Nothing the cops found when they were here." Josh scanned her from head to sneakers. "All I can say is, anyone shorter than you would have found it a stretch to ride those bikes, even after adjusting the seats."

Paula was five foot five. That eliminated only a small portion of the adult population.

Josh moved to the door between the helmet racks and the restroom. "Kelsey handles accounts. She spent yesterday afternoon digging up receipts for the stolen stuff. I'll look for her file on the computer." He unlocked the office door and headed for the desk in the middle of the room.

Paula stopped inside the door. To her left, several stacks of boxes were piled haphazardly to the height of her shoulder. Helmets, backpacks, water bottles, and other accessories sat on shelves along the remaining three walls.

Josh sat behind the desk, tapped the computer keyboard, and peered at the screen. "Kelsey started putting price tags on our new shipment yesterday, but we needed her to serve customers in the main room. Maybe she didn't get around to the receipts. I don't see them."

Paula turned toward a noise coming from the main room. A little girl ran in and bumped Paula into a box.

"Olivia," Josh said.

The girl darted around the desk and leaped onto his lap, rocking the chair backward.

A woman halted in the doorway. Her gaze passed from Paula to Josh. "I'd hoped to get Olivia settled here before you started work. She was a chore to drag out this morning."

Olivia jumped off Josh's lap. He stood and looked at Paula. "This is Zabrina, my former life-partner."

Zabrina's dark eyes flashed at him. She wore a long cashmere sweater over multicolour scrubs. Paula introduced herself while Olivia skipped around the far side of the desk to the boxes and disappeared from Paula's peripheral view. Paula guessed Zabrina was in her early thirties, at least ten years younger than Josh.

"Paula's the insurance adjuster for our burglary claim," Josh said.

"What burglary?" Zabrina's eyes grew wide.

"In Canada, the police call it break and enter," Paula said, to their apparent disinterest.

Josh stared at his ex. "People broke into the store Wednesday night and stole two bikes."

Zabrina's gaze shot toward the boxes behind Paula. "Olivia, get down from there." She looked back at Josh. "Why didn't you tell me this when I called?"

"I didn't have time before you hung up." He dug his hands into his pockets. "It's no big deal."

Paula turned from them to Olivia, who looked about seven or eight years old. The girl climbed onto a table that supported a tower of boxes. Paula moved closer, to catch her if needed.

"If I'd known," Zabrina said, "I wouldn't have brought her today."

"You told me there was no other choice."

Olivia reached for the box on the top of the stack. Paula grabbed her.

Zabrina marched toward them. "Olivia, get down."

The girl squirmed in Paula's arms and slithered to the floor. Zabrina blocked her daughter's exit from the room while Josh dashed to the side of the desk, seized Olivia's shoulders, and held on until she was steady. He straightened. Zabrina faced him eye level, thanks to her high heels.

"What's the plan, Josh? Olivia can't do her schoolwork in here."

"Why not? We'll set up a kids' desk. Kelsey can keep an eye on her."

"Except when she's not in the store or she's out there serving customers. Josh, the office is a mess. You saw Olivia climbing on the boxes."

"I plan to clear them out."

"When?" Zabrina sniffed.

Olivia loosened herself from Josh's grip and ran out of the office. Paula slipped around Zabrina to see what Olivia was up to. In the showroom, Olivia straddled a child's bike near the counter.

"We'll figure something out," Josh said to Zabrina. "You only called me this morning."

Paula left them for Olivia. "You can't ride that in here."

"Daddy lets me take them outside." She raised her feet to the pedals.

The bike tipped into Paula, who clutched one handlebar. "Let's wait to ask your daddy when he comes out."

Voices flowed from the office, but Paula couldn't make out any words. The front door opened and a man who looked to be in his late fifties walked in. He wore bib jeans, a checked shirt, and a ponytail, which was greying. His white beard extended to the middle of his chest.

"Herb." Zabrina emerged from the office. "I'm counting on you to make sure Olivia survives the day."

"Me?" Herb stepped backward.

Josh appeared behind his ex. "Put a sock in it, Zab."

"I don't want her alone in the office for one minute without supervision," Zabrina said. "I have to get to the hospital. I'm already late. You deal with this, Josh."

"I said I would." Josh's lips tightened.

Herb pressed the keypad to activate the Open sign.

Olivia rocked the bike side to side against Paula. Zabrina strode over, her boots clacking on the hardwood floor. She leaned down and managed to kiss her child's moving cheek. "Be good, sweetie. Do what Daddy says." She glanced at Paula. "If I had a choice, I'd take her with me."

"If I had a choice . . ." Josh muttered, as his "former life-partner" marched outside. He shared a glance with Herb and apologized to Paula for the interruption. Josh's flushed face suggested either embarrassment or more anger than he'd let on.

"No problem," Paula said, grateful to be a good seven years past that kind of domestic tension. Her ex-husband had set things off by cheating on her, but after two years of brooding, Paula realized she'd cooled toward their marriage first and had been nastier in their breakup arguments than he deserved. She still wasn't sure that her older daughter had completely forgiven her.

A crash jolted her alert. Olivia was off the bike, which had fallen on the one beside it, toppling both on the floor. Josh rushed to his daughter, who cringed beside the service counter but didn't seem physically hurt. Paula chided herself for taking her mind off the child, even though Olivia wasn't her responsibility. She couldn't remember her daughters being that out of control. Olivia might be hyperactive or have an attention disorder, or maybe she was acting up because her parents were at each other's throats. Zabrina was right. Olivia couldn't be left alone. Paula surveyed the store for a place where Olivia could do her schoolwork. The corner between the walls of helmet and accessory racks would be out of the way yet visible from much of the showroom. The location would work as long as someone kept Olivia in sight.

The front door chimed a couple into the store. Herb went over to serve them.

While Josh set the bikes upright, Olivia skipped into the office. Paula followed her to the table she'd climbed on earlier and pulled her down again, to little resistance this time. Moments later, Josh appeared beside them.

"The table would make a good desk for her," Paula said. "You could move it to the main room, near the accessory racks. Do you have a low-enough chair?"

Josh's brow knit, and then his face brightened. "Herb keeps a stool under the platform in the workshop. I'll get it." He left for the main room.

Paula took the child's hand and coaxed her to the service counter. She warmed to the touch of little fingers enclosed in hers. Grandchildren were years ahead for her, at best. Both of her daughters claimed no interest in having kids, although they had time to change their minds. Leah was twenty-eight, but she wanted to start a business, and who knew when COVID would let that happen? Erin had four years of veterinary school ahead, starting this fall. Would COVID delay her studies? Paula was happy they were focused on careers, but she wouldn't mind a child joining their family. She pictured Sam spending hours building towers and bridges with LEGO, enjoying it more than the child. The thought made her smile. It was after six p.m. in Hamburg now. Sam would be wrapping up his work for the day and heading back to his apartment. Paula wanted to leave Cycle Life well before noon to fit in a Skype call with him.

Olivia yanked her hand away and darted to the racks of bicycle gloves. As Paula chased her, so she wouldn't wreck the carefully arranged display, a strange thought formed. Maybe Olivia was the person Paula was destined to rescue from death. Ridiculous, but hadn't she already saved the child from falling off a table? Yet she'd failed to stop the tumble from the bike.

Paula caught up with Olivia before she reached the racks and held the struggling body away from them.

* * *

Detective Brian Novak attempted a stride into the Major Crimes office, but achieved no more than an awkward shuffle. He nodded at colleagues along the way. There were fewer of them on-site than he'd met during his first month of working on cold cases. Almost overnight, COVID-19 had made his desire to avoid human beings normal. He stopped at the coffee centre and fiddled with the machine. Who would invent pods when drip worked and tasted better?

"Want some help?" a voice said.

Novak turned around. The tall detective behind him had told him her name several times, along with assorted personal details. All he remembered was that she'd recently transferred to the Robbery unit from . . . ? He wished detectives wore uniforms with name tags. The machine hummed into action.

"Got it," he said, and hoped this was true.

"Are you still living with the Vincellis?" she asked.

Had he told her this? Had Mike? Novak attempted a joking reply. "Good of them to put up with me." He forced a smile.

The humming stopped. He took out his cup and sipped. Not terrible. He stepped aside so she could make her brew. Robbery didn't have a coffee machine on their side and used this one Mike had set up years ago. Everyone chipped in on an honour system.

"I'm sure they enjoy having you there," she said.

They pretended they did to be kind—Mike, his sister, her boyfriend. Even the kid had once crawled on Novak's lap with a book for him to read, treating him like a grandpa. When Novak stumbled over the blurry words, Eli recited the picture book to him, pretending to read. Novak's eye doctor had said vision problems were common with depression. As was every kind of problem, it seemed.

She stirred milk into her coffee and turned to leave for the Robbery side of Major Crimes. "Have a great day."

"You too," he said, to her back.

Novak shuffled to the far corner and entered the cold-case room, which was enclosed in glass interior walls and windows along the outside ones. He settled at his desk, which faced outside, its view of Nose Hill and the Calgary skyline backdropped by mountains wasted on him. His inability to appreciate beauty was common for depressives, his doctor said. Novak turned on his computer. He opened the folder to the first cold case on his list. Someone had ranked them in order of likelihood to be solved. Novak had reviewed the case when he first returned from retirement, but none of the details were familiar now. What was the point in him reading the files anyway? His mind was too muddled to pick up any detail a detective in his prime had missed.

He opened Mike's email with the police report on the bike store break and enter. Cycle Life. Novak plugged the store's name into the search navigator of the first cold-case file.

Detectives in their prime could screw up plenty. Novak certainly had. How many people had gone to jail due to his tunnel vision? Or prejudice? No doubt assumptions about suspects' race, financial status, gender, or sexual orientation had steered him to wrong conclusions. Someone innocent goes to jail and hardens onto a criminal path, a life ruined by his screwup. He stared outside at the vista that was obstructed by a highway overpass and pictured the ranch he'd left behind. Grass, cattle, horses, fresh air, endless sky—all of them healthier than police work.

The search turned up no reference to Cycle Life. He copied the bike store's address into the navigator of the first cold case. *1988. A woman robbed and beaten to death by an unknown assailant.* Thirty-two years ago. If the perpetrator had been twenty at the time, he'd be . . . fifty-two now. Four years younger than Novak and not too old to pay for his crime. Novak would gladly put a ninety-year-old in jail if he deserved it.

The address search came up blank in the folder. And the next case, and the next. He realized the keywords were too narrow. Officers spelled names wrong or reversed numbers, or digital transcribers entered them incorrectly. He returned to the first cold case and broadened his search. *Cycle. Cicle. Cyc. Life.* Some yielded a few results that went nowhere upon further search, others too many long shots for him to sift through. He had to be efficient or this would drive him nuttier than he already was. He gave up on words and number combinations for the first case, although he was starting to remember a few details about it, and dived into the second-highest-ranked cold case.

"Feel like a break for coffee?"

Novak spun around. The detective he'd spoken to earlier stood in the doorway.

"I just got here."

"It's been over an hour."

Novak glanced at his mug. It was almost full. He stretched his arms up straight and rubbed his back.

She peered beyond him at the wall of windows. "You've got the best office in the unit, and all this space for yourself with everyone at home."

"Or out on a call, like Mike."

"I've noticed you refer to him by his first name, but he calls you Novak."

"Everyone does." Including his wife Christine, as a term of endearment. He didn't know why, and he never would now. So much he wished he'd asked her, both trivial questions and important ones. "I called him Vincelli before I moved into his place."

"I admire your dedication, giving up your retirement to return to the force."

He would have set her straight about that, if he cared about what was true. The worst thing about this emptiness was that he couldn't feel enough to grieve. His soul, which he'd never believed in, had shrivelled to a twig. He belonged in a windowless room, dealing with cases that were dead like him.

Joining her for another coffee would involve getting up from this chair, shuffling to the coffee machine, talking with her—all way too much. This rote work was easier.

He shook his head and glanced over his shoulder, at his computer. "Thanks, but I'm on a roll here."

"Good luck." She smiled. "I'll leave you to your work."

Novak opened the next folder and typed *cyc*.

Chapter Four

Paula studied the setup she'd helped arrange in the corner of Cycle Life. The stool Josh had brought from the workshop was the perfect height for the table, and Olivia was so comfortable that she'd sat quietly for ten minutes. She leaned over the table, doing addition and subtraction in a workbook. The school area was away from the store's main traffic, but there was space behind Olivia for customers to check out accessories on the walls. It helped that Josh had been able to clear the area thanks to two customers who'd bought bikes and taken them home. While Paula had no direct reason to hang around the store, doing so confirmed that business was booming too much for her to suspect Josh of staging a break and enter to collect the insurance. From the steady stream of customers, she had no doubt Cycle Life could have sold the two stolen e-bikes by the end of the weekend.

Josh came up beside her. "Olivia's okay." His gaze settled on his daughter. "She acts hyper sometimes to get my and Zabrina's attention. Our separation has been stressful."

"It's tough for kids, at any age," Paula said. "How old is she?"

"Eight, going on eighteen." He grinned and left to help a customer select a saddlebag.

Paula checked her watch. She had plenty of time to talk to Herb before her Skype lunch with Sam. Herb stood behind the service counter dealing with a racing bike sale. When the buyer wheeled his purchase out of the store, Paula took the opportunity to ask Herb about the break and enter.

Herb started, as though he hadn't expected this. "I can't tell you more than Josh. He's the one who discovered it."

"What time did you get to work yesterday?"

"About ten minutes after him." He looked around the store, which was now experiencing a rare lull. "We can talk in the workshop, if you want."

Paula followed him down the back aisle. His grey ponytail bobbed on his flannel shirt. In the workshop, the fat-tire bike still sat upside down on the platform. Since the room had no chairs, Herb suggested they use the bench between the platform and the wall that separated the workshop from the restroom.

He sat on one end, Paula on the other, closer than two metres away. From what she'd observed, Cycle Life's COVID protocol was limited to a bottle of hand sanitizer on the service desk. She should be worried for her mother's sake, but she'd barely thought of the global pandemic for the past hour. Things felt refreshingly normal.

She asked Herb what he remembered about the previous morning. He repeated what Josh had told her, adding that Josh was usually the last one to leave the store, except on Mondays, his day off. They each took a weekday off so they were all there Saturdays, their busiest day of the week. Sunday the store was closed.

"Do you have shares in the company?" she asked. "The insurance policy lists Clayton Little and Joshua Chapman as co-owners."

Herb shook his head. "I had some but sold them along the way. Clayton's retired and doesn't take an active role anymore."

"Have you worked here long?"

"Clayton hired me going on forty years ago." His fingers fidgeted on his lap.

Paula considered asking his permission to record their conversation, but that might make him clam up. She'd make notes later.

"Was Clayton the store's founder?"

"Back in the early sixties," Herb said, nodding. "Josh joined some twenty years ago. Make that twenty-four. It was the year Kelsey was born. She's Clayton's favourite granddaughter and was here all the time as a kid. Old Clayton spoiled her." Herb smiled. "Kelsey could be a holy terror, like Olivia."

"Do you know Clayton's current share of the business?"

"Fifty-two percent. The store's his baby. Josh says it's time he gave up control, at age eighty-four." Herb flushed. "Don't get me wrong. He leaves Josh to run things his own way. It's not a problem." His flush deepened above his beard.

Paula nodded, but was it a point of conflict between the co-owners? She shifted her position on the hard bench and glanced at the boarded back window. "Josh said you took care of repairs right away."

"Luckily Home Depot's open. I went out and bought the right-size board. Hammered it on by lunchtime. Should be good enough until we can replace the window—and get bars."

"Do you expect more intruders?"

His shaggy eyebrows rose. "Why would I?"

"Have you had past break-ins?"

"None I recall in forty years."

"Thieves often strike the same business twice," she said. "I've encountered a few cases in my claims work."

His eyebrows lowered, reducing his eyes to slits. "We'll be extra careful." He turned sideways to stare at her directly. "The police asked if I'd noticed customers who acted odd—anyone who might be checking out the place, or someone with a grudge." He shook his head. "I've thought about it since yesterday and still have to say no. We get the occasional customer complaining, but we deal with it quickly and fairly. I can't think of anyone who's walked out angry in the end. My guess is it was kids out on a lark, possibly low-level professionals. High-level ones would have broken the keypad instead of the window." He smiled wanly. "From what I know from watching TV."

"Kelsey's here," Josh said from the doorway.

Herb turned toward him. "She's early."

"I told her to come in as soon as she could. A new flood of customers is arriving." Josh looked at Paula. "She'll give you the receipt details."

Paula and Herb left the workshop and retraced their route to the service counter. Herb pointed out Kelsey, who squatted beside Olivia's table to watch her colour on a sheet of paper. He continued past the counter to deal with a customer. Kelsey stood as Paula approached her. Olivia looked up from her colouring while Paula introduced herself. Kelsey was petite, no taller than five foot two, and slim. Her tank top and mid-thigh-length skirt showed off her toned arm and leg muscles. Maybe she biked everywhere.

"Can I take a bike out while you're busy?" Olivia asked Kelsey.

"Your dad or I will go with you later," Kelsey said. She led Paula into the office. "I don't know how Josh thinks we can homeschool and serve customers simultaneously."

"Perhaps it's temporary until they find a new arrangement."

"Let's hope." Kelsey pursed her lips. "I like Olivia, but I'm not increasing my work hours to babysit." In the office, she took the chair behind the desk.

Paula sat in the visitor's chair and felt a tug on her pant leg. Olivia had followed them in. The child dropped to the floor and nestled against Paula's leg, like a cat. At least she and Kelsey could keep an eye on Olivia while they talked. An angel figurine sat on the desk, behind the computer monitor. Paula hadn't noticed it earlier this morning. Was this Kelsey's personal touch?

Kelsey squinted at the computer screen. "To be honest, I didn't get far with finding the receipts for the stolen items. It was crazy busy here yesterday."

"I understand. You can email them to me, when they're ready. Here's my card." Paula took one from her purse and placed it beside the figurine.

"I'll get on it when the crowd out there thins," Kelsey said. "Do you need anything more from me?"

"I gather you weren't present when Josh discovered the break and enter."

Kelsey nodded. "I'm only supposed to work afternoons this week. By the time I arrived yesterday, the store was business as usual. Josh was with a customer and Herb was in the back repairing a bike. It was fifteen minutes before Josh told me people broke in. It freaked me out." Her eyes flickered. "It feels like a violation. I know that's weird."

"Not at all."

"This place is kind of my second home." Kelsey looked around the room.

Olivia felt heavy against Paula's leg. Paula looked down at Olivia's head, which bobbed forward. She'd have outgrown napping, but maybe she was up late last night or was tired from today's changes in her young life. Since Kelsey showed no signs of leaving, Paula decided to question her further.

"Josh said you're studying at university."

Kelsey nodded. "I'll get my Bachelor of Commerce next fall, with a concentration in business. I registered for the spring term to speed my degree up. It's all online now, which saves the time of travelling to classes. Easy to fit my store work around them."

Josh poked his head in the doorway. "There you are."

Olivia bolted upright. "Daddy, I want to ride a bike."

"Okay, honey, when this lady is finished here." Josh looked at Paula.

She took that as her cue to leave. Almost time for her lunch date with Sam. She stood and thanked Josh and Kelsey for making time for her during their hectic day.

In the showroom, Olivia ran to the bicycle she'd tried out earlier this morning, Josh following. Meanwhile, Kelsey greeted a new customer. Herb was occupied with a man at the store's far end, so Paula let herself out and texted Sam to see if he was home from work. Josh's bike was still the only one in the rack. She guessed the Jeep parked in the lot belonged to Kelsey, rather than the pickup truck or BMW.

In her car, she saw that Sam had replied. *Ready when you are.* She'd noted a shawarma takeout place on her way to the industrial park and picked up a sandwich and diet cola there. Since the weather had warmed to comfortable-with-a-jacket, she set up her tablet on their outdoor table, with a view of the downtown skyline and mountains beyond.

Her heart lifted at the sight of Sam's face on the screen. His usually short, spiked hair was growing out, but the crinkled eyes and upturned lips were comfortingly familiar. After three and a half years together, she found it hard to believe now that when they met, he had been a murder suspect.

He began by saying he was happy to have her mother use his studio for making her masks, which lifted Paula's heart further. But it sank with his next sentence. "My colleague's brother, who has a top job in a German hospital, says that flight advisories and shutdowns will continue into the fall." They had planned for Sam to fly home then for a visit. He sipped his red wine. "Who knows when I'll get back? Someone might as well use the studio."

To shift the subject to one more upbeat, Paula asked how his work was going. She ate her sandwich while he updated her on Hamburg's HafenCity harbourfront, the largest urban redevelopment project in Europe. A German architecture firm had hired Sam to work on several mixed-use projects. One had run into a zoning glitch that frustrated Sam, but he was sure he'd work it out. Paula was equally confident he'd find a way to solve the thorny issue. His devotion to his work was one of the things she loved about him, even though it had taken him away from her.

Sam paused to twirl his spaghetti around his fork. "Your turn. What's new at work?"

To save time, she gave him the short version. "At last, we have a new claim—a break and enter. It seems run-of-the-mill so far." She shifted to the personal. "Mum has agreed to risk us inviting Leah, Erin, and Isabelle for an indoor dinner tomorrow night. I'm starting to like having the whole weekend off, now that most of my claimants are available to meet online on weekdays. Will this become a new way to do business, long-term, do you think?"

"If it does, you'll be able to work remotely from Hamburg."

Sam was always looking for ways she could live in Hamburg for extended periods. A goal of her cancelled trip this spring had been to help determine if that was doable.

They finished their meals and signed off with "I love you. Talk again soon."

As always, Paula's chest tightened when Sam's image froze then disappeared. From the restaurant, she drove to her office to clear her work plate for the weekend.

In her cubicle, she drafted a statement for Josh to approve, grabbing details from the police report and her recollections of their conversation. She sent the document to his work email address, with instructions to make any changes and corrections and return it to her for final typing. She then emailed the officer in charge of the break and enter case to see if there were new developments. It was unlikely the stolen goods would turn up, and a long shot that the police had a lead on the crime or had apprehended the culprits. All she could do now was wait for Kelsey's receipts.

While the information was fresh in her mind, Paula typed up the Cycle Life history that she'd learned from Herb, for her future reference.

Clayton Little, born 1936. Founded Cycle Life 1960s. Retired, owns 52% share. Josh Chapman owns 48%. Herb (surname?), hired 1980 approx. He might have been fresh out of high school. *Josh hired 1996. Clayton's granddaughter, Kelsey, born same year. Questions: Is Clayton keeping his share in the store to pass down to his children? Does Kelsey intend to stay on after she completes her Bachelor of Commerce degree?*

A thought struck her. Tipsters who called the police sometimes had an involvement in the crime. This likely applied to "psychic" tipsters too. Josh and Herb had come across as down-to-earth types disinterested in the spiritual world, but there had been an angel figurine on the office desk, probably brought in by Kelsey. The psychic had wanted Paula to get involved. Herb had said he couldn't think of any customers with a grudge against Cycle Life, but Paula's company had its share of dissatisfied and angry claimants. Did one have a grudge against her? Connor had kept a spreadsheet listing every claim they'd handled, which included the names of the people involved. Paula glanced at her computer clock. She had an hour before she had to get home to help prepare dinner. She went to Connor's desk in the reception area, located the USB, and returned to her cubicle to open it.

* * *

"Good luck with Connor, babe."

Isabelle cringed at the term. Unaware, Habib kissed her goodbye and sauntered out the front door. Her other housemates, Erin and Nick, had left earlier for work. Isabelle had the place to herself. She stooped to pet Salt. The golden cocker spaniel mixed with something mutt had become as much her dog as Erin's now that Isabelle was working from home.

In the kitchen, Salt wove around the room and barked as Isabelle chopped vegetables for tonight's chili dinner. The bad part about not going out to work was that the others assumed she had time for all the cooking and cleaning, especially since Gran had left to live with Paula. Isabelle did have time, with her insurance work running down and no commuting, but that wasn't the point. Sure, the others were doing important jobs on the front line. Erin worked in animal health, and their boyfriends were grocery store clerks. Food was essential, but . . .

Isabelle hated how Habib called her babe. She wasn't a baby. Her fault for letting him get away with it from the start. After three years, it was too late to break his habit. She whacked the last carrot into pieces, dumped the vegetables in the Crock-Pot, and set the heat to low.

Salt followed her to her office, barking all the way. He lay down beside Pepper, a black cocker spaniel mutt mix, who was Erin's old dog. Isabelle sat at her desk and logged on to her computer. Connor wasn't Active on Skype yet. This morning at breakfast, she and her housemates had discussed his claim to be in Rome. They all agreed that Isabelle's evidence suggested he was in Calgary. Nick asked why she hadn't clued in earlier when Connor told her he'd found an overseas flight, when every airline in the world was grounded. Habib and Erin had nodded along with Nick's put-down. Yes, they all had university degrees— the dudes were working toward advanced business degrees and Erin would start veterinary medicine next fall, but Habib used to say Isabelle was "street smart." If he'd told her this lately, she hadn't noticed.

Connor now showed as Active. Isabelle took a breath. The four of them had also agreed she should talk to Connor before telling Paula he was in Calgary. He might have a good reason to keep it a secret.

They'd urged her to confront Connor right away, before she lost her nerve. And she wanted to do it without the others hovering around, listening in. Now was the time, with Pepper and Salt snoozing nonjudgmentally on the office floor. She checked the World Clock website. Nine thirty p.m. in Rome, which probably didn't matter.

Connor answered her call, his background a picture of the Trevi Fountain. He wore his contacts instead of his glasses. "What's up?" he asked. "How's it going with your new claim?"

"I haven't heard any more from Paula." Isabelle's leg moved up and down under her desk. She pressed her thigh to stop the nervous tic. "What did you do today?"

"Shopped for canvasses and art supplies. It took me all day to find an open art store. In the end, I took a bus to the suburbs and, since the restaurants are closed, I picked up groceries at a big supermarket. It's cheaper than eating out."

Too much detail. A sign of lying.

"Tomorrow, I get started on painting," he continued. "I want to create images of the deserted streets in Rome to evoke the pandemic isolation. I've taken tons of photos on my phone to work from."

"Calgary's streets are deserted too. If you were here."

"But I'm not." His eyes flickered.

"Your room looks bright for nine thirty."

"The apartment has high-wattage lighting. I'll dim it for painting to get the colour even."

A cat meowed.

"Finnegan's still there?" Isabelle asked.

"It's not Finnegan," he said, sounding irritated. "I haven't named her yet. Or him, I should say. This cat's male."

"You called it 'her' the last time."

"Did I?"

Isabelle wasn't sure. The cat leaped in front of him. He shoved it to the floor. So Isabelle couldn't check the gender? She was flubbing her indirect questioning. "Connor, I know you're in Calgary."

Connor's face blanched. He was a worse liar than she was.

"Why did you lie to me?" Her leg moved up and down, but why bother to stop it?

Finnegan reappeared in front of the camera. Connor let her stay. "If I told you," he said, from behind the cat, "you'd spill it to Paula."

"I wouldn't if you asked me not to."

"You would."

Isabelle suspected he liked hiding behind the cat. "Paula doesn't care where you are. You don't work for her anymore or keep in touch. Do you?"

Finnegan hissed at the screen.

"Paula felt so bad about firing me," he said.

"You weren't fired. They laid you off."

"A euphemism."

She'd have to look that word up. Finnegan moved away, revealing Connor, his bearded face less pale now. Maybe he felt better, having told the truth.

"Paula was thrilled to hear I was exploring the world," he said. "And taking up painting again. Pursuing my dreams. It made her feel less guilty, I think. I'd hate to let her down."

Isabelle couldn't see why Paula needed to know. "I won't tell her, if you want."

"I want," he said. "I planned to go, had my ticket to Rome, but the airline cancelled. I thought about looking for another flight, but Gabe was a mess. It didn't feel right to leave him. Now I'm sure my nagging drove him away."

"You haven't heard from him yet?"

Connor shook his head, his eyes red. Isabelle felt bad for him, but if she had a nagging older brother, she'd probably get tired of him too.

"What do you do all day?" she asked, hoping to lighten the mood.

"Look after Finnegan. Buy groceries. The usual."

"You could paint Calgary in the pandemic."

"I've run out of supplies, and the stores are closed."

"Order online."

"I could," he said. His mouth sagged.

She doubted he'd order anything without a push. Even when he wasn't depressed, he didn't have confidence in his painting. "I'll come over to visit sometime."

"Don't worry about me," he said. "Just don't tell anyone, especially Paula."

Isabelle realized the first thing he'd asked her about was work. He must miss it more than he let on. Now, she felt Paula's guilt. Weird how he always wanted to impress Paula. When they were all working together, he'd asked Isabelle not to tell her that his brother was a drug addict. Isabelle could see him not telling Nils, their older, higher-up boss, but Paula wasn't that uncool. Anyway, Isabelle hadn't told either of them. She could keep secrets.

"I've gotta go," Connor said. "Finnegan's rubbing my leg, wanting her lunch."

"Call me the minute you hear from Gabe. You will soon. I feel it." She didn't know if she was lying or not.

* * *

The psychic hadn't made it easy for Mike to track him down. All he had to go on was a name, Gabriel, which could be a first name, a surname, or a name the psychic had adopted. The voice on the phone had sounded young, but voices, like everything else, could be deceiving.

Mike glanced at Novak, whose gaze was fixed on the tonight's binge show, *Friends.* Mike preferred dramas, but sitcoms were the one thing that could make Novak smile, even chuckle on occasion. Lucy was spending the night at Kyle's apartment, and Eli was asleep. Mike took out his phone to do another search of "Gabriel." *The archangel?* Most likely a well-meaning fraud. Mike had learned in Homicide that "mostly likely" was usually true, but not always.

Novak snorted. The episode ended with a final laugh-track laugh and an abbreviated roll of credits. The next episode began.

"Researching a case?" Novak muttered.

"Unofficially." Mike saw no reason to lie. "I realize I pushed that break and enter case on Paula without properly vetting the alleged psychic."

"I wish you hadn't pushed the cold cases on me."

"Pardon?" Mike hoped he hadn't heard correctly.

Novak glanced at the TV screen. The friends were hanging out in Monica's kitchen. Novak repeated his remark.

"You said you were getting into your search."

"That's the problem," Novak said. "It bugs me to leave it for the weekend."

Mike nodded, relieved. He'd worried the work was too much for Novak. Like these binge shows, Homicide work was addictive—and it had to be. Time was an enemy, for new cases anyway. Novak's cold ones had no urgency, but his getting hooked might be a good sign.

Novak adjusted his position on the sofa. "In my day, if they'd stuck me with cold cases, I'd have plowed through them until I dropped. My wife hated my obsession."

Mike's last girlfriend had too. They'd broken up three years ago. Lucy regularly urged him to look for someone new, especially now that she'd found Kyle, but single life freed Mike to pursue every suspicious thread. Official ones had priority, though. "That reminds me," he said. "I have to go to into work tomorrow, clean up some paperwork."

On TV, a pot exploded on Monica's stove. She was the only *Friends* character Mike could see himself wanting to spend any time with. The others were too self-absorbed, and at least he and Monica could have fun cooking together.

"I'll tag along," Novak said.

"To Westwinds? They don't pay you to work weekends."

"Who gives a shit?" Novak stared at the TV and smiled at a lame joke.

Novak wanting to work weekends was another hint that the old Novak lurked beneath his current shell. Mike returned to his phone, his chest lighter.

If he'd taken Gabriel as seriously as other callers with potential tips, Mike would have asked him for contact details at some point during the past few years. In the Bible, archangel Gabriel wasn't so much a psychic as a messenger, delivering communications from God. This Gabriel wanted to prevent a future death. Did he have inside information?

A barber. The memory came from nowhere. The first time Gabriel had called, about two years ago, he'd begun by saying he was professional psychic. Mike had skeptically asked if he earned a living from this. Gabriel replied that his barber work paid the bills.

Mike returned to his phone and searched *barbers Calgary*. There would be hundreds of barbershops in the city, every one of them closed by the pandemic restrictions. Even if his search turned up a place called Gabriel's Barbershop, Mike wouldn't be able find Gabriel at work. Still, he had nothing better to do tonight. He scrolled through several pages of results. Too many barbers. One shop alone, boasted a staff of twenty, but none named Gabriel. It was probably a psychic name anyway and Gabriel was Joe or something in his regular life.

Friends segued into yet another episode. Novak got up to use the washroom and get sodas for them both.

Partway through their fifth *Friends* episode of the night, Mike's search hit on a possibility, Emilio's Easy Cuts. The site included several customer reviews. One praised the proprietor, Emilio, for his service and attention to clients' needs. A second reviewer wrote *Gabe's haircut was unreal.* Gabe, short for Gabriel.

Unreal would be his style. The shop was located in Forest Lawn, a neighbourhood not far from Paula's office and home. That meant next to nothing, and this was a long, long shot, but Mike carried the phone into the hall and called the number listed on the site. He turned his back to the living room so Novak wouldn't hear. After a few rings, the voicemail kicked in. "We're currently closed due to COVID-19 rules. Please leave your contact information, and we'll phone you with a special offer when we reopen."

"Brian Novak," Mike said. He left his own personal number, but what had made him give Novak's name? Hopefully a gut instinct. The latest news report had said nonessential stores, including barbershops, wouldn't open for weeks. Too late for the bike store break and enter, but if this Gabe was psychic Gabriel, Mike could learn more about him for future cases.

The next morning, when Lucy returned, Mike suggested they make brunch while Eli watched cartoons. Novak hadn't emerged from the basement and probably wouldn't before noon. They cooked pancakes, sausages, bacon, and eggs; sliced strawberries and bananas; and popped toast. Like the old days, before Kyle. Mike was scum for wishing those days back for his sister.

While he made coffee, his personal cell phone rang. "Brian Novak? This is Lee, from Emilio's Easy Cuts. We're closed, but we want our customers to know we're thinking of them."

Mike moved to his bedroom. Would Lee offer him a haircut under the table? If so, he'd ask for Gabe's services.

"Thanks for your support," Lee continued. "I'm adding you to my customer list and will be sure to call when we reopen."

"Actually, could you put me in touch with Gabe, one your barbers, now?"

"Gabe? I haven't seen him since COVID shut us down." Lee sounded like an older man.

"Does Gabe still do psychic readings?"

Lee laughed. "Does he do that? It sounds like him. We're strictly barbering here, but he might still be doing that stuff from home."

"Could you give me his phone number or email address?"

"Sorry, I can't," Lee said. "But if you want, I'll send him your details."

"That would be good." Mike heard a tapping noise at the other end of the line.

"I'm looking at my employee records," Lee said. "Strangely, I don't have Gabe's phone or email address, only his emergency contact—a brother. Do you want me to forward your name and number to him?"

"Go ahead." Mike had a hunch. "Tell him I'm calling about Cycle Life. Gabe will know what I mean."

"Cycle Life?"

Mike spelled out the store's name and repeated his contact details twice, to ensure Lee had them right. Was Mike's hunch correct? Would his message result in a return call from Gabe? Or prompt him to avoid the mysterious Brian Novak? It was a crapshoot.

Chapter Five

Paula and her neighbour from across the street manoeuvred the sewing machine cabinet up the exterior staircase to Sam's studio above the garage. They set the awkward piece of furniture on the floor between the kitchenette and futon. Paula's mother followed them in with a bag of fabrics.

The neighbour offered to get the sewing chair from the house, while Paula and Theda debated the best location for the cabinet. Placing it against the west window would block access to the large desk, which would be her mother's work area for cutting material and assembling the masks. The east wall, under the mounted TV, was an option. When Sam left for Europe, they'd cancelled his cable subscription. He watched light TV shows to let his mind drift and allow his subconscious to brainstorm solutions, but Theda said she'd rather watch TV in the main house. In the end, they agreed that placing the cabinet against the south window would work best. Already, the sun travelled high enough that it wouldn't shine in directly from the south to blind her while she sewed.

When the neighbour returned, he and Paula set the cabinet in place. Next, they carried boxes of Sam's books back to the house to store in the basement, leaving her mother to arrange her fabrics on the vacated shelves. All this walking up and down stairs and lugging items would serve as Paula's exercise for the day, and it was a refreshing break from insurance claims and sedentary work.

Yesterday, she'd combed through Connor's spreadsheet of recent files, looking for a male claimant who might be angry about his claim settlement and could get the notion to pass himself off as a psychic. A few had rejected traditional whiplash treatments in favour of alternatives such as acupuncture and mind-body therapies. A married couple she'd dealt with for damages to their collapsed roof had stated the incident happened while they were conducting a séance in their living room. The crash upstairs had jolted everyone out of their collective trance. They'd thought the sound was from the deceased relative they'd been attempting to contact. The man had chuckled over this, despite being a believer. Paula had been impressed that he could view the spirit world with humour. He might think it funny to draw her into the break and enter claim with his vision of her butterfly scarf. Had she worn the scarf any of the times they'd met? She couldn't recall. In the file for his claim, she couldn't find any connection between Cycle Life and him. He lived in Evergreen, in the southwest, the opposite end of the city. Should she call the man and bluntly ask if he'd drawn her into the case and, if so, why?

Sam might say that her subconscious would brainstorm the answer while the rest of her was preoccupied with physical labour.

In the basement, she led her neighbour past the treadmill and elliptical machine to the guest room, where they placed the boxes of books on the bed. She wouldn't have any guests down here until COVID was over.

On their way back, her neighbour stopped to admire the home gym. "I need a setup like this so I can lift weights and work out while watching TV. I miss my fitness centre."

Paula nodded sympathetically. She wished she could invite him to use her equipment during the day, but it would be intrusive for her mother, and he had teenage children who might bring the virus home. Her gaze lit on a small table, which Sam had brought with him when he moved in two and half years ago. She went over and picked up the solid wood table. "It's a challenge to convince Sam to get rid of quality items we don't need. Mum might find this handy for her masks at some stage in their process."

"I've put in an order for a mask with a fishing design," her neighbour said. "She's on the hunt for the right material. My payment, she says, for helping move her stuff."

Paula smiled. "I'll contribute a case of beer."

Upstairs, he grabbed the ironing board to take to the studio, while Paula carried up the oak table. She and her mother could handle the rest of the move on their own. They thanked their neighbour, who left them to their midmorning tea break in the studio. They settled on the futon with Sam's Corelle cups and set her mother's second-best teapot on the coffee table.

"What time are the girls coming today?" her mother asked.

"I told them six," Paula said. "After lunch, I'll scoot out to buy a few groceries. Would you be up for trying vegan lasagna?"

Her mother's nose scrunched. "Can you make lasagna without cheese?"

"I found a recipe with soy mozzarella and herb ricotta."

Her mother sipped some tea. "I got used to trying those foods when I lived with Erin, but Walter doesn't consider meatless dishes real food."

"Good thing he won't be here."

"I invited him. Didn't I tell you?"

"No." Paula set her cup on the coffee table harder than necessary. "Mum, you were the one who wanted to limit it to the girls."

"Walter has no contact with people, aside from his walks with me and trips to the occasional store."

"He hits a store every day," Paula said. "This was supposed to be our family gathering." Strictly speaking,

Isabelle wasn't family, but Paula and her mother included her because she had no relatives in Calgary. Since COVID, Walter had none he could visit with in person. "Okay," Paula said. "But he'll have to eat vegan."

* * *

The aroma of fried bacon urged Novak up from his basement bedroom. He followed the scents to the kitchen, where Mike, Lucy, and Eli sat around the table.

Mike picked up a piece of bacon. "There's still plenty for you."

Novak took his chair opposite Eli, helped himself to the bacon, sausages, eggs, pancakes, and sliced bananas, and doused them all with maple syrup. Some meals, he had no appetite; others, like this, he scarfed food down. His doctor said both were effects of depression. Throw in the medication that slowed down his metabolism and the net result was a twenty-pound weight gain since January.

When Lucy had finished relating her plans for the day, Novak asked Mike what time they were leaving for Westwinds.

Mike raised a brow. "You're coming?"

"I told you yesterday that I was."

Mike shared a glance with Lucy. Novak hated when they did this, as though he were a nutcase. Which he was.

"I'd planned to leave after eating," Mike said. "We can go later, when you're ready. It's only paperwork. I can make my own time."

Novak forked up a huge bite of pancake and spilled syrup on his shirt. He wiped it with a napkin, creating a smear. He considered changing before going into work, but few would be there to see him on a Saturday.

On the drive to the station, Mike asked if he'd made any progress with his search for a cold case connection

63

to the break and enter at Cycle Life. Novak recalled Mike asking that yesterday on the drive home.

"No change," Novak said.

"Let me know if you do."

So that Mike could take over? Novak had to admit that this would give both cases their best chances. He stared out his window at a passing car. Novak hated depending on Mike to drive him to work, but even on near-empty streets, Novak didn't trust his reflexes and slightly blurry vision. More symptoms.

With few cars in the parking lot of Calgary Police Service Headquarters – Westwinds, they got a spot close to the entrance of the Investigative Services Building. Inside, they walked through the huge atrium to the Major Crimes section. Novak forced smiles and greetings at the occasional officers they met but didn't recognize any of them, let alone remember their names. He used to be sharp with names and details, such as wedding rings. Did the female detective wear one? She was too young for him, and he was too old for romance, but what about her and Mike? Novak glanced at Mike, who had slowed to accommodate Novak's shuffle. She and Mike were around the same age, had work in common, and most cops liked sports of some kind. They'd be bound to find one to do together.

They passed unoccupied cubicles, stopped at the coffee centre, and made themselves cups. Mike said he'd come get Novak when he was done and departed for his cubicle.

If Novak could drive, he'd be free to search as long as he wanted, into the evening, to the end of the last case file. What was the point of being a widower if he was still beholden to someone? There was no point to this search anyway. He'd spent all day yesterday scanning files until his vision blurred so much that he couldn't make out the letters. This afternoon, time would be short.

In his glass office, he set the paper cup on his desk and opened the file he'd stopped partway through yesterday. Outside, it was so cloudy that he could barely see beyond the highway overpass. Nose Hill and the Calgary skyline were blurs, the distant mountains invisible. He pressed *Find* and typed *cyc*. No results. *Cicle*. None. *Life*. One result. His heart skipped. He read the highlighted text. No relevance to Cycle Life. Back to *Find*. He searched the address numbers. No luck.

He moved on to the next file and repeated the search drill. Soon, he was into the mechanical routine. His fingers stiffened on the mouse. He stretched them back and forth, looked his watch. *Holy shit*. An hour had passed. Impossible. He gulped some cold coffee. Any minute now, Mike would show up and drag him away from the finish line. Novak blinked to refresh his eyes. He returned to the screen. *Cyc* and then *cicle*. He went through all the words and opened the next case—a suspicious death in 2013.

Cyc. Five results. That would be a lot for typos. Novak's hand shook on the mouse, but he managed to click on the first highlighted *Cycle* in the text. *Employer: Cycle Life, 920-29 St. NE*. His heart raced. He clicked on the next section of highlighted text. *Location of death: Cycle Life.* His head grew dizzy. He blinked. Was this real? Wishful thinking? He returned to the start of the file and skimmed. *Cause of death: opioid overdose.*

Novak looked back at his office door. Seven documents remained in the file, in addition to any hard-copy material filed somewhere in the storage room. No way he'd get through it all before Mike arrived. Novak fumbled in the desk drawer for a USB to copy the documents to but couldn't find one buried among the mass of writing supplies. *Shit.* He grabbed a pen and a piece of paper and jotted down the date of death. The case was probably online. He'd search his computer at home before deciding whether to hand over the information to Mike. This was Novak's discovery. He deserved that much. He scrolled down to the deceased's name and wrote *Omar—*

"Ready?" Mike said from the doorway.

Novak stopped writing. He swivelled his chair around.

"Find something?" Mike asked.

Novak glanced at the paper he held in his hand and hoped his head blocked Mike's view of his computer monitor. "Just noting the point where I stopped so I can pick up here tomorrow. Good timing. I've had enough for today." He turned back and clicked the mouse. The file disappeared from the screen. "Give me a few minutes to clean up."

Mike remained in the doorway. Novak couldn't stash the paper in his pocket without explaining why he was taking file information home.

He downed his cold coffee, dropped the cup in the garbage can, opened his desk drawer, and slipped the paper in. He mentally repeated the date of death. *May 14, 2013.* The deceased's name . . . ? *Fuck.* He'd forgotten already. It wasn't a common Canadian name. He'd never dredge it up.

Mike eyed him as though he suspected Novak was up to something. Or was that Novak's guilty mind playing tricks on him? It would be right to tell Mike about the case for the sake of the deceased's family, who'd been waiting seven years for answers.

* * *

Paula carried three dining chairs into the living room and arranged them into a conversation oval with the sofa and armchair. Her mother divided the jar of mixed nuts into six individual bowls so people's hands wouldn't mingle. The doorbell rang. Walter, ten minutes early. That figured. Paula opened the front door.

He handed her a bottle of red wine. "I prefer beer, but Theda says you like your daily nip."

Paula's grip tightened on the bottle. She was drinking less with Sam away, thanks to her almost-teetotalling mum.

"You're looking well, Paula," Walter continued. "Sam's absence agrees with you." He grinned.

She swallowed a scowl so he wouldn't think his jab had hit the mark and asked if he'd like a beer now.

"You bet. No glass is good." He ambled to the living room.

Her mother directed him to the armchair. "The other chairs are for the girls. Paula and I will have the sofa, to separate us into our bubbles."

"I haven't felt this bubbly since COVID began," Walter said, presumably as a joke.

Paula headed into the kitchen. The aroma of baking lasagna wafted from the oven. Her mother had insisted they make a second pan with meat for Walter. Paula set the wine on the island and opened the bottle for herself and the girls. The label was unfamiliar, but knowing Walter, the red blend was cheap. She poured a glass and tasted it.

Hmm. Not bad.

From the fridge, she selected a can of Grasshopper beer. The local craft brewery brand would be wasted on Walter. She filled a glass of water for her mother and returned to the living room, where Walter and Theda were engaged in a conversation about Walter's wife. One of the staff in the long-term-care residence had tested positive for COVID-19. Once the virus spread in those places, he said, vulnerable residents were helpless. A quiver in his tone prickled Paula's sympathy for him.

Noises outside the front door drew her into the hall. Erin and Isabelle breezed inside. Paula moved forward to hug them before remembering and stepping back. "Gran insists no body contact."

"I keep forgetting," Isabelle said.

"Will we remember to hug again when life is back to normal?" Paula said.

"What's normal?" Erin asked.

Paula offered to get them glasses of wine and sent them to the living room as a text notification beeped from her phone on the console table.

A message from Leah. *Too tired to go out tonight. Sorry.*

Paula's stomach clenched. She worried about her daughter's despair over losing her business dream and her boyfriend. Leah had said she filled the empty hours walking five or six hours a day, usually alone, listening to music. It sounded like bone-weary fatigue. And obsessiveness.

Her shoulders heavy, Paula carried the two wine glasses to the living room. Isabelle was telling everyone how much she enjoyed working from home. At their office, Isabelle's main job had been adjusting small claims on the phone. Now she met claimants face-to-face on RingCentral. "It's practically like in person," she said.

Post-COVID, Isabelle might be able to continue her online meetings, using headphones to block out other office sounds. Seeing faces on a screen was a step up from phone calls in terms of reading body language. Why not use the new technology to their advantage?

"I like doing Connor's admin work, too," Isabelle added.

"Has he Skyped with you from Rome?" Paula asked.

"It's hard with the time difference." Isabelle leaned forward to grab a handful of nuts. "Is Leah coming tonight?"

"No." Paula relayed Leah's message.

"I hope Leah's not getting more depressed." Theda echoed Paula's fear. "When we talked yesterday, she sounded interested in my masks."

"Masks?" Erin asked.

"I forgot." Theda rose from the sofa. "I meant to hand them out when you arrived. They're in the dining cabinet drawer."

While her mother went to get the masks, Paula described the project that had taken over Sam's studio. "The experts say we'll all be wearing masks this summer."

Erin nodded. "We already are at the animal clinic, to protect our clients."

Walter snorted. "Can dogs and cats catch COVID?"

"Not that we know yet," Erin said. "It's to protect their owners."

Humour wasn't Erin's strong suit—perhaps that acorn didn't fall far from Paula's tree. Sam thought her problem with Walter was that she took him too seriously.

Her mother appeared with a handful of colourful masks. "I've ordered better fabrics but made these with what I had in the house." She held up a mask. "This is a wine-glass design for Leah, for her wine and tapas bar."

"Paula can take that one." Walter laughed. "A mouth cover will stop her nipping."

Would Sam find that funny? Paula ignored Walter. "Mum gave me one with flowers, to go with my scarf." She fingered the silk draped around her neck.

"I gave Walter his earlier," Theda said. "Stripes. The most masculine material I had on hand."

Walter set his beer can on the coffee table then retrieved the mask from a pocket in his jeans and put it on.

Theda passed one to Erin. "Yours has little cats."

"It's cute," Erin said, studying it. "My clients will love it."

"Will the cats notice?" Walter's voice was muffled behind his mask.

Another benefit of masks—muffling Walter.

"I'm still working on improvements." Theda handed one to Isabelle. "You'll have to make do with cats as well, until I find a fabric for you."

"This is like Christmas." Isabelle looped her mask behind her ears.

Erin tried hers on too. "It's more comfortable than the masks at the clinic."

Paula looked at her mother, who beamed with pleasure. Leah's wine mask dangled from her hand. Paula was glad her mother had this support from those closest to her, while she hated the thought of her daughter alone in her apartment, probably moping, missing this rare time together.

The oven timer dinged, and Paula left the room. Before taking the lasagna from the oven, she replied to Leah's message. Paula had no plans for tomorrow, the forecast called for sunshine and warming temperatures, and she had to make sure Leah was okay. Bone-weary wasn't normal.

Enjoy your rest, honey. I'm not working tomorrow and could use a walking partner. Want to meet at Nose Hill? The park's glorious views of the mountains and downtown skyline would lift her daughter's spirits, she hoped.

* * *

Mike guessed he was the only one in the living room watching the movie. Novak was slumped in the armchair, his eyes closed. Lucy and Kyle were making out on the sofa. From the corner of his eye, Mike glimpsed Kyle drape his body over hers. *Get a room*, Mike wanted to tell them, although he agreed with their decision that Kyle wouldn't sleep over until he officially moved in. It made the situation clearer for Eli. That move was less than two months away. If Mike didn't start looking for an apartment, he'd be sleeping in his room across from Lucy and Kyle or sharing the basement with Novak.

On TV, the thriller's mood music rose to a fever pitch. The hero's car barrelled through city streets, knocking down safety barriers, tires screeching. Mike's cell phone rang.

"Brian Novak?" a male voice said.

"Yes." Mike rose from his chair.

"You're looking for Gabe Riley?"

"Yes." Mike lowered his voice. "Am I talking to his brother?"

"What do you want Gabe for?"

Mike crossed the living room on his way to the hall. Novak stirred then resettled. Was the brother hiding Gabe for some reason? Or naturally cautious of strangers? From the hall, Mike went into his bedroom and closed the door behind him. Maybe Gabe was missing? Mike took a stab. "I have knowledge of his whereabouts."

"Where is he?" The tone was sharp, but the voice reminded Mike of Gabriel's.

"I have to tell you in person."

"Why?"

Mike paced his bedroom to wait out the pause.

"Okay," the guy said.

"Give me your address."

"Are you joking?" the brother said. "It has to be public, safe, but all the restaurants are closed." Another pause suggested he was thinking through options. "Chestermere," he said. "Do you know it?"

A satellite town east of Calgary, linked to the city by a canal. Mike recalled going to Chestermere as a kid to visit a friend's cottage. Now, the town was on its way to becoming a Calgary suburb.

"There's a park on the east side of the lake," the brother said. "It's busy Sunday afternoons nowadays with everyone hanging outside."

The lake community outside of Calgary was a peculiar choice of meeting place, but outside of Calgary might be the point.

"How will I recognize you?" Gabe's brother asked.

"I'm tall." Mike needed a better identifier. He pictured his clothing in the front-entrance closet. "I'll wear a Calgary Flames ball cap. How about you?"

"That's good enough," the brother said. "Let's make it two, tomorrow afternoon, near the postal boxes between the parking lot and the street." He hung up.

Mike's heart quickened. This could be the break.

Chapter Six

A scream jolted Novak's gaze to the television screen. Someone was falling off a cliff. He had no clue how the person had gotten there. A song he didn't recognize kicked in. The credits rolled. On the sofa, Lucy and Kyle decoupled.

Mike entered from the hall and glanced at Novak before turning to the pair seated inches apart. "Lucy, I arranged for an afternoon meeting tomorrow but forgot you were working." He looked at Kyle. "Can you fill in for Eli duty?"

"No problem." Kyle smoothed his rumpled hair. "What time should I come by?"

Novak bristled. He'd be here, but Mike didn't trust him to look after a six-year-old.

"One is good," Mike said.

Kyle smiled. "Do you ever take a full day off?"

Lucy nudged him. "Some of us do real police work."

Her job in the child abuse unit was often too real. Kyle's job was to instruct new recruits, nine to five on weekdays. When he went home, he left his work at Westwinds. Now, he clicked on the TV news. Mike returned to his chair across the living room.

Novak's thoughts drifted to the cold case. Before dinner, he'd spent an hour searching for it online. The single news report he'd found stated that on May 14, 2013, a Cycle Life customer collapsed in the store. An ambulance drove the unconscious man to hospital, where he died two hours later. He was identified as Omar Bashar, age thirty-four. Cause of death was a suspected opioid overdose. His wife, Farideh Bashar, stated that her husband had been prescribed opioid medication for a back injury and became mildly addicted. Calgary police were investigating the incident.

Was mildly addicted comparable to slightly pregnant?

Kyle said it was time for him to get home. Lucy walked him to the front door, and Novak and Mike left the room to give them privacy. Mike carried their beer glasses to the kitchen. Christine would have chided Novak for not doing his share of cleaning up.

After saying his goodnights, Novak headed to the basement, wondering about his next step. The obvious one was to tell Mike. *Not yet*, Novak's inner voice said. *What's the rush for a seven-year-old case?* Besides, knowing police bureaucracy, it was possible Homicide had ruled out suspicious death but neglected to close the file. The news report had made it sound only mildly suspicious, like mildly pregnant. Novak chortled.

In his bedroom, he stripped off his clothes and got into his pyjamas. His laptop sat on the desk, luring him back to the search. He'd found no Omar or Farideh Bashar listed on the internet White Pages. Had she remarried? If he contacted cell phone providers through official police channels, the staff sergeant would find out, and Travers abided by the book. Novak would have to explain about the cold case. *Not yet.*

He went to the bathroom to brush his teeth. Looking in the mirror, he saw his eyes were red from hours of staring at computer screens. He'd been searching social media sites when Mike called him to dinner. On Facebook, women often included all their names so their friends from the past could track them down. Novak itched to get going on it again, but he was drained. Better to wait until he was fresh.

As he crawled into bed, he wondered if Omar and Farideh had had any children. Novak got up and made a note to search for Bashars of the appropriate age. Social media pages for younger people often popped up in searches. There might be cousins as well. He set the paper and pen on the bedside table, in case he thought of something else during the night, and snuggled under the covers.

Cycle Life. He'd found reviews from satisfied customers on several retail rating sites. Nothing lower than four stars. *Knowledgeable and friendly staff. Quick to diagnose problems. Best bike shop in Calgary. Josh is awesome at his job.* The Cycle Life website had basic information about the store's bikes and accessories, along with its location and hours. They were closed tomorrow, Sunday, which would make it a good day to snoop around. Small chance Novak would find anything, but he'd get a sense of the place. Cycle Life wasn't far from Lucy and Mike's house. He'd plotted the directions on Google Maps. Sixteen minutes by vehicle. If he could drive and his pickup truck weren't at the ranch. An hour on public transit. Sunday service was crap, and Novak didn't do transit at the best of times. Walking would take two hours and twenty minutes. Out of the question. But a forty-minute bike ride was doable. He'd overheard Mike and Lucy talking about tuning up their bikes now that spring was here.

When Novak and Christine moved to the ranch, they'd thought they might ride their bikes on quiet country roads. They hadn't.

The next time Novak looked at the clock it was after ten in the morning. Faint light flowed into the basement window. His head ached. He dragged himself out of bed and to the bathroom, where he found his eyes narrow and redder than they'd been the previous night. Upstairs, Mike and Eli were in the living room building a structure with LEGO.

Mike looked up from the floor. "Good morning. Lucy's off to work. We're all on our own for breakfast. Help yourself."

Novak nodded.

"Care to join us here afterwards?"

"Thanks, but I had a rough night sleeping." Novak rubbed his head for emphasis. "Think I'll head back down for a nap."

Mike's eyes flickered, either with pity or concern for the basket case. "I might be gone by the time you're up for lunch, but Kyle'll be here."

To look after Novak as well as the kid.

Novak grabbed a piece of toast and a mug of coffee then carried his breakfast to the basement and logged onto his computer. A half hour later, he'd located a Farida Bashar on LinkedIn. The news report could easily have spelled her name wrong. Farida owned a sports clothing boutique in Canmore, over an hour's drive west of Calgary. He should send her a phony message related to her store in hopes she'd bite, but he couldn't think of what to say. He went with the truth.

I'm Calgary police detective Brian Novak and am investigating the unsolved suspicious death of Omar Bashar. Can I phone you, or could we meet in Calgary, at the coffee shop of your choice?

With that done, he set his focus on getting to Cycle Life. Novak checked the basement furnace and storage rooms but couldn't find any bikes. He'd check the garage and backyard shed when Mike was out this afternoon. There was a good chance Kyle would take Eli to a park at some point. If the shed was locked, he'd find a way in. People, including cops who should know better, usually kept their keys in obvious places or used easy-to-deduce combination codes. Novak was back in the game.

* * *

Mike arrived at the park in Chestermere with its long row of post office boxes between the parking lot and the main street. All the residents in the older core of this lake community probably picked up their mail at this spot. He put on his Calgary Flames baseball cap and got out of his car.

About twenty people were scattered through the grassy park beside the lake. A group ate lunch at a picnic table. A man and a boy tried to fly a kite in the mild breeze. The sky was more cloud than sun, but already, the day was warmer than any had been the past week. A car pulled into the lot. The driver was male. Gabriel's brother? Two toddlers leaped out of the back seat. They raced to the playground, the man following them.

Mike loitered beside the postal boxes, enjoying the view of the dark-blue lake. A motorboat sped by. Since his childhood, most of the cottages here had been torn down and replaced by luxury homes that ringed the lake. The streets fanned into new development.

A bicyclist rode into the lot. He stopped at the bike rack on the far side, locked his bike up, and removed his helmet. From his movements, Mike guessed the stocky man was in his twenties. He wore shorts, a fleece sweater, and running shoes. From a distance, his beard and dark glasses looked like a dollar-store disguise. Mike walked toward him and stopped a couple of metres away.

The man clutched the helmet to his chest. "Are you Brian Novak?"

Mike nodded. He scanned the park and spotted a vacant picnic table near the lake, away from people. "Can we talk over there?"

They crunched over grass, which was still mostly brown from winter. As they drew closer to the lake, the breeze picked up to a wind, which explained why the table at this prime location wasn't occupied. Mike was glad he'd worn his jacket and jeans. He sat on the bench, facing south. Gabriel's brother settled across from him. He set his helmet on the table, top down, like a turtle on its back.

"When did you last see Gabe?" the young man asked, his dark eyes narrow.

"He phoned me three days ago," Mike said.

The man's face relaxed. "No one else has heard from him that recently. Did he say where he's living?"

"No." Mike zipped up his jacket against the wind and decided to come clean, more or less. "I've never met your brother in person, but he calls me every few months, typically about a vision concerning a case my unit is working on. Brian Novak is actually my partner in Calgary Homicide. I'm Detective Mike Vincelli."

"Oh shit." The man grabbed his helmet and rose, as though he intended to make an escape. Mike could tackle him before he reached his bike, but he wanted Gabriel's brother to think he was on his side—and Mike was at this stage. A couple with a little girl passed behind the brother, who dropped back to the seat. His brow furrowed. "Oh fuck. You didn't hear from Gabe at all. It was me who phoned you Thursday morning, not him." His hand slid from the helmet to the table. "I'm no further ahead at finding him. You're no help at all."

Mike blinked. "You called me pretending to be Gabriel?"

The man stared at the lake.

"Why?"

He kept staring.

Mike changed course. "When did Gabe go missing?"

The brother inhaled, perhaps considering how open he should be. He turned to Mike. "Gabe went out one night close to four weeks ago and wasn't home in the morning. I tried calling him. No answer. I wonder if he turfed his cell phone. He doesn't answer emails." He drummed the table. His fingers protruded from his bicycle gloves. "My neighbour told me he saw Gabe in a grocery store line last weekend, so I know he's alive—at least, he was then. The neighbour tried to talk to him and found him evasive." His gaze returned to the lake. A family stood at the edge, throwing stones into the water.

"But you haven't reported Gabe missing," Mike said.

The brother shook his head, his gaze on the shimmering lake. The sun was breaking through the cloud. "He's only missing from our apartment, and from me, and he probably has his reasons."

"Such as?" Mike studied the man's profile. Hook nose, unkempt beard, black curls, which ruffled slightly in the wind. Gabriel was a barber. He might have cut his brother's hair shortly before he left. "Why did you call me and impersonate Gabe?"

"Why did you impersonate your Homicide partner?" he snapped back. "Same reason, I expect. To get what we wanted. When I saw the news blurb about that bike store theft, I figured there'd be an insurance claim. If something fishy's going on there, Paula will ferret it out."

Mike started. "Paula Savard?"

"I used to work with her."

"You mean . . . at her office?"

The brother nodded.

Paula's colleagues were Isabelle and the company owner, Nils. They'd recently laid off an administrator. Paula had referred to him by name. What was it?

"That's why I recognized you when Gabe told me he'd call you about his visions," the brother said. "Your name got tossed around the office a lot."

"Were you the office administrator?"

He nodded.

"What's your name?"

He stared down at his helmet.

"Come on," Mike said. "I'm going to tell Paula about this."

"She'll be pissed that I tricked her." He looked up. "Isabelle said the insurance company assigned Paula the claim. Did you convince them?"

"You've been in touch with Isabelle?"

He nodded. "She didn't know, at first, that I wasn't travelling, but she guessed."

"And she didn't tell Paula?"

"I asked her not to."

Typical Isabelle, to follow an instinct that contradicted sensible behaviour.

The brother raised a hand to his forehead and massaged his temple. "All right." His hand dropped to the helmet. "I'm Connor. I tried to copy Gabe's indirect premonition style by giving you hints leading to Paula. You're a detective, after all."

Mike gritted his teeth at having been played. "Are you aware, Connor, that Paula doesn't want to deal with potentially dangerous claims?"

Connor's lower lip grew slack. "We don't know this is dangerous. I hope it's not. All I want is to know he's okay." His voice wavered.

Mike shifted direction. "What do you think is going on at Cycle Life?"

Connor fingered his helmet straps. "Drugs." He looked up. "From things Gabe's mentioned, I suspect that's where he gets his supply."

Mike tried not to look startled by the blunt revelation. "What things?"

Connor shrugged.

"What type of drugs?"

"I won't get my brother in trouble. That's why I wanted to get Paula into it, not the cops." Connor picked up the helmet, placed it on his head, and fastened the strap under his chin. "You got what you wanted, Detective. And I came all this way for nothing." He adjusted the helmet and set off for the parking lot.

Mike caught up with him. He'd heard there was a bike path along the canal from Calgary to Chestermere. "Did you ride here on the canal path?"

Connor nodded. "I figured if you were a weirdo, I could ride back without you following me in your car." He veered toward the bike rack without saying goodbye.

Mike couldn't think of anything to do except to phone Paula.

* * *

Paula's cell phone rang while she was walking in Nose Hill Park, doing her best to keep up with her daughter. Leah forged ahead seemingly unaware her mother had stopped.

"You sound out of breath," Mike said.

Paula explained and watched Leah disappear down a slope. Beyond, the mountains straddled the horizon, glistening white with snow.

Mike apologized for disturbing her weekend. "Would you be able to meet later today, at your office or home?"

"Is this about the bike shop break and enter?"

"That's right."

His tone sounded serious. Paula chose the office so they'd have privacy. She opened her waist pouch to make sure she'd brought the key chain that included the keys to her office building.

Leah reappeared at the crest of the slope and marched toward her. Paula told Mike she'd text him a meeting time and tucked her phone away.

"Mom, I thought you were right behind me," Leah said.

"How much longer do you want to walk?"

"If you're done, I'll walk you to the parking lot and then head up on another path."

Paula hated to cut their time together short, but two hours on Nose Hill was enough with the sun beating through her spring coat. She took it off and finished the water in her bottle.

They walked east. Leah's head thrust forward, her face a frown. Excessive exercise certainly kept Leah fit, and it beat brooding in an apartment, but Paula could see no joy in her daughter's movements. Leah hadn't glanced once at the glorious skyline beside them.

81

The parking lot was now crammed with cars to the edge of Fourteenth Street. The hilly park was so vast that Paula had been unaware of the crowds arriving. She'd enjoyed the prairie grasses and views but wished her conversation with Leah had touched on something important. Leah had answered Paula's gentle probes with "I'm fine" or "I'm dealing with it, okay" or "Stop hassling me, Mom." She'd barely listened to Paula's summary of the dinner party and had shown only a mild interest in her grandmother's mask-making venture.

Paula stopped beside her car. "Mum and I are thinking we'll celebrate my birthday next Saturday, if that works for us all."

Leah blinked. "Yah, right, your birthday's Tuesday. I doubt I'm busy any day coming up."

Paula longed to hug her goodbye. She watched Leah's ponytail bob against her back all the way up the hill and swallowed the lump in her throat, feeling less reassured than before about her daughter's emotional state. With a glance at the time, she texted Mike, telling him to come to her office at three p.m.

On Deerfoot Trail heading south, Paula found her thoughts shifting to Mike's call. What had the police found? Until now she was convinced all she wanted was to settle a routine claim, but she couldn't deny a rising excitement. What was wrong with her, that claims connected to Homicide gave her a rush? Without them, she wasn't sure she wanted to continue her adjusting work. Yet she'd vowed to do without them. This had been her dilemma since her decision to protect her loved ones from dangers associated with her job, and nothing, not one single thing, had changed.

Parking was always available Sundays on Inglewood's Ninth Avenue, especially now with so many businesses closed. Paula parked in front of her building, let herself in, and climbed the stairs to her floor. She stopped to use the restroom her company shared with the optometry and real estate offices.

In the office, she set her sunglasses and waist pouch on the reception desk. As she made coffee in the kitchenette, the downstairs buzzer sounded. She jogged to the reception area to let Mike in and went out to greet him. The creak of his footsteps coming up the stairs reminded her of his visit about the bike store case three days ago, although more light streamed in today. Mike rounded the top of the staircase dressed casually in a T-shirt and jeans under his unzipped spring jacket. His overgrown hair was windblown. She ushered him into the office.

Mike halted at the reception desk. "Is this desk Connor's? The office administrator you let go?"

She nodded. "That reminds me, I haven't answered the email he sent from Rome."

"He's not there," Mike said. "Two hours ago, I met him at Lake Chestermere."

That wasn't possible. "What do you mean?"

Mike sniffed. "Let's have some coffee and sit."

Since peppering Mike with questions would be a waste of time, she led him to the kitchenette. Connor had said nothing about coming home early from his trip. How had he managed to get a flight? And why would he meet Mike? They didn't know each other.

Their mugs filled, they sat at the mahogany table in the same chairs as they had on Thursday, allowing Mike his cop view of the outer door. Paula stared at him. He took a sip of coffee, set the mug down, and told her what he knew.

Floored by his report, Paula touched her bare neck. "That explains how your psychic knew about my scarf. I'd suspected one of my claimants from this winter and planned to call him tomorrow." She shook her head. "I can't believe this. I knew little about Connor's personal life aside from the fact he has a younger brother. He was much friendlier with Isabelle. They're the same age."

Mike glanced over her shoulder, at Isabelle's desk. "Connor says they've been in contact, and she eventually figured out he'd lied about his trip."

"She didn't tell me." Paula said, her chest tight. "What's the big secret?"

"Beats me."

"Does she know Connor's brother is into drugs?"

"You'll have to ask her."

Paula leaned back in her chair. "You think Cycle Life is a front for drug dealing?"

"So far, it's only hearsay from Connor," Mike said. "It could also be a legitimate bike business."

"From what I've seen, it seems to be." Paula drank her coffee, reflecting. "Assuming the bikes and equipment were actually stolen, they'd still be covered under the store's policy."

"Technically, the break and enter should be handled by Community Policing. I'll suggest to Drugs and Missing Persons we get Robbery to take over the file. That way, Major Crimes will keep on top of it."

"Can you do that?"

"It's happened for financial cases. This is arguably more worthy."

Paula nodded. Gabe was missing, and drug dealing took numerous lives.

"Where are you at in the claims process?" Mike asked.

"Waiting for the owner's signed statement and receipts for the stolen items. I'll follow up first thing tomorrow."

Mike rubbed his mug with his palm. "I'd say don't rush them to settle, and stay away from that place. Drugs are a dangerous business."

Paula pictured the Cycle Life showroom bustling with customers; Josh, Herb, and Kelsey dealing with their booming business. "So far there's no death, suspicious or otherwise," she reflected aloud. "All we're going on is a pseudo-psychic's prediction about me preventing a death. Connor made it up to rope me in."

"Still, drug dealing is something to steer clear of," Mike said, his tone firm.

"I don't have to go to Cycle Life again," she said. "What's left on the claim can be handled by email or phone, but I want to talk to Connor. He got me into this, and I want to know what's going on."

"I do too," Mike said. "What's his address?"

Paula finished her coffee, stalling.

He cocked his head. "It will save me the effort of looking him up or requesting his phone records."

She clunked her mug on the table. Mike drained his mug, showing no sign he'd caught on to her annoyance. The police had access to so much information. Her inequality relative to them bugged her when it came to working with Homicide on cases. Another reason for her to avoid them. She left the table to get her cell phone from her waist pouch on Connor's desk. Mike carried their mugs to the kitchen and joined her in the reception area. She gave him Connor's details, including his address in Forest Lawn, a short bus ride to the office. In good weather, he'd biked to work.

"Connor was perfect for his job," she said. "Accurate, reliable, pleasant with clients on the phone. His flaw, if it was a flaw, was his lack of ambition in this line of work. I got the sense he was marking time until he saved enough money to travel and paint full-time. That's why his flying to Rome in the midst of a pandemic was credible. His goal, he said, was to live his dream inexpensively in a warm, beautiful country."

"Meanwhile, he's in Calgary," Mike said. "I won't keep you anymore. The bottom line for you is no rush to settlement, be careful with Cycle Life, and, I'll add, hold off on contacting Connor."

"Why? He's my former co-worker and a friend." Acquaintance would be more accurate. "His brother's the one involved with drugs, not Connor."

Mike's eyebrow rose. She caught his meaning. She couldn't be sure Connor didn't use or deal illegal substances. Isabelle was bound to know more about this. Paula would talk to her before contacting Connor. Despite his manipulative act, Paula felt a pang for him. With a missing brother and no job, Connor would be as lost as Leah.

Chapter Seven

Novak steered the bike onto the sidewalk to avoid disrupting the street hockey game. Eli slammed the ball against the curb beside Novak. It bounced back into the street, where Kyle intercepted it. He jogged to the net at a slow pace, presumably to let the pack of kids close in on him. Novak pedalled past the net, confident he and the bike were in riding shape. It wouldn't hurt to do a fourth spin around the block, to be sure.

Ahead, a black Mazda approached—Mike, back from his afternoon meeting. It couldn't have been a formal interview, since he'd worn jeans and a T-shirt. Novak drew to a stop. Mike turned into the driveway, got out, and strode over the brown grass to Novak.

"Where'd you find the wheels?" Mike held a shopping bag in one hand, a baseball cap in the other.

"In the shed." Novak nodded in the direction of the backyard. "Kyle said it's Lucy's old bike." When Novak saw the bikes through the shed window, he decided it would be easier to ask Kyle to open the shed rather than try to crack the combination. Riding a bike wasn't suspicious, after all.

Mike squinted at the blue-and-gold frame. "So it is."

"Kyle fixed it up, repaired a few spokes, adjusted the seat. He says he and Lucy won't have much time for biking this spring, with his move to the house."

A cheer rose from the street. Mike turned to look at the game. Novak raised his leg over the rear wheel to dismount. He remembered his thought about another ride around the block. Too much trouble to get back on. A pull in his groin area suggested a bike style with a lower centre bar might work better for a man his age. The next time he went to the ranch, he'd get Christine's step-through bike.

Mike raised the bulging shopping bag. "I'll get started on supper."

"Kyle made chili."

Mike frowned then nodded. "I picked up a loaf of sourdough bread. That'll go with it."

"Actually, Kyle's got the bread maker going for rolls. He made coleslaw too."

Mike lowered the shopping bag to his side. It occurred to Novak, for the first time, that Kyle's superman role might be getting on Mike's nerves. Not so different from Mike's supplanting Novak, his former senior partner, in police work.

"In that case," Mike said, "how about a beer before dinner? It's warm enough to sit out back. I'll take these groceries in and meet you there."

Novak walked the bike through the side yard, lodged it in the shed between Mike's bike and the lawn mower, and locked the door. Mike emerged from the patio door wearing sunglasses, a beer in each hand. He placed them on the coffee table and sat on the sofa that faced the yard. Novak took the armchair to his side. This weather-resistant furniture was almost as comfortable as the living room set.

Mike took a sip of beer. "Remember the psychic I told you about, the one who lured Paula and me into the bike store break and enter case?"

Novak nodded and drank some beer to hide his expression. He really should tell Mike he'd found a cold case linked to Cycle Life.

"Turns out that psychic was a fraud."

Novak forced a grin. "Who'd have guessed?"

"I mean, he was impersonating my usual psychic to get Paula on the case."

Novak swirled his beer, struggling to grasp the relevance.

Mike explained that the imposter psychic wanted Paula involved in the Cycle Life break and enter for personal reasons unrelated to a cold case. "Sorry to send you down that blind alley."

"No problem," Novak said. "It gave me a goal. Does this mean Paula's insurance work has nothing to do with a past unsolved murder?"

"It's unlikely, unless you find something."

"I'm almost through all the cold cases." This was true. "What kind of personal reasons?"

"Nothing reported to the police yet."

Mike wore his *I'm not saying any more* look, but obviously his meeting today had been related to Cycle Life or the psychic or both.

Between Mike's reticence and Novak's muddled mind, Novak still didn't understand—did this mean he was off the hook about coming clean? He owed it to Paula to confirm. "Good to know Paula isn't in danger."

"She says there's no need for her to visit Cycle Life again. I think she'll be fine if she stays away."

Still confused, Novak affected an ironic smile. "You think Paula will do that?"

Mike looked at his beer bottle. "I think she's serious about steering clear of our suspicious death cases and so, yes, I think she'll avoid that store and the people there."

Novak took a slow sip. Odds were there was no connection between the cold case and this new personal matter. It would be a shame to hand over the file to Mike and the other active-case cops, now that Novak had wheels to pursue it on his own. If he found anything critical, he'd refer it to the regular channels. Surely his mind wasn't so far gone that he couldn't recognize critical. "Let me know if she's getting in deeper than you expect."

Mike stared at Novak, who took another sip as casually as he could.

"Paula was instrumental in my last big case before I retired," Novak said. To add that he cared about her would sound soppy.

Something vibrated against his chest. He set his bottle on the coffee table and took his cell phone out of his shirt pocket. An email from Farida Bashar.

"Good news?" Mike said.

Novak realized he was smiling. "My daughter wants me to Skype with the kids. I'll take it on my computer downstairs. Better than trying to see them on this tiny phone."

"I'll stay here and enjoy the sun."

Novak left him and went down to the basement, gripping the rail to avoid falling on his unsteady legs. He opened his laptop. His hand shook on the computer mouse as he navigated to his email and read Farida Bashar's message. *I would like to meet you in person. Can you come to Canmore?*

It was too far to bike, and there was no public transit from Calgary. He continued reading. *Alternatively, I have to be in Calgary on Tuesday, but coffee shops are closed for indoor dining.*

Damn COVID. He'd forgotten about that when he'd suggested a coffee shop meeting.

Are you at police headquarters, in the northeast? If you'd prefer that I go there, Tuesday 11:30 a.m. would work for me.

Novak stared at the screen. How would he explain a visitor coming to see him at Westwinds? His cold case work didn't involve meeting people. They'd have to do this the modern way, on Skype or Zoom. It would beat a phone call. He shook his head. No, in person was best, real-face-to-real-face, and he wanted the best for this stranger, Farida Bashar. He recalled his first car ride to a crime scene with Mike, his novice Homicide partner. Novak had spouted pearls of useless advice, but one grain still rang true. *We do it for the victim's family.* Seven years after her husband's death, Farida Bashar was willing to meet Novak and resurrect her pain because he'd offered her the remote chance of closure, to use the modern term. Fuck Zoom and Skype.

Good for me too, he wrote. *I'm in the Investigative Services Building, the smaller building to the west of main headquarters.*

Minutes later, she replied, *I remember. Meet in reception.*

When she showed up, he'd tell his colleagues the truth, unless he could figure a way out of it.

* * *

During dinner, Paula told her mother Mike's news about Connor. "At work, Connor struck me as a solid, sensible type. He must feel desperate."

"You would be, too, if your brother were in trouble."

He had been, three months ago, due to Paula's carelessness.

Her mother cut her pork chop. "Now you don't have to worry that this claim will put us in danger."

"Because the spirit world had nothing to do with the threat?" Paula scoffed. "I wasn't worried about that." Although she had thought about the bogus prediction occasionally. She pictured Olivia's near fall from a pile of boxes. The eight-year-old might be doing her schoolwork surrounded by people who were dealing or buying drugs. While Paula's priority was to protect her loved ones, she couldn't brush off dangers to a child. "Tomorrow morning, I'm going to Isabelle's house to find out what she knows about Connor. She'll wriggle out of this less in person."

"Can you drop me at David's on the way?"

It would be only a slight detour. Paula took a bite of mashed potatoes. She'd hoped her mother had given up on the idea of trying to reconcile her differences with David when it came to how they viewed the pandemic.

"We'd planned to go this weekend," her mother continued. "But you were busy."

Paula did owe Sam's father a visit, and COVID-related excuses to avoid social contact would only last so long. "I'll join you for the first half hour or so. If he annoys you with his conspiracy theories and put-downs about listening to science, you can come with me to Isabelle's. I'm sure you can amuse yourself while she and I talk business."

Theda nodded. "There's always tidying to do there."

While Paula loaded the dishwasher, her mother phoned David to ask if he'd be fine with them stopping by after breakfast tomorrow.

"He says he's not doing anything," her mother reported. "I'll take that as a yes."

A typically David backhanded welcome. Paula would have a lot to discuss with Sam on tomorrow's Skype call—Mike's discovery about Connor, her concerns about Leah's isolation, and whatever she gleaned about the state of their parents' relationship.

Monday morning, Paula's mother insisted on baking David a loaf of banana bread. "We can't go empty-handed."

Paula thought you could with family like David, but she helped her mother make a second loaf for Isabelle and Erin. They set off later than Paula had hoped, but breezed through downtown and crossed the Bow River to Bridgeland before ten.

David opened his front door as they walked up the steps of his bungalow. "I happened to look out the window."

Couldn't he admit to anticipating their visit? Inside, Paula handed him the banana loaf.

His eyebrows rose in delight, the same way Sam's sometimes did. "I knew Theda would bring a homemade treat."

They followed David to the kitchen, where he made tea and took out plates for the banana bread.

According to Sam, the décor of the house hadn't significantly changed since his mother died in 1984. Almond-coloured fridge that still worked. Lacquer countertops, only slightly stained. White cabinets, which had come back in style. Paula and Sam wondered if any hopes Theda had of romance with David were muted by the thought of competing with the ghost of a wife he'd adored. An aggressive cancer had taken her. It still disturbed Sam that she'd probably endured more pain than she'd let on. Rather than bring David and their two sons closer, her suffering and death distanced them from each other—to avoid dealing with their pain, according to Paula's private psychological assessment. David displayed no family photos, but the living room wall bore prints and paintings of northern Manitoba, where his late wife had grown up.

Paula carried the tray of food and tea to the living room. She and her mother settled on the plaid sofa and David on the recliner chair that faced the smart TV, one of the few recent additions to the home. David had never mentioned his appreciation for this gift from Sam. Paula gathered that David spent much of the day flipping through news and sports channels, with longer stops at *Jeopardy*.

He crossed one leg over the other and munched banana bread while Paula passed along Sam's report of his Sunday day trip to Bremen with a colleague and his wife.

David washed down the food with tea. "Travel rules in Germany must be less strict than here."

"We can drive wherever we want," Paula said.

"Only with our bubble-mates." David snorted.

Her mother set her teacup on the coffee table. "That reminds me, David, I made you this." She picked up her purse and took out a mask made from the same flowered material as Paula's and placed it beside her teacup. David loved gardening, a passion he shared with Theda.

"Won't hurt to wear it when I'm grocery shopping," David said. "I see a few people with them on already."

"Sam told me you were having your groceries delivered," Paula said. Sam called his father on Skype most weekends.

"There's always a few things unavailable when I order." David sniffed. "Or so they claim."

What would be the point of that conspiracy? Every time she shopped, Paula witnessed the unavailability—shelves and freezers stripped bare of frozen vegetables, meats, canned goods, milk, eggs. Her gaze rested on the flowered mask. "I'd have thought you'd be against wearing masks."

David's top leg moved up and down. "I'm in favour of protecting myself without government rules."

"Not everyone's a natural hermit," Paula said. He'd take this as a matter of fact, not an insult.

He looked at her mother. "Social butterflies, like Theda, can look after themselves too. Isolate if they're higher risk, while the young and healthy live life as normal."

"And COVID runs rampant through society," Paula said.

"And builds herd immunity," David said. "Why destroy the economy and people's jobs and mental health for the sake of a few old folk who are past our prime?"

"More than a few," Paula said. "And vulnerable younger ones as well."

Her mother leaned forward. "David, don't forget the people in long-term-care homes. The staff will be certain to bring the virus in. It spreads through group residences like wildfire."

He grimaced. "Most of those old folk are too gone to be much use. If I ever need to go into one of those places, shoot me first."

Paula had heard him say this before and didn't doubt he was sincere. She too didn't want to ruin life for the next generations, but she couldn't give up on people like Walter's wife. And how would the hospitals cope with a virus out of control? They'd have to decide whom to treat and whom to let die.

She finished her cup of tea. "I have to get to Isabelle's. Let me know when you're ready, Mum."

Her mother looked over her teacup at David. "I'll stay, if you want company."

"Sure do." His wrinkled face brightened. "I don't mind isolating with my TV, but it's becoming too much, even for an old hermit."

Paula left them to their detailed discussion of garden ideas. Theda planned to plant vegetables and flowers in Paula and Sam's backyard.

While cruising west on Memorial Drive, Paula wondered where her mother would live when COVID was over. Her mum wasn't as negative about long-term-care residences as David was, but she did want to postpone that lifestyle as long as possible. Perhaps she'd move in with David, if they made up. Or maybe she'd stay on with Paula, especially if Paula and Sam wound up spending most of the year apart. Paula doubted her mother would move back in with Erin and Isabelle and their boyfriends. While Theda had enjoyed her years in a house full of lively, younger folk, she'd complained about doing their housework. Paula had advised her to let the place go to force them to do their share.

"Paula," she'd said. "I can't see a mess and not clean. They don't seem to see it."

Paula understood. She'd be the same in that situation. Her mother also found that their music hurt her ears, she disagreed with most of their political and social opinions, and she didn't enjoy their television shows. "The stories move around too much, no one is likeable, and it's all sexual innuendo and people being abused or killed." Paula could agree with half of her mother's points, being between the generations.

When she and Sam had built his studio, their long-term idea had been to make it a granny flat for her mother, when the time came. But Sam loved having a den separate from the house. If he decided the Hamburg job wasn't for him, he'd want the studio back.

She entered Brentwood, her neighbourhood for nineteen years, where she and her then-husband Gary had lived after their move from Montreal. When they separated, she'd stayed in the house with their daughters, until Leah moved out and Erin was settled at university. Paula had moved to Ramsay, for an urban lifestyle, and sold the house jointly to Leah and Erin for nominal amounts. Paula held a mortgage for the full value of the home. Her daughters had been paying off their debts, Erin with rent from her roommates, Leah from her bartending work, which had crashed with the pandemic. Paula put both daughters' payments on hold until COVID was over. If it ever were.

She parked on the street in front of the house, a bungalow with an extension above the attached garage. The extension housed the master bedroom suite, which Erin and her boyfriend had taken over after her grandmother-cum-den mother left. Isabelle and her boyfriend had the basement bedroom and rec room. The students renting the other three bedrooms, on the main floor, had returned to their family homes when university instruction went online. Isabelle used one of the front bedrooms as her office.

On the front porch, Paula rang the doorbell and heard Salt bark. Isabelle answered, led Paula to her office, and proudly pointed out the room's features. One of the students had left behind an "awesome" workstation, including an ergonomic chair and a bookcase. Isabelle had painted the wall behind the chair green, to make her backdrops show up clearer on Skype, RingCentral, and the other online platforms.

Paula patted her old dog Pepper and suggested a COVID-safe talk on the front porch. They brought out kitchen chairs, the dogs following them all the way. Salt wove around Paula's legs so tightly she almost tripped, reminding her of another reason for her mother not to move back here. One time, her mother had tripped on a backpack a student had left on the stairs. Miraculously, she hadn't broken or strained anything. Pepper shambled to the entrance. Every time Paula saw their family dog, she wondered if this would be the last time. She'd told Erin that when it came time to put Pepper down, she absolutely wanted to be present.

She and Isabelle settled on the porch, angled toward each other. Isabelle wore a pink baseball hat to shade her eyes; her blonde ponytail protruded from the back. Paula put on her sunglasses. The temperature had risen remarkably the past few days, but they still needed sweaters and long pants before noon, even in this sunny and sheltered spot.

Paula stared at Isabelle and got to the point. "Why didn't you tell me Connor isn't in Rome? He's in Calgary."

Isabelle's gaze darted sideways. Her face flushed. She waved at a woman walking her dog on the sidewalk and shouted a "great day" greeting. Paula waited out her stalling.

"He asked me not to." Isabelle's gaze followed the woman walking away.

"Why?"

"You already felt guilty for letting him go. He didn't want you to know he'd also lost his chance to go to Europe, like you lost your chance to go see Sam there. He thought it would make you feel guiltier."

"He made you lie to protect me?"

"I didn't lie," Isabelle said. "I haven't talked to you since I found out." She wrinkled her nose. "How did you find out?"

Evidently, Connor hadn't told Isabelle about his meeting with Mike the previous afternoon. "When was the last time you talked to Connor?"

"Saturday. I texted him yesterday, but he said he wasn't up for Skype. He's really worried about his brother."

"What do you know about him? Gabriel?"

"Connor calls him Gabe." Isabelle squinted, either in contemplation or from the sun shining into her face. "He's a couple of years younger than Connor. They share an apartment. Their dad split when they were kids. Their mom looked after them okay until she took up with this hippie dude and moved with him to BC somewhere off the grid. Connor and Gabe didn't go with them."

"Why not?"

"Connor was in college, studying art," she said. "He didn't graduate," she added. "Gabe was in high school and didn't want to leave his friends. They got an apartment with money from their part-time jobs, and moved to a better one after we hired Connor and Gabe took up barber work."

"When did Gabe get into drugs?"

Isabelle started. "You know? Connor asked me not to tell you that, either, when he was working with us. He didn't want you to think he came from a grubby family."

Paula's chest tightened. "I wouldn't think that. I hope I'd have sympathized. Lots of families deal with this."

"Yeah, well, he was embarrassed about the whole thing. I wasn't even supposed to tell you about his parents taking off on them."

"Connor has too much pride."

Isabelle shifted on the chair. "He doesn't know when Gabe's serious drug use started. Their mom always smoked pot, and she gave it to Connor and Gabe before they were even in high school. Connor didn't like how it made him feel out of control. When they got older, he suspected Gabe had gotten into harder stuff but couldn't prove it. You'll have to ask Connor about it. I didn't ask too much." Isabelle's wide-set eyes narrowed. "Connor really meant to go to Europe, if he could find a flight, but then he didn't feel right about it with Gabe missing." She looked sideways at Paula. "Did Mike tell you all this?"

Paula kept her expression neutral. "Why do you ask that?"

"Mike would find out from the Missing Persons cops, if Connor finally reported Gabe missing. I told him to, but he didn't want to get Gabe in trouble with the people who . . ."

"Gabe might be working for, dealing drugs?"

"Connor doesn't know he is, for sure." Isabelle stared, her eyes wide. "What do we do now?"

"*We* do nothing," Paula said. "Mike will handle it as he sees best. Have you met Gabe?"

Isabelle shook her head. "Connor showed me pictures. They look kind of alike, except Connor's dark and Gabe's pale. Connor's also heavier. Gabe's thin, which might be the drugs."

Did the brothers sound alike on the phone? That might have inspired Connor to impersonate Gabriel. Since the "psychic" message hadn't come from another world, Isabelle wouldn't freak if Paula told her about it. But there was no reason for Isabelle to know. In any case, the minute Paula left, Isabelle was bound to contact Connor. He'd tell her himself, or not. Paula hoped he didn't coax Isabelle into a foolish next step.

Chapter Eight

Isabelle rocked in her office chair and ate her cheese sandwich while waiting to Skype with Connor. His text had said he'd call half an hour ago. No reply to her follow-ups. At last, the notification came. Connor's face appeared against a backdrop of Roman gladiators.

"What kept you?"

"Let me guess," he said, ignoring her question. "You heard from Paula?"

His beard looked bushier than it had two days ago, and his curly hair was growing raggedy. His clear glasses made her wonder if he really were in Rome, where it would be evening. But why would he lie about not going? She noted dark shadows under his eyes and set her backdrop to a forest scene, to soothe him. "Paula was—"

"I've done something stupid," he said and told her about calling Mike and pretending he was Gabe.

"Wow," Isabelle said. "I didn't know your brother was psychic."

"He's especially psychic when he's high. I don't take it seriously."

"Paula doesn't either."

"Mike does, or he listens, at least. That's why Gabe got into calling him, of all the cops in the Homicide unit."

"Mike's smart."

Finnegan climbed onto Connor's lap and blocked the lower half of his face. Her yellow eyes staring at Isabelle seemed to say, "I clued you in to Connor's being in Calgary. You owe me for this." Connor and

Gabe had adopted the cat during a freezing spell a few months earlier when she'd meowed all night on their patio. They'd posted notices in the neighbourhood, but no one contacted them.

Connor peered between Finnegan's alert ears and recapped his meeting with Mike. "Stupid of me to tell a cop about Gabe's dealing. Stupid to get Paula into it, and pointless, in the end. Now that she knows there might be shady business at the bike store, she'll wrap up the claim and split."

Finnegan leaped off Connor's lap, revealing his full face. His eyes looked less shadowed than before. Sometimes spilling the truth made people feel better.

"All this has got me curious about the bike store," she said. "What's its name again?"

"Cycle Life."

She'd research it later. "Do you want to go there and scope the place out? We'll pretend we're shopping for bikes."

Connor leaned back on his chair. "I can't do that."

"Why not?"

"What if they recognize me, as Gabe's brother?"

From the photos she'd seen, Isabelle doubted anyone on the street would pick them out as related.

Connor pulled on his beard. "Mike wore a baseball cap to the park. I guess that would help disguise me, if we went." He glanced behind him. "I really am interested in a new bike, if I could afford one."

"I've got work to do this afternoon but could go tomorrow."

He shook his head. "No, Isabelle. We can't do this. Gabe has a friend who works there. I've met her, and she'd blow my cover."

"Who's that?"

"Kelsey." Connor rubbed his forehead. "I called her after Gabe took off, in case she knew anything. She didn't and hasn't heard from him in over a month. I called her again yesterday, after meeting Mike. Still no word." Connor's voice cracked. "Kelsey denies the store is dealing drugs. She says Gabe gets them elsewhere."

"But she knows he takes them."

"I guess. We don't talk about it directly. I don't know her well." Connor rubbed his forehead harder, above his left eye. "On top of all this, I'm getting a migraine. The Chinook blowing in."

He'd explained that the barometric pressure changes related to warming weather precipitated the migraine headaches he got several times a year. "Bummer," she said. "Are you taking meds?"

He nodded and blinked. "I've got the aura now. Light flashes, weird shapes."

Finnegan's head popped up. Apparently, she'd returned to Connor's lap. She lowered herself again. Isabelle could see only the top of her head and ears.

"The meds might kick in by tomorrow. Is that Tuesday?" Connor's face brightened. "I think Kelsey said she gets Tuesday off in exchange for working Saturdays. I'll phone her to make sure, on the pretext of commiserating about Gabe. She'll buy it. Kelsey knows I'm worried about him. I got her worried too, yesterday, when we talked."

Finnegan's orange-white-and-black fur filled the screen. She padded over the keyboard.

"You pest," Connor said.

"Let me know if tomorrow works." Isabelle picked up her phone and searched "Cycle Life." She checked the driving distance. Twenty-three minutes from her house. "Do you want me to pick you up?"

"I'll bike," he said. "It can't be far. Gabe discovered it as his local bike store."

According to Google Maps, Connor could bike there in about twenty minutes, depending on where in Forest Lawn he lived. "Do you think Gabe's drug dealing began with him going to the store to buy a bike or parts?"

"Could be," Connor said. "He likes the idea of buying local, rather than from big chain stores."

Finnegan meowed. "I've gotta go feed her. All this cat does is eat. Me too. I'm putting on weight staying home all day."

"Tell me about it," Isabelle said, to be sympathetic. She patted her flat stomach.

* * *

Paula adjusted her position in her office chair. For the past half hour, she'd done all the talking on her Skype call with Sam. They had so much to cover since they'd last spoke, on Sunday morning. Sam had listened with interest, but now his hazel eyes glazed over. Their call was later than usual, since he'd stayed at work into the evening. It was past ten thirty p.m. in Hamburg, and Sam was a morning person.

She brought her recap of Isabelle's limited information about Connor to a close. "I'm sure she's talked to him already. Who knows how much they'll both keep from me."

"Does this store sell bikes and equipment manufactured in China?"

"I gather that's the case with most bike shops in Calgary," she said. "Why?"

"I've heard China's the main manufacturer of synthetic opioids and other laboratory produced drugs," Sam said. "Exporters could easily slip powder or pills into bikes or parts shipped overseas to the store. Customs officers might not think to check a bike pump or, if they did, not notice the tiny grains."

Paula pictured the boxes stacked in Josh's office—Olivia climbing on top of them, almost falling. Kelsey still hadn't emailed the receipts for the stolen goods, but that wasn't unusual for claimants, even for claims of larger amounts. Still, if the store were a front for illegal drugs, their bike-related sales might be relatively small potatoes.

"I'm only guessing," Sam said. "I'm no expert on the drug market."

"Me neither." She fiddled with her scarf, a striped one this time. "I should research this or, better yet, assign Isabelle. With her skills on the net, she'd unearth more than I would. That is, if I were to get more involved, which I'm not."

Sam laughed.

She let go of the scarf. "You're right. I'm tempted to dive in, but that rabbit hole could lead to . . . I don't know where, which is the point."

His expression sobered. "I won't tell you not to dive."

"You should."

"Sorry," he said. "Your choices are your own. What time shall I call tomorrow?"

"Whenever you're finished with work and dinner."

He shook his head. "It's your birthday. You tell me when, and I'll be here."

Most people wouldn't view that as a gift, but it was one from Sam, given his devotion to his work. They signed off.

Paula finished her afternoon tasks and checked her business email a final time. No reply to her follow-up message to Kelsey. Despite Mike's advice to avoid the Cycle Life, why not stop by the store to give Kelsey a nudge, but no more than that? Paula had driven her car to work that afternoon so that she could buy a new ironing board on the way home. Her mother found Paula's board too wobbly for properly ironing masks. Cycle Life would be a short detour.

She closed up the office. As she entered the hallway, she heard footsteps above her. Someone coming down the stairs.

A woman stopped on the landing. "I thought everyone in the building was working from home."

"I'd thought so too," Paula said, "apart from me."

"I just came in for a few things." The woman drew closer. "Are you Paula?"

Paula nodded. The woman had frizzed bangs and grey hair tied in a braid that reached her waist. She wore layers of colourful clothing. Paula didn't recognize her, and she'd met almost everyone in the building.

"I'm Valeria." She motioned toward Paula's office. "Isabelle mentioned you. Fun girl. Real chatty."

"That's her." Paula remembered Isabelle had befriended a woman who worked for a company that made hemp products. Their premises were on the top floor. Valeria's earth-toned shoulder bag was probably made from hemp.

"Would it be legal for us to walk down the stairs together?" Valeria asked.

Paula smiled. "Fortunately, this old building has a wide staircase."

Valeria shifted her shopping bag to her right hand so she could hold on to the railing. Paula kept close to the wall, but they were less than two metres apart.

She recalled something Isabelle had told her about the woman. "You're the one who saw the ghost rumoured to haunt this building."

Valeria glanced at her. "It wasn't me who saw her. An optometrist who worked in the office next to you told me about a few sightings by others. This was some years ago."

Second- or third-hand information. "What kind of sightings?"

Valeria looked over again. "Why? Have you seen her?"

"Just curious." Such beliefs were so beyond Paula's understanding that they intrigued her, in a way some might call academic. Her university major had been anthropology.

"I thought you might have had an apparition," Valeria said, "since you're alone in the building. She seems to favour this, from the reports."

"What do people see?"

They exited the building and faced each other.

"Fluttery visions in the halls," Valeria said. "A couple were outside your office. Isabelle shivered at that."

"I'll bet." Paula felt cool in the shade of the building.

"Each report described her differently. Age, clothing, contemporary or period dress."

"People seeing what they expect." The building, which was over a hundred years old, could prompt someone to see a ghost in historic dress.

Paula made sure the building was locked and told Valeria the owner had designated her responsible for the premises in the absence of everyone else.

Valeria nodded and pointed west. "I'm parked down the street. Paula, it's been great to talk with a human being in the flesh. We should meet for coffee when this is over."

"I'd like that."

Valeria looked about her age, and Paula had lost touch with her closest girlfriends during her transitions—her shift from school to work, marriage, and parenthood; her move to Calgary; her divorce and move to Ramsay; and her new life with Sam. Valeria might be too New Age for her, but so was Callie, and Paula still thought of Callie as her best friend even though she'd died over three and a half years ago. If Paula were ever to see a ghost, it would be her.

"Bye now." Valeria startled Paula from her reverie. "See you on the other side."

Paula drove to Walmart and bought an ironing board that she hoped would satisfy her mother. From there it was fifteen minutes to Cycle Life. By the time she arrived, the clouds had blown away, turning the sky bright blue. It seemed foolish to worry about danger.

Three vehicles were parked in the lot. Josh's bike was in the rack outside the front door, which was propped open. Paula entered the store and spotted Josh and Herb serving customers. The number of bikes in the showroom had thinned by about a third since she had been here on Friday. Olivia's table and chair were in the corner between the helmets and bike accessories, but no Olivia in sight. Some hooks on wall racks behind the table were bare of items.

Josh left the woman he was serving and came over to Paula. "You're here for the receipts? Kelsey said she left them for you to pick up in the office. Let's go have a look."

Paula was sure Kelsey had said she'd email them, but this was equally good. "Have you had a chance to look over the draft I statement I sent?

"Not yet. Too busy," he said. "Monday's usually my day off, but I couldn't afford the time." He started toward the office.

Paula caught up to him as they passed the table. "Olivia's not here today?"

"Zabrina, my ex, had an early shift." His lips narrowed. "Our plan to homeschool her here isn't working."

The pile of boxes in the office looked unchanged since Friday. Paula would love a peek inside them, although any drugs hidden in bicycle parts were probably too well concealed for an amateur like her to find. Papers, envelopes, and file folders were stacked haphazardly on the desk, covering the bottom of the angel figurine.

Josh rifled through the mess. "She mentioned an envelope. You might have to come back tomorrow for it. I don't want to bother her at home when she's sick."

"I hope it's not serious."

"She started coughing during lunch and thought she should leave in case it's COVID."

"I hope it's not, for your sakes and that of your customers." She'd noticed Herb and a man leaning close together examining a bike.

Josh opened a desk drawer and took out a manila envelope. "Here it is." He handed the thin envelope to Paula.

Since the flap wasn't sealed, she pulled out the contents partway. The top two sheets were receipts for e-bikes, and there were a few receipts for accessories underneath. No list of items, as she'd requested. She slipped the papers back in. "There should be more than this."

Josh nodded. "Clearly, she didn't finish. I forgot. Tomorrow won't work. It's Kelsey's day off. Her first week of working full-time this spring, she's not off to a roaring start." His tone was nonchalant rather than critical.

Paula glanced at the angel on the desk. "Is that Kelsey's figurine?"

He followed her gaze. "Mine. Olivia gave it to me for my birthday."

The eight-inch ceramic figure wore white and held something out in her hands, as though offering it as a gift. "What's that she's holding?"

"It does look like a "she" in this apparition." he said. "I read angels gender-shift."

"Do they?" Clearly, she'd been wrong to assume Josh dismissed the spirit world.

He looked up. "Do you need me for more?"

"Not now." She fluttered the envelope. "I'll follow up with Kelsey by email. No rush for her to deal with this."

"Sorry for the delay. My fault, really. We've needed her to deal with customers."

"Sales look impressive," Paula said, as they re-entered the showroom.

"I worry about new supply coming to replenish our stock," Josh said. "COVID's causing manufacturing and shipment delays that back everything up. Excuse me." He left to talk to a woman and man with two children who milled around some kids' bikes.

Across the room, a man wheeled a bicycle toward the exit, Herb beside him. His ponytail flowed down the back of the checked shirt that looked like the same one he'd worn on Friday.

She followed them outside, where the customer mounted the e-bike. Herb pointed past the furniture store next door and told him to do his test ride around the whole building, keeping a watch out for any cars. Paula realized that on Friday, she'd looked at the rear parking lot from the Cycle Life workshop deck but hadn't gone into the lot. Presumably, the police had checked it for clues, but she had nothing to do for the rest of the day. She put the envelope in her car and strolled past Furniture Sellers, its storefront windows concealed by blinds. A notice on the front door apologized for the store's indefinite closure.

The street beside the building sloped down to Furniture Sellers' basement level. The store's delivery door and a regular steel door faced the rear lot, now bathed in afternoon sun. Paula put on her sunglasses. From the furniture store, the lot sloped upward to Cycle Life. A whirring sound made her turn to the e-bike behind her, the cyclist on his second lap of the building. He pedalled uphill with ease, rode past Cycle Life and Countertops, and disappeared around the far corner. In her peripheral view, Paula noticed the regular door to Furniture Sellers open. A man emerged into the sunshine and lit a cigarette.

She went over to him. "Do you work here?"

"Used to," he said. "We're closed for COVID." He wore a T-shirt, shorts, and flip-flops.

"Why are you here, then?"

He drew on his cigarette. She guessed he was in his forties. Brown hair curled over his forehead and ears. Tattoos covered his lower arms—one of the abstract designs was a bird. The investigating police hadn't found any witnesses. Maybe they'd missed him. His visits to his workplace would likely be sporadic, like Valeria's.

"Did the police talk to you about the break and enter at Cycle Life?"

The man's eyebrows shot up. "It was burgled?"

"You didn't know?"

"How would I? We're closed." He looked up at Cycle Life's deck, one storey above them. "I haven't seen Herb since, well, before COVID."

"You know Herb?"

"We run into each other outside for a smoke, or lunch, when the weather's good. I thought I might see him this week, now that it's warming up."

So, this wasn't the man's one-off visit. "I'm Paula Savard," she said to prompt him to offer his name.

He flicked cigarette ash to the pavement.

"I'm the insurance adjuster for the break and enter," she continued. "Have you noticed any activity around here the past week or two?"

"I told you—we're closed. My manager asked me to meet a delivery here today." Smoke billowed from his nose with his words. "We still get the odd shipment, items previously ordered. They're late, as usual." He took another drag. "When did you say this break and enter was?"

"Wednesday evening or Thursday morning, between six p.m. and nine a.m."

He scanned the staircase leading up to Cycle Life. Light bounced off the workshop window, which had evidently been replaced during the past three days. "I was here early morning last week," he said. "I forget which day. They all blur together. I saw a couple of people going up those stairs. They stood for a few seconds on the porch. One of them disappeared behind the other then reappeared, and they both walked in. I knew Cycle Life had stayed open, so I assumed they had business there, maybe dealing with stock."

Paula's heart beat faster at the prospect of a witness, but she decided not to take out her notebook or ask to record him, since he seemed a bit skittish. "Can you describe them?"

"It was dark." He puffed the cigarette, apparently reflecting. "But there was some light from the moon or stars. I don't remember a deck light. Might be burned out. I had a better angle on the one who stood farther back. The way they moved, I thought the back one was a man and the other a woman. That's all I can tell you." He dragged on the cigarette.

"The police would find your information useful."

"I don't even know which night it was." He dropped the cigarette butt to the pavement and mashed it with his flip-flop sole. "Wait. It *was* Thursday morning. I was up early because I'd fallen asleep Wednesday night watching *Survivor*. I woke up at five or six the next morning."

"And came out here right away?"

"After puttering around."

She looked beyond him, at Furniture Sellers. "You slept overnight in there?"

He stared at her; his eyes narrowed. "I had to meet an early morning delivery. Come to think of it, that's why I woke up. Thursday. That's right. It was my manager's idea I stay over, to make sure I wouldn't miss it." He looked away. *Liar.* "We'd been waiting months for this important shipment." He nodded over his shoulder, at the store. "Why not sleep over? There's plenty of beds in there to choose from. Why let them lie vacant?"

Too much defensive detail. Probably a squatter, although if the man knew Herb, he might be a Furniture Sellers employee, or a former employee, with a key to the place. Maybe he'd moved in after the store closed for reasons that didn't matter to her. Would the police kick him out of his temporary home? She didn't know the break and enter officers in this district well enough to trust them to see the value of accommodating this witness to obtain his information, and Mike might have succeeded in bringing the case into Major Crimes. She'd talk to him first.

"Nice meeting you," the man said. "I've got to get back to work. That's a joke." He whirled around and disappeared inside.

Paula took her phone from her purse and texted Mike, *Can we meet today?*

Chapter Nine

After his call to Westwinds, Mike put the casserole in the oven so supper would be prompt and then returned to the back patio. Paula sat on the outdoor sofa keeping an eye on Eli and his friend Aria, who were playing one-on-one soccer in the yard. Mike told her that he and a couple of colleagues in Drugs and Missing Persons had convinced Robbery to take over the Cycle Life break and enter.

"It helps that they aren't busy at the moment, with robberies down in the city," he added. "They're sending a guy to Furniture Sellers tonight at seven, after Cycle Life closes, to not give them a heads-up. I'll tag along, since I initiated the involvement of Major Crimes." He had also got Paula into this and owed her his attention.

She held up her phone. "While you were inside, Isabelle sent me about twenty pictures of Connor and his brother, which she found on Instagram and Facebook. All taken before Gabe disappeared."

"Send them to me."

"Will do."

After Mike confirmed he'd received them, Paula tucked her phone into her purse and said she'd leave by the side yard, to minimize their indoor contact.

As they stepped down from the deck, Mike dodged a ball which Eli had kicked wildly. Aria raced after it.

"Can you be goalie?" Eli shouted at Mike.

"Okay, after I see Paula out." Mike straightened to exaggerate his height. "You two will never get one past me." He continued toward the side gate.

"I was hoping to catch Novak before I left," Paula said.

Mike checked his watch. "He's been biking almost an hour. Good to see him keen on any activity." They walked to the front yard, and Mike thanked her for bringing her news. "Once more, you uncover something we missed."

She smiled. "I'll take the compliment, but who'd have thought to check a closed store for a squatter?"

Down the street, Novak was pedalling toward the house. "Wait a sec and you can see your old friend."

"It's been three and half years . . ." She trailed off and stared at a point beyond Novak. Mike knew she was thinking of Callie, whose murder had brought Paula into his and Novak's circle. They'd shown up at her house to question her, and not altogether kindly, since they'd viewed her as a suspect.

Novak rode onto the sidewalk and stopped in front of them. He blinked at Paula a few times before his face lit with recognition. "Paula? It's been a long time, but Mike's been keeping me up to scratch. How's your break and enter claim coming along?"

"Almost settled," she said. "I don't hold out much hope we'll recover the stolen items. Bikes sell quickly in today's underground market."

Novak got off his bike. "I'm thinking I'll buy a good lock for this one so I can stop for a milkshake or something. A saddlebag would be handy, too. My way of repaying Lucy for the loan."

Mike loved hearing his friend full of plans. He told Paula he'd let her know what happened tonight. After she left, Novak asked why she'd been visiting. Mike saw no reason to withhold details from his comrade in the Homicide unit.

"She located a witness," Mike said and summarized Paula's findings as they walked to the backyard.

While Novak stored the bike in the shed, Mike reminded the kids that Aria's mother would arrive soon to pick her up. If Lucy and Kyle were late, would Mike trust Novak to babysit? This revived-Novak, who was now sauntering into the house.

Goalie-Mike planted himself in front of the side fence between two flowerpots that served as goalposts. He fended off several shots but allowed each kid to score once—the right balance of obstacles and success, in his view, although Lucy would say blocking the majority was Mike being competitive. Kyle would have let in a few more. If Mike were less competitive, he might consider if Lucy's and Kyle's approach was better for kids' self esteem, rather than dismiss it as modern pampering.

Mike called the game to halt so they could clean up Aria for her mother. Their shared homeschooling arrangement was working reasonably well. Tomorrow, he and Lucy would unload Eli on Aria's family.

Lucy and Kyle arrived in time for dinner. During the meal, Novak chatted about his discovery of a bike path near the airport, a good forty-minute ride from here. Novak's rave review reminded Mike to get his own bicycle in shape so they could ride together before Novak recovered enough to go back to his ranch. CPS had hired him on a three-month renewable contract, so he could decide to leave next month.

After dinner, Mike drove to Mountainview Industrial Park and arrived ten minutes before the appointed time. A sign announced the building's three stores, with Furniture Sellers listed at the top in the largest letters. Cycle Life was below it, and CounterTops, curiously, was at the bottom. No cars were in the front lot, which had north and south entrances.

Mike continued to the back of the building in case the Robbery guy was early. No cars or people in this lot either. He cruised by the furniture store and up a slope, for a view of Cycle Life's rear entrance. A half-flight of stairs led up to a deck with a door and window. There were no doors or windows at the basement level, as Paula had observed. The deck faced a currently deserted alley between two other industrial buildings. The alley led to a craft brewery restaurant, where Mike had eaten one time. From here, the brewery blocked any mountain view for which the park had been named.

As Mike passed CounterTops, which also had no basement entrances, he spotted a Ford Taurus in his rearview mirror. That would be Bonneville from Robbery. Mike made a U-turn and pulled up beside the unmarked car, now parked behind Furniture Sellers. A woman got out—a new transfer to the Robbery unit, Megan Molina.

Mike got out of his vehicle. "Bonneville didn't come?"

"He decided he'd better go home one evening before his wife divorces him."

Mike nodded. Bonneville was a workaholic, even when work was slow. Megan—the few times they'd met, she'd asked Mike to call her by her first name—stood close to six feet tall. She wore a blue jacket, open at the front, and a beige shirt and pants. Her dark hair was tied up in what might be called a French twist. Mike had last spoken to her when he was looking into women in the Robbery unit who fit Connor-the-psychic's description. But she was too young, in her early thirties. Her eyes were brown, not blue. Officers were unlikely to wear butterfly scarves on the job, which had steered Mike's search to civilian staff and Paula. Clever of Connor.

They walked to the door. No windows to look into. Megan rang the buzzer. This was Robbery's case; Mike was her sidekick.

She frowned when no one answered. "Your friend, the insurance adjuster, must have scared him away."

"Or he's not answering." Mike had anticipated both possibilities, but he hadn't thought Megan knew about his friendship with Paula. Megan had joined Robbery after Paula's last case with Homicide. "The company might be checking messages to not lose business. We can try to contact him through them."

Megan nodded. "They'll also want to know about a squatter."

Mike brought up the store's phone number and handed his phone to Megan, so she could leave the message and her phone number, if and when voicemail kicked in.

"I'll give them the squatter's story, at face value," Megan said to him, before speaking into the phone. "This is Detective Megan Molina from Calgary Police Service. We're looking for one of your employees, who might have witnessed a break and enter at the adjacent bicycle store, when he was present at Furniture Sellers' northeast branch." She returned the phone to Mike. "What are the odds we get a reply?"

"Less than fifty-fifty."

"You're on," she said. "If they call, you owe me a free coffee from Homicide's coffee machine."

"That's worth less than fifty cents." He wasn't sure that qualified as a joke but was quite sure he liked the crooked eyetooth revealed by her smile.

* * *

The next morning at Westwinds, Megan appeared at Mike's cubicle entrance. "You lost," she said. "The manager of Furniture Sellers returned my call. She said to hold off on approaching the squatter until she makes an arrangement."

"What does that mean?"

"She hung up before I could ask. Are you free to try the store again, after she gets back to me?"

Mike fumbled for his coffee cup. "I've got a meeting at noon. Otherwise, nothing on the schedule today."

"Good. I'll keep you posted." She smiled. "I'll hold you to that free coffee." She left before he could think of a witty reply.

He took a gulp of coffee. She was attractive. Her blue pantsuit followed her curves, and he liked women who approached his height. Since he hadn't noticed her at Westwinds before this spring, he assumed she'd transferred from one of the district offices. He had no clue about her relationship status. She didn't wear a wedding ring, but many officers didn't, as jewellery could interfere with their physical tasks. Maybe he'd ask around. Was dating coworkers allowed these days? He and Megan worked in separate units, although in the same division in this relatively small Investigative Services Building. But neither was the other's direct superior in the CPS hierarchy. Their involvement might not be prohibited, but it would be tricky. Police relationships usually tanked. He was proof of this. And breakups within the division were usually awkward, messy. Sometimes one person transferred out. He brushed the ruminations from his mind and got into his paperwork.

Twenty minutes later, Megan reappeared in his doorway. "All set—ten a.m. at Furniture Sellers. We can take my car and should easily be back for your meeting." She fiddled with her paisley tie. "One condition. The squatter, Dustin, has asked us to wear masks. His manager says we'll understand when we meet him."

"No problem." Mike kept a mask in his suit jacket pocket in case anyone he interviewed made this request. This was the first, so far.

"Let's meet in the atrium at nine thirty."

She was waiting when he arrived precisely on time. On their way through the reception area, she asked how his friend Novak was enjoying his return from retirement.

"He's settling in," Mike said. He'd shared Novak's psychological troubles only with the division head.

"They say he was your mentor in Homicide."

"I think of him as that. He coached me through my first case." Strangely, Mike wanted to tell her more. "Indirectly, it relates to my interest in this B and E. That earlier case was where we both met Paula, the insurance adjuster handling the Cycle Life claim."

"I heard she's been a big help on some homicide files," Megan said. "I think it's good to outsource certain police work to qualified civilians. They offer a different perspective."

"I agree, but we need to be mindful of the risks. And so do they." Risks Paula didn't want anymore, understandably.

They arrived at Furniture Sellers before ten and parked in the back lot. Again, Megan rang the bell. She'd lead the questioning, and he'd take the notes for the Robbery file. The door opened, and they flashed their badges at Dustin, who plucked a disposable mask from a box on a console table beside the door. A giant bottle of hand sanitizer, boxes of antiseptic wipes, and a pack of cigarettes sat beside the box of masks. Dustin stepped back but didn't shut the door in their faces. He fit Paula's description—a wiry man with close-set eyes and tattooed arms.

Megan and Mike put on the masks they'd brought, hers a disposable type, his plain black, and with Dustin's next step backward, they entered the basement. Mike closed the door behind them. To their right were sofas and chairs arranged in conversation nooks. Beyond were dining room arrangements and then darkness. The area looked vast enough to extend under Cycle Life. To their left, behind the garage doors, were cartons and furniture wrapped in plastic and stacked in piles.

"Still getting deliveries?" Mike said.

Dustin nodded. "Previous orders that were delayed for the usual reasons. They build up with no customers coming in to buy."

"Are you staying here for work?" Megan asked.

"Not exactly, but the manager's given me the okay. Turns out it's good you came by, to be up front about it. We can talk upstairs."

Dustin grabbed the hand sanitizer and the wipes then led them down an aisle straight ahead to a staircase. Mike followed Dustin and Megan up to the ground level. The closed blinds at the front of the store were so thick that Dustin's silhouette wouldn't be visible from outside. Mike noticed Dustin held his right arm stiffly to his body. Could be a shoulder problem.

They settled in a conversation nook, Mike on a leather sofa that was more comfortable than the one he had at home. Perhaps he'd shop here if he got his own place. Megan sat on a love seat to his left, and Dustin on the matching chair across from Mike. Dustin sprayed sanitizer on his hands and rubbed them thoroughly. Megan did the same. Mike took the hint, to help put Dustin at ease. Two months ago, he'd have labelled Dustin neurotic. Now, this was normal.

Above them, a chandelier illuminated their nook, which struck Mike as pure showroom. No signs Dustin used this space. Mike took out his notebook and pen. Megan asked Dustin if he minded her recording their conversation.

"I have nothing to hide." Dustin crossed his arms and legs.

Megan looked at him. "Why don't you start by telling us if you're living here full-time?"

"My manager gave me permission last night." Dustin's voice was muffled through his mask, but Mike could make out most of the words. "She called me after you contacted her, suspecting it was me. I'd told her about my problem." Dustin explained that he and his wife had separated at the start of COVID. The day the World Health Organization declared COVID-19 a global pandemic, she told him she wanted him out by the end of the month.

"Wasn't her timing perfect?" Dustin said. "March 11. I'll never forget the day." His beady gaze darted between Megan and Mike as he described his commiserations with the store manager. "Customers trickled away with the health order," he said. "We had plenty of time to talk."

The manager had offered to help him find an apartment and joked that if the government forced them to close, Dustin could move into the store. It had all the furnishings he'd need, plus a staff kitchenette and a bathroom with a shower. "The previous manager suffered from profuse sweating," Dustin said. "He had the shower installed so he could use it and change his shirts several times a day to avoid putting off customers, and even then . . ." His mask bunched up, presumably from his wrinkling nose.

Mike's nose wrinkled too. He felt a sneeze coming on; mask material irritated his nostrils.

As he talked, Dustin uncrossed his arms, seemingly growing relaxed. He said that when the Alberta government ordered nonessential businesses closed, he still hadn't found an apartment he liked and remembered his manager's joke.

"I thought, why let this go to waste?" He looked around the showroom. "I had a key for meeting deliveries. That part of what I told your adjuster was true. She was the one who put you on to me?" He raised his eyebrows. Megan and Mike remained silent. "I left my car at my wife's, to not invite questions," Dustin continued. "I get my groceries delivered. Who needs more than this?" He extended his arms, taking in the whole showroom. "Beats being locked up in an apartment."

Mike could relate to that. He'd miss his spacious house. He glanced at the tables, which were set with candle and flower centrepieces, salt and pepper shakers, napkin holders, and place mats. "Where do you eat and sleep?"

"Over there." Dustin gazed beyond Megan's love seat. "I keep to one bedroom and living room display, to not mess up the others."

Mike couldn't see signs of Dustin squatting. Either he was neat or closer displays concealed his sleeping and living quarters. Near the far wall, Mike glimpsed a door. "Is that your bathroom?" he asked, pointing.

"It was put in for customers," Dustin said. "The one with a shower's in the basement. So's our lunchroom, with a fridge and microwave. That's all I go downstairs for, except to meet deliveries and go smoke outside. Someone might see me out front." His eyes crinkled. "I guess that doesn't matter now that I'm here legit."

"You went outside early Thursday morning to smoke," Mike said, then remembered Megan was supposed to lead the conversation.

"You noticed two people enter Cycle Life's workshop?" she said.

Dustin folded his arms then winced, as though the movement had caused him pain. "First, are you booting me out? Because if you are, I won't say another word. My manager called Bob Sellers, the owner, last night. He approved my staying here until the store reopens. What harm am I doing? I offered to pay him enough to cover water and electricity, but he said it was fine as long as I keep my usage minimal. Decent guy, Bob."

Megan shared a glance with Mike. He couldn't recall the legalities of living in commercial zones. Much would depend on the situation, he supposed. He'd pulled some overnighters at Westwinds and would have crashed on a sofa if he'd had one. Would it be different if he slept there a week, or a month? He couldn't see how Dustin's presence was harmful. He could arguably be called the company's security guard, working for the cost of accommodation and utilities. Mike nodded at Megan.

She turned to Dustin. "We'll confirm with Bob Sellers, of course, but the police have no problem with your living here as long as the owner agrees."

Bob *Sellers*. Mike had been slow to grasp the play on Bob's surname. *Cellars*, a synonym for basement. Furniture Sellers. The store's basement showroom was larger than this main floor.

Megan asked Dustin to describe what he'd witnessed after five on Thursday morning. With her gentle steering, he related the events he'd told Paula. Mike took notes while stifling the tickle in his nose.

"Last night," Dustin said, "as I drifted to sleep, it hit me that I'd gotten a view of the man's silhouette, when he looked sideways for a second. From the shape of his profile, I think he had a beard and wore glasses."

Mike sat upright. An image of Connor in Chestermere flashed through his mind.

"He was young," Dustin added. "I got the sense from his movements."

"How would you describe his build?" Mike asked.

"Normal," Dustin said. "Not overweight but not thin, since he blocked out the woman most of the time. He was bigger than her, but not huge, if you know what I mean."

Stocky, like Connor? Mike took out his phone and found the pictures of Connor and his brother that Paula had sent. "Would you recognize him from a photograph?"

"I might," Dustin said. "I can't for the life of me describe people I've seen, but I'm quick at recognizing return customers. They appreciate this."

Mike scrolled through the pictures, some of each brother alone and others of them together. Gabriel was slimmer and had red hair. Connor had dark colouring, but that difference wouldn't be noticeable in the near dark. Neither one had a beard in the pictures. Evidently, Connor had grown his after he was laid off, a common occurrence these days. But Gabe could have grown one too. Both brothers wore heavy-framed glasses in some pictures and none in others when they were likely wearing contact lenses. Mike paused at a picture of one of them in silhouette, standing on a ridge after sunset or sunrise, in a three-quarter pose. The silhouette looked more stocky than slim.

He rose to show the picture to Dustin, who recoiled in his chair. *Right.* Mike set the phone on the table and cleaned it with an antiseptic wipe, avoiding all contact between the phone and his skin.

"I'm used to safe handling of evidence," he said, to reassure Dustin. In a pandemic, the whole world was a crime scene.

Dustin rolled his right shoulder. To relieve some stiffness, or was he hesitating? He picked up the phone. Mike returned to the sofa, so as not to intimidate Dustin by hovering over him. Megan fixed her gaze on Dustin as he stared at the phone. Mike appreciated that she'd remained silent when it was appropriate for him to intervene. Ego and chatter could kill interviews.

He turned to Dustin. "Scroll through the other pictures, if you want."

"I think this is him." Dustin looked up. "I can't be sure without the beard, but the way he stands. I think so."

Connor?

Megan thanked Dustin for his help and asked for his contact information.

"I'm trusting you guys to keep your word," Dustin said, and provided his cell phone number and email address.

"We might ask you to come to the station for a more complete ID," Megan said.

Dustin shuddered. "It's not right for you to make me come to a crowded indoor place."

"We'll take care to keep you away from social contact."

"We'll see. Is that all? I could use a smoke."

"Do you ever smoke in here?" Megan asked.

He shook his head. "It's a devil to get the smell out of the furniture. That wouldn't be fair to the owner and manager. They've treated me well during this tough time."

Mike thought about asking him to show them his living space, but Dustin was already heading for the stairs. In the basement, he strode to the console table for his cigarette pack. Mike could make a second trip to confirm the basement did extend under Cycle Life, if this became relevant.

Outside, Dustin looked up at Cycle Life's deck. It was possible he'd remember more details with the help of a police artist. Megan and Mike wished him well and left. They didn't speak until they were driving out of the lot.

Mike told her that Dustin's ID pointed to Connor. "I'd have put money on Gabe. He's the one with the link to Cycle Life."

"Is the next step to interview Connor?"

"I'd prefer to act on a more conclusive ID but don't relish trying to get Dustin to Westwinds for harder evidence."

"I can't say Robbery will go ahead without evidence this is more than a break and enter," Megan said.

"Nor Homicide or Missing Persons, without an official report." Or drug trafficking without more than Connor's hearsay account. "Questioning Connor is worth a shot, but I don't expect he'll be forthcoming. Do we have enough to haul him into Westwinds?"

"Probably not. But we could go to his place this afternoon, after your meeting."

He nodded. She assumed they'd go together, without a directive from their superiors. He liked all that, but a question nagged.

"Why would Connor break into Cycle Life?" Mike said. "And then scheme to get Paula on the claim, knowing she'd dig deeper than most and might discover he was the thief?"

"That is odd."

"He must really want to find his brother. Clearly, according to Connor, Gabriel's disappearance relates to whatever is going on at Cycle Life."

"And Paula is the best one to dig that out." Megan stopped for a red light. "It makes sense in a twisted way."

"Paula was Connor's colleague and friend. He trusts her," Mike said. "She might convince him to be honest with us."

"You mean, we bring Paula along for the interview?"

"That wouldn't be protocol," Mike said. "But she told me she'd like to pay him a visit. She could easily be present when we show up this afternoon."

"If you arrange that, I'm game."

First, he'd have to think this plan through—the ethics, the risk of screwing up the case. The potential danger to Paula. And balance these against his opportunity to spend the afternoon with Megan. He looked at her profile, at her pleasantly curved lips that might be soft and warm to touch.

"I'll mull it over for the next few hours," he said. "If it seems right, I'll call her."

Chapter Ten

In his glass office, Novak racked his brain, but he couldn't come up with an alternate plan to meeting Farida Bashar in sight of the entire Homicide unit. Already, it was almost eleven a.m. She'd be here in half an hour. He'd run out of time to tell the staff sergeant that he'd arranged for the widow of a cold-case victim to come into Westwinds without running it by the team first.

Beg for forgiveness rather than ask permission. He'd also beg to participate in the interview with her, arguing that he was familiar with the file. In reality, the case notes were so minimal that he could brief anyone on the pertinent details in five minutes. Omar Bashar, age thirty-four, customer of Cycle Life, had died of an opioid overdose in May 2013. The store owner and manager, Clayton Little, called 911 when Bashar collapsed and stopped breathing, his lips blue. Dispatchers immediately sent an EMS vehicle to the store. Bashar died en route to the hospital. The official autopsy confirmed trace levels of opioids, no other contributing factors to his cause of death. Bashar's wife had said he'd become addicted to prescription opioids, but she had thought he'd recovered. The police investigation found no evidence of wrongdoing. Novak couldn't recall the case from his former days in Homicide. He wouldn't have been lead or file manager. At most, he had been on the periphery. It seemed Homicide had reached a quick resolution. Why was the case left open?

He took a drink of coffee. *Cold.* He'd been so distracted that he hadn't taken a sip during his past hour of brooding. On his way to the staff sergeant's office, he stopped for a fresh cup. There was no one at the coffee centre after the early morning flurry. He spotted Mike entering the Homicide office, speaking animatedly to a woman—remarkably expressive for Mike. He and the woman drew closer.

Mike introduced her. "Detective Megan Molina, in Robbery."

"We're friends." She smiled at Novak.

"Friends" was an exaggeration, given that her name had already slipped Novak's mind. Mike asked her if she wanted a coffee and brewed himself a pod when she said she'd had enough for today. When she left, Novak would talk to Mike privately and confess his discovery about Cycle Life. Mike had gotten him into the search and deserved to be the first to know.

"The weather's turning fabulous," she said. "Sunny and warm, with a Chinook breeze. I'll take my lunch outside to a bench."

Mike stirred his coffee. "I'd join you if it weren't for my noon meeting. I need to prepare." He looked at her. "We'll talk afterwards."

Novak exhaled in relief. Mike's meeting—an excuse to put off talking to him.

"See you later," she said, and headed out to Robbery.

Mike followed her as far as his cubicle.

Outdoors. Novak could waylay Farida Bashar outside the entrance to the Investigative Services Building and spirit her to a bench. Would she find that strange? Rather than go back for his coat, he took a chance his suit jacket would keep him warm.

He raced through the atrium and reception area. Outside, a woman approached the entrance. Black hair, dark complexion, in her forties, dressed in a spring coat and pants. He went up to her and asked if she was Farida Bashar. She nodded. Another exhale in relief.

"I'm Detective Brian Novak," he said. "I'd love a break from this stuffy building and the day has warmed up. Let's talk over there." He glanced to his left, at the lawn.

"That would be safer."

The word had taken on a new meaning. The pervasive fear of succumbing to a lethal virus had its benefits. They walked onto the grass. No one sat on a bench or at the single picnic table, the farthest sitting area from the building entrance. Farida Bashar walked beside him to the table without question.

"Coming here disturbed me more than I'd expected," she said. "I'd thought I'd moved on during these seven years."

They sat across from each other, Novak facing the building, the sun high in the southern sky. Farida kept on her sunglasses. He hadn't brought his and would appear more approachable without them. Gusts of this warm breeze blew Farida's short hair across her cheek. She tried brushing it into place with her right hand.

Her left hand with no wedding ring rested on the table. "My understanding is that you've reopened the investigation into my late husband's death. Is there new evidence?"

"No." He'd expected this question and decided a simplified truth would be easiest. "A recent break and enter at Cycle Life, where he died, led me to search our cold cases for any prior incidents at the store. So far, I've uncovered no connection between the two events, but I asked to meet you to see if our file left out something significant."

She balled her left hand into a fist. "Cold case. So Marty's case wasn't resolved. I assumed it had been, when you didn't contact me after your first visit."

Marty. Presumably Omar's Canadian nickname. "The autopsy report noted trace opioids in his blood."

"Trace?" Her lips tightened. "It was more than that. Marty told me he was off oxycodone, and I believed him until he died. I was so angry at him for lying, but now we know how addictive they are."

Novak waited for her to continue. He noticed Megan exit the building and walk to the bench closest to the exit.

Farida brushed back her blowing hair and told him she and Marty had bought their first house a year before his death. While carrying in a used refrigerator they'd bought, his back went into a spasm. He could barely move for the pain. Over the months that followed, his doctor prescribed painkillers of increasing strength. Nothing worked until oxycodone, in its various brand names. His doctor recommended surgery as a long-term solution, but Farida and Marty preferred natural remedies—massage, yoga, and exercise. This led Marty to biking. He credited Cycle Life with finding him a seat and handlebars at the right angle for his back. With time, his pain subsided, and he didn't need surgery.

"I resented his daily bike rides for taking time from our family," she said. "But it seemed a healthier addiction." She gave up on taming her hair and slid her hand down her cheek. "Marty led me to think all he needed was the occasional over-the-counter medicine. I was stunned when you told me he was still using." She narrowed her eyes. "I didn't recognize you at first, or your name. It hit me now, your expression as you're listening. You and your partner came to my house that one time. He did most of the talking."

Novak leaned back. Nothing she'd said was familiar, aside from the general situation of a person becoming addicted to prescription meds, which he'd encountered in other cases. Seven years ago, Farida would have been in her late thirties. He didn't recognize her, even though she probably hadn't changed that much since then. His name hadn't appeared in any of the reports in the file, and he hadn't partnered with the primary detective, who'd transferred to another department after the Bashar case. Perhaps Novak had substituted for the detective's regular partner that day.

Farida rubbed her cheek. "I realize for you it was just a job."

Not "just," he wanted to argue. It was his job and he'd done it adequately. That would be an epigraph for his gravestone. *He was adequate.*

She folded her arms across her chest. "I'm getting cold sitting out here. It's not quite spring yet."

Novak was sweating.

Her remark seemed to signal the end of the conversation, and he couldn't think of any pertinent questions. Both rose from their seats. Across the grass, Megan sat at her bench, her attention apparently focused on eating her sandwich.

"One thing I remember from your visit." Farida adjusted her handbag over her shoulder. "While we talked, I kept wondering why Homicide detectives were involved."

"We investigate suspicious deaths."

"I saw nothing suspicious then. I assumed that Marty's doctor had continued to prescribe the drugs or Marty had found another, more-willing doctor. It never occurred to me he'd buy illegally. He didn't have those kinds of connections. Am I naïve, or what?"

Novak joined her at the end of the table. "It's good to be trusting." He wasn't. A side effect of his job.

"Lately, all I hear about is the opioid crisis. Doctors overprescribed strong pain medications, realized too late how addictive they are, and stopped prescribing. A sensible response, except it drove addicts underground. A huge supply market emerged, which any motivated person like Marty could find." She toyed with a strand of blowing hair. "But what I was going to say—this is why I remember you—at the end of your visit, when your partner was talking on the phone, I asked you why this was a homicide case. You looked at me as though you were debating how much to share with the mere civilian whose life was turned upside down and said that someone had called in an anonymous tip."

Novak started. That wasn't in the file. "What else did I say about the call?"

"Nothing I remember." Her hand dropped to her handbag's strap.

"I'm sorry if I came across as arrogant."

She clutched the strap. "It would have helped if you'd followed up and told me the outcome, or that there was no resolution."

"I will this time." He had assumed he wouldn't contact her again, until now.

She glanced across the grass to the parking lot. "I'll take the shortcut to my car."

"I'll walk you there." This way he'd avoid passing Megan.

"No thanks. I've had to learn to get by on my own."

Novak repeated his promise to call to let her know the outcome. Her nonresponse seemed to say, "I won't hold my breath."

He watched Farida tread over the grass before he took the direct route back to the entrance. On the way, he mentally debated what to say to Megan. He stopped by her bench. "You're right," he said. "This is better than being stuck inside."

"Meeting a friend?"

"An old acquaintance."

She stuffed the garbage from her finished lunch into a paper bag. "I'll go in with you."

A trusting person would assume she was being friendly rather than wonder if she wanted to know what he was up to.

* * *

"I'd love a third helping, but I'm stuffed." Walter scraped his chair back from the dining table and patted his stomach.

Paula offered to pack containers of pancakes, sausages, and eggs for him to take home. She was enjoying his presence at her birthday brunch more than she'd expected and was glad her mother had pushed to invite him. It made her first event of the day more celebratory. She rose to collect the dishes. Sam would be calling soon.

"I'll take care of it, Paula," her mother said. "It's your birthday."

"I'll help, Theda," Walter said, to Paula's amazement.

"If you insist," she told them both.

"Say hi to Sam from me," Walter called after her, as she made her way upstairs, the one part of the house where she could be sure of privacy.

She changed into a blue sweater that Sam especially liked and looked through her scarves. The butterfly one had been a favourite before Connor's phony psychic prediction. Time to rehabilitate that scarf. She draped it around her neck and tied a loose bow high enough for Sam to see on his laptop screen.

Her laptop sat on the table by the front window. She'd purposely avoided taking it downstairs that morning so she wouldn't be tempted by work. This would be a day off, an easy treat given her light workload. Even if Kelsey sent her the receipts and Josh sent his amended statement, dealing with them could wait until tomorrow.

She settled on the rattan chair, where she had a peripheral view of the street. The sunshine hadn't yet moved around the house, so glare on the screen was minimal. It was a few minutes until noon. Her email icon showed five messages waiting. She did a quick check. Nothing from Cycle Life, or anything else important. She turned off her email notifications as his call came through on Skype.

Sam appeared on the screen, his whole face a grin. "Happy birthday!" He wore his almond-coloured business shirt that picked up the gold flecks in his eyes.

She smiled back. "Did you just get home from work?"

"A half hour ago," he said. "I thought I'd dress classy. How was brunch?"

"So good I probably won't have room for dinner. Mum and I are doing takeout. Walter says hi, by the way. Seems his birthday gift was not needling me. Maybe he's too worried about his wife."

She summarized the COVID situation at his wife's long-term-care residence. The single case was now an outbreak, with another staff member and three residents testing positive. One was in hospital, in intensive care. Walter was glad the residence had taken the step of confining everyone to their rooms. His wife was trying to occupy herself with her hobby of making dollhouse furniture, but her fingers were becoming too arthritic for the delicate work.

"Crafting tiny tables and beds requires less space than mask-making," Paula said. "You'd cringe if you saw Mum's materials spread all over your studio."

Sam chuckled.

She told him how Walter visited his wife daily and stood outside her window, talking on the phone to her. "It's sad to picture it, but the upside is the pandemic forced him to learn how to use a cell phone, like Mum with her computer." She segued to her mother's latest thoughts about Sam's father. "Mum calls their situation a truce. She thinks they'll manage to respect each other's views on the pandemic if they limit their visits to every week or two. We haven't decided if we'll invite him to my birthday party this Saturday. So far, we're only definite about the girls."

Since she'd hogged the conversation so far, she asked Sam about his work. While he detailed his immediate project, she stole glances out the window. Walter sauntered out of her house carrying his bag of leftovers. She decided that if her mother brought it up, she'd agree to invite him to her party. Perhaps now that she was fifty-six, officially in her late fifties, she was becoming mellow.

Sam paused and lobbed the focus back to her, asking about her work. She told him about the previous day's trip to Cycle Life to follow up on the receipts.

"And snoop." His eyes crinkled. "So much for not getting involved."

She faked a scowl. "Turns out Kelsey, their clerk, misunderstood and thought I was going to pick them up. She had some ready for me, but other information was missing from the envelope she left. Cycle Life doesn't seem in a hurry for money, which could suggest their real business is drugs. But they are busy with customers and might be generally lax about their accounting. Josh doesn't seem interested in that kind of detail."

"Sadly, you'll never know, since you won't be involved."

She scowled, for real this time. "I think I prefer Walter's teasing."

Sam laughed.

Paula described her discovery of a witness to the break and enter, the squatter living in the furniture store. When she finished, she asked if Sam had plans for the rest of the week.

"Work," he said. "Would you mind if I spent Saturday night at a castle hotel we'd booked for your cancelled trip? One, in particular, fascinates me, architecturally."

"Go ahead." She meant it. Why should he give up something enjoyable because she couldn't have it? "You can vet the place for when I get there, hopefully this summer." She glanced outside and noticed a car parked in front of her house. "That looks like Leah's Civic. She didn't say she'd come by, unless she emailed or phoned in the past hour."

"I'll let you go," he said, but they continued talking for another twenty minutes until he said it again. "I really should let you go. Happy birthday."

"A different kind of birthday for me.

"Nothing like what we'd planned." No castle for her.

"I'll do my best to latch on to the bright side, like time with Mum and Leah, to make it the best day I can under the circumstances."

"I love you," Sam said.

"I love you too." It was a truly bright moment.

Downstairs, she discovered her mother and Leah weren't in the kitchen or living room. Paula called down to the basement in case Leah had come by to use the gym. That effort would be a sign Leah's spirit was back. When no one answered, Paula returned to the kitchen. She looked out the back window and saw a figure in the studio. Perhaps her mother was showing off her new project to Leah. The outdoor thermometer indicated it was fifteen degrees Celsius, so Paula ventured out to the sunshine without a jacket. Feeling only mildly chilly, she crossed the lawn and trotted up the staircase to the studio. Her mother and Leah turned around. They'd been studying the materials strewn on Sam's desk.

Paula stepped forward to hug Leah and halted. "Great to see you, honey."

"Happy birthday, Mom. Gran brought me here rather than disturb you and Sam." Leah held up a piece of fabric with a pattern pinned to it. "Isn't Gran's mask-making great?"

"Fabulous," Paula said. "I didn't expect you until Saturday."

"I brought you dinner for tonight, coconut curry. It's in the fridge. My neighbour's drumming up business for takeout meals from her restaurant. I wanted to support her."

"That's good of you, honey. Can you stay and share it with us?"

Leah shook her head. "I'm meeting a friend for a walk." She set the fabric on the desk. "Gran's showed me her whole operation. It's a real assembly line." She stretched her arm to take in the desk, ironing board, sewing machine, coffee table, and futon, all topped with masks in various stages of preparation.

"I gave Leah her wine-glass mask," Theda said, "but I've improved my methods immensely since making it."

Leah picked up a finished mask from the futon and pinched the nose bridge. "These are really well made."

"Of course they are," Theda said.

Paula smiled at her mother's indignant tone. "Gran's making them for all her friends."

Leah looped the mask over her ears. "This is more comfortable than any I've tried." Her voice was muffled through the material. "In the next few months, there'll be a huge demand for masks. They'll likely become fashion and personality statements. People would lap these up." Leah took off the mask and let it dangle on one ear. "I told Gran she could easily sell these for ten dollars a pop."

"I hadn't thought of it as a business," Theda said.

Leah looked at her. "I could work up a marketing plan. We'd start with word-of-mouth, like my neighbour with her meals." Excitement crept into her voice. "Meanwhile, I'd set up your website, for future mail orders. Postage would be cheap, since the masks are so thin and light."

Paula moved toward them. "Leah, I know you mean well, but turning this into a business will spoil the fun for Gran."

Leah whirled toward her. "Don't worry, I won't crack the whip. Gran can work at her own pace."

"I'm not interested in managing a website," Theda said.

"I'll handle all of that," Leah said. "Marketing, sales. That's what I do, or did, when I planned my restaurant."

Paula's heart tugged at the thought of her daughter's failed dream. She loved Leah's enthusiasm, but it wouldn't be fair to let her take over her grandmother's project.

"Gran, run me through your whole process again," Leah said. "I'll take some pictures we might use on the website."

Paula heard enough about the process every day at dinner. She left them alone, intending to talk to her mother later to make sure she wouldn't sacrifice her own needs for her granddaughter's sake. Leah would have to find another way to bounce back.

Outside, the chill was gone from the air. Paula glanced at the shed. Maybe she could pump up her bike tires for her first ride of the season after Leah left. Until then, she'd enjoy the sunshine on the front porch. She entered the kitchen and spotted her phone on the island. It had been hours since she'd checked for text and phone messages. To stay away any longer would require a superhuman effort. She carried the phone out the front door, settled on the wood bench, and leaned into its comfortable backrest.

One phone message, a text, and several new emails, including one from her brother in Montreal with the subject *Happy Birthday*. She'd save it for last.

Mike had texted, *Want to catch up on the case? Free tonight?*

This didn't sound urgent, and he wouldn't know it was her birthday. She typed, *Tomorrow okay?*

He replied before she'd opened her voicemail. *Good. I'll touch base in a.m.*

She returned to the phone message. The sound of Connor's voice startled her.

"Happy birthday. Do I get credit for remembering? You told me you were going to Europe for your birthday and somehow the twenty-eighth stuck in my head. I'm sorry for the mess I caused you. I must have been smoking Gabe's weed when I came up with that crazy plan. It's legal, heh?" His forced laugh sounded rueful. "If you're ever my way, to meet a claimant or something, stop in to chat. It gets lonely here, sitting around thinking about Gabe. Scratch that. I'm not looking for sympathy. Anyway, have a good birthday, and sorry for screwing up."

Paula's shoulders slumped. His words were full of remorse, worry, and loneliness. Her brother was safely in Montreal, but not long ago, concern for his well-being had kept her awake at night. Like Connor, she'd done her share of stupid things and didn't have the excuse of youth and weed for the ones connected to her Homicide work with Mike. Connor's apartment in Forest Lawn wasn't far from her home. Leah had taken care of her birthday dinner, and hadn't Paula wanted a bike ride today?

She found Connor's address and plugged it into Google Maps. Thirty-three minutes by bike, if she took the longer route on river pathways that avoided busy streets. She always liked a destination for a ride, and making amends with her former colleague would cap off her birthday afternoon.

She sent him a text to make sure he'd be home later today and then dived into her brother's birthday greetings, waiting for Connor's answer.

Chapter Eleven

Isabelle drove into the Cycle Life lot and parked between a Prius and a pickup truck. If Connor was late, the truck would help hide her from passersby who might wonder why she was sitting in her car. She took out her phone to pass the time and opened an email reply from a claimant. He'd agreed to postpone their four p.m. RingCentral meeting until this evening. Now there'd be no rush to get home.

She jumped as someone rapped on her window. Connor peered in. He moved sideways so she could squeeze out of her car and into the tight space beside the white pickup. Connor wore his contacts and a blue baseball cap with the insignia *Viva Italia*.

"Why the cap?" she said. "You told me it's Kelsey's day off."

"I still like that it hides me a bit." He unzipped his bulky jacket. "The walk was warmer than I expected."

She was glad she'd dressed in a T-shirt and capris. "You didn't ride?"

"I decided that shopping for a bike would look more authentic if I didn't ride here on one."

"Don't be paranoid," she said. "People with okay bikes buy better ones all the time." She sidled out of the space between the vehicles. "How's your migraine?"

"Better." He followed her to the handicapped parking spot in front of the store. Cycle Life's door was propped open. One bike was in the bike rack in front of the window. They stopped in the empty handicapped spot. "On the way, I got a text from Paula," he said. "She wants to come to my place."

"Why?"

"Because I invited her," he said. "Don't tell her we're doing this."

"Of course not." Why did people always think she'd blab? "Why did you invite her?"

Connor glanced at the door. "When we're in there, call me Ryan. I doubt Gabe mentioned me to them, except to Kelsey, but in case he did . . ."

"Okay, Ryan." Isabelle headed for the doorway.

"No, actually, Ryan's too close to our surname, Riley."

Too late, she was already inside. Connor shuffled behind her. In the store's front corner, to their right, a woman scanned racks of bike shorts, shirts, gloves, and shoes. A changing room divided the clothing area from a back corner full of bike accessories where a child stood at a table stacking helmets into a pile. Near the service counter, directly ahead of the door, two older men studied an e-bike. Bikes occupied the larger left-hand side of the store. Above them, wheels hung from beams along the high ceiling.

"Wow," Connor said. "They've sold a lot of bikes."

Isabelle had thought the room was packed, but now she saw the spaces between the bikes. She guessed there were at least fifty total. They approached the service counter.

The man with the white beard and ponytail patted the e-bike's seat. "You're good to go."

She'd assumed the little girl was with the buyer, but with no glance at the child the man wheeled the bike past Isabelle and Connor and out the door.

The ponytail man approached. The name tag on his flannel shirt said Herb. Isabelle elbowed Connor as a message to stop fidgeting with his cap brim.

Connor's arm dropped to his side. "I . . . I'm interested in a bike."

"Regular or electric?" Herb said.

"Regular."

"That's good. I just sold the last e-bike on the floor. We can order you one, but no guarantee you'll get it before June."

"Regular's good. I need the exercise." Connor touched his stomach. It looked paunchier than it had when Isabelle last saw him in person, at work.

"What will you be using the bike for?" Herb asked.

"Mainly riding around town, to get to places. I don't have a car. My friend drove me today." He nodded at Isabelle. Too much detail.

Her gaze strayed to the girl, who carried another helmet to the table.

"I've got a few left that might work for you," Herb said.

"Sales have been good this spring?" Connor asked.

"The best I recall in all my years here." Herb tugged his Santa Claus beard. "People are looking for simple activities to ride out this pandemic. I'll show you what we've got."

Connor gaped at Isabelle, begging for her support. But they'd learn more if they split up.

"Ryan, you check out the bikes," she said. "I need a new helmet."

She ignored his pleading expression and walked to the girl, who concentrated on balancing a fifth helmet on the stack. As her arm drew away, it bumped the middle helmet. The two on top of it rocked but settled.

"Great job," Isabelle said. "Are you a clerk who can serve me?"

The girl looked up and giggled. "No."

"What's your name?"

"Olivia." She looked about seven or eight years old.

"I'm Isabelle. That's a cool tower you're making." Isabelle turned toward the sound of voices behind the rear wall of helmets. A woman came out of a back room. Her boots clacked on the wood floor.

"What do you want to buy?" Olivia drew Isabelle's attention back to her.

"A helmet, but not one that's crashed from your tower. You know why?"

Olivia shook her head, her dark pigtails flapping against her cheeks.

"Because the helmet might get cracked, and then it's no good." Isabelle glanced at the tower. "If they hit the floor, those helmets won't be safe to sell to customers."

"They won't fall."

Isabelle grinned. "Yes, they will. That's the fun of towers."

She sensed someone standing behind her and turned around. The woman from the back room. Maybe in her early thirties, black hair to her waist. Her red sweater dress looked awesome against her olive skin. A man came out of the back room and walked to the service counter.

"You're good with kids," the woman said to Isabelle. "I don't have the patience."

Isabelle shrugged. "They're just people."

"Josh." The woman called the man over. "Your customer's given me an idea." She nodded toward Isabelle. "We could hire someone to look after Olivia in the store."

"A babysitter?" Josh said.

"Homeschooler, but anyone could supervise her work. I'm thinking a student. They'd be available with the schools closed and might want pocket money. High school. Junior high would be okay too, since you'll be around to keep watch, in your fashion."

Josh's face scrunched. At her idea or her dig at him?

Olivia picked up the top helmet and carried it to the back wall as Josh stared at the woman, his eyes baggy, with dark circles underneath. "Do I pay for this, Zab, or do you?"

Zab's scowl was prettier than his. "We split it. What's the minimum wage?"

"Fifteen dollars an hour."

"We offer ten, cash, under the table.

"Sounds reasonable." Josh looked at Isabelle. "You're hired."

Isabelle opened her mouth to say she had a job and wasn't a teenager. But her insurance workload was shrinking every day, and she might learn if the store's business was shady or not by hanging out here. She could easily arrange RingCentral calls around homeschooling Olivia, who was now patiently jiggling the helmet onto a hook. She seemed a quiet, studious child, easy to look after.

"Josh, we can't hire someone off the street," Zab said. "We'll have to conduct interviews to make sure the person's suitable."

He rubbed his forehead. "You conduct them. I don't have the time."

"Like I do." Zab turned toward the front door, which a customer was entering. "I've got to go. I'm late for work."

"Me too." Josh left to greet the customer.

Zab grabbed Olivia on her way back from the helmet wall and bent over to give her a hug. "Bye, sweetie. You behave for Daddy." Zab clacked by Isabelle and out of the store.

Olivia ran to the stack, lifted the next helmet off, and left the table. Across the room, Connor and Herb leaned over a bike, white beard and baseball cap brim almost touching. Both Herb and Josh had their backs to Olivia, who struggled to force the helmet onto a hook. Isabelle wondered if she should go over to help. Or should kids be left to figure out things for themselves?

"Don't let her manipulate you."

She whirled around and found herself facing Josh. He'd snuck up on her, like Zab had. Their creepy family trait? And was he referring to Zab or Olivia? Isabelle nodded toward Connor. "I . . . I'm just waiting for my boyfriend, Ryan."

"I know, and I appreciate your help with her."

Olivia appeared at the table. She picked up another helmet.

"About what you and . . . Olivia's mom were talking about," Isabelle said. "I have nothing to do for the rest of the day. I could stay if you want help."

"Don't let me manipulate you either," Josh said.

From his deadpan expression, Isabelle couldn't tell if he was joking or not. Olivia brushed against her leg cradling the helmet to her chest. Isabelle really could use a new helmet. Hers had a hairline crack from being dropped a few times. She recalled a recent claim for water-damaged merchandise. The owner's wholesale cost was a lot less than retail. For Josh, a helmet might be worth a few hours of babysitting.

"If you want," she said, "you could pay me with a helmet."

He squinted at her. "You're serious?"

Was she? "Sure."

"It's a deal."

"Yay." Olivia jumped up and down and clapped her hands.

Josh grinned. "See what I mean about manipulating."

All three of them had manipulated her, probably. Josh excused himself and returned to his customer. Connor broke away from Herb and made a beeline to Isabelle.

"Did you buy a bike?" she asked.

He shook his head. "Too expensive."

She lowered her voice. "What did you learn?"

He looked around. Isabelle followed his gaze to Olivia, who was at the racks jiggling the helmet onto a hook. Josh and his customer moved to the far end of the bike area. Herb was gone.

"Herb loves his job," Connor whispered. "He raved about his work, but they're busy and he hopes Kelsey shows up tomorrow. He didn't use her name and referred to her as their female staff person."

"Why wouldn't she show up?"

"He thinks she faked sick yesterday and might do it again," he said.

"Did she say she was sick when you called her?"

Connor's brow knit. "She didn't answer my calls, but I phoned the store pretending to be someone she'd served. They told me Tuesday's her day off. From the voice, I think it was Herb. Anyway, we can leave now and get out and relax."

"I . . . I can't." Isabelle glanced at Olivia, skipping toward them. "Seems I have a new job."

* * *

Connor's three-storey apartment building was U shaped. Paula glimpsed its courtyard through the vehicle entrance gate, which could only be opened with a code. She secured her bicycle to a fence bar, grabbed her fleece sweater from the basket, and headed up the sidewalk to the building's front door. Two children ran past her, followed by a woman carrying shopping bags. The boy punched the entry code and held open the door for them all, including Paula, and dashed to open the interior door for her and the other two.

Paula located Connor's unit number, three, on the building's ground floor, on the courtyard side. He answered her knock. She started at the sight of him with a full beard.

"That grew quickly in six weeks," she said.

"My mother's family tends to be hirsute." He ushered her in.

The main room had an open floor plan. A counter with two barstools divided the kitchen and living room area. Two recliner chairs in the middle of the living area faced a wall unit with a large-screen TV. A cat perched on the farther chair and stared at Paula, its ears alert.

145

Connor had told her about the stray that he and his brother had taken in over the winter. He was probably glad for the company now.

"What's the cat's name?"

"Finnegan. Gabe and I chose it for our Irish heritage. Who knows her original name. She turned up here with no ID tag, but she wore a collar, so she must have belonged to someone. One night, she clawed her collar off and I thought, she's really ours."

Finnegan leaped from the chair and padded over the carpet to Connor. He leaned down to pick her up. The cat nestled against his chest. Her orange-white-and-black colouring was calico, but Paula noticed the M shape on her forehead characteristic of tabby cats. The calico-tabby mix squirmed in Connor's arms.

He wore his contact lenses along with a T-shirt and faded jeans with genuine, rather than fashionable, rips. His dark curls reminded Paula that his brother was a barber. Gabe had likely cut Connor's hair shortly before his disappearance, judging by the curls' reasonably trim appearance. Connor's stomach bulge and fleshed-out cheeks above his beard suggested he'd been spending too much time inside, close to his fridge.

He let Finnegan slither to the floor. "You want a drink or something?"

"Water would be good." She looked past him to his patio, which would look out to the courtyard. "Should we sit outside rather than mask up in here? It's mainly to protect my mother. She's living with me now."

He nodded. "Isabelle told me."

"May I use your bathroom first?"

He pointed at a short hall. "Door on the left."

Paula set her helmet on the main room counter. She guessed the accordion door in the hall was for a linen closet and the other two closed doors led to Connor's and Gabe's bedrooms. The bathroom was clean and neat for a man in his twenties living alone, or with a brother. No hairs in the sink or food particles on the mirror from brushing and flossing. It fit with

Connor's precision at work. Paula took out her comb from her waist pouch, did her best to fluff up her hair flattened by the helmet, used the toilet, and returned to the living area. Connor had set two glasses of water and a bowl of wrapped chocolates on the counter. She picked up one glass and the bowl, even though both would be covered with Connor's potentially COVID-laden fingerprints. She hated this shift to viewing human beings as virus carriers more than people.

They carried the items past the chairs and the small table set against the back window. Judging by the placemat and salt and pepper shakers, Connor ate his meals here, looking out to his deck, which was enclosed on three sides by four-foot brick walls. He told her that the paved courtyard led to an underground garage for residents. Rather than pay extra for parking, he kept his bicycle on the deck, trusting his neighbours not to steal it. The bike leaned against the far side wall.

They set the bowl and glasses on the outdoor table between two red Muskoka chairs that backed against the living room window. Seated, all Paula could see above the wall was blue sky. Finnegan eyed the distance to the top of the wall then leaped with grace and settled on the wall like a sphinx. Her eyes closed in apparent contentment.

From the bowl, Connor took a chocolate ball wrapped in gold foil. "I'm sorry I tried that stupid psychic stunt. Maybe I should see a shrink again."

"Have you seen one before?"

"Once." Connor twisted the ends of the wrapper to release the chocolate. "She helped me see that my father's absence and my mom's benign neglect led me to assume responsibility for my younger brother." He shrugged. "Gabe's kid problems got more serious. The shrink would probably say it's beyond my control now and I have to let it go."

Paula nodded, relating as a parent. "It drives you nuts to be responsible and care when you can't do anything." She smiled. "But let's forget about that and move on."

"To where?"

Good question. While he chewed the chocolate, she tried to think of subjects other than work. "Have you used your time off for painting?"

"I can't get into it," he said. "Too depressing." He picked up another chocolate.

She glanced at his bike. "How about cycling? My ride here made me eager to do more this summer."

He chewed and swallowed. "I get out now and then." He glanced at her. "Have you settled their break and enter claim yet?"

It would be hard to get away from work, the main thing they had in common. But the subtext of his question was, had she ended her involvement with the place he connected to his brother's disappearance?

"They're slow on sending receipts and signed statements," she said. "There's also a slim chance the police will recover the stolen items, which could prolong things."

"Have they got any leads?"

Finnegan meowed, and her ears perked up. She looked at the door to the apartment.

"Turns out a squatter's been living in the furniture store next to Cycle Life," Paula said. "He happened to go outside early Thursday morning and saw two people on Cycle Life's back porch."

Connor's eyebrows shot up. He looked over his shoulder. "Was that the doorbell?"

"I didn't hear it."

"I'll go check." He went inside, leaving the door ajar.

Finnegan leaped down. Paula stood and followed her back inside. Connor stared at Paula from the counter, his face pale. "I buzzed them in. It's Detective Mike, with a partner. On TV they come in pairs to tell you—" His voice broke, and he teetered sideways.

Paula rushed past the chairs, but Connor leaned back into the counter for support and avoided falling. Damn COVID, which made her hesitate to grab his arms. She watched his shaking muscles grow steadier. Someone knocked on his apartment door.

"You have to answer," Paula said.

Connor shook his head. Paula went and opened the door to Mike and a tall woman dressed in a blue pantsuit. Mike's jaw drop would have been comical if it weren't for Connor's terror about Gabe.

"Is there word about Connor's brother?" she asked.

Mike blinked, as though startled again. "It isn't that."

Her shoulders relaxed. She stepped back and bumped into Finnegan. The cat screeched and scurried away.

Mike introduced Detective Megan Molina, from Robbery.

"Call me Megan," she said. "I've heard so much about you, Paula, that I feel we're on a first-name basis."

"Why are you here?" Mike asked Paula.

"There's no news about Gabe?" she said, to be sure.

"No."

She glanced at Connor and repeated Mike's answer, in case Connor had been too stressed to hear it.

"Gabe isn't dead?" Connor sounded stunned.

"Not that we're aware," Mike said.

"Thank God." Connor slumped against the counter.

Paula told Mike and Megan that she'd come for a social visit. "Why are you here, if it's not about Gabe?"

"We spoke to the witness you located," Mike said. He looked at Connor. "We have a few questions."

"For me?" Connor stepped backward, toward the hall.

Megan looked around the room. "Let's sit on those recliners. I'll get the chair." She walked through the living area to the table.

Evidently, the police had talked to the squatter, but what could he have told them that related to Connor and not Gabe? Paula longed to stay to find out, although the criminal investigation wasn't her direct business. She also wanted to stay to support Connor.

She faced him. "Connor, I don't know what's going on, but the best way to help your brother is to tell them the truth. They'll find out eventually, anyway, and every minute you slow the process, the worse it will be for Gabe."

Connor straightened. "I thought you'd come here to visit, as a friend."

"I did," she said. "I am your friend. That's why I'm telling you this."

"Funny." He squinted at her. "Minutes after you mention your witness, two detectives show up. Were you prepping me for them? Softening me up, so I'll admit to something?"

"What's there to admit to?"

"I knew it, you're on their side." Connor spun around and marched to the hall.

Was he planning to escape out a bedroom window?

Instead, he remained in the hall, scooped up Finnegan, and cradled the squirming cat in his arms. Mike moved toward Paula as Megan set the dining chair in front of the TV, facing the recliner chairs. Three seats, four people in the room.

Mike stared at Connor. "Paula can stay for our questioning, if you want."

Connor looked up from his cat. "I don't need the three of you against me."

"I'm not against you," Paula said. "I'm *for* you and Gabe. Honestly, Connor, I don't know what this is about."

He snorted. "Except you agree with what they're doing here."

"Yes, if it's relevant." From Connor's perspective, that would feel like three to one. Giving him control might prompt him to go along. "I'll stay or leave. Your choice entirely."

His gaze returned to Finnegan, now nestled in his arms. "I'll deal with this on my own."

"Okay," she said. "Connor, I did come here as your friend, and I'll be there for you, whenever and with whatever you want and need."

"You can let yourself out." Connor didn't look up from the cat.

Chapter Twelve

Mike settled on the recliner chair, Connor on the recliner beside him. The apartment setup reminded Mike of Chandler and Joey's apartment in *Friends*. Megan faced them both, on the hard chair in front of the TV. The cat purred on Connor's lap. Mike took out his notebook and pen while Megan went through the courtesy of asking Connor for permission to record their interview.

"I have nothing to hide," Connor said.

Of course, he did, but who knew if his secret was important? Mike felt a tickle in his nose and hoped it wasn't his cat allergy acting up. He'd noticed some cat hairs on this comfortable leather chair. If this were a social gathering, he'd crank up the footrest.

Megan began by showing Connor the photo of the man in silhouette. "You posted this on Instagram." She held her phone across the space so Connor could see. This was awkward, but easier than spraying everything with sanitizer.

Connor leaned over the cat and peered at the screen. "That's me on Lynnwood Ridge," he said. "Gabe and I went there to see the sunset a week or so before he left. Our last walk together." He slumped back in the chair, bouncing the cat. "What of it?"

The tickle in Mike's nostril grew worse. He set his notepad and pen on his lap and rifled through his pockets for a tissue. Nothing but the pair of latex gloves he always carried for unexpected searches.

"A witness identified you as a man he saw outside of Cycle Life before dawn the morning of the break and enter."

"Paula's witness." Connor stroked the cat. "Who is this person? None of the companies nearby open that early. And most are closed full-time."

"How do you know that?"

Connor's beard quivered. "I'll be honest with you," he said. "I went to Cycle Life earlier this afternoon on the pretext of shopping for a bike, but really, I went to snoop, on account of Gabe's involvement there." He glared at Megan. "Nothing illegal about that."

Mike couldn't hold in the tickle. He twisted toward the window and sneezed—again and again. He rubbed his nose with a latex glove then turned back toward Megan and apologized. "Cat allergy."

Megan compressed her lips, but her eyes crinkled, as though supressing a smile. *Humiliating.* The cat stared at Mike, its yellow eyes seemingly claiming innocence for the dander that permeated the room. It slid to the floor as Connor stood.

"I'll let some air in," Connor said. "There's Kleenex in the bedroom."

Connor was stalling, but at the moment, Mike didn't care. He felt another sneeze coming on, and latex gloves were useless for wiping nose drips. They were also ridiculously bright purple. Connor opened the door to the deck then loped through the living room and disappeared around the corner to the hall. Mike looked at Megan. Apartment walls were notoriously thin. They shouldn't talk about anything they didn't want Connor to hear.

"I had a cat," Megan said. "My boyfriend got custody when we broke up. I miss the cat sometimes."

But not the boyfriend, Mike found himself hoping. He also hoped Connor wasn't crawling out his bedroom window. That would work against him if they hauled him into Westwinds and laid charges. Connor might have committed petty theft, but he didn't strike Mike as bad. Paula had worked with the dude for three years and judged him decent. The cat leaped onto the table not far from Mike and curled into a cat-ball.

Connor returned with a box of tissues, which he handed to Mike before resettling in his recliner. He checked his cell phone, which he'd evidently picked up along the way.

"She should have replied by now." Connor stared at the screen. "Normally, she answers within minutes."

"Who?" Megan asked.

"Kelsey. A friend of Gabe's. She works at Cycle Life. I got in touch with her after he took off, to see if she'd heard from him." Connor glanced at Mike. "After meeting you in Chestermere, I talked to her a couple of times, but since yesterday, nothing. The store told me she went home sick yesterday. It must be bad if she's not picking up her phone." His eyes grew wide, and his gaze shifted between Mike and Megan. "What if Kelsey's gone missing, like Gabe? You have to do something."

"We are," Megan said. "By getting you to tell us what's going on."

"And I've told you," Connor said. "I don't know what you're talking about." He crossed his arms.

Mike wiped his nose and wondered if Connor's apparent concern for Kelsey was a strategy to shift the focus away from the robbery. But someone young not answering texts and emails promptly, when this was contrary to her habits, could indicate something serious, especially given her workplace's suspected involvement in drug dealing.

"Are you taking me to the police station?" Connor asked.

Mike looked at Megan. Her call.

She stared at Connor. "Will you answer more questions related to our witness' statement?"

He shook his head. "Not without a lawyer present. I've watched enough cop shows to know this."

"Then it's a trip to headquarters," Megan said. "The ID is enough to hold you for questioning." Borderline true, and they might make it stick.

"Can we stop by Kelsey's house on the way?" Connor said. "She lives with her grandfather. I don't know his phone number."

"Do you have their address?" Megan asked.

"It's on my phone," Connor said. He looked it up and read it aloud. "It's not far from Cycle Life. Her grandfather founded the place."

Mike wrote the address in his notebook. "Do you know her grandfather's name?"

"I forget," Connor said. "She always calls him Grandpa, and his surname's different from hers—Tedesco. Her mother's his daughter."

Mike looked at Megan. "The B and E's your deal. I'll drop you both at Westwinds and then swing by the grandfather's place. I think it's worth checking out."

Megan nodded.

On the way to Westwinds, Mike remembered he had to drive Novak home from work. After he'd parked and Megan and Connor got out, Mike sent Novak a text to let him know where he was then caught up on his messages until Novak arrived. During the ten-minute drive home, neither one brought up work. Mike appreciated the brief respite from the case, while Novak chatted about the warm weather.

"Since you picked me up early," Novak said, "I'll take the bike for a spin before dinner."

Spin wasn't a word Mike associated with Novak's recent gloomy mood. Another sign life was looking up for his friend. He dropped him off and continued to the address Connor had supplied, another ten-minute "spin" by car.

Kelsey's grandfather's house in Mayland Heights was similar in size and age to Mike's 1970s bungalow, but the overgrown trees were a contrast to the single evergreen and sparse shrubbery in Mike's front yard. He rang the doorbell. After a second ring, Mike considered leaving. Then the door opened halfway, revealing a man wearing wire-rimmed glasses and a red plaid shirt. He looked in his mid-eighties—wrinkled forehead, strands of white hair combed across his crown. Mike introduced himself and asked to speak to Kelsey.

"She's not home." Her grandfather's forehead lines deepened. "You said you're a detective?"

"I'm investigating a break and enter at Cycle Life, where Kelsey works."

The man blinked several times. Then his forehead relaxed. "Kelsey told me about that." He shook his head. "The world's changed. I remember a few times, in my day, we forgot to lock up at night. Not a blessed thing stolen."

"I understand you're the store's original owner."

"I still own the majority share. Clayton Little." He pulled the door fully open and extended his right hand.

Mike thought of virus germs, but for goodwill, he shook the gnarled hand. Clayton's handshake was firm.

"When do you expect Kelsey home?" Mike asked.

"I never know with her," Clayton said. "Could be tonight. As she puts it, 'We give each other our freedom.' What is it you want her for, exactly? Don't you do your interviewing at the store?"

"When did you see her last?"

Clayton's brow lines deepened again. "Yesterday, I think. Morning, when she left for work. I expected her home after supper."

"You didn't see her this morning?"

"I told you, already. No." Clayton's tone was sharp. "Sorry," he said. "But now you're getting me worried."

"There's no cause for concern. This is routine." Mike hoped this was true. He removed a business card from his pocket. "When Kelsey gets in, could you have her contact me?"

Clayton stared at the card as though scrutinizing Mike's contact details. "You're sure she's not in some kind of trouble?"

Mike couldn't be sure.

Clayton looked up. "If I understood texting and whatnot, I'd try to reach her that way. Kids today are always on a leash."

Mike was here because Kelsey's leash to Connor had broken.

* * *

Paula found the afternoon too beautiful to ride directly home. She stopped on a side street in Forest Lawn and called her mother to say that she was prolonging her outing but would be home in time for dinner. The extra exercise would also burn off steam after her troubling visit with Connor. Rather than make amends, they'd ended up wider apart than before. Worse, it seemed Connor might have some involvement with the Cycle Life break and enter. She looked up at the clear blue sky. Where did she want to go?

Cycle Life.

Specifically, she wanted to talk to her witness and saw no reason to stay away. The police had what they wanted from him. She wouldn't be interfering with their case and would need his statement for the insurance claim, anyway. True, she'd vowed not to work on her birthday, but, if she were honest, this was more about curiosity. She checked the map on her phone. Fourteen minutes by bike and, afterwards, thirty-two minutes to her home. Doable, when her spirit was pumped.

In precisely fourteen minutes, she turned in to the rear entrance of the three-store building and slowed behind Cycle Life. A person sat on the bottom of the staircase smoking a cigarette. The squatter? He gazed upward, talking to a man sitting on the deck. Beard, plaid shirt. Herb. Naturally, both would come outside for this year's first burst of warm weather. The man on the stairs looked at her, his nose shrouded in cigarette smoke. It was definitely him.

He rose and dropped his cigarette butt to the pavement. On the porch, Herb stood, waved at Paula, and went inside. She got off her bike and kicked down the stand.

The squatter remained in place, a good three metres from her. This time, his T-shirt, shorts, and flip-flops suited the weather. "You're the insurance woman."

"That's right," she said. "Paula Savard."

"Dustin. Herb was telling me about the theft." Dustin scanned her from head to toe. "You don't look dressed for work."

She went for the truth. "I was visiting a friend who lives nearby and detoured here on my way home. My police contacts said they talked to you."

He nodded. "This morning. I squared things with my manager and Furniture Sellers' owner—I can live here until we reopen. The cops have no problem with it."

"That's good." She honestly agreed. "Might as well make use of the space."

"Yeah, gives me time to find a tolerable apartment that fits my budget. Meanwhile, the store works amazingly well as a residence. Pity it's not permanent."

He was their sole witness to the break and enter. It wouldn't hurt to forge a small connection. "I can imagine," she said. "My office building has effectively become my home office, since I'm the only person in the building. I love having the huge place to myself, and it's quiet for working."

He nodded. "Quiet's good for sleeping too. I was telling Herb that there's everything I need in there. My pick of bedroom and living room setups, the employee kitchen and tables, a bathroom with a shower that the previous manager installed."

When she'd told Sam about meeting the squatter, he'd been intrigued by the alternate living arrangement. "My partner's an architect," she said. "He loves seeing unique ways people use space."

Dustin glanced down the slope, at Furniture Sellers' basement. "I'll show you around, if you wear a mask and keep a proper distance."

She hadn't been hinting at a tour, but since he'd offered, why not? It would be interesting to know if sounds travelled through the walls to Cycle Life, although Dustin's reference to quiet implied that he heard no noise at night, when drug-dealing activities might take place.

She walked her bike down the slope with Dustin, fastened her helmet over the bike's handlebar, and took her flowered mask from her waist pouch. No racks or poles for locking the bike, but the only passersby would be Cycle Life customers on test rides. During her visits here, she hadn't noticed any people or trucks in the alley between the two buildings behind this one. Had the police thoroughly checked those premises for potential witnesses? Maybe not, since they'd considered it a minor B and E.

Dustin opened the door to Furniture Sellers. Inside, he plucked a mask from a box on the table by the entrance, put the mask on, and picked up a bottle of hand sanitizer. "It's kind of fun to have a visitor, besides your two cops. My manager and grocery guys leave their deliveries outside. Talking with Herb reminded me I miss people."

Paula squirted sanitizer on her hands and rubbed them to what she believed would be Dustin's—and her mother's—satisfaction. The numerous crates and furniture behind the garage door were probably the deliveries that Dustin had talked about on Paula's previous visit.

"Are you a salesman here?" she asked, now that she knew he was an employee.

"Yep. Long story about my making this a temporary home. I told your cops about it."

She'd get the story from Mike. The living room and dining room displays to her right continued so far that she couldn't see to the end of them. The far section was dark. "Do you make use of the whole store?"

"Only a small area upstairs, plus the kitchen and bathroom down here. I try to keep most of the store pristine so it will be ready for customers when we reopen. We'll start with the kitchen." He led her down a passage between the delivery door and the pile of items and stopped at a service elevator in the building's northwest corner.

"It's for transporting deliveries to the main floor," Dustin said. "Customers with strollers or who need assistance appreciate it. We also bring down older furniture to the basement showroom. The newer and higher-quality furnishings are generally on the main level, where customers enter. If they want something cheaper, we send them downstairs."

Paula remembered Josh saying that Cycle Life didn't have basement space. "Does your basement continue underneath Cycle Life?"

"Partway, as far as the furnace room." Dustin turned the corner to a side passage. "Here's the kitchen." He entered a room and switched on the ceiling light, illuminating three tables and a counter with a microwave, kettle, and toaster. "I'll ask you not to touch any surfaces. Sanitizer isn't foolproof. It would be nice to have a window, but getting the walls painted white brightened things up. If it stays warm, I'll move one of these tables outside. When Herb's out, he'll be company."

Salesmen were usually sociable people. That could account for Dustin's chattiness with a stranger like her, and, moreover, his willingness to risk her bringing in the virus. She returned to her question about the basement layout. "Does this mean the furnace room is underneath Herb's workshop?"

He squinted, seeming to reflect. "I guess. And their restroom. Their access is from there."

This meant the far section of Furniture Sellers' basement was beneath Cycle Life's office, service counter, and clothing and accessories areas. "I assume your store and CounterTops have direct access to the furnace room?"

"We need to, in case of heating or other problems."

"Can you show it to me?"

"The furnace room?" He blinked. "Why?"

"I'm adjusting the Cycle Life claim. The more I know about their premises, the more we'll be able to recover their stolen goods." She couldn't see how viewing the furnace room would help but hoped Dustin would buy it.

"We'll need the key. I keep it here." He crossed to the kitchen counter, opened a drawer, closed it, and turned around. "Bob Sellers, the owner, wouldn't like me taking outsiders there, since the furnace room's a shared space. Besides, from what Herb told me, the thieves entered through his workshop and took the bikes out front." His gaze darted sideways, in the direction of the furnace room.

Was he hiding something there? Although his excuse made more sense than her alleged reason for seeing the room.

Dustin strode past her to the doorway. "I'll show you the full bathroom next." He switched off the kitchen light. "I do my best to save Bob the cost of utilities."

"Is that why the far end of the basement is dark?"

He nodded. "I don't need that area. Why waste electricity?" He turned left in the passage and opened the door to the bathroom. "Have a look in, but let's stay out here. It's hard to keep from touching anything."

Dustin made her mother seem reckless about COVID. Paula peeked at the cozy room with a glass corner shower stall. To her right, the pile of delivered items extended halfway to the ceiling and all the way to the wall that ran along the front of the building.

"If it weren't for this junk," Dustin said. "We could go from here straight to the staircase, but we'll have to circle back the way we came to get upstairs."

Paula glanced at the tower of deliveries. "Where will you put all these things?"

He shrugged. "We don't usually have this problem. Now, we have no customers buying the existing stock. Are you in the market for furniture?"

Before she could reply, he started back down the passage. They turned left at the elevator. Her house was full, but maybe her mother could use another small table for her mask-making. They arrived at the rear entrance.

"Mother's Day is coming up," she said. "My mum's notion of the perfect gift is a surprise that's thoughtful, practical, and a bargain."

"We're bound to have what you want." He nodded at the pile. "To help clear things out, I'll kick in my employee discount."

"Thanks. I'll browse another day, when I have the time." It would be an excuse to come back.

"Do you have time now to see my quarters upstairs?"

She made a show of checking her watch but wouldn't miss this. "Sure."

His bright eyes above his mask suggested he was keen to show her the areas he used. Was it overly suspicious to think he might be purposely keeping her from the furnace room? And if he were hiding something there, it was likely personal and unrelated to the break and enter. Mike had told her witnesses often skewed their testimony by withholding their irrelevant secrets.

Dustin picked up the bottle of sanitizer. "It won't hurt us to clean again."

Paula massaged the liquid over her hands, peering at living and dining room displays that faded to darkness. Above the farther ones, Cycle Life customers would be milling around, wheeling bikes to the entrance. Possibly Olivia was running all over or knocking a bike to the wooden floor. If sounds carried through the ceiling, Dustin must hear them occasionally, even from here.

Their hands re-sanitized, Dustin led her down the main passage to the staircase, which abutted the front of the building. He started up the stairs, but she paused at the bottom.

He stopped at the midpoint landing and looked down. "Do you have trouble with stairs? You should have said. We'll take the elevator. No problem."

"It's not that." A passage to her right followed the wall. "I'd like to check out the rest of your basement, to get a full picture of Cycle Life's layout."

Dustin barrelled down the stairs. "I 'spose it'll only cost Bob a few pennies," he said, his tone light.

She stepped back to let him go ahead of her down the passage. He flicked on a series of wall switches. Mini living rooms flowed into dining rooms into bedrooms to a distant wall with a door, presumably to the furnace room.

"What's that smell?" Dustin said. "I hope it's not a dead mouse or squirrel." He continued toward the furnace room.

Paula sniffed through her mask. Now that he mentioned it, she could detect an odour. Familiar. It took her back to another time she'd entered a house. She edged toward the odour.

Dustin gasped.

She stopped behind him, couldn't see around him.

"Is he dead?" His voice rose several pitches.

That smell. *The sphincters relax after death*, she recalled from the past occasion. Her heart pounded. "Who's 'he'?" She stepped sideways, hitting a chair.

A body lay in the passage, twisted, splattered in red. Paula swayed. Images flashed. Legs twisted as they couldn't be in life. Callie, her friend, dead on the river path. *Not again.* Paula gripped a chair arm, her skin clammy, her vision blurred. Dustin's fuzzy shape moved to the body on the floor.

Don't disturb a scene that might be suspicious. "Don't touch him."

"We're trained in CPR, for customers," Dustin said and mumbled something more.

Her head spun. She sank to the chair, gulped for breath.

He squatted, blocking her view of the body. "It's a woman."

Paula looked down at her blurred waist pouch. *Do something.*

"She's cold, stiff. I don't feel a pulse." He stood and retreated toward Paula. "Her head is covered with blood. Did she fall? Who is she? Why is she here?"

The pouch came into focus. *Call 911.* Her shaking hands struggled with the zipper. She reached in, grabbed her phone, punched digits. A voice answered.

"I . . . I'm at." She blanked.

"Furniture Sellers," Dustin said, from beside her. He supplied the address.

She repeated it into the phone, her voice growing steadier. "A woman. Seems dead. Looks like she fell. Send EMS immediately. From Eighth or Ninth Avenue Northeast enter the store's rear lot, go into the basement level."

"On it," the woman said. "How many people are there?"

"Only two. The store's closed, officially."

"Both of you, go outside now, stand far from the building, and wait for EMS."

"Oh God," Dustin said, his back to her. "There's a candlestick on the floor. Did someone bludgeon her? Oh God."

Paula spoke into the phone. "Did you hear that?"

"I did," the dispatcher said. "Don't touch anything and leave the minute I hang up. I'm hanging up now, okay?"

"Okay."

The line clicked.

Dustin looked around the room. "What if he's still in here?"

"Who?" Paula said.

"If she's killed, then . . ."

Hiding places were everywhere in these displays. Dustin had said the woman's body was stiff. Rigor mortis started an hour or two after death, but the killer could have lingered in the dark, might have been here since she'd arrived.

"We have to get out." She rose, slowly to avoid dizziness.

Dustin didn't move. "I touched her. What was I thinking?"

"That doesn't matter," she said. "But avoid touching anything else." She braved a glance at the body, which Dustin had touched, forgetting his worries about germs. Red sneakers on the feet, jeans on the bent legs, head drenched in blood. A woman, he'd said. Paula couldn't tell the person's gender from this distance.

She turned to Dustin. "Follow me."

He nodded. She zigzagged between chairs and sofas down the diagonal route to the exit. No footsteps behind. She looked over her shoulder. Dustin raced down the aisle by the wall, taking the longer route. Had he not understood? She stopped at the console table by the door and tapped her foot, waiting for him to reach the staircase.

"This way," she shouted. "It's faster."

He bounded up the stairs. Idiot, heading for the front exit. He wasn't thinking straight. Neither was she. In her early moments of panic, she'd handled the situation badly.

But now she was astute enough to carefully lift a mask from the box of disposables on the console table and cover her hand with the mask when she opened the door. The police would be checking the entry points to the basement for incriminating fingerprints.

Chapter Thirteen

Novak biked into the industrial park. A truck was parked in front of an automobile-glass repair shop, but the other businesses he passed looked closed. Behind him, a siren shrilled. He hugged the curb to let the patrol car speed by. The warmth of the sunshine and exercise made his back sweat, which justified his legitimate reason for visiting Cycle Life—to buy a saddlebag, so he wouldn't need a backpack while riding. A lock would be useful, too. Also, a water bottle to fasten to a holder on the bike's crossbar, although bending over to grab it might make him swerve all over the place. Bikes were fine recreation, but he preferred getting around in a car or truck, protected from the weather and with space for everything he needed.

He approached a building sign that listed three retail outlets, the middle one Cycle Life. The patrol car that had passed him was parked in the lot, near the north entrance, and an officer and a civilian stood nearby.

Novak pulled up next to them and stopped. "What's going on?"

"Murder in Furniture Sellers," the civilian said.

The officer glared at him. "Nothing has been determined yet." She looked at Novak. "Sir, we need to ask you to move on, to clear the area."

Novak glanced at the storefront window covered with blinds. The door was open. "I'm Detective Brian Novak, in Homicide."

"Homicide's here already?" The mask over the civilian's nose wrinkled with his words. "On bike patrol?"

The officer's walkie-talkie buzzed. "You two stay here while I take this." She moved a few metres away.

Novak looked past her to the building's middle store, which would be either Cycle Life or CounterTops.

"Cycle Life had a break and enter last week," the civilian said. He wore flip-flops, shorts, and a T-shirt. Tattoos decorated his forearms.

The man's backpack made Novak aware that his own back was sweating even more than before, the old adrenalin rush of encountering a crime scene. He told the civilian this was his afternoon off and he'd ridden here to buy bicycle supplies.

"A break-in and now a murder," the man said. "Maybe it's good to get out of here, but where will I go?"

This morning, Mike had talked about trying to track down a witness who was squatting in the store next to Cycle Life. Was this the man?

The officer strode back to them. "Novak? I think you spoke to my recruiting class."

"That must have been years ago."

"Ancient history." The officer laughed. She looked to be in her thirties. "They want me to set up the perimeter. Can you stay with Dustin until we can take him to Westwinds for his statement?"

"Where's Paula?" Dustin asked.

"She's on her way up." The officer looked from Dustin to Novak. "You two stand back on the sidewalk, to make space for EMS. They'll be here any minute." She jogged to the patrol car.

Across the lot, Novak saw a man emerge from the middle store. "Is that Cycle Life?"

Dustin followed his gaze. "Yeah. Doesn't look like Herb, though. The manager's Josh. I don't know him as well."

The man got on a bicycle parked out front and rode out of the lot's far entrance. They shouldn't be letting potential witnesses go like that. What if he'd seen or heard something happening next door?

Novak dismounted his bike and walked it to the sidewalk, Dustin by his side. They stopped about midway between the north entrance and the sign pole, which would be good for securing his bike . . . if he had a lock. The officer carried a box past them to the lot's south end. Novak nudged down his kickstand. He wished he had a bottle of water.

"I don't know what's keeping Paula," Dustin said. "She'd have got out ahead of me."

Presumably, Dustin had discovered a suspicious death in Furniture Sellers. Novak longed to grill him, but Dustin's fresh account would be more useful to Homicide. Wait, Paula? Was that the name he'd said? Paula Savard was the adjuster handling the Cycle Life B and E. Had she gone to the store to interview the squatter?

A siren wailed the EMS van into the lot. It drew up in front of Furniture Sellers, blocking Novak's view of the door. The driver leaped out and ran to the rear of the van.

"Will we see them bring her out?" Dustin asked.

Her.

People spilled out of Cycle Life, likely drawn by the sounds. The officer left her perimeter tape and ran to the group, to contain them. They needed more cops to deal with this.

"There's Paula," Dustin said.

Novak turned. A woman and a uniformed officer crested the sloped street that likely led to the rear of the building. They stepped into the front lot. The woman wore a T-shirt, capris, and sunglasses. She had dark hair and looked to be in her fifties.

"Paula," Dustin shouted.

The woman looked over at them and then spoke to the officer. Both walked toward Novak and Dustin. The officer told Paula and Dustin to wait on this spot for their ride to police headquarters and left to talk to EMS.

"Detective Novak?" Paula said. "I didn't expect to see you here."

"You know him?" Dustin's eyebrows rose.

Novak repeated the story he'd told Dustin.

Paula glanced at Novak's bike. "They made me leave mine in the rear lot. It's part of the crime scene. While I was inside with Dustin, someone might have touched the handlebars if they left while Dustin was showing me the premises."

Dustin shuddered. "It's creepy to think of that."

Paula's gaze shifted from him to Novak. "They told me not to talk to anyone about what happened."

"Me too," Dustin said.

"Does that include talking to you, Detective?" Paula asked.

"It does," Novak said. "And it includes discussing it with each other."

Paula nodded and stared at Dustin. "Why did you run upstairs?" She looked at Novak. "This happened after the fact. Does it count?"

"Afraid so," Novak said.

Dustin shrugged off his backpack. "I don't know why I kept this on so long. It makes my shoulders ache." He set the bulging pack on the grass. "I ran upstairs to pack some clothing, thinking they won't let me live here now. Damn, I forgot my jacket. It'll get cold tonight, and maybe tomorrow. My mind was a mess."

"Mine too," Paula said. "I was in shock."

"You thought enough to call 911."

"How about you talk about something else," Novak intervened, reluctantly. He ached to learn more about what went on inside Furniture Sellers.

At Cycle Life, the officer had managed to hustle everyone inside. A neat accomplishment.

"How long will they keep us at police headquarters?" Dustin asked.

"That depends," Novak said.

"Could it be overnight?"

"Possibly." Depending on Homicide's workload and how suspicious they judged Dustin's behaviour.

The paramedics stood behind the van, talking with the officer who'd come up with Paula. They were probably waiting for word that the building was safe for them to enter. Novak asked Paula how many patrol cars were at the rear of the building.

"One, last I saw," she said. "When I called, I sent them to the back lot, to the basement level, since . . ."

The body was in the basement.

An unmarked Ford Taurus pulled into the lot and parked behind the EMS van, leaving space for the paramedics to pull out a stretcher.

"Is that Homicide?" Paula asked.

Two men in suits got out, neither one of them Mike, to Novak's relief. He didn't relish having to provide a third explanation for his presence.

"I hoped Mike would be here," Paula said.

The tall guy was Oscar Furey, a recent transfer to Homicide. Novak's involvement with him so far had been limited to nods on their way to and from the coffee centre.

"That's Detective Shearer." Paula referred to the shorter one. "He interviewed me during our first case together, Detective Novak. He rubbed me the wrong way."

Novak got along with Shearer, but some colleagues called him an asshole. Shearer and Furey huddled with the paramedics.

"I'll have to call my manager." Dustin squatted beside his pack and got his phone from an outer pocket. "She'll put me up for a night or two. I'm already dreading it. She has three teenagers, who are out partying all the time, from what she says. But a hotel would be worse, and they're expensive." He carried the phone toward the sign pole.

Furey broke from the huddle and walked their way. "You're the witnesses?" His long jaw dropped. "Detective Novak?"

Novak launched into his third explanation.

Furey glanced at Cycle Life. "We wondered about the cars parked in front. Aren't nonessential stores closed?

"Bikes are essential transportation," Paula said. "Shouldn't you interview the people there, even if the death was . . ."

Hours ago?

Dustin returned, tucked his phone in his backpack, and stepped a few metres away. Several people came out of Cycle Life. The officer stringing the yellow tape reached the sign pole. She knotted the tape to the pole and continued stringing to the north entrance.

Furey told Dustin that the officer from the second responding patrol car would drive him to Westwinds when she was finished securing the perimeter.

"What about her?" Dustin jerked his thumb at Paula.

Furey turned to her. "The plan is for me to take a video statement from you, here at the scene, if you're agreeable."

Paula nodded. "It will save me a trip to Westwinds."

"Why does she get special treatment?" Dustin said.

Rather than answer, Furey glanced at the gathering outside of Cycle Life. "Meanwhile, I'll take care of the bike store gang."

"I can do that," Novak said. The words had popped out. He wanted to stay on this side of the yellow tape. "Might as well use me while I'm here so you can focus on your key work. I'll keep those gawkers out of your way, take everyone's name and contact details, interview them, and send them home." He hoped he hadn't sounded rambling or desperate.

Furey rubbed his jaw. "That would be a help."

A person left the group at Cycle Life and started in their direction. Novak lurched forward to waylay the curiosity seeker.

"Take your bike," Furey said. "It will be safer parked over there."

Novak retreated, gripped his handlebars, and quickstepped his bike diagonally across the lot toward the woman. Slim, long blonde hair, young—in her twenties, he guessed.

"You have to go back into the store," he told her.

"Was there a break and enter or something next door?"

"I'll explain when we're inside."

She stood her ground. "Who are you? Cops don't wear cargo shorts."

"I'm off duty." If he mentioned suspicious death, she looked the type to be on her cell phone calling friends and posting on social media within seconds.

She cocked her head. "I've seen you before. Were you at Cycle Life this afternoon?"

He shook his head. "Officer Novak."

Her face brightened. "Detective Novak. I knew I'd met you. Remember me?"

Wide-set blue eyes, lively expression. An image from his past began to take shape.

"Isabelle," she said. "You investigated my aunt Callie's death."

Callie, Paula's friend. He remembered Isabelle now. She was a wild card but had contributed somehow to the resolution.

Isabelle's eyebrows rose. "You're here. That means it's a homicide." Her gaze shot to Furniture Sellers.

"I'm off duty," he said. "Here by chance. I'll explain when we get inside."

She stepped sideways for a better look at Furniture Sellers. "It's a B and E, then, like at Cycle Life?"

A child separated from the bike store group and trotted their way. Novak had barely arrived and had already lost control of the situation. He recalled Isabelle was inclined to stick her nose in every pie. "Isabelle," he said. "You can help the police by getting everyone back into the store."

"Isabelle," the child called. She looked about seven, his granddaughter's age.

Isabelle pivoted and grabbed the little girl around her shoulders. "Olivia, this nice man wants to talk to us in the store."

"I want to talk to him here." Olivia stamped her foot.

"It's something he has to tell us in the store. I know I really want to hear it." She reached for the child's hand.

Olivia drew back and then tentatively accepted Isabelle's hand, which enclosed hers. Novak's grip on the handlebars relaxed. He followed them both to Cycle Life, his steps light on the pavement. Amazing. He was inside.

* * *

When her mother didn't answer her call, Paula left a message saying she was delayed and to eat dinner without her. She added that her reason related to work—true—and would be easier to explain in person. She returned the phone to her waist pouch.

Across the lot, Detective Novak was shooing the curious Cycle Life customers back into the store. From this distance, Paula didn't recognize Josh, Herb, or Kelsey in the group. A last man remained outside with Novak. Then a woman came out, handed something to Novak, and went back in. She looked too tall to be Kelsey. As Novak spoke with the man, Paula realized he was interviewing him and jotting notes on the paper and clipboard the woman had given him.

The officer setting up the yellow tape tied it to a post she'd brought to the lot's north entrance. Dustin stood on the sidewalk, his mask lowered to his chin so he could smoke. Smokes would have been among the personal items he'd dashed upstairs to collect before leaving his temporary home. Paula kept rehashing his behaviour and couldn't decide if it was suspicious or not. He'd welcomed her into the store's basement and had seemed eager to give her a tour of his dwelling—but not into the darkened area where the body lay. His instinct to collect his clothing and any valuables was plausible, but wouldn't a panicked person more naturally run to the nearest exit?

An image of the body on the basement floor flashed into her mind. Bloodied head, red sneakers. *It's a woman*, Dustin had said.

Paula took a step toward him. "Are you sure the victim was female?"

He drew on his cigarette, perhaps reflecting. "We're not supposed to talk about this."

True. But also convenient for avoiding an answer.

Admittedly, Dustin had stood closer to the victim than she had, and he'd remained there several minutes, but the head was covered in blood. What about the chest? In the photos Isabelle had found of Gabe, he was slim and androgynous looking. Dustin might associate red sneakers with women, but men wore them too. If Gabe had been looking for a hideout, what would be better than a closed store with bedroom and living room furniture? Dustin, by his own account, lived on the opposite side of Furniture Sellers. But could they have shared the premises for the past month without becoming aware of each other's presence? It was unlikely.

In front of Furniture Sellers, the paramedics manoeuvred the stretcher out of the rear of the van. The tall detective followed them into the store. Detective Coyote Face strode toward Paula. Since their last encounter, she'd learned his surname was Shearer, but her nickname for him still fit. Pointy nose, narrow face, beady eyes on the lookout to pounce, regardless of a person's innocence or vulnerability. When she'd shared her view of him with Mike, he'd defended his colleague by calling him competent. It wasn't a ringing endorsement.

Shearer stopped in front of her, closer than she would have liked. "We meet again, Ms. Savard. You have a knack for stumbling upon dead bodies."

She fought the urge to glare at him. It was only her second instance of doing so, and she'd had good reason to be there both times. Shearer's face was more lined than it had been three and a half years ago. He still wore a thin moustache. His reddish hair, once short, now draped COVIDly over his ears. They hadn't crossed paths during her Homicide-related insurance work, but he was the unit's second-in-command and would be aware of her involvement.

"At least we already have your fingerprints on record," Shearer added. "It'll save time at Westwinds."

"You have a record?" Dustin held out his cigarette as if it were a tiny shield.

"I was a witness." She tried not to sound defensive. "Like you are now."

"A suspect, too," Shearer said, about her, or them both.

"How long will I be at police headquarters?" Dustin asked. "I need to tell the friend I'm staying with when to expect me."

Shearer moved to Paula's left, where he'd have a better view of Dustin. "That depends on when I'm finished here. It could take hours."

"Your partner said he'd interview me here," Paula said.

Shearer scratched his moustache. "Right. Furey mentioned taking a video-statement on his tablet." He pivoted and strode back to Furniture Sellers.

"This could take all night," Dustin said. "For me, anyway."

She nodded. "The police can move slowly."

He took out another cigarette from his pack. "Why are they treating us differently? Is it to keep us separate? But, then why aren't they separating us here?"

Paula shrugged, evading an answer. She guessed—hoped—the reason was that Shearer didn't view her as a suspect in this case and was either careless about leaving her with Dustin or, less likely, trusted her not to contaminate the witness evidence by discussing her shared experience with Dustin.

She turned to check the situation at Cycle Life. The man Novak had interviewed walked to his car. Novak opened the store's front door, and a woman came out. It seemed he was interviewing customers individually and then sending them home. She guessed he'd leave Josh, Herb, and Kelsey until the end. Were all three working today? Paula recalled Josh saying Tuesday was Kelsey's day off. Yesterday, she'd gone home sick.

"There's another van," Dustin said.

It drove into the north entrance and pulled up in front of the EMS vehicle. Two men leaped out of the unmarked vehicle. Was this the Forensic Crime Scene unit? The men put on Hazmat suits. Must be.

Paula's cell phone rang. Her mother.

"When you called, I was on the front porch, enjoying the sun with Walter. I hope you don't have a serious work problem."

How to explain without worrying her? "It's a long story, Mum," Paula said. "I'll tell you when I get home tonight. The bottom line is, go ahead with supper on your own. I'll keep you posted."

"We'll save your birthday takeout for tomorrow. I'm still full from our big brunch."

"Me too." Paula realized this was true. She said goodbye and hung up.

While she had her phone out, she checked to see if she'd missed a text or call from Mike. Nothing. She'd have expected him to contact her when he learned that she and Dustin had discovered a body at Furniture Sellers. Maybe he hadn't heard. News occasionally got lost in police bureaucracy. She sent him a text.

Mike and Megan sat across the table from Connor in the interview room. Connor's body language said it all. Arms crossed, beard jutting toward them, veiled eyes. Zero chance he'd talk about the break and enter at Cycle Life until his lawyer arrived. Mike considered slipping out to grab a bite to eat. Once this finally got going, it could drag into the evening. Luckily, Mike had wrapped up his Homicide work for the day and wasn't needed at home. Lucy and Kyle were there to look after Eli, and Novak could look after himself. He seemed to have stumbled back onto his feet.

Megan's text notification sounded. She read the message and looked at Connor. "Your lawyer's here. I'll take you to a room where you can consult privately."

When they left, Mike decided not to chance getting food in case the consult was quick. He'd hate to miss his first impressions of the lawyer Kelsey had promised Connor, should he ever need one.

"Just came out in general conversation," Connor had told them, while fidgeting with his beard. "She's Kelsey's cousin. Kelsey didn't give me her number, though."

Mike had tracked her down easily by searching Clayton Little's address in the online White Pages. His phone number was listed. When Mike called, Clayton remembered his visit. He agreed it wouldn't hurt for Mike to contact his other granddaughter about Kelsey's whereabouts and supplied the cousin's phone number.

Mike took out his cell phone to pass the time. A text from Paula. He'd missed the vibration.

In case you don't know, Dustin and I found the body at Furniture Sellers.

Mike started. *A body?* He phoned the Homicide administrator to ask if they had a new case of suspicious death, at Furniture Sellers.

"Yes," she said. "Came in less than an hour ago. Shearer and Furey are at the scene. They haven't reported back yet. The staff sergeant put the rest of the unit on alert. Didn't you get the message?"

"No. Let me know when they report. Right now, I'm working with Robbery, waiting to interview someone about a case at the store next to Furniture Sellers. There could be a connection."

"Will do."

He signed off and replied to Paula, *Thanks for the heads-up. Occupied with Connor, but send me any updates.* Strange he'd heard this from her. That's what he got for hanging out with Robbery.

He scrolled through several routine messages until Megan reappeared. She returned to the seat beside him.

"What's the lawyer like?" he asked.

"Under thirty. I gather she and Kelsey are reasonably close cousins."

"Had Connor met her before this?"

"Not unless they're both talented actors."

"I have other news." He summarized the little he knew about the homicide case. "So much for Paula's vow to stay away from suspicious deaths."

Megan frowned. "I'm sure a body was the last thing she expected to find there." Her forehead creased. "In fact, you and I walked through that basement this morning without giving the possibility a thought."

"The person must have died later. We couldn't have missed that." He recalled a dark section of basement they hadn't entered. *Fuck.* If a body had been there, his instincts were off.

Megan's phone rang.

She listened to the caller, hung up, and looked at Mike. "Connor's lawyer has called off his interview. She wants us to meet her in the consult room to explain. Connor won't be present."

Chapter Fourteen

Isabelle crouched beside Olivia, who sat at her table in the back corner of Cycle Life. Together they traced the drawings on the workbook's first two pages. Images of unicorns and dragons took shape on the tissue paper. Olivia followed the lines underneath with care and precision.

"Awesome," Isabelle told her, and meant it.

She'd been at Cycle Life almost three hours now and could hardly keep up with Olivia's abrupt shifts from hyper to obsessively focused. Was that normal for kids? Isabelle wouldn't know. She didn't have younger siblings and none of her friends were parents yet.

Isabelle set down her pencil, stood, and withdrew from the table. When Olivia didn't look up or stop drawing, Isabelle sidled through the clothing corner to the entrance door so she could keep an eye on both Olivia and the door to Herb's workshop. His interview with Detective Novak couldn't take much longer, unless Herb had tons to say about the incident at Furniture Sellers. *Incident.* So far, the detective hadn't called it more than that.

In all the excitement, she'd been too busy to call Connor to tell him what he'd missed. She reached into her right back pocket for her phone. Nothing there. She tried the left pocket, although she'd never put it there.

She looked at the door. After Novak had interviewed the last customer, Isabelle had gone outside to photograph the crime scene. She'd gotten a shot of the police car with Paula standing behind it. *Paula.* Another person she hadn't had time to call. Why was Paula here? Isabelle had started to take a picture of the officers setting up the yellow tape when Novak stopped her—because "crime scenes were confidential." He told her to delete the first picture, which she pretended to do. After they went inside, she'd taken the phone out a few times to check her messages. Had she set it on the service counter? She dashed over and rifled through every receipt and piece of paper. What would she do without her phone? Her whole life was in it.

At her table, Olivia turned a page and resumed her tracing. Her school workbooks were piled on the table corner. Isabelle looked under each workbook in the stack, although she had no idea why her phone would be there.

"Olivia, have you seen my phone?"

Olivia kept drawing, staring downward, her dark hair hiding her face. "It's in my schoolbag."

Relief flooded through Isabelle. "How did it get there?" Isabelle squatted and opened the backpack slumped against a table leg. Books, pens, pencils, erasers, a purple stuffed rabbit. She unzipped the front and then a side pouch and touched metal, touched screen.

"I borrowed it to call my mom." Olivia looked up and brushed her hair from her face. "I was going to give it back."

Then why was it in her backpack? She must have lifted it from Isabelle's pocket seconds after she'd placed it there, before the password protection kicked in. Olivia had gone to the bathroom shortly after they re-entered the store. She must have made the call in there, while Novak was explaining his plan to Isabelle. After the customers, he'd interview Isabelle and Herb, and they'd have to close the store until the crime scene tape was down, which could take a few days if the incident was serious. Herb had ranted—this was bad for business, why should they be punished, why couldn't the police run the tape from the street to the wall dividing them and Furniture Sellers?

Olivia gazed up at her, her child eyes innocent.

Isabelle opened her phone and pressed random apps. Everything seemed the same. "Why did you call your mom?"

"She'd want to know police are here."

Isabelle nodded. Her parents would freak if they knew she was in a store surrounded by police tape and blaring sirens. Actually, they weren't blaring anymore. She could risk a look outside before Herb and Novak came out.

She left Olivia to her tracing and padded back to the store entrance. Sounds from the farthest corner made her whirl around. Novak stood in the workshop doorframe. She'd have to check outside and phone Connor later, when there might be more to tell him.

Novak wove through the bikes and stopped in front of her. "Your turn, Isabelle."

"When is it my turn?" Olivia stared up at them from the table.

"After her," Novak said. "I save the best for last."

Olivia smiled, for the first time Isabelle had seen. Good to let kids think they're important.

Novak asked if there was a private space for them to talk. "Herb wants to work on a bike, and the workshop seems to be his domain."

Isabelle glanced at the office door. "The office is free with Josh and Kelsey gone."

"I'll be contacting them after this," Novak said. "Herb gave me their details."

"Only my dad and Kelsey are allowed to use the office," Olivia said. "And my mom when she wants to yell at my dad."

Isabelle stifled a smile and thought Novak was doing the same. The office wouldn't give her a view of Olivia anyway, but the bench that people used for trying on biking shoes would work. Isabelle hadn't seen anything weird going on and had nothing to say that Olivia shouldn't overhear. "We can sit here."

"It will have to do," Novak said.

Olivia returned to her drawing. Novak sat on one end of the bench, reminding Isabelle about social distancing. She sat at the other end, her back to Olivia, but Novak would notice if Olivia got hyper again. His position, closer to the door, gave him a better view of the whole room. Cops liked that. Isabelle recapped her shopping trip with her friend Ryan—best to stick with that name in case Herb told Novak about him—and left out their motive of coming here to spy.

"What did you want to buy here?" she asked.

Novak leaned back, maybe not expecting her to be the questioner. "A saddlebag and a lock. Maybe a water bottle."

"We've got some stock of them all, but they're going fast."

Novak stared. "Do you work here?"

"Not really." She told him about Olivia's mother's worry about leaving her in a busy store for homeschooling. "I had nothing to do today and said I'd look after her until the store closed and Josh could take her home. He's paying me with a helmet." That made her offer to stay more innocent and believable. Before he left, Josh had told her that Herb would drive Olivia home at the end of the workday.

Novak asked what she'd heard and seen during her almost three hours here. She could honestly say, "Nothing you wouldn't expect in a store." Since the detective didn't ask, she assumed Herb had told him all he needed to know about Josh and Kelsey, including that Josh had left early because he was tired and that Tuesday was Kelsey's day off and she'd gone home sick yesterday. Had Herb said he suspected she was faking sick? According to TV crime shows, her mentioning this would be hearsay.

Novak took her home address and cell phone number. He repeated them to make sure he'd got them right. She was grateful to feel her phone against her bum now.

He leaned forward and called, "Your turn, little girl."

Olivia hopped up and over to the bench. Isabelle half expected her to jump on his lap. Novak made Isabelle wish she had a kindly grandfather. One of hers had died when she was a baby; the other was a grump she saw once a year when her mother forced her into duty visits. Olivia plunked herself down between Isabelle and Novak on the bench. Isabelle got up and edged to the service counter. She took out her phone to call Connor but instead decided to scroll through messages so she could eavesdrop. Since Olivia's back was to her, Isabelle could hear Novak's standard cop questions but not Olivia's answers. Was that why Novak had gotten Isabelle to sit with her back to Olivia? Clever.

Olivia turned toward Isabelle. "I listen to everything in the store." She scanned the display of bikes, the counter, the office door. "Hearing is my superpower."

"Is it?" Novak looked as if he believed this. He'd be a cool granddad.

Isabelle hadn't noticed anything super about Olivia's hearing. But she also hadn't been looking for it.

"I'll listen more now," Olivia said.

"No need to do that," Novak said. "Be your usual fun self."

Olivia leaned forward and looked at the entrance door. "Someone's outside."

She was obviously trying to prove her superpower. Isabelle heard nothing, and then a knock on the door. Novak stood to answer. Someone pounded. Olivia leaped up and ran to Isabelle, who wrapped her arms around the trembling child. Novak opened the door.

"What's going on?" a woman said.

"Mommy!" Olivia tore away from Isabelle's arms and ran to the woman, brushing Novak so hard he teetered sideways.

Olivia's mother—Zab, as Josh had called her— leaned down and squeezed her small daughter to her chest. Isabelle had noticed the name Zabrina

Chapman and a phone number written on some of Olivia's workbooks.

In her peripheral view, Isabelle saw Herb come out of his workshop. He shuffled toward the store entrance.

Zabrina clutched her long sweater to her chest, a red cardigan over red scrubs. She wore dangly ruby earrings. "After Olivia called, I was frantic and got a co-worker to fill in for me." She glanced at the storefront. "Olivia mentioned police but not a whole crime scene blocked off with caution tape."

"How did you get past the police and tape?" Novak asked.

Zabrina ignored his question. "I noticed an EMS van."

"There was an incident next door," Novak said. "We don't know the details yet, but police err on the side of caution."

"Not always, in my experience," she said.

What was her experience? Isabelle drew closer to the group at the entrance.

Zabrina looked at Novak. "Who are you? A customer? The store sign says Closed." She narrowed her eyes. "You talk like police but don't look like one."

"I'm an off-duty officer, lending a hand." Novak scanned the group, including Isabelle. "We're finished here. You're all free to go. I'll leave with the last person."

"That'll be me," Herb said. "I need to lock up. How will we know if we can open tomorrow?"

"Assume closed," Novak said. "Until you or Josh hears otherwise."

"Where is Josh?" Zabrina looked around, and beyond Isabelle to the office.

"He was tired and went home," Herb said.

"Humph," Zabrina said. "And he wants me to trust him to watch Olivia." Her gaze settled on Isabelle. "What if you hadn't been here?"

"Josh would have stayed." Herb sounded defensive. "He's not irresponsible."

"Humph," Zabrina repeated.

Olivia stared up at her. "I want Isabelle to teach me tomorrow."

"She can't, sweetheart," Zabrina said. "Since the store will be closed, Daddy can look after you at home."

Herb snorted. "Like the store closure will keep Josh away."

"He can't get past the police tape," Zabrina said.

"You did," Isabelle said.

Zabrina squinted at her and turned to Novak. "Tell Josh that you cops will fine him if he crosses the tape. Not that a fine will do any good. All I know is, Josh will *not* bring Olivia into this place, and I have to work tomorrow. I'm an essential worker, in health care. They won't let me take time off."

"She'll teach me." Olivia darted to Isabelle and clutched her legs.

Isabelle rested her hand on the girl's head. Maybe Zabrina could drop off Olivia at her place? It would be weird, but . . . Isabelle could easily fit tutoring and childcare around her insurance work. And she'd learn so much about these people, who might be involved in the incident at Furniture Sellers, and more.

"She can't, sweetie," Zabrina said. "We'll work something out with Daddy."

"I want Isabelle." Olivia squeezed tighter.

"Olivia." Zabrina's tone was firm. "Pack up your things, so we can go home. It's been a long day." She rubbed her brow.

Isabelle wished she'd jumped on her weird thought and offered to homeschool Olivia. Thinking it through had been a mistake. She'd lost her chance. Olivia let go of her legs and loaded her schoolbag, curiously obedient, while Herb sold Novak a saddlebag, a lock, and a water bottle. Zabrina asked Isabelle what she wanted for payment. Isabelle said Josh had offered her a helmet.

"Have your pick." Zabrina's tone turned warm. "You were a lifesaver."

Like Olivia, Zabrina seemed to blow from one extreme to the other. For Olivia, it was from hyper to focused. For Zabrina, nasty to friendly, although maybe Josh pressed her buttons. Isabelle's mom was the same. She loved Isabelle's dad, but his quirks were high maintenance.

After Zabrina and Olivia left the store, Herb said he had a couple of things to finish before closing and went back to his workshop. Novak moved toward the office and talked on his phone, reminding Isabelle that she hadn't called Connor yet. She went outside so she could show him the crime scene. Zabrina and Olivia stood beside a pickup truck and watched the action in front of Furniture Sellers. Two uniformed officers talked with a man in a classy suit. Was he a detective? This was more than an "incident." As Zabrina took out her phone, Olivia ran to Isabelle.

"One of the cops said a woman died," Olivia said.

Isabelle looked at the huddle. She couldn't hear more than snippets of voice tones.

"My superpower," Olivia said.

Isabelle nodded, although Olivia had probably made that up.

"Olivia!" Zabrina yelled. "We have to go home. Now."

Olivia raced to her mother, who took her hand and hustled her toward the yellow tape. They ducked underneath, crossed the street, and got into a red car parked in front of the closed hot-tub store. Their car backed out. Isabelle turned to white pickup, which was the only non-cop car left in the lot. It must be Herb's. Her cell phone rang. Connor.

"You're psychic," she said as a joke. "I was going to call you."

"I can't talk long." His voice was raspy and low. "I'm at Westwinds, police headquarters. They're keeping me overnight."

"Why?"

"It's about Cycle Life."

Isabelle looked at the store. Novak and Herb were still inside.

"My lawyer had to leave to deal with a personal matter," he said. "That was her excuse, anyway. I didn't plan to be here this long. Would you go to my place to feed Finnegan tomorrow? You can get my key from my neighbour in unit two, next door. He's always home in the morning. I left Finnegan enough food until then."

"If he's home, why can't he feed Finnegan? I mean, I want to help, but—"

"There's another thing." He coughed. "I overheard the cops talking about warrants. It reminded me that there're some bags of Gabe's drugs in my underwear drawer. I confiscated them from his room before he left and meant to throw them out. Can you take them out of the apartment, in case the cops go looking?"

"You want me to throw them out?"

"I guess. It seems a waste, though. That's why I didn't pitch them before. I thought, travel's expensive and I don't have a job and they're easy money . . ." The line went silent. "But what if I need them for a more expensive lawyer, if mine doesn't work out? Let's hold off on getting rid of them."

A second man who looked like a detective came out of the store next door.

"I can't bring them to my place," Isabelle said.

"No one would check there."

Her roommates would think this was terrible, but she could hide them in her office. They never went in when she wasn't there. "Are they illegal drugs?"

"What do you think?" he said. "If the cops find them, they'll assume they're mine."

"You can tell them they're Gabe's."

"Like they'd believe me. It would also get him in trouble, if he ever shows up."

And this could get her in trouble. But right now, the risk of trouble was greatest for Connor. "Okay," she said. "Would tomorrow morning be soon enough?"

"I don't think the cops will do anything tonight. There's something big going on here in Major Crimes."

"That's why I was calling you." She quickly summarized the events of the past few hours. "Detective Novak calls it an 'incident,' but I think someone died, and maybe was killed."

Connor gasped. "Gabe."

"Why him?" Isabelle tightened her grip on the phone.

"He hung out in Cycle Life. Oh, Gabe." Connor's breathing turned heavy.

Isabelle tried to calm him. "It's not Gabe. Olivia heard them say it's a woman."

"A woman?" Connor's breathing eased. "Not Gabe?"

Olivia likely had misheard or made it up, but Connor had to get through tonight, alone, in the police station. "Don't worry. I'm sure it's someone else."

"Oh no . . . She's missing too." Connor's breathing got heavy again. "Not her."

* * *

Paula wished Dustin good luck as he got into the back seat of the patrol car. She watched the vehicle drive out of the north entrance of the lot and hoped Mike would call tonight to fill her in on what happened with Dustin at Westwinds.

At Cycle Life, the young woman who'd come outside returned to the store. From her movements, Paula would swear she was Isabelle, who had no reason to be here. The only other vehicle parked in front of the store, a white pickup truck, might be blocking Paula's view of a car. She moved onto the sidewalk to check. Sure enough, there was a station wagon, same make and colour as Erin's. Isabelle frequently borrowed the car. Paula started toward it to inspect the dusty front licence plate.

"Paula."

She halted.

Detective Furey jogged across the lot. "Finally, I have time for our interview," he said. "I hope you haven't been bored waiting."

"Hard to be bored at a crime scene."

"You said it." Furey held up a tablet computer. "Are you comfortable with this method of interviewing? I'll do a video recording."

"I haven't experienced it yet, but sure."

"We might still ask you to come in later for a further statement if things change or if you think of something else." He scanned the police vehicles and officers nearby. "The south entrance will be quietest."

On their way to the CounterTops end of the lot, Paula glanced at the station wagon's licence plate and made out a paw print shape under the dust. Erin's animal-rescue décor plate. Why was Isabelle here?

"I've heard a lot about you, during my month in Homicide," Furey said. "They can't praise you enough for your help solving the January hit and run."

Paula stiffened at the positive police verdict on her involvement, which had cost a man his life. She shifted the subject. "What was your area of policing before?"

"Traffic. I was familiar with your hit and run from that end."

She couldn't get away from it but tried again. "How do you like Homicide work?"

"Love it," he said. "It's tragic and painful but gets to the meat of people."

She silently agreed. They stopped in front of the police tape. Furey took the position that allowed him a view of the crime scene. Paula faced him, the police activity behind her. All she saw in her periphery was the storefront of CounterTops, the third store in the building. It had drawn nobody's attention. She guessed Furey was in his late thirties. He was over six feet tall and slim. His wavy hair fell over his forehead and ears, softening the oblong shape of his face.

A car rounded the corner onto the street, made a three-point turn, and pulled up beside them. The passenger rolled down her window and asked what was happening. Furey told her the stores were closed.

"When will the bike shop reopen?"

"That's uncertain," he said. "Please move on."

The woman held up a cell phone.

"No photographs." Furey stepped sideways to block the camera view.

The car drove forward slowly and disappeared around the corner. Furey shook his head at Paula.

He started the recording, held the tablet in front of her, and began the interview by asking what had brought her to Furniture Sellers today. She related her experiences from the time she'd left Connor's apartment to Dustin's and her discovery of body, doing her best to stick to the facts. No doubt Homicide would read between her lines and question Dustin's behaviour. Why would he have invited her into Furniture Sellers if he was concealing a dead body? Was his reluctance to show her the furnace-room end of the basement innocent or not? Was his instinct to leave by a farther exit solely due to natural panic and a desire to get his belongings? She'd love to dig into this meat.

Furey asked if she had anything to add before he turned off the recording.

"Not that I can think of, for now, except . . ." She looked at CounterTops. "Gabriel Riley, the brother of my friend Connor, went missing a month ago, although this wasn't officially reported. My first thought was, he's the victim. But Dustin says she's female."

"This is speculation." Furey concluded the interview in his formal voice and pressed the tablet.

"Gabriel has a connection to Cycle Life," Paula continued. "After seeing Dustin's living arrangement, I can say that this building seems a likely place for Gabe to hide out. Dustin would have noticed another squatter in Furniture Sellers, and Cycle Life doesn't have a basement area, but have your people checked CounterTops, the other store?”

Furey’s chin quivered. Did this mean they’d checked? They hadn’t? He didn’t know?

He gazed past her shoulder. “I should get over there.”

She turned around. The paramedics carried a stretcher out of Furniture Sellers. Paula noticed the bulky shape of a person on top. Uniformed officers and Detectives Shearer and Novak milled around the EMS van. Erin’s car and the pickup truck were gone from the lot. While Paula was occupied with Furey, Isabelle and Herb had driven out the north entrance.

Paula and Furey headed back in the direction of Furniture Sellers. He gave her his card and told her to phone him any time, day or night, if she remembered anything she hadn’t mentioned in the interview, however insignificant it appeared. “You know the drill,” he said. “Call your friend, Mike Vincelli, if you prefer. We’ll be working 24/7 for the next few days. It’ll be exhausting.”

“You’ll love it.”

His eyes brightened in agreement. “Oh, and I forgot. Your bike’s in the crime scene. I’ll find someone to drive you home.”

“Thanks, but I’ll call a cab and leave your guys to their work.” She looked at the group now moving to the rear of the EMS van. She caught Novak’s gaze and waved.

Furey thanked her and left to join his fellow officers, who obstructed Paula’s view of the paramedics loading the stretcher into the vehicle. A text notification chimed. She took her phone out of her waist pouch. Isabelle.

Why were you there?

Paula typed a reply, *Phone you tonight.*

Is it Kelsey?

Chapter Fifteen

From his seat across the desk, Novak described his afternoon with an enthusiasm Mike hadn't seen in him since Novak's wife took sick.

"Shearer accompanied EMS to the morgue," Novak said. "I'll have to wait until he gets here to see what he wants me for next."

"How about a well-deserved evening at home?"

Novak slumped back in the chair. "No fucking way. Did I mention they found a wallet on the deceased with the phone number of an emergency contact?"

Mike nodded. "Her cousin, who's a lawyer on the Cycle Life B and E. She got the call before we started Connor's interview and went directly to the morgue."

"Shearer wouldn't tell me the victim's name, for fear it gets out before the ID." Novak frowned, perhaps at being excluded. "Cause of death appears to be blunt force trauma to the back of the head. Forensics found a candlestick nearby, next to a dining room setup. Furey says he'll never play Clue again." Novak chuckled. "Nice guy, Furey."

Everyone said that and Mike agreed, based on his few small-talk chats with Oscar Furey. Homicide's newest member was a few years older than him, pushing forty, and was catching on well to the work, by all accounts. Mike had once seen him talking with Megan, both too engaged in a joke to notice Mike walk by.

Mike shook the memory from his mind. "When I was in Furniture Sellers, I noticed some tall candles on dining tables. A heavy brass candleholder would make a solid weapon."

"Which someone wielded on a girl. How old is she?"

"The cousin said twenty-four, a few years younger than her. They grew up in the same neighbourhood, almost as sisters. Kelsey's parents are doctors. They moved to Kelowna a few years ago and bought into a medical practice. Her brother lives on the west coast. They'll all arrive tomorrow, but the cousin insisted on doing the ID now, to spare the immediate family and remove the agony of waiting. If the ID's positive, she'll arrange for her mother, Kelsey's aunt, to spend the night with the grandfather Kelsey lived with."

"Kelsey?" Novak said. "An employee at Cycle Life?"

"That's right."

Novak scratched his nose. "Herb mentioned her during his interview. Her grandfather founded the store. His daughters had no interest in it, but Kelsey had hung out there since she was a kid. She planned to take over eventually. I asked what Josh, the part-owner and manager, thought about that. Herb said—"

Furey appeared in the doorway. "Am I disturbing something?"

Mike glanced at Novak then looked at Furey. "Go ahead."

Furey entered the office, his expression grim. "Positive ID. Kelsey Tedesco."

"Jesus," Novak said. "Her family."

"Her cousin, who made the ID, will inform them," Furey said. "But Shearer wants someone to talk to Kelsey's grandfather tonight to find out about her recent activities." He pursed his lips. "Seems an intrusion on an old man's grief."

Novak spun his chair toward Furey. "That's true, but the quicker we learn what we can, the more likely her family will find closure, for want of a better word."

"I'll go," Mike said. "I met the grandfather, briefly, earlier today."

Furey cocked his head. "Why were you there?"

"In connection with the Cycle Life file that Robbery's handling."

Furey's eyes lit up. "With Megan? Have you forwarded the details to Homicide?"

"I'll do that now that we have the ID."

"There might be a link." Furey stared at Mike. "I interviewed your friend Paula at the scene. She suggested Forensics check out the other store in the building. We hadn't thought of that. Assumed the victim and killer entered Furniture Sellers directly. Forensics is on it now." He waved. "I have to get going. Talk to you later."

Novak watched Furey leave. "I think he'll make it in Homicide."

Mike didn't know if he wanted or hated to agree.

"I'll go with you to the grandfather's," Novak said. "If you want a partner."

"Officially, you're on cold cases."

"Make it unofficial then. Furey was game to assign me the Cycle Life interviews." Novak looked down at his casual shirt and shorts. "I'm not dressed for meeting the victim's family. Let's stop at home on the way, so I can change into my suit. First, I'll use the restroom." He got up to leave before Mike could reply.

Mike finished his paperwork and concluded it made sense to take Novak along. Novak was part of the Homicide unit. His depression had improved. Shifting detectives out of cold cases for short-term needs wasn't unprecedented. Why deny his friend the thrill of the case? What could possibly go wrong, except everything?

"Okay," Mike said, when Novak returned. "But we make it a quick stop at home for clothes and food."

In the car, Mike steered out of the parking lot. "Before Furey arrived, you were talking about Kelsey's plan to run her grandfather's business. What does Josh think of this?"

"He wasn't there," Novak said. "Josh left work early, around the time I got there."

"Was that usual for him?"

"I gathered not."

"We'll bring him into Westwinds for an interview." Mike stopped at a red light. "What did Herb say about Josh's view of being usurped by Kelsey?"

"That Josh would be happy to hand over the reins to her when she's ready."

"Hmmm."

"Herb pointed out it wouldn't happen soon. Kelsey was still at university and needed time to cut her business chops. They've also floated the idea of opening a second store, which Josh would manage. Herb thinks Josh will prefer the new place. He can make it his own and leave the family baggage behind. My impression was Herb is loyal to Josh, to the core. We won't get any negatives about Josh from him. On the other hand, our Miss Scarlet . . ."

"Who?"

Novak laughed. "Josh's estranged wife burst in while I was there. She was wearing all red. Seemed a tad hostile toward him."

At the house, while Novak changed into his suit, Mike made ham-and-cheese sandwiches for them to eat on the way to Clayton Little's bungalow. When they arrived, Mike parked in front and gobbled the last of his sandwich.

"Clayton stayed close to his store," Novak noted. "An easy bike ride from here."

They went up to the door and rang the bell. The numerous trees in the front yard cast longer shadows than they had when Mike visited three hours ago. He started to press the bell again when the door opened.

Mike introduced Novak as well as himself, in case Clayton had forgotten him.

"You were here earlier, looking for Kelsey." Clayton's eyes watered behind his wire-rimmed glasses. "My other granddaughter says you found her. I had two granddaughters. Now one." He let go of the doorknob and stumbled backward.

Mike lurched to grab him, but Clayton regained his balance. Novak closed the door behind them all. His bowed legs shaking, Clayton shuffled to the living room and sank into the closest chair. Mike took the sofa facing a front window draped with sheer curtains. Novak sat in an armchair between the window and fireplace on the far wall. Photos lined a mantelpiece above it—weddings, graduations. The console TV in the corner looked as old as this 1970s house. The bike store business might be doing well, but Clayton clearly hadn't used the profits to upgrade his furnishings or buy an expensive home.

Clayton tapped his chest, as though getting his heart to settle. His hand slid to his belt. Mike leaned forward to read the stylized initials on the buckle—CL, for Clayton Little. Or Cycle Life.

"I don't understand," Clayton said.

Mike waited for him to continue. The grandfather clock in the hall ticked through the silence.

"Yesterday morning," Clayton said, "after breakfast, Kelsey went downstairs to get ready for work and then waved on her way out the kitchen door. I had my hands in the sink, washing dishes, barely nodded goodbye. It was the last—" His voice broke.

This was cruel to make him remember, but regardless of them, he'd relive his regrets many times over. "Can you think of anything that might have led to what happened?" Mike asked.

"All I've done since you were here is think. Only one thing comes to mind." Clayton glanced over his shoulder, at the front window. "There was a day this winter, or early spring. It was snowing, dark, dusk. A man stood across the street, staring at the house. I didn't think much of it at the time."

Mike looked at Novak, who took a notebook and pen from his suit pocket.

"Could you describe this man?" Mike asked.

"It was dark, snowing. He was too far away, across the street. Not a person I recognized from a distance. Makes me think he was a stranger, or someone I didn't see regularly."

"You're certain the person was male?"

"I thought that, from his bulk, or the way he was standing. He wore a jacket and a toque. It was snowing. Did I say that?"

Mike nodded. "Did any male friends of Kelsey come to the house?"

"Now and then," Clayton said. "She broke up with her last boyfriend after Christmas. He was last here for our company party. Nice fellow, but I sensed he didn't turn her crank." Clayton chortled, perhaps forgetting about Kelsey's death for a moment. His face sobered. "I wondered if the man across the street might have been the young chap who was here a few times. A friend, not a boyfriend. He had a different name. Gabriel."

In the corner, Novak looked up from his writing.

"Except Gabriel was a skinny chap. His brother came with him once or twice. He was heavier and darker complexioned than Gabriel."

Clayton had noted the starer's bulk. "Did Kelsey ever say anything to you about the brother?"

"All I recall is her saying he looked out for his brother, whom she called 'vulnerable.' Her living here kept me up on those modern terms." Clayton wriggled in his chair, gripped the armrests, and hoisted himself to his feet. "I need a spot of tea before I show you."

"What?" Mike said.

"Would you have a cup?"

"No, thanks," Mike said.

"I'll join you." Novak tucked his notebook and pen into a pocket.

Tea would take time. Mike could leave it to Novak to find out if Clayton wanted to show them something important. "Would you mind if I had a look at Kelsey's bedroom?" Mike asked.

"It's in the basement."

Mike left them in the hall and went down the stairs. At the bottom, he took the pair of latex gloves from his pocket and put them on.

The stairs led to a sitting room. Two game controllers lay on the coffee table between a sofa and a flat-screen TV. While it was possible Clayton had come down here to play with Kelsey, it was more likely she played with visitors, perhaps Gabriel or Connor. Four doors led out of the room. Mike checked them all. A furnace room, a storage room packed with boxes. The bathroom was reasonably clean, aside from a dark hair coiling in the sink. The medicine cabinet contained birth control pills and menstrual pain medicine. The fourth room was Kelsey's bedroom.

A blurred print of a speeding cyclist greeted Mike from the entry. The wall behind Kelsey's bed displayed a print of a robin on a bare tree branch. A half dozen pillows with moon-star-and-Aztec-sun designs were propped on her bed. Business school textbooks filled her desk hutch, and fantasy novels lined her bookshelves.

Mike zeroed in on the two jewellery stands flanking her dresser mirror. Necklaces dangled from one of the jewellery trees, earrings from the other. Many featured moons and stars, and all were pairs, aside from one with a cat sitting on a crescent moon. He thought of the cat in Connor's apartment and bagged the single earring on the chance it was connected to Connor in some way. A Chinese lacquer box stood in front of the dresser mirror. Inside were hair clips and scrunchies. Nothing remotely significant there, based on his current information, nor in her dresser or desk drawers, in particular, drugs, to his relief—not even cannabis.

He returned to the sitting room. An enviable setup for a woman starting out in life. Privacy downstairs, but a house with companionship. Mike could have that situation, too, if he stayed in his current place, except he was a decade older than Kelsey. He pulled off his gloves and went upstairs to the main floor.

From down the hallway, he could see Clayton sitting in the kitchen, facing the rear of the house. Mike took the opportunity to peek into the rooms in the hall. The first one was a formal dining room. An oak table and a China cabinet. Too neat for daily use. Mike guessed the largest of the three rooms, decorated with stripes and dark shades, was Clayton's bedroom. A double bed and a desk with a computer on top crammed into the smallest bedroom. Footsteps drew Mike back to the main hallway.

A woman approached from the front entrance. She halted, a suitcase in one hand, a computer bag in the other. Mid-fifties, Mike estimated. Kelsey's cousin had said her mother would spend the night with her grieving father.

Mike introduced himself and held out his badge. "My partner and I are here to investigate the circumstances surrounding Clayton Little's granddaughter."

"I'm his daughter, Kelsey's aunt," she said. "We're all stunned over this. Kelsey." She set her bags on the floor and scanned the hall and living room as though her niece might be there.

"Alison," Clayton called from the kitchen.

She wove around Mike toward her father, who rose from his chair. They hugged, clutching each other, and then parted. Mike entered the kitchen. Alison looked like an older version of Kelsey's cousin. Her bobbed haircut, parted in the middle, outlined her heart-shaped face.

"While I'm up," Clayton said, "I'll use the washroom."

Alison watched him shuffle to the hall. Novak remained at the table and poured tea into his cup. Mike stood in the middle of the kitchen, which looked like it was renovated within the past twenty years. The granite countertops reminded him of the search underway in CounterTops' basement. He took out his phone in case he'd missed a vibration notifying him of a report. No word.

"I don't know if Dad will survive this," Alison said quietly, moving to the arched entrance between the kitchen and hall, which would give her a view of the bathroom. "Kelsey was Dad's future. For some reason, she loved the store. It was Dad's life when my sister and I were kids. He was disappointed that neither of us wanted to take over the business, but I told him that was his fault for encouraging us to enter the professions."

Mike made a reasonable guess. "Are you a lawyer, like your daughter?"

"That's right. My specialty is contracts. I handle Cycle Life's legal matters."

"What will happen to Cycle Life now?" Novak asked.

Alison's brow knit; she kept her gaze on the hall. "Dad might sell his controlling share to Josh, if he wants it and has the money. Herb might buy some. He's a follower and wouldn't want to be in charge, but a quarter or so share doesn't come with responsibility."

"In effect, Josh would control it all," Novak said.

"You know them?" she said.

Novak looked up at her, over his teacup. "I interviewed Herb at the store today."

She nodded. "Herb was Dad's man in his time, now he's Josh's, and I assume he'd have become Kelsey's. He doesn't seem to be the chauvinistic type, from what I know of him."

"You seem to know them well," Novak said.

"I wouldn't say well." Alison moved into the hall, perhaps for a better view of the bathroom. "Dad hosts a Boxing Day gathering for the staff every year, even though he's retired. I attend as the company lawyer. Maybe this past one will have been the last."

"They all come?" Novak asked. Mike also wanted Alison to continue. "With their spouses and kids?"

"Herb's divorced, and his daughter's grown up. They keep a certain distance from each other. In the past, he had gambling problems."

Mike shared a glance with Novak.

"Herb seems to know his bike stuff," Novak said. "Olivia, Josh's daughter, was in the store this afternoon. She's a handful."

"Isn't she, though?" Alison returned Novak's rueful smile. "She gets worse every year, tearing all over the place, Josh letting her get into everything, Zabrina angry at him for not disciplining her—not that she tries herself." Alison shrugged. "That was their relationship, her leaving things up to Josh and then blaming him for it. Kelsey told me they separated after the holidays." Alison took another step into the hall. "I just remembered something. Talking about this reminded me. It probably doesn't mean anything—it's hearsay at best."

Mike wanted to say, "Tell us. Let us decide on its importance," but this lawyer would be aware of police practice, and his push might prompt her to clam up. Novak stayed quiet as well. So far, Novak had manoeuvred this interview ball deftly.

"Last Boxing Day," Alison said, "Kelsey and I saw Josh and his family off at the door. When they drove away, Kelsey said to me, 'She's the brains of the operation.'"

"Olivia?" Novak said.

Alison smiled. "That's possible, but I assumed she was referring to Zabrina. I knew what Kelsey meant. Zabrina's smarter than Josh, but I found it an odd way to phrase it." Her smile broadened. "That's the lawyer in me. My husband constantly teases me about my precision with words." She paused. "I better go see what's keeping Dad." She walked away.

Novak drained his teacup. "I'd thought Zabrina was peripheral to the operation. Wish I'd paid more attention to her."

"Did Kelsey mean a drug operation?"

"Or the kid, Olivia. She's an operation in herself."

"You'll have to tell me about these people."

"I only met Herb, Zabrina, and Olivia. The absent ones—Josh and Kelsey—loomed large in Herb's conversation. Josh was a focus for Zabrina's anger."

Voices sounded from the hall. Clayton's muttered words grew clear. "Can't a man poop without someone hovering? Kelsey didn't fuss over me."

"All right, Dad." Alison returned to the entrance and picked up her suitcase and computer case. "I'll get settled in my room."

Clayton looked at Novak. "Is there more to discuss?"

"You were going to show us something." Novak rose from the table.

Clayton frowned. He turned to Alison. "You should see this too."

"You can show me later, Dad. I need to freshen up after my drive here." She carried her bags down the hall.

Clayton ambled between Novak and Mike to the kitchen's back door. He plucked a ring with several keys from a wall rack and fumbled with the doorknob.

"Let me do that," Mike said.

Novak shot him a glare, *Don't hover.* They followed Clayton outside to the deck, and Mike closed the door. Clayton gripped the railing and started down the steps to a path leading to a garage that opened to the lane.

Clayton stopped on the bottom step. "You'll see better from the garage-door end. I'll get the remote." He turned around.

This would take forever if they went back. "I'll get it," Mike said. "Is it on the rack?"

"In the top pocket."

Mike returned to the kitchen, found the remote, and checked his phone on his way out again. Still nothing. He caught up with Novak and Clayton at the fence that ran along the back lane.

"I don't drive anymore," Clayton said. "Only Kelsey uses the car. Used." He struggled with the key as he unlocked the gate. Mike refrained from offering to do it.

In the lane, Mike held up the remote control, silently asking for permission to open the double garage door. Clayton nodded.

Mike pressed the button. Inside was a Jeep surrounded by shovels, a rake, and other yard equipment, as well as bicycles.

Clayton's shaky finger pointed at the two bikes on the driver's side of the vehicle. Mike drew closer. They had batteries on the crossbars. Electric bikes. New ones, judging by their shine and the sales tag tied to the handle of one. Helmets rested in the other one's front basket. Saddlebags bulged over the bikes' rear wheels. Mike had come to accept Connor as the Cycle Life thief, but why would he bring the stuff here?

"Kelsey told me about the break-in at the store," Clayton said. "She acted like it was news to her. I didn't find these until . . . After you came by earlier, I looked in here, in case . . . You hear of people leaving their car running in an enclosed space. Kelsey wasn't depressed, far as I knew." He turned toward the bikes. "After this, I don't know her at all."

Clayton's glasses were smudged, with sweat or tears. He'd assumed the obvious, that Kelsey had taken the bikes. Mike asked if he could photograph the items, to compare them to the information in the police report. Clayton nodded. Mike took out his phone. The angle and lighting were poor, but he didn't want to disturb anything. He told Clayton to stay away from the garage until the police completed an official investigation.

Clayton's nod shifted to a head shake. "I can't believe she'd steal. Not from the store. My store. Our store. Her store, the plan was, for when I'm gone."

A bike store clerk would know the value of these items on the underground market, but how sad Clayton had to discover this about his granddaughter, on top of her death. Another possibility was that someone had framed Kelsey. A person with access to the remote, who'd been to the house. Connor, who might be Kelsey's stalker, lurking across the street?

Mike's phone vibrated in his pocket. After they returned through the gate, Novak and Clayton continued to the house while Mike stayed behind to take the call.

Chapter Sixteen

Paula devoured her plate of leftovers and recapped her day to her mother, who sipped a cup of tea, her forehead wrinkles growing deeper as Paula reached the ending. She hated dumping this on her mother, but her mum had to know everything so she could be prepared.

"I've learned danger can hit from any direction," Paula said. "Suspects have been known to show up on my doorstep. Mum, there are times I'll have to be out—phone me right away if a stranger comes to the house while I'm gone. Don't let anyone in. That includes Connor, if and when they let him go. In fact, he's the most likely to show, since he views me as a friend—at least he did."

"You are his friend."

Paula speared some lettuce that had grown rust coloured. She was probably overreacting, but she couldn't take the chance of some horror happening to her mum.

"Paula." Her mother set her teacup on the saucer. "I appreciate your concern for me, but you promised Connor you'd help him however you can. A person's word used to matter."

Paula bristled. "It has to adapt to changed situations."

"In the old days, we were loyal, regardless."

"This isn't the old days." Paula finished her plate of food. Despite her argument to her mother, she couldn't leave Connor to deal with his multiple problems alone.

After her late dinner, Paula checked her phone. No message from Mike since her text to him about finding the body. She'd put off calling Isabelle as long as she could and went upstairs to phone her.

Isabelle answered instantly. "Was Kelsey killed?"

"First, why were you at Cycle Life?"

"Connor's sure it's her, but there's nothing on the internet about a murder, or 'incident,' as Detective Novak called it. Why were you there?"

I asked you first would sound childish. Paula explained that she'd gone to speak to Dustin, the witness to the Cycle Life break and enter, leaving out the part about their discovering the body. "When did you talk to Connor?"

"A few hours ago. He called to ask me to feed Finnegan, his cat. They're keeping Connor overnight. Something about his lawyer being busy with a personal matter. I'll go to Connor's place tomorrow morning."

Paula paced from her bed to the front window. The risk to Isabelle seemed slim, but *danger could hit from any direction*. "I'll do that. It makes sense, since I live closer to his apartment. Do you have a key?"

Isabelle paused before speaking again. "He said to get it from his neighbour."

"Which apartment number?"

"I don't mind going," Isabelle said. "I'm not busy with work."

"Neither am I." Paula looked out at her quiet street, glowing red in the pre-sunset light. Isabelle always loved to leap into action. "I'll sleep on it and let you know in the morning."

"But was it Kelsey?"

"No one's told me this." True.

After hanging up, Paula got into her pyjamas before going downstairs to watch the news with her mother. Her cell phone rang. Calgary Police Service. She answered.

"Paula, it's Connor. I'm still at Westwinds. My interview's postponed to tomorrow. That's why I'm calling. I need a lawyer. Since you worked with some, can you recommend one that's not too expensive?"

"I thought you had a lawyer."

"She withdrew from my case, citing conflict of interest." His voice quivered. "She's Kelsey's cousin. I'm sure now Kelsey's dead. The cops won't tell me anything."

Paula's heart skipped, although Connor's feeling and the cousin's withdrawal weren't confirmation. "Mike hasn't contacted me. I think he would if it were Kelsey, since I was dealing with her through work." Paula hoped this would reassure Connor more than it did her. "Try not to think of it and get a good night's sleep."

"In jail?" he scoffed.

"I'm surprised they didn't send you home for the night."

"I've got a migraine," he said. "Been throwing up, the light's killing me. My vision blanked for a few minutes."

Her heart went out to him. "I'm sorry. You seemed okay this afternoon."

"It went away, but now it's back and worse. They want to keep an eye on me here, and I'd be useless at home." His flat tone continued. "About the lawyer. They'll give me a pro-bono dude, but I want someone who gives a shit about doing a good job."

Emily Wong popped into Paula's head. A new, young lawyer. Her handling of a whiplash claim had struck Paula as clever, efficient, and caring. Since *Calgary Police Service* had appeared on her call display, the police must have Connor's cell phone and he was calling from the general line in the holding area. "How can I get in touch with you?"

"I don't know. Leave a message with the holding-cell guard?" He sounded bitter. "Who knows how long I'll be here? I need to phone Isabelle next to ask her to pick up some clothes when she's at my place tomorrow to feed my cat. Underwear and socks. My contact lens solution and case. Maybe a couple of shirts . . .”

“I’m thinking I might go instead of Isabelle. What’s your neighbour’s unit number, so I can get the key?”

“No. Let Isabelle do it.” His tone was sharp.” She loves to help. You know how she is. You’ll do enough if you find me a lawyer.”

All of that was true, but Connor had seemed especially eager for Isabelle to go, or for Paula not to go. Was there another reason for this? A question to ruminate on overnight. She told him she had a good lawyer in mind and would contact her immediately.

* * *

When the front door clicked open, Isabelle bolted from her office chair. The guys were finally back from their shifts at the grocery store. She ran to the entrance and kissed Habib hello. Salt barked his greeting.

Habib drew away from her. “What a day, babe.”

“Now they want us for the morning shift tomorrow,” Nick added. “There’s no relief on the front line. Where’s Erin?”

“In the bedroom watching a movie.”

“All I want to do is crash,” Habib said.

Nick loped upstairs, Salt behind him. Habib described his day to Isabelle on their way down to the basement. Customers complaining about lineups and unavailable foods. Hoarding toilet paper—a man had tried to sneak five packages in the bottom of his shopping cart through Habib’s cash. “Like I wouldn’t notice,” Habib said. “When I insisted on confiscating them, the guy stormed out. Meanwhile, the lineup’s growing and more people are pissed.”

Isabelle muttered appropriate comments but had heard all this before. She suspected that underneath their gripes, Habib and Nick loved being in the thick of the COVID-world action. She paused in their sitting nook. “Can we talk about something, for me?”

"Always." Habib's gaze strayed to the table, where their one-thousand-piece puzzle was laid out. "I wouldn't mind winding down with the puzzle."

She couldn't search for little pieces and explain at the same time when she knew that Habib would think hiding drugs was worse than stealing toilet paper. "Let's sit." She dropped to the sofa.

Habib nestled beside her, his arm around her shoulder. He squeezed tighter as she told him about Connor's call from police headquarters and Paula's offer to maybe go to his apartment instead.

"There's your answer," Habib said. "Let Paula take care of it."

Isabelle drew back. "She'll take the drugs to the police."

"That's the right thing to do."

"But wrong for Connor. The cops will think they're his."

"If they aren't, why are they in his drawer?"

"He took them from Gabe and meant to throw them out but didn't."

"That doesn't make sense."

It had when Connor said it. She realized she'd moved away from Habib on the sofa.

He dropped his hand to his thigh and angled himself toward her. "The cops must have serious evidence against Connor if they're locking him up overnight."

"They have to wait for his lawyer." She folded her arms. "Lawyers are busy and slow. I know that from work."

"The cops will give Connor the third degree. What if he caves and blabs about you hiding his drugs? In our house?" He looked around the room. "We'll all be in shit."

"Connor's in real shit now. I don't want to get him in deeper." But Habib was right. Connor was so messed up—there was a good chance he'd crack under questioning. She could find a good hiding place for the drugs, but what if the cops brought sniffer dogs? Was Connor in enough shit for the cops to do that? She didn't know. Someone had been murdered, but Connor wouldn't be into something that bad.

Habib studied her, his dark eyes kind but firm about her doing the thing he thought was right. They'd been together almost three years, and this was their biggest disagreement. Relationships were about compromise—she'd read that in an online article.

She uncrossed her arms. "Paula said she'd message me in the morning. If she's going, that's it. If I go, then I'll decide what to do with the drugs when I'm there."

"Flush them down the toilet."

She'd see.

"I like that, leave it to fate," Habib said. "I could do with a little relaxing before bed. How about some puzzle work, babe? It's almost half done."

Isabelle wriggled her stiff shoulders. She could use the drain of tension.

* * *

In the morning, Paula woke to a text from Mike. *Can you come by my office? Ten thirty?*

Now it made total sense for her to detour to Connor's apartment, since it was on her way to Westwinds. Paula replied *Okay* and texted Isabelle, telling her what she'd decided and asking for the building entry code and unit number of the neighbour with the key.

While she showered, Paula wondered why Mike had asked her in. If Homicide wanted to question her further, most likely Shearer or Furey would be the contact. Her thoughts kept returning to Kelsey. Paula pictured her petite form and the angel figurine on the office desk which Josh had said belonged to him. If Kelsey was the victim, presumably she had entered Furniture Sellers' basement from Cycle Life, via their stairs from the restroom to the furnace room. But why would she go down there?

Paula updated her mother over breakfast and repeated her advice about taking care before heading to Connor's apartment building. When she arrived, she checked her phone. No reply yet from Isabelle, who tended to sleep late now that she was working from home. On her way to the building entrance, Paula considered phoning Isabelle. A man approached from inside and held open the door for Paula.

Since she still didn't know which neighbour kept Connor's key, she took a guess and knocked on the door to the right of his unit. No one answered. She tried the unit to the left. A man dressed in pyjamas opened the door. She explained she was Connor's friend, that he'd been called away unexpectedly and had asked her to feed his cat. "Do you have his key to loan me?"

"That cat." The man shook his head and went to get the key.

She entered Connor's apartment. Finnegan sat upright on the closest recliner chair and stared at Paula. Once more, she was struck by the neatness of the place. Since his kitchen had no dishwasher, before going to Westwinds he'd evidently washed and put away the dishes that they'd used on the deck. She searched his organized cupboards and found the bag of cat food in the upper one beside the sink.

Finnegan padded to the counter. Paula preferred dogs to cats, but she scooped the cat up and leaned into her face. "Hey Finnegan, do you miss Connor?"

Finnegan hissed, and her front paw shot out. Pain seared Paula's face. She dropped the cat to the floor and touched her pulsing cheek. No blood. Finnegan arched her back and pawed the air.

Paula glared at her. "I'll feed you anyway." She filled the cat bowls with food and water and returned them to the floor. Finnegan wove between her legs before tasting a dry morsel.

"Smart girl to be wary of a stranger." Paula left Finnegan to her breakfast, carried her purse and the empty tote bag she'd brought with her to the bathroom, and looked in the mirror. A dry scratch sloped diagonally down her cheekbone, but the pain had stopped. Hopefully, makeup would prevent questions. She collected Connor's contact lens gear and would stop at a drug store for concealer on her way to Westwinds.

In the side hall, Finnegan pawed one of the closed doors. Fifty-fifty this was Connor's bedroom. Paula opened the door and Finnegan scooted in.

An easel stood in the far corner by the window. Finnegan had guided her correctly. No canvas sat on the easel, but finished paintings were stacked along the side walls.

Paula studied Connor's work. Isabelle had said he was shy about showing her pictures of his paintings on his phone. Calgary street scenes glistened in watery tones. Paula recognized a side street in Inglewood. While the painting was a bit abstract for her taste, she wouldn't mind it hanging in her living room. She'd do more to encourage Connor's artistic endeavours.

Finnegan curled up on the bed, purring, as Paula selected three shirts from Connor's closet—conservative business wear that would impress the police and Emily Wong, who'd agreed to take his case and had offered a reduced rate thanks to her relationship with their adjusting firm. Paula added a fleece top for Connor's release, since the weather had turned colder today, and draped the shirts over Connor's desk chair to avoid the cat hair on the bed. She opened the top dresser drawer, lifted several pair of boxer shorts, and touched plastic. A bag of round blue pills stamped with the letter *M* on one side and the number *30* on the other. Fingers trembling, Paula rifled through the drawer. A bag of pinks, one of greens.

Connor had said—he'd definitely implied—that he didn't take illegal drugs, that his brother Gabe was the one who used. She glanced at Finnegan, purring on the bed, her face buried in her fur. She'd get no answers from that cat.

Paula dumped the clothes and drugs into the tote bag. Another reason to talk to Mike at Westwinds.

* * *

Over breakfast, Isabelle reread the text from Paula and decided again not to answer. Paula would believe she wasn't up yet. It was passive-aggressive, and Paula would probably try all of Connor's neighbours until she found the one with the key, but what else could Isabelle do when she'd screwed this up? She should have gone to Connor's apartment last night or really early this morning to keep all the options open for him.

She cleared the table and loaded the dishwasher while Habib, Nick, and Erin scrambled to get ready for work. As they all gathered at the front entrance, Isabelle kissed Habib goodbye.

"I'm glad things worked out," he said, which was his annoying code for he was happy with Paula's decision. She and Habib hadn't told the others about what was happening. The morning had been too rushed.

After they all left, Isabelle went to her office and checked the local news feed. Still only the basic report of a suspicious death at Furniture Sellers, the name withheld pending notification of next of kin.

The doorbell rang. Salt barked. Isabelle looked out the window. There was no car parked out front, and she couldn't see anyone on the front porch. She jogged to the hall and down the stairs to the entrance, the dog brushing against her legs. She looked out the peephole. No face stared back, but Salt kept barking.

Isabelle opened the door and looked down at a person gazing upward. "Olivia?"

213

"I was worried you weren't home." The wind blew Olivia's dark hair over her face.

"Why are you here?" Definitely no car. "How did you get here? How did you know where I live?"

"I wrote it down when you told the policeman," Olivia said.

"When? At the store?"

"I took a bus and the CTrain." Olivia's eyes lit up at the sight of Salt. "You have a dog."

Isabelle shivered. "Come in, it's cold out." She stepped back, banging into yapping Salt. Olivia must have meant she'd overheard Isabelle give Detective Novak her address. Maybe Olivia really had superhearing. Isabelle couldn't imagine getting around a city alone on public transit when she was eight. Plus, her parents wouldn't have let her. She closed the front door behind Olivia. "Do your parents know you're here?"

Olivia bent to pat Salt, who grew quieter. "I want a dog or gerbil, but Mommy says they're too much work."

"Olivia, why did you come here?"

She stared up at Isabelle. "Someone died in the store beside Daddy's. I'm scared." Olivia's eyes watered, and her little face contorted. She shook all over and started crying.

Isabelle squatted to hug her. A shocking death was terrible for Isabelle as an adult. How could a kid stand it? "Oh, Olivia." Isabelle squeezed her tightly. The shaking reduced to trembles.

Olivia pulled away and rubbed her eyes, sniffing. Tears glistened on her cheeks. Isabelle offered to get her a tissue as Olivia took off her backpack and coat and dropped them both to the floor. At least she'd come dressed for the weather. Underneath, she wore a T-shirt with hearts all over it.

"We need to call your mommy," Isabelle said.

Olivia shook her head. "She doesn't like me to bother her at work. Daddy took me to Uncle Herb's because he had to go to the police station. Why do they want to talk to Daddy? Uncle Herb won't tell me." Olivia sniffed again and brushed her hand over her nose. "I couldn't hear them talking, even with my superpower. Mommy won't tell me anything, but she doesn't know I heard her and Kelsey talking at my house."

Connor's friend Kelsey? "When was that?"

"Saturday. Or Sunday. I forget."

Olivia wiped her dripping nose with her forearm. She really needed a tissue. It would be yukky to take her hand. Isabelle directed her up the stairs, told her to sit in the living room, and got a tissue from the bathroom. She returned to find Olivia tossing a rawhide bone for Salt to fetch. When he scampered back with it, she hurled it into the dining area. Isabelle handed Olivia the tissue. Salt trotted back, dropped to the floor, and chewed the bone as Pepper limped into the living room.

"You have two dogs!" Olivia crouched and stroked Pepper's fur. "I asked my daddy for a dog, but he said Mommy's the boss. What's wrong with this dog's leg?"

"We don't know. She's old and gets lots of sicknesses." Isabelle sat on the sofa. "Olivia, how did you figure out what bus and CTrain to take here? I can barely do that."

Olivia kept stroking Pepper. "In winter, Uncle Herb's truck wouldn't start. He took me home on the bus and Ctrain. Your stop is earlier."

"You remembered the route?"

"I printed it from his computer. He has Calgary Transit in his computer Favourites. His truck is always broken. It's crap, Daddy says."

"Does your daddy or Uncle Herb know you're here?"

"He's not my real uncle." Olivia left the dogs and crawled onto the sofa. Salt came over to sniff her dangling legs. "After Daddy left, Uncle Herb told me to stop asking him questions and wait for my parents to tell me. He went outside to work on his truck before it snows tonight."

Salt rested his head between the two of them on the sofa. Olivia rubbed his fur.

"Did you tell Herb you were leaving his house?" Isabelle asked.

Olivia leaned over Salt. Her hair hid her expression.

"He'll be looking for you by now and going ballistic. Do you have his phone number?"

Olivia shook her head.

Isabelle took out her phone. "I have to call your mom. What's her number?"

"She'll be mad at me. She's busy at the hospital. She's a nurse."

Isabelle had seen the number on Olivia's workbook, which might be in her backpack. But it could be hard to get hold of a hospital nurse, and calling might annoy Zabrina, who had seemed easily annoyed, and also worry her. Josh was occupied with the police.

"Do you have Herb's phone number in your backpack?"

"No." Olivia stared at Salt. Was she lying?

Rather than waste time hunting through the pack, Isabelle could look Herb up. "What's Herb's last name?"

"Gray, I think."

Isabelle looked up the White Pages on her phone and found Herbert Gray, with no phone number listed. She Googled the name, and a few pages popped up for an actor, Herb Gray, who lived in Calgary. The guy in the photos looked like Herb from the store, but with a goatee instead of a beard. A three-quarter view revealed his ponytail. Was Herb an actor on the side? Actor-Herb had a website with a contact number. She phoned and listened to the ring. Olivia slithered off the sofa.

A man answered and Isabelle asked if he was Herb from Cycle Life.

"Yes. Why are you calling?"

She explained the situation as quickly as possible. Olivia held out the rope toy to Salt, who gripped it with his mouth and ran around the room in circles. Olivia spun with him and laughed.

"For God's sake," Herb said. "What is the matter with her? I searched everywhere and was about to call Josh." His voice grew calmer. "I should be glad she's alright. Where do you live? I'll come right away."

Isabelle supplied her address, with directions. She remembered now that Detective Novak had repeated it back to her when he interviewed her at the store, giving Olivia a second chance to hear the numbers.

"That's not too far," Herb said. "But my God. Did she take a taxi?"

"A bus and Ctrain."

"I'll be there in about twenty minutes." Herb ended the call.

Olivia let go of the rope toy and Salt skidded backward, regained his balance, and took the rope to the dining area. Olivia wobbled to the sofa, her face flushed.

"Would you like milk and cookies?" Isabelle asked. They seemed like a kid thing.

While Olivia settled on a dining chair, Isabelle poured them each a glass of milk and set four Oreos on a plate. She carried them to the dining table and sat. Since they had time to kill, it wouldn't hurt to ask what Olivia had overheard. "Kelsey came to your house on Saturday or Sunday?"

Olivia nodded, her mouth full of cookie. She washed the food down with milk, leaving behind a white moustache sprinkled with chocolate bits. "They sent me to the basement to watch TV. That's how I know they wanted to talk about things they didn't want me to know, so I snuck upstairs." She bit into another cookie.

Paula's approach was to let people talk, and she got results. Isabelle ate a cookie to keep herself quiet.

Olivia chewed and then wiped her mouth with her arm. "I hid behind the top of the stairs. They couldn't see me, but I could hear because of, you know."

"Your superpower."

Olivia nodded. "They talked about a boy who loves Kelsey, but she doesn't love him. He's after her all the time. Mommy told her to watch out for him."

Isabelle drank some milk, willing herself not to push. Olivia ate the last cookie.

"Kelsey said he was harmless, she could handle him." Olivia paused to finish her glass of milk. "Mommy said 'Psssh,' like she thought Kelsey was being dumb. Then I went downstairs and watched *Powerpuff Girls*." She described the program, which seemed to involve biologically altered superhero girls.

"Did you hear the boy's name?" Isabelle asked when Olivia finally stopped talking. "The one who loves Kelsey?" She held her breath, fearing it was Gabe or Connor, who'd kept other secrets from her.

Olivia shook her head. "Do you have more cookies?"

Isabelle got the package from the kitchen and refilled Olivia's glass of milk. The doorbell rang. Herb? He was quick.

Cold air whooshed in as Isabelle opened the front door. Herb apologized for Olivia's disturbance. Isabelle noticed his pickup truck parked on the street.

"She's been no problem." Isabelle told Herb to come inside to wait for Olivia to finish her snack. "Do you want some too?"

"That would be great. I skipped breakfast in the kerfuffle of Josh dropping off Olivia."

In the store, Herb had seemed quiet. Now, Isabelle found him livelier and more interesting—maybe because she knew about his acting. Olivia had left the table to run around the living room with Salt. Pepper limped behind them. Olivia ignored Herb and Isabelle walking past her to the dining area. Isabelle offered him coffee or tea. He said milk and cookies would suit him better. She got him a glass of milk and dumped the rest of the cookies onto a serving plate for them all to share.

"I found your phone number on your website," she said. "You're an actor?"

He nodded. "Amateur—community theatre, musicals. Mostly for kids." He spoke between bites of cookie. "I earn a little money as a movie extra. Of course, the pandemic called a halt to it all. Lucky that I dropped my agent, so you got me directly." He drank some milk. "Did your boyfriend decide on a bike?"

Boyfriend? Oh, right. Ryan, aka Connor. "Not yet."

"No pressure," Herb said. "You rescued things yesterday, with Olivia."

"I had the time. My work has fallen off with the pandemic."

"Do you work from home?"

"For now, with my office closed."

He shook his head. "The store is no place for a kid. Olivia's obviously taken to you, to pull a stunt like this. You deal with her well."

Isabelle warmed to the compliment. "Have Zabrina and Josh figured out her homeschooling?"

"Not yet. You'd be perfect." He caught her gaze.

Once again, Isabelle considered the idea of homeschooling Olivia here. It would solve Josh and Zabrina's problem and get Olivia out of the store. Isabelle would earn some extra cash. The house was free of other people most days, and she had lots of time. She could set up a kid's table in her office to keep on top of Olivia's schooling. Playing with Salt and taking him for walks would be like recess for Olivia. And it would be fun for Isabelle to have company during the day. These were all super reasons to manoeuvre Herb into suggesting to Josh and Zabrina that they offer Isabelle the job, and this didn't include the best reason—Isabelle would learn things about them.

* * *

Paula stopped outside Mike's cubicle. He sat behind his desk, talking on his cell phone, but motioned her in. She took the visitor's chair across from him and set her purse and tote bag on the floor. Mike told his caller that he had to go and placed his phone on the desk.

"Did you ask me in to get my detailed statement about finding the body yesterday?" Paula hoped this was the reason.

"That was the plan, but the team has other priorities now." He rested his hands on his desk, fingers linked. "There is some good news, from your insurance perspective. It looks like we've recovered the goods stolen from Cycle Life."

"You don't look happy," she said. "Did Connor steal them?"

"We don't know yet. Kelsey might have been involved too."

"An inside job?"

"Would that be covered by Cycle's Life's commercial crime insurance?"

"She's not an owner," Paula said. "If she has no history of theft from the company, it's covered." Her stomach knotted at Mike's grim expression.

"In any case, that's a small matter in the grand scheme."

The knot tightened. "Have you identified the victim?" She knew what he'd say next.

"Kelsey." His fingers separated. He pressed his palms to the desk. "I found out last night but saw no reason to make your rough day worse. There's more."

She clutched the armrests, waiting through the silence. No sounds from outside of his cubicle. Were all his colleagues out investigating the new developments?

"We followed through on your suggestion to search the building's overlooked store, CounterTops. They found another body."

"Who?" When she and Dustin found the body in Furniture Sellers' basement her first thought had been the person was—

"Gabriel," Mike said. "Gabe. Connor's brother."

She slumped back in the chair. "Murdered?"

"There's no indication of this. We're waiting for the autopsy. We took Connor to the morgue this morning to identify him. He's on his way back now."

Connor shouldn't deal with this alone. "Can I see him?"

"I'll look into that for you," Mike said. "We postponed his interview for the break and enter again but can't do this indefinitely. I hear he's not well."

"This will make things worse for him." Paula reached for the tote bag.

Chapter Seventeen

In the cold-case office at Westwinds, Novak reviewed the preliminary report on the body discovered in the basement of CounterTops at 7:38 the previous night. Based on the scattered stacks of takeout containers, officers speculated the young man had camped there for more than a week. He was found slumped on a pile of blankets and pillows that had apparently served as a makeshift bed. No evidence of foul play. Since rigor mortis had passed through the body, time of death was more than thirty-six hours earlier, but not much before seven a.m. Monday, judging by the relatively unadvanced state of decomposition. A health card in the victim's wallet bore the name Gabriel Riley. Officers couldn't access his cell phone, which would be sent to computer forensics. The Forensic Crime Scene unit dusted CounterTops' basement for fingerprints. Report to follow. Due to the homicide in the nearby store, the case was ruled a suspicious death. Once again, Mike wasn't the team lead in this new homicide case.

On the drive to work that morning, Mike had said he would be next on the lead rotation but certainly wasn't hoping for a third death. He also preferred leading cases with his usual partner, who was currently on leave with a broken leg from a skiing accident. Mike had added that Megan would accompany Connor to the morgue to identify the body. Novak looked at his watch. They should be finished by now.

He checked his emails and texts. No messages from anyone in Homicide. If it weren't for Mike, Novak wouldn't know about this second death. Mike had forwarded him the report and told Novak to ask the staff sergeant to include him on this active case, arguing he'd become involved inadvertently, had knowledge and experience to contribute, and was part of the Homicide unit. Novak would have talked to Travers in a flash if he hadn't covered up his cold-case findings. For that, he deserved to be kicked out of Homicide.

Novak stared out the window. Dark clouds glowered above the highway overpass and the hazy views of Nose Hill, Calgary's downtown, and the mountains in the distance. His thoughts strayed to his conversation with Clayton Little over tea in his kitchen, while Mike was in the basement searching Kelsey's living area. Novak had raised the issue by saying he recalled an incident at Cycle Life in 2013—a case of suspicious death.

Clayton had nodded, his teacup trembling in his hands. "I was still managing the store part-time. The customer was a regular. His name escapes me now. He was looking through the racks for something and started weaving, gasping for air. We rushed over to help him." Clayton blinked and swallowed. "He was on the floor, passing out. I said I'd call emergency, but Josh said, 'No, it's probably the heat.' The man went unconscious, and Josh changed his mind and said 'Yes, call.' Josh slapped him to try to wake him while Herb shooed out our other customers and closed the store. EMS came and took him away." Clayton paused for a sip of tea. "We followed up and learned he'd died. A tragedy for him and his family, but not the first time a customer died on our premises."

Through the story, Novak clenched his China teacup so hard the handle shattered. He apologized, dumped the mess into a nearby garbage can, and wiped the table.

Clayton got him another teacup and brushed off his offer of payment. "These cups are old and fragile, and I have more of them than I need. Where were we?"

"A customer died in your store," Novak prompted.

"The earlier case was a heart attack," Clayton said. "This one seemed similar, but something about the way Josh and Herb kept emphasizing the man's 'natural cause of death' and putting other little things together gave me a lightning-bolt thought—the man died from drugs." Clayton exhaled. "And we supplied him."

"By we, you mean . . . ?"

"Josh or Herb or both." Clayton's lips tightened. "They were like sons to me."

Novak waited out Clayton's sip before asking his next question. "What little things had you noticed?"

"Herb was always short of money for his gambling debts."

No surprise that Herb hadn't mentioned his gambling to Novak in his interview.

"And Josh experimented with hallucinogens," Clayton said. "Magic mushrooms, I think, and only outside of work. If the man died of drugs, I assume it was another type, but if Josh was inclined toward one kind, he might not see the harm in another. It happened I'd recently read an article about drugs manufactured in places like China being smuggled into the country. In that lightning-bolt moment, it hit me how easy it would be to hide them in bicycles and accessories. Most of ours come from China."

During the next pause, Novak finished his tea. "Any other things?"

Clayton set his cup on the table. "I forget them now. Pieces that added up."

A thought struck Novak. "You were the anonymous caller. You phoned the police and told them to investigate the customer's death as suspicious."

Clayton's mouth dropped. "I've never told a soul this." He shook his head. "Afterwards, I wished I hadn't. It was a mistake to betray the store."

But Clayton hadn't betrayed his store. He'd wanted to cleanse it of wrongdoing. Was this his reason for maintaining a controlling financial interest and part of his desire for his granddaughter to take over from Josh?

Mike's footsteps in the hall ended Clayton's confession. Novak had intended to tell Mike about it later, but the news about the second body had derailed that.

The second body was really the first, Novak reminded himself. Gabe had died earlier than Kelsey. Did she know he'd set up residence in CounterTops' basement? They were friends. And Cycle Life had been her second home since childhood. Novak's gut said that when Gabe wanted to move out of Connor's place, Kelsey suggested CounterTops, which was unoccupied—and rent free. Furniture Sellers, with its comfortable beds and sitting and eating areas, would have been a more logical choice, but perhaps she'd known Dustin had claimed it. After a month or so of living in the same building, did Dustin and Gabe really not know of each other's presence? Were the two deaths a coincidence or related?

Novak's phone beeped. A text from Mike, asking him to come to his cubicle. For an assignment on the Kelsey case or to discuss something mundane, like what time Mike could drive him home? Novak hated his dependence on Mike's driving almost as much as he hated being out of the Homicide loop. He checked his phone and computer again. No new messages or reports.

On his way to Mike's cubicle, Novak's thoughts shifted to Josh's estranged wife, Zabrina. Novak had paid her little attention at Cycle Life, but now a couple of comments she'd made struck him as interesting. In the store, she'd said that cops didn't always err on the side of caution *in her experience*, and she'd noted that Novak, despite his casual clothing, talked like a police officer. What was her experience with cops? Maybe her father or brother was one, or she'd been involved in protests or something like that. This didn't necessarily point to a criminal past, but it was worth pursuing.

He halted at Mike's cubicle. A woman sat in the visitor's chair. She turned around. Paula.

"Hi Novak," she said. "Mike and I are done." She rose and looked at Mike. "Let me know if they'll let me see Connor, and when."

Mike glanced at the tote bag she held. "Drop his things off at admin, and they'll get them to him in the holding area."

"I'll wait to give them to him personally, if I can."

"What will you do until then?" Mike asked.

"Pick up lunch for my Skype with Sam." She said goodbye to them both and left.

Novak took over her vacated chair. "You wanted to see me?"

Mike leaned back and rested his hands on his chest. "Are you up for sitting in on my interview with Josh? Travers agrees your second set of ears and eyes would be more useful there than on cold cases."

Novak was sure Mike had talked their staff sergeant into this. Mike would be less trusting if he knew about Novak's withheld information relevant to their two most-recent cases. While Mike took a phone call, Novak mentally debated the pros and cons of doing the right thing, the biggest con being the likelihood of Travers booting him back to cold cases— or completely out of Homicide. Though Novak reported to Travers, Mike had requested the specific search of Cycle Life in the cold-case files. Novak owed both an explanation, and it would be easier to get them over with together.

"There's something I need to tell you and Travers," Novak said after Mike ended his call. "Would you have time now?"

"Can this wait? We're all crazy busy."

"It relates to Cycle Life."

Mike glanced at this watch and stared at Novak. "Tell me, and I'll decide if we disturb our staff sergeant right away."

Novak took a deep breath and floundered through his confession, trying to keep to the pertinent facts, that four days ago he'd unearthed a cold case—a suspicious drug overdose—connected to Cycle Life. He'd tracked down the deceased's widow and talked to her outside Westwinds to avoid anyone in Homicide seeing, and had discussed the cold case with Clayton, all without their staff sergeant's knowledge or approval.

Mike's eyebrow rose as Novak talked, but he said nothing.

"I knew it was wrong. There's no excuse." Novak took a breath. "I'm telling you now because we owe the widow our best efforts for dropping the ball before." And for his dismissing her husband's death as not important enough to remember.

Mike's cell beeped on his desk. He gave it a glance. "This explains your trip to Cycle Life yesterday."

"Pure chance I arrived there with the patrol car. You know the rest."

Another message beeped from Mike's phone. He typed a reply and looked up. "Turned out it was fortunate your faulty approach led you there at the right time. I doubt the responders had the resources to properly interview the Cycle Life staff and customers."

"I didn't get everything," Novak said. "I overlooked Zabrina and realized this morning that she hinted at prior experience with the police."

"We'll check her out. Does she go by Josh's surname?"

Novak shrugged. "Another thing I overlooked."

"We'll get it from Josh." Mike nodded at his phone. "The last message said he's gone through fingerprinting and declined a lawyer since he and his store weren't directly involved. We waited to release both victims' names until after Gabriel was identified, but Josh heard about Kelsey from Clayton's daughter last night."

"So, it is Connor's brother."

"You didn't get the memo?"

"Seems I'm not on the team email."

Mike stared across the desk. "Send me the files on the cold case. For all Travers has to know, you unearthed it today."

Novak leaned back. Was he really off the hook? This was too easy, but he was grateful to Mike for letting this go. "Could you send me the report on Dustin's interview?"

Mike nodded. "We plan to interview him again. Too much of what he said doesn't ring true." His phone rang. As he talked, he stood to get his jacket. He hung up and placed his phone in his pocket. "Josh is ready for us in the interview room."

Novak gulped. "I haven't prepared."

"I'll brief you on the way."

In his younger days, Novak had "winged it" with no problem. Now, all the way to the holding area, he struggled to grasp the case details. None stuck in his fuzzy brain.

Mike carried a second chair into the interview room. Josh looked up from the table and said "Hi guys" as though this were a friendly encounter. As Herb had indicated, Josh was in his early forties. He had thinning hair and wore a black turtleneck that looked to be of good quality and that fit his muscular form snuggly. It made Novak conscious of his rumpled jacket and shirt. Mike sat across from Josh and set a folder on the table.

Novak took his place beside Mike and away from the small table. Mike confirmed Josh's agreement to an interview without a lawyer present and his awareness the interview would be recorded. Novak glanced at the cameras in the room's corners and the peeled paint on the walls. He sniffed the room's acrid smell. Major Crimes waved Westwinds' no-indoor-smoking rule here to put suspects and witnesses at ease. Despite the dark circles under his eyes, Josh looked at ease without a cigarette.

Mike began by questioning Josh about their building in the industrial park. Josh explained that it was owned by a company whose name escaped him. Kelsey had recently taken over the handling of matters like their rent payment. Josh's shadowed eyes darkened at the mention of her name. Naturally he'd be grieving—or wanted to give that impression.

"I'll get the company's name and contact details from the store computer when we reopen," Josh said. "Do you know when that will be?"

"We'll notify you," Mike said and asked who had access to the building's three stores.

"The owners and managers of the stores." Josh added that he hadn't given the code to enter Cycle Life to the other store owners, nor did he know their codes, and he assumed Furniture Sellers and CounterTops didn't share codes with each other either. To his knowledge, there was no business connection between them, although they shared a crossover market—people updating their homes. Cycle Life attracted some impulse shoppers from among the other stores' customers. "People looking for furniture who realize they could also use a new bike or reflector." He said he saw no reason for Kelsey to be in Furniture Sellers then paused. Another display of subtle emotion.

If Josh were hiding something, he was good at it. In the store, Zabrina hadn't hidden her anger at him. Novak could see Josh as a husband who'd cheat on his wife, get away with it for too long, wheedle his way to forgiveness, and then cheat again until finally she got fed up. Novak hadn't been that husband, although he'd had mistresses—every new and exciting homicide case.

Josh told them that Kelsey had shopped in Furniture Sellers before the pandemic. "She had enough furniture, but during lunch breaks she'd browse their décor stuff."

"Like candlesticks," Mike said.

"That kind of crap." Josh said he'd furnished his apartment through the store when he and his wife separated after Christmas. "It was convenient, and they gave me a discount."

"Who was your salesperson?"

"Candy. She often opened their store around the same time I was opening. We'd talk about the weather and shit."

I'll bet. Novak supposed he shouldn't jump to conclusions about Josh, whose love life probably wasn't relevant anyway.

"Do you know a salesman there named Dustin Fairchild?"

Josh's brow knit. "I might know him by sight." His face brightened. "Is that the dude who was living there? Herb told me about him, although he didn't know about it before yesterday."

"Have you talked to Herb since yesterday, when you left work early?" Mike asked.

"Yeah, I was tired." Josh ran his hands down his face, demonstrating fatigue. "Then Kelsey's aunt calls me last night to say Kelsey died. That didn't help my sleep. I told Herb about Kelsey this morning, and we talked about that when I dropped my daughter off. He's babysitting her while I'm here."

"Wasn't it unusual for you to leave before closing time?" Mike said. "We understand the store was busy, and Tuesday was Kelsey's day off."

Josh met Mike's stare. "She'd left work the day before, saying she was sick." No defensiveness in his tone. "I was worried I was coming down with what she had and didn't want to pass it on to customers." His gaze on Mike didn't waver. "Business has been insane this spring. I haven't taken my usual Monday off for weeks. It catches up with you."

Novak had to give Josh credit for having his answers down pat, and for accounting for his fatigue. You couldn't fake those shadowed eyes. If the store was harbouring drugs, Josh might be up nights getting rid of the evidence in case the police got a warrant. Novak made a mental note to mention this to Mike in case no one had thought of it.

Mike rested his hand on the folder. "Have you noticed any activity at Furniture Sellers since the pandemic closure?"

"Nope," Josh said. "No cars parked in front or people going in and out. None of their usual delivery trucks or customers' cars going to their back entrance. I might have seen one or two vans I'd thought were people turning in by mistake or thinking the store was open. Herb said the dude told him they were still getting some deliveries. He had his groceries delivered too. Is he your suspect?" Josh's eyes widened with seemingly innocent interest. He raised his hands, palms toward Mike. "I know, you can't answer that. You need to do your job. I hope, whoever it is, you get him. I've known Kelsey since she was my daughter's age." His voice shook, slightly.

Mike opened the folder and slid an eight-by-eleven-inch photograph across the table to Josh. "Do you recognize this?"

Josh gazed down at the picture. From Novak's angle, it looked like a multicolour rope resting in a C-shape.

"Is it a bracelet?" Josh looked up. "Kelsey's?"

Mike stared.

Josh studied the picture again. "My daughter makes stuff like this in arts and crafts. I don't know if Kelsey wore that kind." He smirked at Mike. "When it comes to jewellery, I wouldn't notice if she were wearing solid gold. Ask my wife if you don't believe me. Or Kelsey, if she weren't dead." He shoved the photo back, his first show of impatience. "Could I please have a drink of water? My throat's dry from all this talking." He fiddled with his turtleneck top.

Mike returned the photo to the folder and asked Novak if he'd like a drink.

"Water would be good." Novak said, his first words since the interview began. Josh's confidence and skill at lobbing police balls revealed the obvious—Novak was no match for the bad guys.

Mike phoned admin to order two bottles of water and a coffee and suggested they take a break. He and Novak went into the hall.

"Josh seems to have a temper when provoked," Mike said.

"Was that item found at the crime scene?"

Mike nodded. "A short distance from Kelsey's body. It was in the crime scene report."

Novak had read the report and missed that detail. In the interview room, he'd thought of something to suggest to Mike. What was it?

"We think it's part of an animal collar," Mike said. "For a small dog or a cat."

Novak nodded as though he grasped the significance of this.

"You must have noticed Josh didn't bat an eye at my reference to candlesticks," Mike said. "Innocent or cool customer?"

Novak hadn't noticed. What was special about candlesticks? Right. The murder weapon. That key detail had slipped his mind.

"Let's send Josh home for now," Mike said. "We'll bring him in again after we gather more information, including what we learn from his estranged wife. I'll make sure we get her surname and contact details. Meanwhile, we'll bring you up to scratch. I'll forward you the forensics and medical examiner reports."

If Novak could read them through his brain fog. Mike was talking as if they were back to being partners. Novak had asked for this. He'd longed for the whole deal. Now he wanted out.

* * *

Paula ducked out of the cold wind into the relative warmth of her car. Around her, vehicles occupied about half the parking spaces in the Westwinds lot, which would normally be full on a weekday during noon hour.

Sam showed as Active on Skype. She set her sandwich on her lap and her phone on the dash mount and called him.

His face on the screen warmed her more. She said she only had a half hour to talk before her one o'clock appointment. Where to begin? Too much had happened since her birthday call twenty-four hours ago. Sam didn't even know that Connor had been brought to police headquarters for questioning. "There's been a development in the bike store claim. The police think they've recovered the stolen items."

"That's great." Sam grinned.

She didn't want to deflate his smile, and once she brought up one piece of big news it would snowball into the next one, and the next . . . "I'll save the full report for the weekend, when we'll have time."

"Looking forward to that," he said. "Is your appointment about the recovery?"

"Indirectly," she said. Mike had arranged for her to see Connor, the suspected break and enter thief. She shifted the focus to Sam. "How was your day?"

"Don't get me started."

She ate her tuna sandwich while watching his animated face and listening to his changing voice tones, hardly trying to grasp his words. She soaked in his joy, his frustration, his determination to complete the work—all the things she'd felt about helping Connor until she'd discovered his drug cache. Mike was almost certain the pills were opioids. He'd taken them from her, but they couldn't be used as evidence, since they hadn't been found in a proper search. *Good* had been her first thought. Evidently, she was still more on Connor's side than that of the police—if those sides were opposing.

The half hour raced to an end. "Love you," they both said, and hung up.

Paula grabbed the tote bag and battled the cold wind on her way back to the Investigative Services Building. The receptionist waved her into the atrium. The large, oval-shaped space struck Paula as unusual for a police station. Calgary Police Service bought the building from Nortel in 2009, when the telecommunications company filed for bankruptcy. Mike had told her he found the Homicide office cubicles cramped, but he liked the building's overall spaciousness and its location a short drive from his home.

A woman entered from the direction of the Homicide office, the detective Paula had met at Connor's apartment. Megan wore a green sweater and pants. They stopped a couple of metres apart and exchanged greetings. One-on-one, Paula was more aware of Megan's six-foot height than she'd been in the apartment.

"Did you get the list of recovered bicycle items?" Megan asked.

Paula thanked her for promptly sending it. "I'll check it against the partial receipts I got from Cycle Life." Partial because Kelsey hadn't completed the work. Heavy with sadness, Paula held up the tote bag. "I'm here to bring some personal items to Connor."

Megan's face fell. "You've heard . . . ?"

Paula nodded.

"I volunteered to go with Connor to the morgue, so he'd have someone he vaguely knew with him." Megan tucked her short hair behind an ear. "He acted stoic, but I could almost see him crumbling underneath. On top of it all, he's got a terrible migraine."

"Stress related?"

"I think so."

The heaviness returned. "Have you contacted his parents?"

"His father is out of the scene. Connor insisted on calling his mother himself. Last I heard, he hasn't been able to reach her. She lives off the grid in BC."

"Have you rescheduled his interview?"

"Mike and I managed to push it back to tomorrow morning, to give Connor a night's sleep. He told me he didn't sleep at all last night in his cell."

"Who could?"

"We think it's best to keep him here tonight to monitor his migraine." Megan said. "If it doesn't improve, we'll call in a doctor."

Paula started. "It's that bad?"

Megan nodded, her lips tight. "I've got to run. Work." She wished Paula luck with Connor and crossed the atrium to a side room.

Paula took the elevator down to the holding-cell area. The dreary hallway to the cells mirrored her mood about seeing Connor. At the security desk, an officer checked her ID and tote bag. He rummaged through Connor's clothing for sharp objects and peered at his contact lens solution as though it might be poison.

They walked down the corridor between the two rows of cells, with only peepholes for looking out and into. Two detainees in adjacent cells talked loudly and rapidly to one another through their mutual wall.

"Getting their stories in sync," the officer said, deadpan.

All she could understand were swear words. She asked if Dustin had gone home.

"This morning," the officer said. "Too bad for Connor. He and Dustin chatted back and forth more pleasantly than that noisy pair." He stopped at the last cells, looked into the peephole of the one on the left, and opened the door. "Your visitor's here." He stepped aside so Paula could enter, left the door ajar, and stayed in the corridor, presumably to keep watch on Connor, or them both.

Connor lay on a padded bench, facing the wall. The bench was too narrow for him to curl up his legs.

"I'm sorry about your brother," she said.

He rolled onto his back. Sunglasses with side shields covered his upper face, his dishevelled beard the lower part. He wore a loose shirt, jeans, and running shoes. "The light's killing me," he said.

The room was dim, its only furnishings a toilet, sink, small table, and benches along the side walls. The other bench had no padding. He evidently didn't have a roommate, one positive in this misery.

She set the tote bag on the table in the middle of the room. "I brought the things you requested from your apartment."

"Isabelle gave them to you?"

"I had to come here anyway, so I picked them up."

His body spasmed. He raised himself to a sitting position and set his feet on the floor. She couldn't see his eyes through his sunglasses, but he appeared to look beyond her to the opposite wall, probably waiting for her to mention the bags of pills in his dresser drawer. She hated that Mike was making her go along with this mind game, but she'd promised.

"I hear you got acquainted with Dustin," she said.

"Your witness." He spoke slowly, in a monotone. "He was in the next cell and knew Gabe."

She'd like to pursue this, but the police might view it as compromising his interview.

"Talking with him took my mind off my headache," Connor said. Each word seemed an effort.

Nothing to distract him from the pain in this stark room. She wished she'd thought to bring drawing materials from his apartment. "Have you got in touch with your mother?"

He gave a faint nod. "It'll take her a couple of days to get here by car."

"She's not flying?"

"She's against planes, on account of their huge carbon footprint."

"But for her son . . ." Paula halted her judgment.

"I think she's really afraid of flying, but her ideal sounds better."

Not when flying would quickly get her to her sons—one dead, the other facing criminal charges. Paula changed the subject. "I gave Finnegan enough food to last until tomorrow afternoon. I'll drive you home after your interview."

"If they let me go."

"Why wouldn't they?" But it wasn't her place to probe. Even if the police found evidence to charge him with break and enter, they wouldn't keep him past the interview for that lesser crime.

"Leave me alone, why don't you?" He lay down again and turned away from her, into the wall.

She scanned the room. The officer had checked the tote bag for anything Connor might use as a weapon against himself or others. If he stood on the table, could he reach the ceiling light and tie himself to it with . . . what? She couldn't see a bulge beneath his untucked shirt. Surely, they weren't stupid enough to let him wear a belt.

On her way out, she'd talk to the guard about suicide watch. She left more weighted with worry than when she'd entered.

Chapter Eighteen

Isabelle gaped at the online news report, which had delivered a double whammy.

Calgary police have identified the two bodies discovered in a northeast industrial park. Kelsey Tedesco, age twenty-four, and Gabriel Riley, age twenty-two.

Two bodies? Isabelle rocked in her office chair. How had she missed the report of a second death? And it was Connor's brother. *Homicide investigating.* They suspected murder.

She picked up her phone from her desk and punched in Connor's number. It rang until voicemail kicked in. She left a message. He had to be home by now and dealing with this by himself. The cops wouldn't release Gabe's name without his closest relative knowing.

She ached for Connor and searched for other news reports. While she'd never met Kelsey or Gabe, it felt as if she had. And what a shock for the people she'd met at Cycle Life, including Olivia. Isabelle glanced at the kid's table beside her desk. After she and Herb had discussed the homeschooling plan, Herb called Josh, who jumped on the idea, but "Zabrina was the boss," Herb reported to Isabelle. She still suggested they carry up Erin's childhood furniture from the basement to see how the homeschooling setup would work. By moving the armchair to the unused bedroom across the hall, the small table fit perfectly beside Isabelle's desk. Minutes later, Josh got back to Herb and said Zabrina was willing to consider the arrangement. Now, she'd be here any minute.

Isabelle got up to make sure Salt hadn't messed up the living room too much, and tripped over Pepper, who yelped. Isabelle squatted to stroke her fur. Where had Gabe been murdered? In the basement, like Kelsey? In Cycle Life? This was more important than a neat living room. Isabelle plunked back into her chair to check for more reports.

The doorbell rang. *Zabrina.*

Isabelle raced down the hall. Salt barked and joined her on the staircase. He'd strewn his toys all over the living room. *Shit.* Isabelle took a few breaths before opening the front door to cold air and Zabrina, who was wearing a fur coat. Snowflakes melted into her dark hair. Isabelle motioned her inside.

Zabrina undid her coat buttons. "You have to admit this plan is nuts."

"Totally" was all Isabelle could think to say. Was she out of the job before the discussion began?

"Well, the whole world is nuts today," Zabrina said. "We all need to . . . What's the word I keep hearing? *Pivot.*" She shrugged off her coat, hung it in the closet, and pushed the next-closest jacket aside so the fabrics didn't touch.

"Is that real fur?" Isabelle asked. "Wolf?"

"Faux lynx." Zabrina's turquoise scrubs followed the lines of her hips. Flowers decorated the rim of the shirt. "Can we sit somewhere? I'm on my feet all day."

Herb had said she was an emergency room nurse at Foothills Hospital, which was a ten-minute drive from here. Salt sniffed Zabrina's leather boots. Isabelle told her to leave them on, since the sidewalks were dry. They went up to the living room. Herb had also said Zabrina lived in Tuscany, the last station on the light rail transit line that Olivia had ridden to Isabelle's house. Josh lived downtown, and he sometimes took Olivia home on the CTrain. Like a lot of kids, Olivia was fascinated with trains and buses. One weekend Josh rode around the city with her for fun, to keep her entertained.

Zabrina apologized for her daughter's intrusion that morning.

"It was something different and interesting," Isabelle said, honestly. *And it could lead to a side job.* She'd worked out a decent payment amount with Josh. Herb had advised her that she'd get a better deal from him than Zabrina. Isabelle offered her a drink.

"No, thanks, I can't stay long. I have to pick up Olivia before Josh loses her like Herb."

Isabelle laughed and hoped it was a joke. She wondered if Zabrina had heard that the woman murdered in Furniture Sellers was Kelsey. They must have been friends, since Kelsey had gone to Zabrina's place for coffee and talked about the dude who was chasing her. Isabelle didn't want to be the one to tell Zabrina the horrible news.

Salt gave up on trying to get Zabrina's attention and trotted to the corner to chew a rawhide bone. Since Zabrina sat on the sofa, Isabelle took the chair across from it, facing the front window. Outside, snow fell lightly, and wind bent the bare tree branches.

"I gather you worked everything out with Josh and Herb," Zabrina said.

Isabelle nodded. "Josh didn't come here, but we talked on the phone."

"Yeah, he's busy with different things, and he'll be busier now with Kelsey gone."

Isabelle glanced at Salt, trying not to give anything away.

"You know she's the one who died in the furniture store?" Zabrina said quietly, as though to herself. "That's what the commotion was about yesterday."

"I saw it on the news, before you came."

"I heard on the drive here," Zabrina said. "It was all I could do to pull into the first shopping mall. I called Josh. He'd found out last night and didn't think to tell me." She scowled, and then her face softened. "I saw her last weekend. She was so alive, with plans for the future." Her voice broke.

"I'm sorry," Isabelle said. "I'll get you a glass of water."

Zabrina shook her head. She touched a strand of hair that had fallen over her chest. "Josh mentioned he knew the guy who died in the other store. The radio said his name, but I was too stunned about Kelsey to hear the rest. This guy and Kelsey were friends. She'd told me about him a few times. He introduced her to his brother, who developed a crush on her. Kelsey thought it was harmless, but I don't know." Her forehead knit.

Connor? A crush? He'd told Isabelle that he and Kelsey were barely acquaintances.

"Kelsey was cute, petite, sporty," Zabrina said. "A lot of dudes like that."

Zabrina was tall, at least five foot nine. Isabelle would call her striking rather than cute. And sporty or not, Zabrina's figure was curvy and trim in the right places. A lot of dudes liked that too.

"I've known Kelsey almost ten years." Zabrina stared at the wall behind Isabelle, her tone mellow, nostalgic. Her eyes looked too glazed to be taking in the painting of cherry blossoms in Japan. "As a teenager, Kelsey worked in the store after school and summers. I'd come by at closing time to meet Josh so we could go for dinner. Kelsey and I would chat while he finished up. Later, after Olivia was born, she became our babysitter—and she also became my friend. I kind of saw her as my little sister. All I had growing up was four brothers." She looked at Isabelle. "Do you have brothers or sisters?"

"No. My roommates are kind of that, except for Habib, my boyfriend."

"Do they work during the day?"

"Usually. When they don't, the house is big enough for them to not notice Olivia."

Zabrina smiled ruefully. "She tends to make herself noticed."

"Do you want me to show you the room Herb and I started fixing up for her schooling?"

"Sure."

Zabrina followed Isabelle down the hall. Salt scooted around their legs in figure eights. They stopped at the doorway to Isabelle's office. Pepper's ears perked up, and she raised her head from her floor cushion. Salt bounded around the room.

Isabelle pointed out Olivia's table and chair and the bookcase. She'd moved her insurance books up to the higher shelves. "Olivia helped me carry up my roommate Erin's childhood books from the basement." She pointed to the lower shelves. "We'll also bring up Erin's old toys. She has some educational ones, like LEGO."

"It sure beats Josh's store." Zabrina's eyes, lined with mascara, grew wide. "I cringe when I think Olivia was there yesterday, sitting above two brutal deaths."

"Was the second one murder?"

"It's serious if Homicide's investigating." She looked at the dogs. Pepper returned to her snooze. Salt was back to sniffing Zabrina's boots. "You'll find Olivia's more like this pup than that old dog. If you're good with that, I am too. Deal?"

Isabelle nodded and grinned then remembered Connor's sadness.

After Zabrina left, Isabelle paced between her office and the living room, bumping into Salt all along the way. Connor didn't love Kelsey. He wasn't her scary dude. But Zabrina and Olivia couldn't both be wrong. Connor had lied to Isabelle and Paula about going to Rome. And his paranoia about Kelsey and other Cycle Life staff recognizing him had been weird. Had he stalked Kelsey at the store? Isabelle's mind spun in circles. She didn't want to dump more shit on him. His brother had died, maybe been murdered.

She checked her phone. Still no reply from Connor. Were the cops keeping him? Why? Paula might know, if she'd taken Connor's things to Westwinds. More importantly, had Paula found the drugs at Connor's place? If so, what had she done with them? Isabelle wouldn't ask that when she sent a text, in case Paula had missed the drugs somehow. Isabelle tried Connor's phone again.

No answer.

* * *

Mike took his seat in the interview room they used when lawyers were in attendance. The room felt spacious and luxurious after the one this morning—twice the size with a table long enough for two chairs on each side, and the paint job and air were relatively fresh. No smoking permitted in here, thanks to a request by one of their regular lawyers. The staff sergeant preferred having two detectives conduct the interviews to maintain a power balance across the table. Mike especially agreed with him right now since Megan sat beside him. She'd lead the questioning on this case that was Robbery's domain.

Connor looked at them across the table through sunglasses that concealed his eyes and half his facial expression. Convenient, Mike thought, but Megan insisted Connor wasn't faking or exaggerating his migraine. She'd bought the heavy-duty sunglasses for him at a drug store. They weren't prescription and, with a migraine, he probably wasn't wearing his contacts. Effectively, Connor now stared at them blindly. Twenty-four hours in custody hadn't improved his appearance. His shirt was rumpled, his beard shaggier, his skin tones grey.

While they waited for Connor's lawyer to return from the restroom, Mike checked his phone. Nothing yet from the guys combing through Connor's apartment. From a work perspective, Mike wished they'd obtained the search warrant before Paula found Connor's drugs. Another side of Mike was glad this

243

miserable-looking young man across the table would squeeze through one loophole.

Emily Wong returned from the restroom and apologized for the interruption. "Eight months of pregnancy takes a toll on the bladder." She took her seat across from him. "When I left, Connor was about to speak."

Connor looked back and forth between Mike and Megan. "After talking with my lawyer—both lawyers—I've decided to not waste time." His tone was flat. "I'll tell you the truth, for my brother and Kelsey, not that anything can help them now." He cleared his throat. "Kelsey and I broke into the store where she worked, Cycle Life. We faked a break-in, actually, because she had the entry code. When we left, we smashed the window from outside, to make it look authentic."

He paused as though he expected a question. When Mike and Megan said nothing, Connor continued. "My excuse is that we were high on cannabis and lack of sleep when we hatched the plan. It's legal." His shoulders stiffened defensively. "Weed, I mean." He explained that his vague motive was to get back at Cycle Life for sinking his brother deeper into drugs. "Kelsey said she wanted to teach Josh a lesson."

"What did she mean by that?" Megan said.

"How would I know?" he snapped. "It made sense when I was stoned." The flatness left his voice as he described their drug-filled night and his realization that their scheme would result in the type of claim his former adjusting firm handled. This led to thoughts of Paula's knack for ferreting out claimants' secrets and solving crimes—and to Gabe's history of calling Mike with psychic predictions. "Paula worked with Mike. People always said Gabe and I sounded the same on the phone. It all merged in my addled mind. Paula, Mike, psychic, similar voices—the connections seemed a miracle." He flashed a self-deprecating smile, which faded. "I was sure, at some point, I told Kelsey my idea to call Mike and draw Paula in. Kelsey insisted later she didn't remember me saying this and would have nixed anything that might make the police dig deeper and hurt Cycle Life's reputation. She had this idea of taking over the business in the future. Maybe her befuddled brain thought the break-in would help drive Josh out. Anyway, afterwards, when I told her I'd called Mike, she got mad and called me stupid. We patched things up, but later, when she ignored my calls, I wondered if she was still mad at me. I never thought she was dead." His voice gave out.

Megan let the silence sit and then suggested Connor backtrack to the break and enter. He cleared his throat and said that they devised the plan in his apartment Wednesday night, while smoking and laughing, and decided to go for it before dawn, before their high wore off and they lost their nerve. His voice and expression grew animated as he described the break-in.

"Kelsey picked out bikes for us. Both of them were too big for her, but she managed to pedal using her toes. She chose electric bikes to get us quickly to her grandfather's garage, which he never used. She said it wasn't really stealing, more like moving them to a storage unit." Connor's wan smile returned. "I was still high enough to believe that. I've never stolen anything before, but I admit I was pumped while we filled the saddlebags with reflectors and little tools and things Kelsey said were overpriced. We also each grabbed a helmet, for safety."

Mike chortled. The other three looked at him. He shrugged an apology. Safety had struck him as an odd concern in that moment, but Connor and Kelsey would have been riding through dark streets, and the expensive helmets were additional items to sell on the underground market.

"What was your plan for the stolen goods?" Megan asked, as though reading Mike's thoughts.

"There wasn't one," Connor said. "In my mind, I thought we might sneak the stuff back into the store, like elves in the night. I don't think Kelsey was in it for the money, but I don't know. I never will." His looked down at the table, then sideways to his lawyer. "That's basically it."

Emily turned from him to Mike and Megan. "Your records will find this is Connor Riley's first offence. Kelsey's too, incidentally."

The police search had confirmed this. Megan suggested they take a break. Emily agreed this would be good for her bladder—more information than Mike needed to know. They left Connor alone in the interview room. Emily power-walked to the restroom as Mike and Megan moved to a quiet area of the hallway to confer. Neither had further questions regarding the break and enter that couldn't be dealt with outside of the interview room.

"We'll charge him," Megan said. "Odds are at the hearing he'll get off with probation and community service, which I view as fitting."

Mike nodded his agreement.

Homicide's turn with Connor was next. Mike spotted Furey loping their way. Megan wished them both good luck and headed for the Robbery department. Furey watched her walk in an interested way that made Mike's gut tense. Moments later, two cleaning staff arrived and said they'd been told to wipe down the room before the next interview.

"It'll be the same people in there," Mike said. "Except Furey."

"I can put up with their filth," Furey said with a smile.

"Administration's orders," the older woman said.

Mike didn't want to cause trouble for the staff, and arguing with admin would add time. He opened the door for the women and supposed they'd clean around Connor.

Furey looked down the hall, in the direction Megan had gone. "Since we have a minute, would you mind if I ask for personal advice?"

Mike's gut grew tighter. He could guess what Furey wanted to discuss. "That's not generally my territory but shoot." He leaned against the wall and kept an eye out for Emily's return.

Furey raked back his thick hair. "After twelve years with the same woman, I'm out of the loop." His hand paused. "I'd like to ask Megan out, but . . ."

Mike's gut was a hard ball.

"Is that okay for colleagues these days? Working together used to be viewed as something you have in common. Now, I don't know."

"Me neither," Mike said, not entirely to stall. He hadn't re-entered the dating scene after his breakup with his girlfriend three years ago, and he'd been far from skilled at navigating the scene before that. All he knew was that work involvements were awkward when they ended, which they almost inevitably did in this high-strain environment.

Furey glanced at the interview room. "On top of that, there's COVID. Are my and Megan's bubbles allowed to merge?"

Mike smiled despite the horrible thought of them merging. "I expect bubbles should take it slowly."

"I'd do that anyway, for the sake of my kids."

Aside from work, the main thing Mike had heard Furey talk about was his two daughters. He spoke with warmth about their skiing, skating, and dance classes. Mike couldn't recall Furey saying a negative word about his estranged wife either, which Mike viewed as taking the high road.

"Maybe it's best to wait," Furey said.

Mike could easily nod and tell him to hold off, maybe throw in a few platitudes. *Work and dating are a bad mix.* But the fact was, Homicide and Robbery were separate sections in the Criminal Investigations Division. Collaborations like their current one with

Megan weren't the norm. And from all Mike had seen of Furey, he was a decent guy and a skilled policeman. Megan couldn't do better.

"I'm the last person who should advise on this." Mike pushed away from the wall. "But neither of you reports to the other, and you won't work together often, if ever again. For what it's worth, I say go for it."

Furey's face flushed, and his eyes lit up. Mike would kill for that moment of joy. He switched the subject to the case and took the folder Furey was holding. "I'll start with the item Josh thought was a bracelet, and the earring." Their other questions would relate to Connor's relationship with his brother and his role as a potential witness to the murder in Furniture Sellers, in case he'd noticed something on his pretext visit with Isabelle to Cycle Life. Those questions could drag past dinner and require postponement until tomorrow. Megan said they planned to keep Connor in holding until then for the sake of his health. She'd scrounged padding to make his cell bench more comfortable and generally seemed the newer breed of cop who viewed herself as part social worker. Furey was a guy who shared his feelings. They were a perfect fit.

Emily approached, and Mike briefed her on what was to come.

She stared up at them both. "I won't hesitate to cut you off, in my client's interest."

When the cleaning was done, the three settled in the interview room. Mike slid the first picture across the table.

Connor picked it up and held it close to his sunglasses. "Where did you get this? I wondered if I'd dropped it there, but no one said anything."

Mike refrained from glancing at Furey and Emily.

Connor studied the photo from different angles. "I'm pretty sure it's Finnegan's collar. My cat. The last night I saw Gabe, she clawed it off. I carried it in my jacket for good luck." Connor's voice trembled. He looked up. "I wore my jacket to Cycle Life that morning and remember being nervous while we were stealing stuff. I kept feeling for the collar in my pocket. But when I checked my pocket later that day, it wasn't there. Did it fall out at Cycle Life? Is that where you found it?"

Mike stared. They'd found the collar in Furniture Sellers' basement, less than a metre from Kelsey's body.

"Connor has answered your question," Emily said. "Move on."

Mike passed Connor the second picture.

Once more, Connor peered at it nearsightedly. "It's a cat on a moon. Might be an earring. So what?" He looked up, his lips trembling. "Is it Kelsey's? She liked moons and cats, or Finnegan anyway, but I can't say I saw her wearing this." He leaned back in his chair. "Gabe had a pierced ear, but he wore plain silver or gold, not fussy stuff. This wouldn't be his. As for Kelsey, I honestly don't know. I'm not into jewellery." Connor shrugged, then he crossed his arms. It seemed he'd taken lessons from Josh on feigned indifference to female apparel but not on feigned nonchalance.

Emily requested a break to consult with her client.

* * *

The gloomy sky outside permeated Paula's office. The building creaked, probably the wind whipping up the forecasted snowstorm. She turned on the light in the reception area, illuminating the desks and cubicle partitions, and phoned her mother to tell her she'd be late for dinner. "Mike called and asked if he could stop by my office on his way home from work, but we can't postpone my birthday meal again. Start without me."

"We'll wait," her mother said. "I invited Walter. There's plenty for the three of us."

For once, Walter's presence was a relief. He'd keep her mother company. Her birthday dinner was ruined anyway. She tried not to speculate on the reasons for Mike's impending visit. His track record for good news this week had been shit.

She tucked her phone in her sweater pocket and packed up her work for the day. The receipts Kelsey had collected lined up with the bikes and some accessories, discovered in Kelsey's grandfather's garage. No doubt any further receipts Josh provided would account for the remaining items. While she and the police needed these receipts to close their files, in the end, the insurance payout would likely be limited to the replacement of the workshop window damaged in the break-in.

Footsteps sounded from the hall. Mike? Paula hadn't heard the front buzzer.

She opened the door to the landing and saw Valeria round the staircase on her way to the entrance. The woman stopped a few steps down and looked up and over the railing. A multicolour scarf was tied over her frizzy hair.

"Picking up more things?" Paula asked.

"You inspired me to give up on working from home with four foster kids running around and the schools closed. My partner does her share, but it's a madhouse."

Paula glanced toward the top floor. "You mean you're back working in your office?"

"Like you said, we've got the whole building to ourselves, if you don't mind sharing."

"Company's good." It hardly made a difference when they worked two floors apart. "I'll let the building owner know, although I don't think he cares."

"Right, he put you in charge. Are you heading home? I'll walk down with you."

"I'm waiting for a visitor."

Instead of continuing to the entrance, Valeria stepped back to the landing. A down vest topped her layered clothes. "I was thinking, since we're two women alone in the building, we should exchange phone numbers, on the off chance one of us runs into a problem."

Paula hadn't thought about that but probably should have since she'd fallen into a murder and a suspicious death. "Good idea." She took her phone from her pocket, and they plugged in each other's numbers.

"We women should stick together." Valeria tucked her phone back into her knit bag as the entrance buzzer shrilled up the stairs.

"My visitor," Paula said.

"I have to get home to rescue my partner." Valeria waved goodbye.

Paula jogged to the reception desk to buzz Mike in and returned to the landing, which seemed to have grown darker during her moments away. She squinted upward. Had a light burned out on the top floor? She'd tell the owner when she notified him about Valeria.

Mike's footsteps, heavier than Valeria's, foreshadowed his arrival. He wore a suit with no overcoat. Paula ushered him into the office, and they stopped in front of the reception desk—Connor's former desk. She leaned against it for support, which she figured she'd need to process whatever Mike had come here to say.

"I can't stay long," he said. "I wanted to tell you in person."

She held her breath. His eyes were shadowed, his olive skin sallow in the office light.

"It doesn't look good for Connor," he said. "Our search of his home uncovered some evidence."

"More drugs?"

He shook his head. "Seems you confiscated his whole stash. With the other things, though, it's enough to move his case beyond break and enter."

To homicide? She touched Connor's desk, the wood smooth and cold. "You can't think he murdered Kelsey?"

Mike's eyes flickered. Was he saying yes? How had Connor's situation steamrolled out of control so fast? "I wish you'd tell me your fucking evidence."

He blinked then resumed his impassive gaze. "We don't have quite enough to charge him with more than B and E but are keeping him overnight due to his severe migraine."

"Megan said you might bring in a doctor."

"Last I heard, his condition's settled enough to make that unnecessary."

"I'm glad *she's* concerned about Connor."

Mike blanched, slightly, at her implied dig. "When you think of it, he might be safest in the holding cell. The alternative is to send him home, alone, to his apartment, his brother and friend dead and him aware that we're on his heels for suspected murder."

She shivered. "I talked to a holding-cell officer about putting Connor on suicide watch. He said the police had already given the order."

"We'll do our best, but as you know, determined people can slip through the cracks." Mike shifted his weight to one hip. "In addition, the autopsy result on Gabe came in. Opioid overdose. With no evidence of drugs where he was found, it raises questions."

"About Connor?"

Mike straightened and sidled toward the door. "I can't say more and have to leave. Novak's waiting in the car. We'll grab dinner, and then it's back to work for me."

"To put the screws on Connor."

She followed him to the landing, where he turned and faced her. "Paula, I'm sorry I dragged you into this."

"You didn't drag," she said. "I leaped at the bait. It's my fault."

"We'll argue that later." He moved toward the stairs. "I'll keep you informed."

"As much as you can," she said and didn't care if that sounded sarcastic.

Chapter Nineteen

Novak plodded through dinner, barely tasting the chicken pot pie and tuning out the chatter around the table. Eli's homeschooling day at his friend's house, Kyle's plans for moving into this house—None of it concerned Novak, except that he'd have to leave soon and stop being a drain on this happy family.

Lucy announced it was time for Eli's bath. Everyone had finished their meals except Novak, who looked at his half-full plate and mumbled he'd eaten too much earlier at lunch. Had he? Kyle offered to take care of cleaning up. He motioned Lucy and Eli off to the bathroom and Mike off to get ready for his return to work. Novak tried to help Kyle and mainly got in his way. Kyle bustled through the kitchen, packing leftovers into containers, loading the dishwasher, and asking Novak how he was enjoying his return to active homicide cases.

"I don't know how officially I'm involved," Novak said, conscious of his droning voice. "They only hired me on contract for cold cases."

Kyle put a detergent tablet into the dishwasher. "Yeah, there might be some union reason, to keep you from stealing the other jobs. I gather your staff sergeant is a stickler for rules."

Travers would be wise to kick Novak back to cold cases.

"My advice?" Kyle winked at him and scanned the kitchen. "Stay under the radar. That's what I do around here." His gaze extended to the rest of the house.

Novak had thought Kyle was already integrated into the Vincelli home. No way could he feel as much the outsider as Novak.

Mike appeared in the kitchen doorway. "Are you sure about skipping tonight's Homicide team meeting?"

Novak nodded. "I'm beat."

Mike squinted at him, back to his former look of concern. "I forwarded you the forensics and medical examiner reports, if you're up for reading." He waved goodbye and left for Westwinds.

Kyle ran water into the sink and told Novak he'd let the hand-washed dishes dry in the rack. No need for Novak in the kitchen. He debated going down to his computer, but what was the point in pretending he could concentrate on forensic and medical verbiage? He ambled to the living room, dropped to the sofa, and scrolled through Netflix. Christine had constantly urged him to watch romantic comedies with her. He'd usually give in and then let his mind roam through Homicide matters. Basically, the stories were all the same, no need to follow the plot. He clicked the first recommended selection.

* * *

Paula, Theda, and Walter agreed that the coconut curry Leah had brought for Paula's birthday was amazing. Walter joked that Leah should ditch Theda's mask-making and go into business with the woman starting up the meal takeout company. Paula would have liked to pursue that idea as a future plan for her daughter, but her mind was on Connor.

Can't bring up that critical matter with Walter around, she fumed, then chided herself. Walter's wife's situation at her long-term care residence was grave. She would be confined to her room for a while.

"Fortunately, she has a private bathroom," Walter had said, with a lightness that sounded forced.

The conversation kept returning to the outbreak in the residence, interspersed with talk of the mask-making business.

Paula found it wonderful to see Leah enthused about something again. "But don't forget, Mum, the masks were your idea. Don't let Leah spoil your hobby."

Her mother's eyes narrowed behind her glasses. "My masks are more than a hobby."

"They're Theda's contribution to the cause of saving us from the virus." Walter chortled, perhaps at his melodramatic words.

"I meant," Paula said, "work on them at your own pace."

"I intend to. A few of my Zoom sewing group friends are interested in filling orders if Leah finds more buyers than I can comfortably supply."

That could end up being the case if Leah's marketing turned their venture into a thriving business.

After the main course they cleared the dishes, and Paula carried the carrot cake her mother had made to the table. The words *Happy Birthday, Paula* and two candles, a five and a six, topped the cake.

"Sadly, we can't light the candles this year," her mother said.

Walter snorted. "We don't want Paula spewing virus germs over the icing."

He and her mother sang "Happy Birthday" with more clash than harmony.

"Two candles—I get two wishes," Paula said. She closed her eyes and made one for Connor and one for Walter's wife, both locked in tonight.

Her mother wished her a good year ahead. "May you and the world be in a better place next spring."

"Amen," Walter said, his expression grim.

"Unfortunately, the birthday present I ordered for you hasn't arrived," her mother said. "It will have to wait for Saturday, when the girls are here."

Three days away. If the police hadn't arrested someone for Kelsey's murder by then, Paula didn't want her daughters and Isabelle here, on the chance the killer showed up for whatever reason. "Mum, I wonder if we should cancel the party."

Theda nodded. "I was thinking that myself, with COVID cases on the rise and indoor gatherings discouraged."

That would make a good excuse.

An hour later, they sent Walter home with half of the leftover birthday cake. After the dishes were done, Paula suggested they relax with tea in the living room. Both sat on the sofa. Paula detailed Mike's visit to her office, her meeting with Connor in his cell, and her drug discovery in Connor's apartment—full disclosure, so her mother would appreciate the seriousness of their situation.

"I'm sorry, Mum, for dragging you into this." Mike's apology to Paula had been similar, and she'd dismissed his assumption of responsibility. There must be a difference between the two, but she had too much on her plate to consider that now.

Her mother set her cup and saucer on the coffee table, beside the vase of daffodils, which she'd bought on her walk yesterday. "Connor's the one to be sorry for."

"What if Connor is guilty, Mum?" Paula said. "I don't know him all that well. Many people kill in a moment of anger. Suppose Kelsey and Connor went to see Gabe in the CounterTops basement and found him dead. How would Connor react?" She sipped her tea, reflecting. "He loved his little brother, felt totally responsible for him. He'd be devastated and angry that the overdose death he'd dreaded had happened. People tend to lash out at the closest person. Maybe he blamed Kelsey for hiding Gabe rather than pushing him to get proper help. She was a small woman, and Connor's a husky man. What if he went ballistic, chased her through the furnace room to Furniture Sellers, and grabbed the nearest object, on impulse?" She stopped herself from mentioning the candlestick, which Dustin had observed at the scene. Homicide might be holding back the weapon detail from the public to rule out false confessions and to potentially trap the killer.

Her mother picked up her teacup. "That is a theory, Paula."

"I know," she said. "My point is, we have to be careful."

"We discussed this yesterday. I won't let strangers into the house, including Connor. I'll phone you if I notice anyone watching the house, or other unusual behaviours."

"Things have escalated since yesterday."

"Those measures should still be sufficient. Paula, I'm not an old woman who can't protect herself."

Eighty-two was old by most definitions.

Her mother peered at her. "Did you scratch your face?"

Paula touched the rough scratch on her cheek. Her makeup must have worn off. She described her encounter with Finnegan. "If the police don't release Connor tomorrow, I'll be stuck feeding that cat again. I don't want Isabelle involved in any way."

Her mother nodded. "The young aren't necessarily better at self-care than us old folk." She finished her tea. "Now, it's bedtime for me."

Upstairs, in her bedroom, Paula emailed the owner of her office building about the burned-out lightbulb and a second person now working in the building, Valeria. If only everything she dealt with was equally nonthreatening. Mere days ago, she'd been excited by her role in a dangerous case, but now the complications wore her down.

She scrolled through Isabelle's numerous texts and emails asking if the police had sent Connor home because he wasn't answering her messages, and had Paula heard that Kelsey was the murder victim, that Connor's brother Gabe was found dead in the CounterTops basement, and that Homicide was investigating his death as suspicious? This was too much for an email. Connor was Isabelle's friend. Paula owed her an update, and ten p.m. wasn't too late to call Isabelle.

She answered right away. "Paula, I'm going nuts with this. Connor's ignoring my texts and calls. He must be nuts over Gabe's death. You know about that, and Kelsey?" Salt barked in the background.

"I know, and I feel terrible for Connor."

"How did Gabe die, if it's suspicious?"

Had the police announced his cause of death? Paula hadn't checked the news tonight, best not to reveal too much. "Mike won't tell me anything. It frustrates me, how he keeps police secrets." That part was true. "Connor has a bad migraine. They're keeping him at Westwinds another night to look after him. I've decided he's no worse off there than he would be alone in his apartment."

"He'd have Finnegan for company at home," Isabelle said. "Did you go over and feed her?"

"I did." Paula touched her scratched cheek. "I also collected Connor's things."

"Oh."

Silence on the line. Was Isabelle waiting for her to mention the drugs? Paula paced to the front window and stared at the falling snow. Connor's apparent preference for Isabelle to go to his apartment could have been that she'd agreed to hide the drugs or dispose of them. If so, it was another reason to keep her out of this.

"I'll phone when I hear more," Paula said. "I'm going to Westwinds tomorrow to drive Connor home after his interview."

"I could do that."

"No." Had that sounded sharp? "I've got to go. It's been a long couple of days."

Another pause on the line. Outside, the wind whipped the snow toward the house.

"Is there something more?" Paula asked.

"Not really." Isabelle's voice quivered. "I just feel terrible about Connor, and Gabe and Kelsey, even though I didn't know them."

"Yes. Me too." Paula signed off with a promise to contact Isabelle the minute the police released Connor. She didn't add "if."

* * *

"Paula didn't tell me everything she knows about Connor." Isabelle sat on the kid's chair that she and Herb had moved upstairs to her office. Olivia would need a cushion to reach the desk.

"How do you know?" Habib said.

To see him, she turned to sit sideways on the chair, which didn't swivel. "A feeling. For instance, she didn't say she'd found drugs at Connor's place."

"You didn't tell her you knew they were there." He leaned over to pat Pepper, who snoozed on her floor cushion.

And Isabelle hadn't told any of them about Zabrina's and Olivia's stories about Connor's crush on Kelsey and that Zabrina had worried he was dangerous. Isabelle's roommates would tell her to report it to the police. Paula would too. She'd probably given the cops the drugs and gotten Connor deeper into shit.

"I'm thinking," Habib said. "If you don't want this homeschooling job, tell these people, babe. You don't owe them anything."

"I said I wasn't sure about it," she said with a huff. "And it bugs me when you call me 'babe.'"

He blinked. "Since when?"

Since lately. She turned toward the desk, so Habib wouldn't see her flush. At the beginning, she'd found the nickname cute, "endearing," her mom had said, when Isabelle took him to Montreal to meet her parents at Christmas. Her fault for letting him get away with it for three years. It was a habit she was stuck with.

Footsteps sounded in the hall. Isabelle tried to swivel the chair that didn't move, which might be good for keeping Olivia focused on her schoolwork. Erin and Nick halted at the doorway. Both held bins full of toys and puzzles.

"I'm surprised my mom saved so much of my and Leah's old stuff," Erin said. "She usually gets rid of things we don't need anymore."

"There's tons of LEGO downstairs," Nick said. "I'll get that next."

Isabelle told them to put the bins in the bedroom across the hall. "The office will be for Olivia's schoolwork."

Erin glanced at the children's books on the bookshelf. "It's funny, you becoming a teacher when you hated school."

Habib laughed. "It's not exactly teaching." He caught Isabelle's glare and wriggled his eyebrows in the cute way that usually made her laugh but not now. "With two deaths in their store basement, I get the impression they want the kid here mainly for you to keep her alive. That's setting the bar low."

"Maybe not in this case," Isabelle said.

"If it's dangerous, tell them to screw it." Habib touched her shoulder.

She shrugged him off.

"Can I help it if I'm concerned about you—"

Babe? She mentally finished his sentence and scowled.

"I'll help them set up the playroom." Habib left to join the others.

At Christmas, her dad had joked that he couldn't believe a guy as smart as Habib would go for her. Isabelle couldn't believe it, too, sometimes. Was she drawn to homeschooling Olivia to prove she was as smart? If she was smart, she'd know what to do about Zabrina's and Olivia's stories.

Isabelle shifted from the kid's chair to her own chair. She didn't want to tell Paula, who was withholding stuff from her. Or make a cold call to Homicide, even to Detective Mike, who bugged Paula by keeping his police secrets.

What about Detective Novak? Isabelle pictured him dressed in his cargo shorts, treating Olivia like his grandkid. He had retired and come back, but not quite as a real detective. He'd given Isabelle his card in case she thought of more information. She rifled through her desk drawer and found the business card.

Brian Novak, Golden Sky Ranch. Under this was a phone number and an email address. The background was a photo of a foothills landscape. No police insignia. She might be able to trust him with what Zabrina and Olivia had said.

A text notification sounded. Isabelle leaped up. Connor? Paula with news? Isabelle grabbed the phone from the pocket of her jeans.

Josh.

Can Zabrina drop Olivia off tomorrow on her way to work?

Her legs shaking, Isabelle texted a reply, *Is the bike store open?*

"Who's that?" Habib stood in the doorway.

Not yet. I have business to take care of.

Josh, Zabrina, and Herb had told her, or implied, the job wouldn't start until the store reopened. Habib was right. She didn't owe them, could tell Josh to screw it. But she'd caught up on her "real" work today and had nothing planned for tomorrow. It would be boring for Olivia to spend the day in front of a screen or get dragged along on Josh's business, which Isabelle hoped was about bikes. If it was drug business, it could be dangerous for Olivia. What was wrong with Isabelle jumping that low bar to help a child?

Josh texted again. *9 am?*

He really wanted this.

"A claimant," Isabelle said to Habib, so he wouldn't hassle her about letting Josh take advantage. *Okay.*

* * *

Mike brushed snow from his overcoat and hung it in the entrance closet. Across the living room, Novak was sprawled on the sofa, snoring. Mike took off his shoes and tiptoed through the room. Novak sputtered and stirred then bolted upright.

"Wha . . . what . . ." Novak's comb-over fanned in all directions, like an exotic bird's crest. "What time is it? I must have fallen asleep." The TV displayed Netflix program selections. "How was the meeting?"

"Took a long time to plan the obvious. We'll decide on Connor after his interview tomorrow." Mike sat on the armchair, his body drained. In many ways, it was harder not being team lead, to have no control of the directions on a case. At the meeting, his suggestion to get a warrant to search Josh's apartment had been brushed off due to a lack of evidence of drug dealing at Cycle Life. "Has Lucy gone to bed?"

"After Kyle left, she said she'd turn in early to read. Do you want to watch the news?"

Mike shook his head. "I'm turning in now too. It's going on eleven."

Novak looked at the TV screen. "Seems the movie ended. I don't remember anything past the heroine's opening despair with her boring life."

"I could use a little boring right now." Mike ran his hands through his hair, still damp from the snow. "The driving will be miserable tomorrow, but I plan to swing by the crime scene on the way to work in the morning. It struck me during the meeting that I haven't seen the place since it became a crime scene. I'd like to get a sense of it before the tape comes down. Care to join me?"

Novak yawned and stretched. "I'll sleep in and find my own way to work."

How? Novak's truck was at his ranch, and his depression still made driving unadvisable in the best of conditions. He never took public transit, and biking would be out of the question, with the snow. None of that would have stopped the old Novak from getting to work on two hot cases, but the old-Novak sparks of the past few days were gone now. "I'll pick you up after I've viewed the scene."

"If you want."

Mike wasn't going to drag him into the cases. He'd done enough dragging with Paula. After the meeting, Shearer had asked him if Novak would want to partner with him on the interview with Dustin and his lawyer. They needed the extra hand, and Mike sensed Shearer had a grudging respect for the old Novak. "Ask him yourself" Mike wanted to tell Shearer now. Mike wasn't Novak's babysitter. Bringing Novak back to work on cold cases had been a Band-Aid solution to Novak's depression, and the Band-Aid seemed to be peeling off. Mike was too tired to try to press it back on tonight. He'd ask Novak in the morning, assuming Novak was up and ready in time.

Novak patted his hair, flattening the bird crest. "Time to move from my nap to bed."

Mike would kill for that luxury, but it wasn't a luxury for someone in Novak's state.

Both went into the hall. Lucy's bedroom door was closed, but light flowed from under it. If Mike transferred from Homicide after these cases wrapped up, he'd have time for reading and other pursuits, like biking and napping. Scratch napping, he wasn't yet into making that a day's highlight.

The next morning, refreshed from a solid night's sleep, Mike drove through increasing snowfall to the industrial park and parked on the street behind a white pickup coated with snow. No one seated inside. With the building area cordoned off and the hot-tub outlet across the street closed, the truck had no reason to be here. Had the driver abandoned it for the time being due to the conditions? Mike snapped a photo of the licence plate to run through the registry later.

From his position behind the caution tape, he surveyed the building's three stores. Furniture Sellers was the largest, which pushed Cycle Life's, in the middle, off-centre. The blinds covering Furniture Sellers' windows made the building look as if it were winking at him. The image made him smile, but this was no joke. Two people, younger than he was, had died in the building's basement. Police had searched the entire place and found nothing to indicate Cycle Life was dealing drugs, but Josh was smart. He would have cleared out the evidence, and he'd had two days since Kelsey's death to do it.

A person came out of Cycle Life and turned around, presumably to lock the door. His ponytail suggested he was Herb. In his report, Novak had described the store's bike repairman as bearded, stocky, in his mid-fifties—a longstanding, loyal employee. Mike couldn't recall anything pertinent Herb had told Novak.

Herb started across the parking lot, his head bent forward against the blowing snow. He beelined toward Mike, seemingly unaware of his presence. A couple of metres away, he looked up and halted. Mike stared at him over the tape, which sagged under its load of accumulating snow.

Mike took out his badge and identified himself. "Do you notice this tape? It means and says plainly, 'Do not cross.'"

"I work at Cycle Life." Herb glanced back at the store. "I figured you cops had finished whatever you were doing in there."

Had he been watching the police work? "I could charge you with obstruction."

"All I wanted was a few specialty tools," Herb said with apparent innocence, "so I could work on my bike at home. I've got the time while the store is closed."

This made sense, and Homicide had in fact done all they'd planned on the scene. Mike took his latex gloves from his pocket, put them on, and held out his hand. "Let me see these tools."

His lips narrowed, Herb shoved his hand in his jacket pocket and dug something out. He turned over his fist, opened his palm, and displayed a tiny wrench, a screwdriver, and a third tool Mike didn't recognize.

"I need to take these."

"Why?" Herb's fingers closed over the tools.

"They're part of a crime scene."

Herb's nostrils flared. "Shit. I should have come earlier."

"You shouldn't be here at all." Mike found a plastic bag in his pocket. He waited for Herb to reopen his hand.

Snow speckled Herb's white beard. His fist tightened. "Come on." His tone grew wheedling. "A brake caliper isn't going to kill anyone."

This gadget probably could, but it hadn't killed Kelsey or Gabriel.

Herb's fingers opened slowly. Mike was no mechanic, but he'd met a few on past cases who'd adored their hardware.

Mike plucked the tools from the man's hand and bagged them before stuffing them in his coat pocket. "Do you have others?"

"No."

"I'll have to search you." Mike raised the yellow tape to the height of Herb's shoulder.

Herb ducked under with agility, a testament to all the biking he did, perhaps. Mike reminded himself to get his bike tuned when the snow was gone, but not at Cycle Life. Herb faced Mike on the street side of the tape.

"It would go best for you if you hand the tools over," Mike said, although he'd still have to request a search.

"If I refuse?"

"You get to visit police headquarters."

"That's a waste of everyone's time."

Maybe, but after this stunt, Mike would recommend bringing Herb in for a formal interview. Clayton's daughter had called Herb a follower—Clayton's man, and currently Josh's man. Herb was a dark horse that Homicide had skimmed over.

Herb turned to the truck parked on the street. "Is this the position?" He leaned against the cab, arms raised, legs planted apart.

Mike patted him down and struck paydirt in the left jacket pocket. An object that resembled a Swiss Army knife. Herb's inside pockets yielded another wrench and a mystery tool.

"Do I get these back after you're finished with them?" Herb asked, his tone snarling now. "Tools of this quality aren't easily replaceable."

"I'll tag them for return to Cycle Life."

"You better not lose or damage them."

Mike would hate to trust police efficiency and care to look after anything he loved.

"Can I go now?"

Herb had been relatively cooperative. Crossing police tape wasn't a major crime, especially when the tape was due to come down later today. Homicide would also be occupied this morning with Dustin's and Connor's interviews. Best to bring Herb in later. Mike nodded his assent.

Herb took out his truck key from his pocket. "It might not look it, but I do want you to get to the bottom of what happened to Kelsey. Her grandfather, Old Clayton, taught me the business. Kelsey and the store meant the world to him."

Mike felt a pang of sorrow for the older man. "I've met Clayton. He'd want any wrongdoings at his store stopped."

Herb's eyes narrowed. His lips pursed and then opened as though he intended to speak. They closed tight. With no more words, he got into his truck. The vehicle disappeared in a cloud of snow. Herb was definitely one to interview again. Mike would love to tackle the dark horse.

Chapter Twenty

"Sure," Novak said in the car, when Mike asked if he'd be available to interview Dustin.

"Did you read the report on his initial interview?" Mike asked.

"Don't know if I got it. Could you send it to me as soon as we arrive? How long do I have to cram?"

"A good ten minutes."

If that wasn't a joke, Novak didn't mind. Nor would he mind being Shearer's largely silent sidekick. It also didn't matter that snow was pounding the car windshield when it was almost May. Novak was mentally back in the action. Ten hours of sleep had helped.

"I woke up to a strange email this morning," he said. "You remember Isabelle? From that first case with Paula?"

"Oh yes." Mike's lip twitched, which it tended to do when he stifled a smile. "You interviewed her in Cycle Life. Curious she was there."

"Evidently Olivia, the eight-year-old, warmed to her. She took transit to Isabelle's house on her own and described a conversation she'd overheard between her mother and Kelsey. I don't think that was the purpose of Olivia's trip. It came up in passing. Isabelle's email was hard to follow."

"That would be Isabelle." Mike slowed to a safe distance behind a fishtailing car.

"I'll forward the email to you," Novak said. "Kelsey and Zabrina discussed a man who was obsessed with Kelsey and might have been a threat to her. The conversation took place a couple of days before Kelsey died. Isabelle thought the man in question sounded like Connor."

"That jibes with the earring and sketch pad we found in his apartment."

"Huh?"

"I told you about them on the drive home yesterday."

Novak remembered now. The earring matched one Mike had confiscated from Kelsey's bedroom, and the sketch pad was filled with drawings of Kelsey. Good likenesses, according to the officer conducting the warrant search. In addition, Connor's fingerprints had been found in Furniture Sellers' basement, on bedroom furniture near Kelsey's body.

"That reminds me," Mike said. "We checked Zabrina's record. She's clean, but your hunch that she's familiar with the police was correct. Her brother's a cop. RCMP in High River."

"High River detachment covers my ranch. What's his surname?"

"I forget. Different from hers. She goes by Josh's name." Mike pulled into the Westwinds parking lot. "Zabrina agreed to have someone come by her house during her window for catching up on sleep after her nursing shift and before Josh drops off their daughter."

"A busy lady." Novak pictured her—Zabrina, dressed in scarlet, storming in and out of Cycle Life. "I don't expect she'll offer much more than she already has, but I wouldn't mind interviewing her."

"Me neither. The Cycle Life gang has caught my attention. I'll tell you about Herb."

Outside, they fought the snow and wind to the Investigative Services Building entrance. Mike described his encounter with Herb while they walked through the atrium to the Homicide office. Novak left Mike at the coffee centre to not waste his limited time.

Cloud and snow obscured the view from his office window. Nothing was visible beyond the highway overpass. Novak settled at his desk, discovered Mike's email had arrived, and dived into the report on the first interview with Dustin, conducted Tuesday evening, a few hours after Dustin and Paula discovered Kelsey's body.

Dustin had evidently viewed himself as solely a witness and hadn't requested a lawyer's presence. Homicide considered him equally a suspect, which would be why Shearer had grabbed that interview. Since then, Dustin had acquired a court-appointed lawyer, who said that Dustin's original account of finding of the body was accurate, but his story's "before" and "after" had changed. Dustin would admit to a minor crime and talk in exchange for clemency.

Novak's phone beeped a text notification. The "luxury" interview room would be ready in twenty minutes. He needed to use a restroom first. So much for his ten-minute cram.

In the hall, Shearer waited outside the interview room door. "They're inside," he said. "Ready?"

Not really.

Shearer, in his forties, had joined Homicide before Novak retired. Back then, Shearer had a crew cut and a moustache. Now he wore his hair looser. He'd kept the lip hair and his trim waist. Since COVID, whenever they talked socially, Shearer complained about the closure of the Westwinds gyms, which Novak had never entered.

They took their seats across the table from Dustin and his lawyer, a broad-faced man in his twenties. Dustin, who looked about twice the lawyer's age, was dressed casually in a shirt rolled up to the elbows.

Shearer began by reiterating Homicide's agreement to go easy on Dustin dependant on the information he revealed. After the preliminaries, he stared at Dustin. "Please describe your situation in the Furniture Sellers store—truthfully this time. We won't be lenient about any more lies."

Dustin rested his arms on the table, hands clasped. Within the multiple tattoos covering the man's right forearm, Novak picked out a vulture. He caught a whiff of cigarette smoke. This non-smoking space might put Dustin on edge.

"I wasn't totally alone at Furniture Sellers," Dustin said. He explained that in early April, less than a week after he moved into the furniture store, he went to the basement to shower and heard a rustling noise at the far end. Thinking it might be a mouse, he turned on all the ceiling lights. A man shot up on a bed. Dustin jumped and probably shrieked. The man sat on the mattress, rubbing his eyes. "He didn't look threatening," Dustin said. "My heart started beating normally again."

Dustin continued his account. The man in his early twenties said his name was Gabe and that he'd moved into the basement of CounterTops after it closed for the pandemic, at the suggestion of his friend Kelsey, who worked for Cycle Life. Though she thought Furniture Sellers would be more comfortable, Kelsey had noticed a furniture delivery van on its way to the rear of the store one day and thought it might still be doing some business.

So, CounterTops became Gabe's rehabilitation retreat, as he called it, a sterile environment without distractions. The plan was to wean him off his opioid addiction. Kelsey would bring him food and pills each day, gradually reducing the amount of oxycodone. The target was for him to be drug free by the end of April. The plan was working, Gabe had said—enough that Kelsey reduced her visits to every couple of days and trusted him to control his drugs. Prior to this, Gabe been living with his older brother, who got on his case about drugs and smoking and leaving his clothes on the floor and not cleaning the bathroom sink after each use. His brother kept pushing him to go to a methadone clinic. Gabe argued against using drugs as a cure for drug addiction. He'd go clean on his own. "But you aren't doing it!" his brother had yelled. He later admitted he couldn't locate a clinic for Gabe in Calgary.

Dustin paused. "It especially pissed Gabe off that his brother had researched clinics behind his back. Gabe felt he was always trying to control his life. I have an older sister who does stuff like that and understood." He scratched his forearm with the tattoos and noticed Novak observing. "I find this building dry."

Shearer stared at him. "Gabe spoke to you openly about his use of illegal drugs?"

"Pretty much." Dustin stopped scratching. "Maybe he thought I wasn't the type to hassle him or turn him in. I'd told him I was living in the store—technically trespassing, at that time. Maybe he saw us as fellow criminals." Dustin snickered and said that by that point in the conversation, he was feeling comfortable enough with Gabe to sit on the adjacent bed. Neither bed had sheets, which bugged Dustin as a furniture salesman. He learned Gabe had been sleeping on the mattress for three nights. Kelsey had set Gabe up with a foam pad and blankets in CounterTops' basement, but the floors were cement. While exploring his new residence, Gabe discovered that the door from the furnace room to Furniture Sellers was unlocked. Since moving in, Dustin had had no reason to check the furnace room. He'd assumed his manager had verified the door was locked when the store closed.

"Was the door kept locked when the store was open?" Shearer asked.

"That wasn't my department," Dustin said. "We had a maintenance man to take care of building matters. I expect he and my manager got their wires crossed about securing the furnace room door. One thought the other did it. Happens all the time." He cleared his throat. "All this talking makes my throat dry. Maybe it's the building or that after spending a month alone, my vocal cords have gotten used to my not speaking much."

Shearer moved on. "What else did Gabe say?"

"That first morning?"

"We'll start with that."

"He said Kelsey had initially brought him food." After the first week, she gave him the door code for Cycle Life. Outside of work hours and on Sundays, he'd let himself out to buy takeout meals. Stairs from the furnace room lead to their restroom. He liked the independence from Kelsey and his brother. Kelsey upped Cycle Life's internet plan so the Wi-Fi would reach CounterTops' basement. Gabe passed hours of time playing video games and streaming movies on the burner phone he'd bought. For exercise, he jogged around in the nearly empty basement. Despite the blankets and foam, his back hurt from sleeping on cement. Dustin explained that he could relate to that, since he suffered from a sore shoulder. He rolled his right arm and winced to demonstrate.

"Gabe said that when he discovered real beds near his living space, it was like heaven." Dustin's voice cracked. "He'd chosen our top-of-the-line mattress. Maybe he noticed the thickness." His voice gave out.

"Would you like a bottle of water?" Novak asked, glad to finally say something.

"That would be great," Dustin croaked.

Novak took out his phone and asked administration to deliver four bottles of water in case the others wanted one. The building was dry in winter, although this was technically spring.

"Where was I?" Dustin said.

Shearer blinked, as though he'd lost track as well. "Did Gabe realize you were living upstairs before you woke him that morning?"

Dustin nodded. "His first night, he heard the TV. The staircase between the two levels is open. The next day, he saw me leave the bathroom after my shower. After that, he limited his time in bed to about seven or eight hours, between eleven and seven, and kept as quiet as he could. I never heard a peep out of him."

"Not one?" Shearer asked.

Dustin shook his head. "I'm a sound sleeper, and there's the geography of the store. My bed and Gabe's were about as far apart as they could be." His voice crackled, but he continued. "When I got up early some mornings, I often forgot he was there. We coexisted, gave each other space, as people say. That's why the girl Kelsey lay dead almost a whole day without my knowing."

"That's hard to believe," Shearer said.

Dustin folded his hands on the table. *One reason I didn't tell you this before."

Mike had walked straight through the basement the day he and Megan questioned Dustin about the break and enter. Neither one had seen the body or considered one might be there, and they were cops, trained to be observant. It needled Mike that he'd missed it, but, by his own account, the basement extended into darkness underneath Cycle Life.

"I never turned on the lights in Gabe's sleep area, to keep the store's electricity costs down," Dustin said. "Maybe I liked the idea of another human being in the place, even at a distance. I agreed to let Gabe sleep there and use the bathroom one day a week."

"One?" Shearer's eyebrow rose.

"To shower," Dustin said. "Gabe had access to Cycle Life's restroom when the store was closed. During store hours, Kelsey would phone him whenever she was available to let him in. She'd wait on the stairs to the basement while he did his business."

Novak stifled a snort. He wished he'd checked the restroom while he was in Cycle Life. In his peripheral view, he watched Shearer's mouth slowly drop as Dustin explained that he allowed Gabe full use of the basement bathroom on Saturdays, let the room lay fallow for four days, and then scoured it clean for his own use on Thursdays and Fridays.

"I don't understand." Shearer's brow knit.

"I had my toilet and sink upstairs," Dustin said. "It was a sacrifice to give up my daily shower, but it wasn't like I was meeting anyone."

Novak laughed. The others looked at him. Novak raised his hands in self defense and wondered if he'd showered at all during his weeks of depression alone at the ranch.

"Oh," Shearer said. "I get it. COVID cleaning. How about we leave this potty talk?"

Novak looked sideways at Shearer. Perhaps the guy had a well-hidden droll side. Someone knocked on the door.

"The bottles." Novak stood to get them.

"How often did your paths cross?" Shearer asked Dustin.

"Not often," Dustin said. "Aside from Saturdays, and the half dozen times we went outside to smoke. By the way, why can't I smoke in here? You let me during the first interview."

"Different room, different rules," Shearer said. "Continue."

Novak handed them each a bottle and resettled in his chair.

Dustin twisted off his bottle cap and winced. "Wrong movement kills my shoulder. Where was I, again? Right. While smoking, Gabe and I stayed close behind Furniture Sellers so anyone driving by or in the alley wouldn't notice us, even though most of the businesses around us are closed." He guzzled some water. "Ah. That hits the spot."

Novak took a sip and agreed. Shearer and the lawyer ignored their bottles.

"Once," Dustin said. "When we were outside smoking, I happened to mention my bum shoulder." He rolled his shoulder again. "Gabe didn't say anything until we went inside. He went to his bed and returned with a bag of pills he said would help. I took one that night, and the pain went away instantly. Even my worries were gone—all my stress about my marriage, my job, COVID, finding an apartment."

"What were these pills?" Shearer asked.

"OxyContin." Dustin's face flushed. "Prescription ones are legal."

"But not to pass around," Shearer said.

Dustin sipped again. "If I give my leftover antibiotics to a friend, is that a crime?"

"You had to know Gabe was getting his drugs illegally."

"I didn't ask." He set the bottle on the table. "That, in a nutshell, is why I lied. If I'd said I knew about Gabe, you'd ask all these questions, I'd start blabbering like this, and you'd charge me for possession of illegal drugs. Do you know what that would mean for me, if Furniture Sellers goes bankrupt from the closure and I have to look for new work? Employers won't hire me with a drug record." He looked at his lawyer. "The deal is no possession charges."

"We'll see," Shearer said.

"You better." Dustin's pink face grew red. "That's why, when we found the body and Paula said we had to leave, my first thought was the drugs upstairs. The cops would search the place and find them. I ran up and flushed the pills down the toilet." His voice broke. He finished the water. "If I'd told you this from the start, would you have charged me with possession?"

"That's irrelevant," Shearer asked.

"Not to me," Dustin said. "I can't see that it hurt me to hold off on telling you, to make sure of no charge."

Did this mean he might be holding back other information for leverage if the police reneged on their deal? Novak opened his mouth to ask but changed his mind. Dustin was bound to answer no whether he was withholding or not.

"Prior to the store closures," Shearer said, "did you meet Kelsey, the Cycle Life clerk?"

"Now that I've seen her picture, I remember seeing her going in and out, over the years. At most, we said 'Hi, have a good day,' or commented on the weather."

"Are you sure that was all?" Shearer asked.

"Yes." Dustin raised his empty bottle to Shearer. "I trust you to honour your agreement. I can live with an obstruction of justice charge but not one for possession of drugs."

Shearer leaned over the table. ""Upstairs, in the area you used, we found a bag of pills hidden in a China cabinet drawer. These didn't go down the toilet."

A flush rose from Dustin's neck. "Fuck. I thought you'd missed them. Why didn't you bring that up?"

Because this was more effective.

"I request a break to confer with my client," Dustin's lawyer said.

"Christ." Dustin folded his arms, the bottle dangling from his fingers. "I was panicked. We'd found a dead body. I don't know what I was thinking, but I wasn't thinking about dealing those drugs. Even if I'd wanted to, I wouldn't know how to go about that."

"That's enough," his lawyer said.

Novak couldn't recall hearing or reading anything about these drugs. He was inclined to think it was a minor case of possession, but his gut said Dustin had withheld something that might be important.

* * *

In the Investigative Services Building entrance, Paula stamped her boots and brushed snow off her spring coat. Despite the slow drive through the storm, she'd arrived earlier than she'd expected, thanks to catching every green light. She entered the lobby and checked her phone. No word from Mike. He'd promised to contact her when the interview with Connor was over. She wanted to be here for Connor's next step, and to learn more about his situation.

Paula told the receptionist to advise Detective Vincelli of her presence. She considered asking to see Megan in Robbery, but there was nothing new to report. As she walked toward a waiting area chair, the interior glass door opened. A man emerged.

"Detective Novak."

He halted and moved closer. "Paula?" He wore a winter jacket, zipped open.

"I'm here to drive Connor home after his interview."

"The interview's been delayed," he said. "Cleaning protocols. Slows our already glacial process. Expect the interview to run past noon."

Paula had arranged to Skype with Sam then.

"Tack on police bureaucracy, Connor won't be out of here until about three."

"How's he doing today?"

Novak frowned. "Not good, from what I hear. His mother's stuck in Prince George. The highways are closed due to the snowstorm—they say it's worse in BC."

"What about his migraine?"

"He has a migraine? I didn't know about that." He looked around her to the building entrance. "How's the weather outside?"

"Getting brutal."

He zipped up his jacket. "After the interview with Dustin, I need fresh air and a leg stretch. That reminds me, I chatted with him afterwards. Did you know he's moved into Connor's apartment?"

"No." She felt a chill.

A couple of officers came in from outside. One nodded at Novak, who ignored him and stepped farther from the reception area. Paula joined him outside the small room with toys and a computer for children who had to wait with their parents.

"I expect it's temporary," Novak continued. "Dustin claims he hadn't met Connor before their mutual stint in the holding section."

"An officer there told me they talked between their adjacent cells."

Novak nodded. "Dustin went on to say Connor offered the accommodation after Dustin's complaints about having to move in with his manager and a host of teenagers."

"That jibes with what Dustin told me at the crime scene," she said. "Is Homicide okay with two suspects sharing an apartment?"

Novak smiled. "No one knew about it until I told them. In any case, not much we can do when we let them go. And Dustin expects Connor to kick him out when he gets home."

"I hope that's soon."

Novak's smile faded; his eyelids fluttered.

Paula raised a hand, palm toward him. "I know, you can't share information."

"Even if I could, I don't know anything. I'm a bit of an outcast in the investigation."

"Join the club."

He snickered and glanced over her shoulder. "I might as well continue on out, finish this trek I started." They said their goodbyes, and he headed for the exit.

Paula decided there was no point in her waiting here or running her car engine in the Westwinds parking lot to Skype with Sam. She'd grab a sandwich on her way to her office and talk to him there. Before leaving, she checked her emails. One from Josh, asking if he could bring the list of stolen items to her office today. He'd had time to take care of it with the store closed and wanted to get the insurance claim off his plate before they were back in business. Plus, he was driving around town anyway.

She sent Josh a reply, *One o'clock?*

He answered before she reached the exit. *Works for me.*

* * *

Isabelle swivelled her office chair toward Olivia, who leaned over her desk multiplying figures in her workbook. Had Isabelle done math that hard when she was eight? She couldn't live without her phone calculator now. Olivia seemed settled—finally.

Isabelle swivelled back to her own desk and read the medical report on her whiplash claimant, whose symptoms had started four days after his minor collision and persisted the past three months. His doctor believed his soft tissue injury was genuine. Should she hire a surveillance company to track his activities? Isabelle would have to consult Paula on this claim that might escalate into something huge. Since Paula would disapprove of the homeschooling plan, the call would have to wait until Olivia left. She'd make background noise or worse, and Isabelle would have to explain what she was doing here.

Her cell phone rang. *Alberta* popped up on the screen with a number Isabelle didn't recognize. She had to be careful with a kid in her care. She let the call go to voicemail.

"Herb here. From Cycle Life." He cleared his throat.

She picked up and cut him off. "Herb?"

Olivia looked over from her writing.

"Hi. Remember me from yesterday?"

"Of course." They'd spent an hour moving furniture up from the basement and arranging it in this room while he told her stories of his acting jobs and Olivia played with the dogs. "Olivia's here now."

"She is?" Herb said. "I thought the store was still closed." He spoke so quietly that Olivia wouldn't have made out his words, even with her superhearing.

"Josh asked me to look after her while he takes care of stuff." Isabelle smiled at Olivia, so she wouldn't stress about grown-ups talking about her.

Olivia resumed writing, her hair draped over her face.

"When do you expect Josh to pick her up?" Herb asked. "Or Zabrina?"

"Josh said it would be him, around three. Zabrina gets home earlier, but she's doing an overnight shift and a half and needs some sleep before dinner."

"Knowing Josh, he'll take advantage and show up well after three." Herb paused. "Don't say anything about this to Olivia. Don't tell her I called."

Isabelle looked at Olivia, bent over her workbook, seemingly absorbed in math.

"This isn't about her," Herb continued. "I'd like to stop by and talk to you about something else. Call me back after she and Josh leave. Don't tell him either. Okay?"

Isabelle realized she was swivelling the chair side to side. *Nerves*. She stopped.

"Isabelle?" Herb said. "It's important you keep this to yourself until you listen to what I say."

She'd started swivelling again. This was all weird, but she had a few hours to think it through. "Okay."

"Thanks." The line clicked. Silence.

Without looking up, Olivia turned to the next page in her workbook. "What did Uncle Herb want?"

What had Olivia heard? Isabelle mentally reviewed her end of the conversation. "Since it's your first real day here, he wondered how you were doing. He says he'd be happy to pick you up earlier if you want. I told him I'd be okay with you staying as long as you like."

Olivia closed her workbook. She brushed her hair back from her face, looking unconcerned. "Can we have lunch now?"

Chapter Twenty-One

Mike and Furey wrapped up their preparation for the long-awaited interview with Connor and walked in silence to the interview room. Mike's thoughts went back to his first meeting with Connor, at the lakeside park in Chestermere. Connor's claim that he didn't know his brother's whereabouts had seemed real, his worry genuine. When Mike saw Shearer standing outside the door to the interview room, he wondered if the case lead would bump him from grilling the person who'd emerged as their prime suspect. But to Mike's relief, Shearer told them Connor and his lawyer were waiting inside and he would watch on camera.

A déjà vu moment hit Mike as he and Furey settled across the table from Emily Wong and Connor, who looked in better shape than he had yesterday. No sunglasses this time, although his thick glasses couldn't hide the shadows around his eyes. His olive skin was pale, his hair as ragged as his beard. At least he'd put on a fresh business shirt.

Emily opened by pointing out that her client hadn't withheld information—a series of events had delayed his forthcoming disclosure.

Mike verbally agreed and moved to his first question for Connor. "On what date did you come to know that your brother Gabriel was living in the basement of CounterTops?"

Connor stared at Mike. "After I met you on Sunday, in Chestermere, I was upset. I felt that by phoning you and pretending to be Gabe and then meeting you in person, I'd screwed things up worse for him. I phoned

Kelsey and told her everything. I must have sounded frantic because, in the end, she said she'd explain what was happening if I promised to keep it secret." Connor paused to adjust his glasses. He leaned back in his chair and looked almost relaxed.

Many people Mike had interviewed looked similarly relieved after finally spilling their story to someone, even to cops looking to nail them on every word. Connor said he had been shocked when Kelsey told him Gabe was living in the closed store adjacent to Cycle Life. Kelsey had admitted that it was her idea. Connor described the detoxification plan that Dustin had outlined in his interview earlier today and added he had been mainly grateful to learn his brother was alive.

"I should have been skeptical," he said, "but Kelsey was enthused about how their program suited Gabe's 'zen' and naturalistic inclinations. She assured me he kept a naloxone kit with him on the chance he overdosed. I didn't see one when I visited him."

Nor had Forensics found any overdose reversal kits in the basement.

"From all I've read about opioid addiction, cold turkey doesn't work," Connor said. "People lose their tolerance for the drugs, they inevitably start using again, and their systems can't handle their former levels. Is that what happened to Gabe?"

Mike hated ignoring his pleading eyes, but that was the interview game. Connor was right that his brother might have survived his final dose if the weaning hadn't reduced his tolerance.

Connor cleared his throat. "That same Sunday, I asked Kelsey to take me to see Gabe." She said part of Gabe's process was to control his own detox regime, so she'd need to get his consent for Connor's visit, and that she'd rather discuss this with him in person, rather than call him on his burner phone. She promised to go after dinner. Connor stressed about it until she got back to him around ten that night to tell him Gabe had agreed to see him. They arranged to meet an hour later, at Cycle Life's front entrance. Fortunately, Connor's bicycle lights worked, and he rode there in the dark.

Inside, Kelsey got the key to the restroom. On their way down the staircase to the basement she talked about hanging out in the building as a kid, discovering all the crannies and nooks. She'd used CounterTops basement as her hideout, where she'd played with her toy horses and blocks. CounterTops didn't bother to lock the door to their basement area, which they only used for storing discarded stock—slabs of countertop granite. From the furnace room, they'd entered the cavernous basement lit only by bare bulbs on the ceiling. It reminded him of a graveyard, with a cement floor in place of greenery. Gabe stood at the room's far end tossing granite chips into a honeycomb of takeout containers, a game he'd devised to occupy his days, complete with a point system. Connor found their reunion awkward. He got the sense Kelsey had cajoled Gabe into seeing him. Gabe said he hadn't called Connor to let him know where he was because he knew Connor would be judgmental.

Connor's voice wavered, but he regained control of it as he explained that he'd tried to act supportive in the basement despite the odours of decayed food in the month's worth of containers scattered everywhere. Gabe had scowled at Connor's offer to collect the ones not used for the game and deposit them in the store's dumpster. When Connor had called Gabe's nest of blankets for sleeping "cozy," Gabe snapped at him, saying that he had a real bed. He marched them through the furnace room to Furniture Sellers' basement, telling them to be quiet so as to not disturb the dude upstairs.

"There's someone upstairs?" Kelsey said.

Gabe whispered that Dustin was good about letting him share the space and he respected his generosity by being quiet and not getting in his way. Gabe switched on a bedside table lamp, revealing a bed with a super-thick mattress, and quietly explained that Dustin had put the sheets on to protect the bed for future customers. "I thought," Connor said, "I'm not buying a bed from this place."

"Me neither." Furey spoke for the first time in the interview.

Connor's story accounted for his fingerprints found on surfaces near Kelsey's body in Furniture Sellers as well as near Gabe's body in CounterTops' basement.

"Gabe's sleeping area was like a mini bedroom," Connor continued. "While Kelsey studied the candles on the dresser, I casually opened the bedside table drawer and saw a plastic bag of pills. I pulled it out and asked what it was, but any idiot knows legit drugs come in bottles. Kelsey said, 'I told you about the weaning plan.' Then I sarcastically said to Gabe, 'What weaning? You leave drugs by your bed to take on impulse at night? If you're serious, you hide them where you have to make an effort to find them.' Kelsey said, 'That's not how weaning works.' Gabe kept telling us to keep our voices down, so Dustin wouldn't hear. I said, who gives a fuck what he hears. I got so mad I grabbed a candlestick from the dresser and threw it at the wall. It almost hit a painting. Well, a cheap print." Connor paused for a few deep breaths.

From the corner of his eye, Mike caught Furey's glance. Emily opened her mouth, as though to speak, but closed it gently. Connor's reference to the candlestick had seemed matter-of-fact, but his action had revealed his temper.

"That shut us up," Connor said. "We all looked toward the stairs, but there was no sign of Dustin. One of us—Kelsey, I guess—turned off the lamp, and I retrieved the stupid candlestick and returned it to the dresser. Then, we all went back to CounterTops' basement. I started collecting containers, preparing to leave, when Gabe said, coolly, that the reason he split from our place was that he couldn't detox with me around, making him feel inferior for his weakness. I swear I didn't do that, or didn't mean to."

Connor's voice trembled. "Gabe said I was the smart one, with the office job and dreams of painting and travel. All he did was waste himself. I argued that this was his choice, that he had as much potential as me and was good at cutting hair. He laughed and walked away to his granite-tossing game. Kelsey followed him. I dropped the containers instead of taking them out—maybe I was mad again. That's the last time I saw either one of them." Connor raked both hands through his hair. "The next day, I regretted we'd left it at that and sent texts, emails, and tried phoning Kelsey. She didn't answer. I didn't have Gabe's burner phone number and didn't know the code to get into Cycle Life." He looked at Mike. "I realized I probably did think he was weak for giving in to drugs and wanted to admit that to him, to apologize." His voice faded to a whisper.

By his own account, Connor had entered Cycle Life twice—Sunday night and for the break and enter the previous Thursday morning. He'd had the chance to watch Kelsey type in the codes for the front and back doors and memorize the numbers, either unconsciously or with the intent to return. Paula had said he was good at his administration work, which included dealing with numbers and details.

"Did Kelsey say where she was getting the drugs to wean Gabe?" Mike asked.

Connor shook his head. "Stress made Gabe turn to drugs."

The argument with his brother would have been stressful and was probably more forceful than Connor had let on, if their words had prompted him to throw a candlestick. People typically underplayed their anger. Was the candlestick the same one that later became the murder weapon? Something to look into further.

"It's no coincidence he overdosed a few hours after that fight," Connor rasped. His hands shot to his face and covered his glasses.

Emily Wong interjected. "I request a break for my client."

Connor's shoulders trembled as he buried his face in his hands. Mike wanted to say, "Gabe's death wasn't your fault," but Mike wouldn't believe that either if he were in Connor's place.

* * *

Within seconds of setting her lunch on her office desk, Paula received a Skype call on her computer. Sam's face filled the screen. They grinned their hellos and chatted about their respective weather. Hamburg was drenched in rain.

"What's the scoop on your break and enter?" Sam asked.

"Josh, the bike store manager, will be by in half an hour with his list of stolen goods. The claim's on its way to being settled."

"Great news."

"What's up with you?" she asked, so she could eat her sandwich before Josh arrived.

Sam was deep into his story of a disagreement with a client when the entrance doorbell buzzed in the reception area.

"Josh is early," she said, sorry to let Sam go. "You'll have to finish that thought tomorrow."

"And you'll have to fill me in on the stuff you've been holding on to."

She couldn't wait. "Be prepared for me to talk your ear off."

"Looking forward to it," he said. "Love you."

"Love you."

The buzzer sounded again. She ran to let Josh in, returned to her cubicle to gobble her last bites of sandwich, and went out to the hall. Minutes passed before she heard footsteps bounding up the stairs. Josh appeared, dressed in a shell jacket over a T-shirt with jeans.

286

He glanced down the staircase. "Does that woman who's leaving now work for your company?"

"Do you mean Valeria? I didn't see her walk by."

"I didn't catch her name. We stopped to chat for a bit. She's cute. Seems sporty."

Paula wouldn't have described Valeria that way. Was someone else working in the building? She ushered Josh into the office and offered him coffee or tea. He said water would be good. In the kitchenette, she showed him the cupboard with glasses and told him to help himself. "COVID protocols," she added.

"Yeah. We should have some in the store."

"Wouldn't hurt." She got a glass for herself.

"What's new with the police case?" he asked.

"Last I heard, they don't have any leads on the people who broke into your store." She and Mike had agreed that all Josh needed to know was that the stolen items had been recovered, but they needed his complete list to make sure everything lined up before they released the goods.

"I mean about Kelsey's murder," he said.

She watched the water fill her glass and turned off the tap. "The news doesn't tell us much."

"No, but don't you have some kind of cop connection?"

"What makes you think that?" She looked over to catch his expression.

He shrugged, seemingly indifferent. "Something Kelsey said gave me that impression. I don't remember what."

She led him across the reception area to her cubicle, and they settled across from each other at her desk. He took a sip of water and leaned back in the visitors' chair, rocking it on two legs. His face was drawn, his eyes shadowed. She noticed he hadn't brought a bag. He must have the list on his phone, or he'd tucked a few papers into his jacket pocket. Nothing threatening about that—but she was alone in the building. She placed her cell phone on her desk in case she needed to call Valeria. Or 911.

"Let's have a look at your list of stolen items," she said.

"I don't have a hard copy."

"No problem." She angled toward her computer. "Read it to me from your phone, and I'll check the items against the police list."

He rocked the chair to its front legs and set his glass on the desk. "Kelsey handled all this stuff before. I thought I'd be able to access the office computer from my home one, through a cloud or something. I asked Herb, but he knows even less about computers than I do. One reason I passed the financials over to Kelsey. I'm not into tech stuff." He touched the glass but didn't pick it up. "Today, I tried again on the computer for an hour. Couldn't get anything to work and got so pissed I quit. You'll have to wait until the store reopens after all."

She did her best to keep her face neutral. Why was he here, then? He could easily have cancelled the meeting. Probably this visit was a ruse to find out what she'd learned from her presumed police contacts. She'd love to know what Kelsey had said to clue him in about this. Perhaps she'd got the information from Connor. Josh might also be curious to know what Paula had learned from Connor about the store's business.

Josh rocked the chair back again. "News reports said Gabriel was the second victim, if you call an overdose that." He held up his hands in surrender. "I don't judge."

"Neither do I." Gabe's death was as sad as Kelsey's, and a tragedy for Connor. "Has the news reported he died of an overdose?"

Josh let the chair clunk to its front legs. "That's the rumour." He reached for the glass and withdrew his hand once more. "I already knew it was him, before I even knew about Kelsey."

"Why's that?"

He cocked his head. "Would you believe he sent me a message from beyond the grave?"

Paula doubted she'd believe that. She sensed Josh studying her skeptical expression. Had he implied he knew Gabe had died first? She didn't recall the news reporting this. "When did you get this message?"

"Tuesday afternoon." He stared at the glass, his brow furrowed. "I was in the store office, tagging helmets, when I heard his voice in my head, telling me he was a real angel now." Josh looked up. "I used to tease him about that, his name, Gabriel."

"There's an angel figurine on your desk," she recalled. "Your daughter gave it to you."

"You have a good memory," he said. "Gabriel's message shook me up so much I couldn't stand being in the store and went home."

She remembered Novak saying that he saw Josh leave the store Tuesday afternoon, around the time the police first arrived at the crime scene. Gabriel's alleged message explained Josh's departure—or provided a cover-up for the real reason.

"Did you know Gabriel well?" she asked.

"I wouldn't say so." He stroked the glass. "We were different types, but we clicked about angels and psychic stuff. Gabriel's name got us talking about that when he'd hang out in the store."

"Why did he hang out at the store?"

"We have our bike groupies." His grin would make no one suspect Gabe had been there to buy and deal drugs. "He was Kelsey's friend. They were around the same age and both into bikes. She told me she got a kick out of his 'ascetic ways,' as she called them. A fancy phrase for asexual, I think." He stared across the desk. "Do *you* think he died of an overdose? It's still a rumour, after all."

Paula tried to keep her expression as casual as his. "Where do you get your rumours?"

"I cruise by the store during my driving around to check out the progress at the crime scene. People hanging around talk."

"Did you know Gabriel used drugs?"

His eyebrows rose. "Like I said, I don't judge."

"Where did he get them?"

"I wouldn't know. Not my business." He rose. "I've wasted enough of your time."

"No rush," she said, hoping to learn more. "You haven't finished your water."

"I'm not really thirsty, thanks. I'll take the glass to your kitchen. COVID protocols."

She met his teasing smile and tried a different angle to keep him talking. "Where did your interest in angels come from?"

His face brightened. "Are you into them?"

She couldn't lie. "I'm curious about why people believe in them."

"I'm not a psychologist," he said. "Haven't been to one either, although my wife probably thinks I should go. People mock me for it, but what's wrong with having an open mind?" He eased back down to the chair. "Gabriel's message was the first real supernatural thing that happened to me. Once, we tried a séance, in CounterTops' empty basement." He caught Paula's glance. "I know, weird that's where Gabriel died—or maybe not. Kelsey was there too, at the séance. Herb thinks it's all crap, but we dragged him down. We tried to contact my little sister. She died when I was nine. She was seven. An accident."

"I'm sorry."

He blinked, as though to bury tears. "It was years ago. I'm okay with it now, but I wouldn't mind contacting her and knowing she was in a good place."

"I understand." She did, although her skeptical side wondered if he'd brought this up to gain the sympathy of a person who might influence the police investigation.

Josh shook his head. "Usually I don't talk about it, but that woman on the stairs made me think of how my sister might look if she'd grown up." He gripped the armrests and raised himself from the chair. "I'll email when I have the list of stolen stuff. Any idea when the cops will take down their crime scene tape?"

"Your guess is as good as mine."

"I doubt that." He smirked.

She wished Homicide kept her in the loop as much as Josh thought they did. His believing this might prove useful. Or put her more at risk.

After he left the office, she picked up her cell phone, glad Valeria had suggested they exchange phone numbers, for safety. While she thought of it, she texted Valeria and asked if she knew of someone else working in the building. Paula had barely sent the message when an email arrived from Isabelle. An agent had assigned them their first new claim since Cycle Life, thanks to the snowstorm. A chain reaction collision west of the city had totalled the insured's car—the driver and two passengers sustained whiplash injuries. Paula suggested she and Isabelle share the work.

Minutes later, Isabelle replied without her usual enthusiasm for opportunities. *I'm kind of busy for the next week.* Paula told Isabelle she'd handle the whole claim and hoped Isabelle wasn't coming down with COVID.

Mike's text arrived next. *Come by 3:00.* The precise time Novak had predicted the police would release Connor.

Paula left the office early to allow extra time for the snow conditions. Her windshield wipers kept a steady pace as she drove north on Deerfoot Trail. She passed emergency vehicles and two sets of cars on the median—the aftermath of an accident. Traffic moved at a crawl, but she entered the Investigative Services Building with twenty minutes to spare. The receptionist confirmed her meeting with Mike, handed her a lanyard with a visitor's badge, and sent her in. Paula made her way to the Homicide office and stopped at Mike's cubicle. He looked over at her from behind his desk. The man seated across from him turned around.

"Detective Novak," she said for the second time that day.

Novak motioned her to take the chair beside him. "We're finished our business here." His jacket was draped over the back of his chair, but she kept her coat on and sat.

"When will Connor be ready to leave?" she asked Mike.

He rested his hands on his desk, on top of a pile of folders, in a movement that made her stomach tense. "We've decided to lay charges."

"For the break and enter?"

He stared into her eyes. "Yes, and murder one."

"That's ridiculous." Her voice was shrill. "Why?"

"An accumulation of evidence."

She crossed her arms. "Which you can't tell me." That was petty, but she didn't care.

"I'm sorry," Mike said.

"You're not. This means you're keeping him?"

Mike nodded. "Until the hearing at least. It will probably be Monday."

"Four more nights in that rotten cell?"

"We'll transfer him to another facility."

"A jail." Her arms tightened under her chest. "Can I at least see him before he goes?"

Mike shook his head. "He wants no visitors, which unfortunately includes you. I think he wants to process this on his own." He paused. "When we told him about the murder charge, he said he deserved it."

"That doesn't mean anything. You know that. People assume guilt for all kinds of reasons." She had to settle her head to deal with this and ordered herself to calm down. "How is his migraine?"

"Better," Mike said. "Telling more of the truth seemed to relieve his stress. If his lawyer hadn't been there, I think we'd have got a confession."

I'm glad she was there. Paula was calm enough now not to say it.

"I have to go," Novak said. She'd forgotten he was present. He stood and grabbed his jacket. "Paula, if you're leaving now, I'll walk you to the parking lot."

"There's no point in my staying." She looked at Mike, in case he thought otherwise.

"We'll discuss this later," he said. "I have some things to do before the team meeting."

She muttered goodbyes and left the cubicle with Novak.

"For what it's worth," Novak said in the hall. "Mike and I think the charge is premature. The team lead's thinking is we've got four days to solidify the case before the hearing. If we can't do it, odds are we'll never have enough to make it stick. It's a gamble."

"With someone's life."

"He also had a psych assessment this morning. For his self-protection, he's safer in custody." Novak stopped in the atrium. "Dustin's protection too. They'd be living together."

"Connor wouldn't lash out at Dustin and harm him." But people did when they were in a bad place.

"I wonder about Dustin." Novak turned to face her. They were alone in this spacious room. "Dustin insists he heard no sounds coming from the Furniture Sellers basement on Sunday and Monday nights. It's an open plan, no doors."

"Their beds were at opposite ends of a huge area, on different levels."

Novak stared, his gaze steady. "Connor described a heated argument that took place in that basement Sunday night or early Monday morning, after Connor found drugs in a bedside table. It was a noisy event."

"People can sleep through all kinds of racket."

"So Dustin said." Novak's wide eyes implied he wasn't breaking any police rules by sharing this information. "It's become clear that Connor had an obsession with Kelsey. She confided her concerns to a friend. Someone saw him stalking Kelsey's house, and he admits he did. Our search of his apartment found an earring of hers in his bedside table drawer and a sketchbook filled with drawings of Kelsey. The cop who found it called them loving images."

"Nudes?"

"No, mostly her face. He said the lines had a tender smoothness." Novak flashed a wan smile. "Don't ask me about art." He moved toward the exit.

She matched his pace. "Why did you tell me this?"

"No reason," he said, with no note of guile.

All the way to her car, she puzzled through Novak's behaviour. He had retired, returned to work cold cases, and stumbled into this active investigation. When they talked this morning, he'd called himself an outcast on the team. What did he have to lose from giving away police secrets? A reprimand? At worst, a boot back to retirement on his ranch. She'd stumbled into this case too and wasn't bounded by protocols. His message to her seemed be, question Dustin, who was staying in Connor's apartment.

Chapter Twenty-Two

Novak decided that icy, snow-covered roads weren't ideal for regaining his driving confidence. A vehicle honked at his abrupt lane change. He'd give the man the finger, if he dared release his grip on the steering wheel. It didn't help that Zabrina lived in Tuscany, on the northwest edge of the city, a curving maze of streets. The GPS with the teacher voice kept directing him in circles. Okay, his fault for muddling her instructions. He cursed his hubris for insisting he could drive, after Shearer called the team meeting. Mike wanted to attend, but thought one of them should talk to Zabrina, so as not to miss the opportunity.

The car in front of Novak's fishtailed. He slammed on the brakes and stopped, inches from rear-ending the car, and sweated under his jacket and suit. At last, he turned onto Zabrina's quiet court. The front of her two-storey home was all garage, typical of these newer neighbourhoods. He parked in front the house, ten minutes later than her specified time. His stupid fault for delaying his departure to talk to Paula because his gut told him she might be able to weasel the truth from Dustin. Sometimes Novak's gut betrayed him.

Outside, the falling snow was refreshingly cool. Zabrina opened the door before he reached the front step. She wore a mauve cardigan that fell to her thighs over a white shirt and jeans. Inside, she stepped back in the hall and told him to hang up his coat in the closet.

"I have two requests," she said. "One is that we maintain a social distance. I work in a hospital and can't afford to get sick. With my exposure, I don't want to pass the virus along to you either."

Novak agreed. Distance would be especially good due to his perspiration from the drive.

"Two," Zabrina said, "please keep your questions brief. My ex-husband will be here with our daughter in less than an hour. I'd prefer you were gone to avoid explaining your presence to Olivia. She's already upset by everything that's happened. Kelsey was her babysitter, like a favourite aunt."

Novak nodded and followed Zabrina to the living room. She sat in the armchair, so he settled across from her on the sofa facing the front window, their distance adequate. A dollhouse, an easel, and a child's table and chair lined the far wall. Zabrina apologized for the mess, although the room was neat aside from the child's area.

"Homes with kids are equally theirs." Novak hoped that made sense.

This home's furnishings were high-quality leather and wood. The abstract paintings on the wall could be valuable art or kindergarten work, for all Novak knew about colours and swirls. Zabrina drew her legs up to the cushion of the broad chair and angled them in front of her, resting a hand on her thigh. Her mauve nail polish matched her sweater. Her dark hair, tied back, flowed down over her chest, where a pendant was nestled. Her shirt was unbuttoned to her cleavage line. The fact that he noticed could be a promising sign for him, albeit a distraction.

Novak recalled her second request and got to the point. "In all your times at Cycle Life, did you notice anything out of the ordinary?"

"I'm not there often, except recently, when it was a solution for Olivia's schooling," she said. "But no, all I saw was the usual bike store operation. It tends to be busy in spring, and more so this year with everyone wanting bikes."

"What about the other two stores?"

"They're closed. No people going in or out, no cars parked in front of them."

"Did you ever go into the basement?"

"No. Why would I?" Her arched eyebrows rose then lowered, perhaps as she remembered that the bodies had been found there. "I'm not sure I was aware there was a basement. Josh didn't use it for the store. Wait— I did shop at Furniture Sellers a couple of times, after we bought this place, and the salesman took me down to their basement showroom, where Kelsey was . . ." Her eyelashes, enhanced with mascara, flickered. "Why would she have been there? It bugs me that I can't think of a single reason. I thought I knew her pretty well. Josh said he knew the man in the other store, through Kelsey. Gabriel." Zabrina's smooth brow knit. "I hadn't met him, but Kelsey talked about him a little. I don't remember specifics."

They'd be hearsay, anyway. Novak had to steer the interview on track to respect her time limit. "When did you last see Kelsey?"

Zabrina's hand returned to her thigh. Her red lips pursed as she reflected. "Monday at the store, when I dropped Olivia off. Kelsey was in the office. We barely said hi. I was in a rush."

Novak believed that from Zabrina's whirlwind movements he'd seen in Cycle Life. "What was the last time before Monday?"

"Sunday morning," she said. "I had the day off and the store's closed on Sundays. Kelsey called and asked to drop by to chat. This wasn't something she often did, which made me wonder if she had something personal to discuss. She saw me as a big sister. When she arrived, I sent Olivia downstairs to watch TV so we could talk." Zabrina glanced beyond Novak at the dining area. "We sat at the table, and I angled myself so I could look out for Olivia coming upstairs. She tends to be nosey. After some chat about work and Olivia, Kelsey started talking about Connor, Gabe's brother. I haven't met Connor, either, but Kelsey mentioned him over the winter. He'd started hanging out with her and Gabe and had—it was obvious from Kelsey's descriptions—a crush on her. She was perky and cute. Certain guys go for that."

Zabrina lowered her legs to the floor and sat upright. Novak could go for her regal air if she weren't almost half his age and way out of his league. She was also so intimidating—or he was so rusty at this—that he'd forgotten to take notes or record the interview. Rather than call attention to his misstep, he'd scribble his recollections later in the car.

"Kelsey thought his feelings for her heated up after Gabe went missing," Zabrina continued. "She wondered if Connor used that as an excuse to call her. Oh." Her face lit. "I see. Gabe had moved into CounterTops' basement. Sunday morning, I got the impression Kelsey didn't know where he was. Connor kept pestering her to help him find Gabe. Well, *pestering* might be an unfair word. I'm sure Connor's worry for his brother was real as well as a ploy to get close to Kelsey. She told me that one night last week, she made the mistake of going to Connor's apartment. They got stoned and he tried to kiss her. He got angry when she turned him down." Zabrina placed both hands on her thighs and leaned forward. "I told Kelsey to watch out for him—try to cool it, hold back. She insisted he was harmless, that she could handle it. I went along, reluctantly, but later I thought, why did she go out of her way to talk to me on Sunday if it was nothing?"

Novak agreed it sounded like Kelsey had felt an urgent need to discuss a situation she feared might go sideways.

Zabrina returned to her upright position. "I work at Foothills Hospital, in emergency. Women come in all the time in bad shape. I learn to recognize the red flags." A beep sounded from her cardigan pocket. She took out her phone, looked at the screen, and frowned. "Josh will be here in five minutes. I told him to give me a heads-up twenty minutes before arriving. He never listens." She looked at Novak. "Do you have more questions?"

He'd got what he wanted—Zabrina's confirmation of her own and Olivia's reports to Isabelle. Which of his other questions was most important? "Did Kelsey have a boyfriend?"

"She broke up with the last one after Christmas." Zabrina rose from the chair. "A nice dude. I met him. Their breakup was amicable. Kelsey had no problems with him, aside from a lack of chemistry. If you give me your card, I'll email his contact details."

"I'd appreciate that." Novak rummaged for one in his suit pocket.

Zabrina was already easing him toward the entrance. "I'll also let you know if I think of something else, however irrelevant it seems. You detectives always say that." She smiled.

"I'm told your brother is RCMP."

"True, but I got that from TV shows."

Novak put on his coat and glanced down the hall toward the stairs leading to the basement. To overhear, Olivia must have tiptoed up and pressed against the wall. Easy to see Olivia being that sneaky.

Outdoors, Novak was pleased to find the snow had diminished to lightly falling flakes and the temperature had warmed up enough to start melting the ice on the sidewalk. When he was halfway down Zabrina's driveway, a blue Impreza Sport sedan pulled in and stopped beside him, Josh in the driver's seat. The back passenger door opened and Olivia leaped out. She dashed to the lawn, grabbed a handful of snow, and moulded it into a ball. Wet, heavy spring snow. Josh joined Novak on the driveway.

"Daddy, can we build a snowman?" Olivia asked.

"Ask your mother," Josh said.

Olivia threw the snowball at a poplar tree. Clumps of snow fell to the white yard. She tromped through snow to the front door. A normal kid.

"How's the case coming along?" Josh asked.

"Progressing." Presumably Zabrina had told Josh why Novak was here.

"You guys don't give anything away after you've swooped in and messed up our lives."

Wasn't it the bad guys who messed up people's lives? The cops' role was to return the world to normal, as best they could. Novak still believed that, more or less.

Josh glared. "Can you tell me when your tape will be down, so I can reopen my store?"

"No idea."

Novak sauntered to his car. Earlier this afternoon, he'd learned the tape would come down this evening, but he had no problem letting Josh stew.

* * *

Isabelle paced her office, looked out the window, paced again, looked. Herb would be here any second. She didn't want to be alone with him in the house and wished she'd phoned Erin to make sure she'd be home on time from work. Finally, the station wagon pulled into the driveway. Isabelle raced to meet her at the front door and rapidly explained that Herb wanted to tell her something that was probably dangerous. They walked up the stairs to the hall.

"Stay in your bedroom with the door closed," Isabelle said. "If you hear me scream or I text for help, call 911. Don't come out for any reason until I get you."

"This is nuts," Erin said. The doorbell rang, and both girls jumped.

"Go." Isabelle nudged her down the hall, watched her disappear into her bedroom at the far end, and trotted down the stairs as the bell rang again.

Herb stood on the front porch. "Is Olivia gone?"

Isabelle nodded and gulped. His pickup truck was parked on the street. He'd cut his long beard into a goatee, like the one in his picture on his actor website.

Yesterday, she'd told him he looked cooler with the goatee.

He glanced at the station wagon. "Who else is here?"

"No one," Isabelle said. "My roommates took our other car. They're working late today." She stepped back to let him enter.

He bustled up the stairs to the living room, leaving his jacket and shoes on, and sat on the chair with a view down the hall. She took the sofa facing him, reached into her pocket, and stroked her phone.

"I don't have long," Herb said. "Here's the deal. You listen to what I have to say, and no taking out your phone. If you so much as look at it, I'm out of here."

Isabelle drew her hand from her pocket and placed it on her shaking thigh. Salt sniffed Herb's work boots, reminding her of Zabrina's visit, which now seemed relaxed in comparison.

"I'm taking off," Herb continued. "They'll never find me. Before I go, I want someone to know the truth."

"Why me?" Isabelle squeaked. She pressed her thigh to stop the shaking.

Herb looked her up and down. "You're not establishment," he said. "I owe this much to old Clayton, to the store, and maybe to my better self." His hands dropped to his lap, fingers splayed. He leaned back in the chair. "It started about ten years ago."

Josh had crashed his bike, Herb explained. Bruises, sprains, a broken vertebra. After it healed, he still couldn't walk without excruciating pain. His doctor prescribed OxyContin. A few pills and his pain vanished. Josh called it a miracle. Whenever customers mentioned injuries—all the jocks had them—he raved about those little pills and gave them a few. He had some left in his bottle. One jock with chronic pain offered Josh money if he could get more— the jock's doctor had told him the pain was something he had to learn to live with. Josh told his own doctor the pain had flared up again to get more pills, which he sold to the jock for a wad of cash. Easy money. Josh hit upon the idea of getting prescriptions from other doctors. He knew the symptoms that would work and couldn't be disproved by objective tests.

Isabelle nodded. "It's the same for our whiplash and other soft tissue injury claims."

"I told you, no phone," Herb said.

She realized she was fumbling for her phone again.

Herb looked at the end table beside his chair. "Put it here, so I can stop you from grabbing it."

Isabelle stood and set her phone on the table, forcing herself not to look down the hall at Erin's room. She returned to the sofa.

Herb glanced at the phone, now inches from his arm. "That's safer."

Not for her. His narrowed eyes seemed to answer *Do you want to hear more or not?* She did, although she could guess where this was going, based the research she'd done online. Opioids were addictive and caused problems worse than the ones they solved. People got hooked. They gave surplus pills to friends, creating more addictions. Some people overdosed. Doctors got wise and stopped prescribing, but the people who were addicted still craved their fixes. Street drugs crept in to fill the void. Bad pills were out there now.

"I've read about the opioid crisis," she said.

"Cycle Life contributed. Insidiously." His face flushed. "I'm as guilty as Josh. I sold them to our customers complaining of pain." He unzipped his jacket, probably from the heat. "My cut paid off my gambling debts, but then I'd gamble my next profit from drug sales. A vicious circle. Eventually, I found a support group." He paused. "The bottom line for me is, I broke the law, but I don't want to do time for that now. I also won't cut a deal with the cops to rat out Josh. He's my friend. We've worked together on legit bike business for years."

"Is he still dealing drugs?"

Salt ran around the room and settled in the corner, chewing a rawhide bone. Isabelle was feeling less panicked—the conversation had shifted from scary to weirdly normal. The websites had said most opioid addicts were regular people—they could be anyone.

As the prescription drug supply shrivelled up, Herb said, ignoring her question, a bike supplier told Josh how to get powder shipped from China in bikes and parts. Josh bought a pill press, legally. Herb became the expert presser for their growing side business.

"I'm not proud of any of this," he said. "My gambling is no excuse."

A turning point came when a regular drug and bike customer died of an overdose in the store. Clayton Little, the store's founder, was semi-retired but came in part-time. Herb had assumed Clayton was unaware of the drug dealing, but his questions to Josh and Herb after the death hinted otherwise. Evidently, Clayton hadn't bought their lies because he later told Herb he called the police with an anonymous tip to delve into the death. Nothing came of it in the end, but it rattled Josh and Herb so much that they limited the store's drug activity to receiving supply and producing pills.

Herb looked down at his lap. "The boy who overdosed in the basement was our runner. He distributed the drugs to street dealers."

Isabelle started. "Gabe?"

"Like me, he did it to feed his addiction." Herb looked at his watch. "Shit. I have to speed this up. Kelsey got wind of something fishy from working on the accounts. She asked Josh about it, and then me, and was appalled by what we were doing. Up to then, she was coasting along, working casually in the business. This fueled her ambition to replace Josh, partly to clean things up."

Salt trotted over to Isabelle, the bone in his mouth. She yanked it out and threw it to dining area.

"I told Kelsey I agreed with her," Herb said. "By then I was cleaning up my gambling, but I also told her not to let Josh know I was on her side. Better I work undercover, secretly supporting her eventual takeover." He shrugged. "My reasoning was that the bike business was doing so well that we'd probably open a second store, and Josh would take the drug business with him. I'd stay with Kelsey and the drugs would be out of our hair." Herb touched the chair's armrests. "Look, I've got to go before the cops track me down. There's a detective I expect to come snooping at my place. I've been driving around the city to evade him. He won't find anything in my home. Josh hid it all."

"Where?"

"Safer for both of us not to know."

Isabelle shivered. "Do you think Josh killed Kelsey?"

"I don't know. He knew she opposed his drug trade." Herb pressed the armrests and pushed himself to his feet. "Would he kill her to preserve the business? You wouldn't believe the money drugs bring in, and the potential would be enormous, if we really got it going. Not me, though. I'm out of it. My truck's packed with all my basic needs. I've got places to go, to build a new life."

Isabelle stood and thought of movies she'd seen. "People get caught when they're on the run."

"Not if you create an effective persona."

"You're an actor."

"Amateur," he reminded her. "But it's taught me well."

She should try to thwart his plan if she could, but she too would hate the choice of going to jail for past misdeeds or turning on a friend.

Herb gazed past her, out the front window. "It might have been our drug runner who killed her when he was high."

"Why was Gabe in the basement?"

"Some stupid detox scheme, Kelsey said. I knew it wouldn't work but went along and helped by letting Gabe into the bathroom when she wasn't at the store." Herb moved to the top of the stairs and stopped. "I wondered about him on Tuesday, Kelsey's day off, when he didn't answer my text about using the john, but young guys can go hours without a piss."

As Isabelle followed him down the stairs, a thought occurred to her. "Did you tell Novak, the cop who interviewed us in the store, that Gabe was in the basement?"

"Of course not. Why raise too many questions?" He opened the door to a blast of cool air and turned to face her. "You're free to do whatever you want with this information. If it were me, I'd do nothing." After a nod goodbye, he jogged down the sidewalk, got into his truck, and drove away.

Isabelle darted down the hall, Salt behind her, and burst into Erin's bedroom.

Erin leaped off the bed. "What happened?"

They hugged and clutched each other. Salt wove around their legs like a rope as Isabelle babbled an explanation.

"Slow down," Erin said. "I don't understand. Let's talk over dinner."

Isabelle nodded. "I'm famished." She knew one thing for sure—unlike Herb, she couldn't do nothing.

* * *

At the team meeting, Mike listened to Furey's summary of their interviews with Connor earlier today. Nothing new so far for Mike, but there could always be a nuance or interpretation he'd missed at the time. Novak slunk into the meeting room and took the seat in the back corner, next to Mike.

No silent clue from Novak on the outcome of his interview with Zabrina. Mike hoped Novak had accomplished more with her than Mike had with Herb, who hadn't answered Mike's phone calls, emails, or texts. That wasn't suspicious necessarily—not everyone lived online—but Mike had a growing sense they'd missed a window to get Herb's version of happenings connected to Cycle Life.

Furey moved on to their second interview with Connor, which had been a slam-dunk situation. Connor had admitted to his obsession with Kelsey. He said he'd been less than up front about this before because it was embarrassing. Mike understood. Who'd want to discuss kissing a woman and being rebuffed, let alone telling cops who were waiting to twist every word you said?

Connor had stumbled through his explanation, which Furey now outlined fairly and accurately. When Gabe introduced Kelsey to his brother, Connor thought she was perfect—pretty, outgoing, athletic, and smart, with clear ambitions and a straight path to her goal of managing the bike store and ultimately acquiring full ownership. Her dream was realistic, since her grandfather wanted nothing more than to pass the store he'd founded down to his favourite grandchild. When Connor visited her home, it was obvious the granddad cherished Kelsey yet gave her independence. Kelsey's relatives were all loving and successful in their different professions.

"'My family is crap,'" Furey said, quoting Connor. "'Losers who only care about themselves and OD on drugs or pursue the addiction of their choice. I had a routine office job, which I lost with the pandemic. And my dream was fuzzy—to see the world and paint, and how many people make a living as artists? I wanted to *be* Kelsey.'" Connor's face had grown increasingly red. "'That's why I followed her around, came on to her, tried to impress her by going along with that bike store theft. But it fell apart Sunday night in the basement, when I saw she wasn't as smart or as perfect as I'd thought. Her stupid plan for weaning Gabe from drugs wasn't working. Even Gabe, the most transparent person in the world, had fooled her into thinking it was. How would she manage against the big guys like Josh? She was too full of herself to know he was playing her. It made me furious at her, and at me, for falling for her schtick.'" Furey looked up from his reading. "At this point, Connor balled his hand into a fist."

Had Connor been angry enough to kill? Not that night, but maybe the next one, if Connor had in fact reached Kelsey with his pleas to visit Gabe a second time, to apologize. Mike could see Kelsey eventually giving in, as she'd done on Sunday.

The Homicide team segued into the current prevailing theory, that Kelsey had taken Connor to the basement Monday night, likely with the goal of the brothers patching things up. But when Connor saw his brother dead, his anger erupted again. He blamed Kelsey for the stupid plan. To escape his wrath, she ran to the furnace room. Perhaps he blocked the stairs to Cycle Life—he was bigger than petite Kelsey. Or she beelined to Furniture Sellers' basement to seek refuge, knowing now that Dustin was upstairs and might come to her aid. Athletic and confident, she might have thought she could outrun stocky Connor. But he caught up with her in Gabe's sleeping area and grabbed a candlestick, as he'd done the night before. People tended to repeat actions. Instead of hurling it to the wall, he bashed Kelsey's head in.

Novak raised a hand. "Dustin claims he didn't hear all that commotion. Should we question him again?"

Shearer chortled. "My wife claims I wouldn't wake up if a truck roared through our bedroom."

"Dustin also says he didn't hear the argument Sunday night," Furey added. "So far we've located no witness who saw Connor, Kelsey, or anyone else enter Cycle Life Monday night. If they used the front door, Dustin states he wouldn't have seen them because he kept the storefront blinds closed and never went out to the street side of the building. A thought I had was to canvass Connor's neighbours in his apartment building to see if anyone saw him leaving or returning Monday night."

Shearer's face lit up. "Great idea. Why did no one think of that before?" He scanned the faces around the long table. "Volunteers?"

Furey and a couple of other guys offered. Mike asked if they'd gotten a warrant to search Josh's apartment.

"Might be time for that," Shearer said.

It was probably too late. Mike decided his next step would be to pay Herb a visit at his home. Novak took out his cell phone, perused the screen, and returned the phone to his pocket. After the meeting had droned to a close, Mike and Novak headed to the hallway.

"While we were in there," Novak said, "Isabelle sent a text. She wants to talk to me about Herb."

"What about him?"

"She didn't say."

"I'm going to his place right now," Mike said. "Are you up for another drive?"

"You drive this time. I'll call Isabelle on our way to Herb's."

Mike was almost certain the window with Herb was gone.

Chapter Twenty-Three

Paula loaded her groceries into the trunk of her car. While she was in the store, the snow had stopped falling and started turning to mush on the pavement. She decided to give Dustin a second try before going home. If he answered, her groceries would keep in the car's fridge-like temperature.

She drove to Connor's apartment building, parked on the street, and walked to the entrance. Like the previous times, a resident might let her in, but that wouldn't force Dustin to open his door. She pressed the intercom button. His voice crackled through the static.

"This is Paula Savard," she said, "the insurance adjuster."

He paused. "Right. You're driving Connor home." He buzzed her inside.

On her way to his unit, she remembered his insistence on indoor masking and put on her mask before knocking on his door. It opened slightly.

"Watch out for the cat," he said from inside. "It ran out when I went for my walk. I had to chase it down the hall."

The walk explained his absence when she'd come by an hour ago. She waited for him to open the door further then realized he wanted her to let herself in to avoid contact. She pushed the door enough for her to squeeze through and closed it behind her.

"Where's Connor?" Dustin said from the middle of the living room. He wore a mask, a shirt rolled up to his elbows, and shorts. Finnegan stood between them, her back arched.

"The police are keeping him longer."

"Why?"

She scanned the room, which looked as neat as it had before the police search. The two recliner chairs would be best for sitting, but she'd be too close for Dustin's seating comfort. "If we sit across the room, we won't need masks," she said. "I'll take the barstool and you can have the table chair." To prompt him, she climbed onto the barstool and set her purse on the kitchen counter.

He padded on bare feet to the chair at the far end of the room and sat. Both removed their masks. Finnegan leaped onto the recliner closest to Dustin and settled into a snooze.

"How are you and Finnegan getting along?" Paula asked, to ease into the main topic.

"We keep our social distance," Dustin said. "I feed her, and she stays out of my way." He rubbed his forearm. "Except when she scratched me after I grabbed her in the hall."

Paula supressed a smile and answered his earlier question. "The police are charging Connor with Kelsey's murder."

Dustin sat upright. "You're kidding. He didn't kill her."

"How do you know?"

He touched his mask, as though reflecting. One reason he'd know would be that he did it. He had opportunity and no alibi and had displayed some suspicious behaviours. She shouldn't let down her guard and was glad she had the seat nearest the apartment exit.

"You're right," he said. "I've known Connor less than two days. I'm not even sure I'd recognize him in the flesh. We only spoke through the wall between our cells. That was weird, talking to a disembodied voice. I first heard his voice when he talked to a guard in the hall, and I thought he was Gabe. This was before both of us knew Gabe was dead. I liked Gabe and Connor too, even though they're different."

Paula waited out his pause rather than disrupt his train of thought.

"Gabe was mellow," Dustin continued. "Connor could have a short fuse, I gathered from things Gabe told me and Connor said about himself. I guess he could have killed her in a crime of passion. Anyone could if the other person pushes him enough."

This made her wonder about Dustin's breakup with his wife. She glanced at the apartment door. Finnegan stirred on the recliner and resumed her nap. "Did Connor talk to you about his passion for Kelsey?"

"Not in so many words," Dustin said. "I read between his mopey lines. How long will the police keep him in custody?"

"Until Monday at least."

"I can't deny that's good for me. On my walk. I took phone numbers of apartments for rent. This neighbourhood's interesting, multicultural, and a short bus ride to my work when it eventually reopens. If a place is vacant, I could buy furniture from our store and arrange for a delivery truck on Monday."

This was ghoulish in light of the charges against Connor.

"Don't get me wrong." Dustin evidently caught her expression. "I don't wish Connor a murder rap. I really did try to help both brothers when the cops questioned me."

"Is that why you lied about not hearing sounds at night?"

"Who says I did?" His flush was obvious, even from this distance. "Supposing I lied, will I be charged? Shit. Now they'll drag me back to headquarters for more questions."

She didn't care about any of that. "Connor has told the police he was involved in an argument in Furniture Sellers' basement on Sunday night."

Dustin jerked upright again. "Did he?"

She nodded.

He rubbed his forearm. "I didn't know that. Who did he argue with?"

"What did you hear?"

"You're sure Connor admitted it?"

"Yes."

"Then what I say won't matter." He looked at Finnegan, who still slept on the recliner chair, purring in contentment. "Okay. Sunday night the voices woke me up. I looked at my bedside clock. It was about a quarter to midnight. Then, I heard a crash that sounded like a person or lamp or something heavy had fallen. I listened for more but heard nothing. I was scared in case it was an intruder other than Gabe. Then I thought, what if he's hurt? I forced myself downstairs and turned on the light. No one was there. Gabe's bed was rumpled, but I don't know how he usually left it. I figured Gabe and whoever was with him went back to his regular place, CounterTops. I meant to talk to him about that the next time I saw him. I was okay with Gabe sleeping there, but not with him bringing in other people."

On the recliner, Finnegan raised her head. Her ears twitched. A text notification pinged from the phone in Paula's purse. "What about the next night, Monday?"

"I swear I didn't hear a peep." Dustin stared directly at her. "It's odd, too, since I was awake half the night with shoulder pain. I couldn't get comfortable." He rolled his right shoulder. "I'd stopped taking the Oxy tablets, from fear I'd get addicted."

"Is that so?" Paula stared at him across the room.

He flushed. "I confess that after your detectives' visited me Tuesday morning I got fed up with the pain and popped one, my last, I swear. But it did the trick."

Finnegan leaped from the recliner. She scurried to the cat tree and scratched a tower.

"Assuming I didn't sleep through a second brawl," Dustin said, "what does that mean for Connor?"

"I don't know." Except that it was less likely he'd killed Kelsey in an impulsive burst of passion. Finnegan jumped up to the cat tree hammock bed.

"I could use a smoke after all this." Dustin stood and glanced at the patio door. "I only smoke outside, in fairness to Connor. He's been good about loaning me his place."

Paula couldn't think of anything else she'd come to ask him, and she wanted to read her text. "I'll leave right after I check my message." She took her phone from her purse.

The text was from Isabelle, asking if she could come over to talk tonight. Usually, she'd handle ordinary work or personal problems with a phone or video call or email.

Sure. 7:30?

Across the room, Dustin leaned over Finnegan and stroked her fur. Since he wasn't rushing out to smoke, Paula checked her email and discovered one from Josh. *Police say tape will be down in a few hours. I'll head to the store to find the receipts. Can you swing by first thing tomorrow morning, before business gets going?*

To assuage a nag of suspicion, she texted Mike to confirm Josh hadn't lied about the tape and replied to Josh. *Yes. Confirm they're ready tonight, along with your amended Statement of Claim.*

Isabelle's answer pinged. *Okay.*

* * *

At home, Paula found her mother in the kitchen making supper with Sam's father. Walter perched on a stool at the island, watching David chop vegetables for salad and Theda fry chicken on the stove. While Paula put the groceries away, her mother explained that David had called that morning to invite her for a visit. Walter had driven her there on his way to see his wife at the residence.

"She's still testing negative," Walter said. "We talked on our phones through her window. When I picked up Theda at David's, they'd come up with the plan of him coming here for dinner. I suggested he spend the night at my place. I'll drive him home tomorrow on my way to the wife's."

"Paula, you go wash up," Theda said. "We have dinner under control."

"Give Walter the task you'd planned for me." Paula flashed him a teasing smile. Sam would be impressed with her new ability to joke with Walter.

She went upstairs and changed into jeans and a T-shirt while wondering if crotchety, loner David and gregarious Walter would become friends. They were the same vintage, and both had working-class backgrounds. Stranger pairings had happened. A light subject to speculate on with Sam this weekend.

Downstairs, everyone served themselves salad and chicken and settled at the table, her mother to her left, Walter to Paula's right, in Sam's chair. She'd love to be joking with Sam at this moment. David sat at the far end, facing the kitchen area. He asked Paula what was new at work.

"Our junior adjuster is coming over at seven thirty tonight for a work-related matter." Paula hoped it was about work and not something more serious. Either way, she didn't want Walter and David listening in. "Mum, would you mind if we use the studio to talk?"

"Of course," her mother said. "It's Sam's."

"Might as well call it Theda's," David said, which launched Theda into a monologue about mask patterns, fabrics, and accessory materials.

Walter's and David's eyes glazed, to Paula's amusement. The three of them finished their meals well ahead of her mother.

Isabelle arrived as they were clearing the dinner table. She seemed less chatty than usual and had uncharacteristically turned down an interesting claim today. In case Isabelle had caught COVID, Paula ushered her quickly through the kitchen and away from the others. On their way past the fridge, Paula grabbed an opened bottle of wine, which she might appreciate after hearing Isabelle's news.

Outside, the lingering daylight startled her after months of dark evenings. Without an overcoat, she wasn't even chilled. Soon, buds would appear on her crab apple tree. A month from now, the tree would burst with white blooms.

They walked up to the studio in silence, another non-Isabelle trait. Paula set the wine on the kitchenette counter and cleared masks from the back of the futon so she could sit without wrinkling her mother's creations. Isabelle sat on the sewing machine chair. She wore leggings and knee-high boots. Her blonde hair flowed over her cut-off shirt. With no preamble, she began her tale about Cycle Life's drug involvement according to Herb. The news wasn't shocking, but the details were too real and close to Paula's heart. She shuddered to think of Erin on watch in her bedroom and was glad to be hearing this now, after the fact.

Isabelle paused for a few breaths. "Did you want some wine? I won't have any, to keep my head straight."

"Smart, when you'll be driving." But Paula could use some to relax her nerves. She rose, got a wine tumbler from the cupboard, and poured herself a glass then returned to the futon with the glass and bottle. "We can't be sure Herb's really gone. If he contacts you again, hang up and call me, or the police. Don't let him into your house." She pushed the mask material aside and set the bottle on the coffee table.

Isabelle chewed a strand of hair. "I don't know why Herb told me all this. Did he think I wouldn't tell anyone?"

"From what you said, he probably expected you would, but after he made his escape. He was up front about not wanting to go to jail or being the person who sends Josh there. At the same time, Herb feels guilty about his role in the drug business and wants to shut it down. I think he handed you that task." Now that she was thinking it through, Paula was fairly sure Herb would stay far away from her girls. "We have to tell Mike this."

Isabelle dropped her hair. "I already emailed Detective Novak and told him everything. He said thanks but didn't say what he'd do about it."

"He'd likely start by passing it along to Mike or the Homicide case lead."

"What about letting Olivia into my place? And Josh comes in to pick her up. He asked me to take her tomorrow." Isabelle touched her hair, as though she meant to nibble it again. "Did I tell you they hired me to be Olivia's homeschooler?"

"No."

"Is there pop in Sam's fridge?"

Paula let her stall so she could check her email. "Go look."

While Isabelle went to the kitchenette, Paula found emails from Mike, who confirmed the tape was down, and from Josh. *All systems go for tomorrow 9 am.*

Okay, she replied to Josh and answered Mike next. *What's the latest verdict on Connor? Isabelle filled me in on Herb's story.* Mike would question the latter if Novak hadn't shared the information with Homicide. Isabelle returned to her chair with a can of orange soda and described her new side job.

Paula finished her glass of wine. "Tell Josh and Zabrina you're not available to take Olivia tomorrow. You have to break with those people."

"What will they do about her school?"

"That's their problem."

Isabelle's chin trembled. "Josh can't look after her in the bike store. He won't even have help, with Herb split and Kelsey . . ." She didn't finish the sentence.

"Zabrina must have a neighbour or relative who can babysit," Paula said. "They aren't your friends. You don't owe them any favours." She stood, too quickly.

Lightheaded from one glass of wine? She steadied herself and carried the empty tumbler and bottle to the kitchenette.

Isabelle followed her. "What if Zabrina can't find someone last minute? They'll have to take her to the store. Two people died there."

And the place was involved with drug dealing.

"She's a kid." Isabelle crossed her arms. "I have to look after her, even if they don't."

Isabelle was right. Paula recalled the autumn she'd met Isabelle, and a similar night of revelation, which had included wine for them both. Isabelle had always been an odd mix of devious and childlike. Now here she was, less than four years later, acting responsibly.

Paula stared at her blue eyes. "When did you grow up?"

"Huh?" Isabelle's nose wrinkled. "I can't say no to Josh and Zabrina this time."

"No, you can't," Paula said. "And thanks for telling me all this."

"What will you do about it?"

Paula's cell phone pinged. She read Mike's text. *I'll fill you in tomorrow morning. Ten?* Perfect timing for her to get to Westwinds from the bike store.

"I'll settle Josh's claim," she said to Isabelle. "Then talk to Mike and take it from there. I'll let you know how it goes."

"Promise?"

She owed Isabelle that much, and Paula would want Isabelle's update on Olivia and her parents.

* * *

The next morning, Paula dressed in her most businesslike skirt and blouse and combed through her rack of scarves. Her hand paused on the butterfly scarf. Connor's fake vision that she'd save a life had proven tragically wrong.

Unless her role had been to draw Isabelle in to save Olivia.

Nonsense.

Still, the purple shades in the flowers and butterfly wings picked up the colours of her clothes, and it seemed appropriate to wear the scarf on the morning that might bring her work involvement in this case to a close. She draped it around her neck, tied a knot and fluffed it into a ruffle, and then put on her black blazer for a finishing touch.

Downstairs, she kept the breakfast conversation with her mother focused on spring plans for the backyard. She gladly delegated the gardening to her mother, who loved digging in the earth. It would also give Theda needed outdoor breaks from the studio.

Paula's drive to Cycle Life went quickly on the mostly car-free streets. Yesterday's ice and snow had melted or turned to slush. A cyclist riding a bike with thick tires made her wonder if Josh would brave a bike ride on today's roads.

He didn't, she discovered, when she arrived at Cycle Life at quarter to nine. There was no bike in the rack—the only vehicle in the lot was a Prius. She wouldn't have pegged Josh as the type to buy an expensive hybrid, but drug dealing was a lucrative side income. He'd have to spend the money on something.

The sign on the door said Open, but they might be able to conclude their business before the first customers arrived. She approached the entrance under a sky so clear and blue it was hard to imagine anything could go wrong. Still, it wouldn't hurt to give Mike a cue to send help if she didn't show up at ten.

She stopped in front of the store. As she took out her cell phone, she recalled her visit to Mike's office the previous day. He'd annoyed her, while Detective Novak had tipped her off about the case. She'd love to do her fellow maverick a favour and was tired of always running to Mike for help or to ask questions, which he only answered if police protocol allowed. Novak had treated her as his equal. She'd return his respect by trusting him to get the subtext of her message.

At Cycle Life now on business. Seeing Mike at ten.

The door opened to the sound of chimes. No Josh among the sparse display of bikes in the showroom. A woman emerged from the office at the back of the store. She halted and stared wide-eyed at Paula.

"You're Zabrina." Paula stopped a couple of metres away. "We met last week. I'm the insurance adjuster, here to settle Josh's claim."

Zabrina cocked her head, squinting. "I remember you now." She wore teal scrubs under a white cashmere sweater-coat, open at the front. "Is Josh expecting you?"

"Yes. He said he'd prepared the documents I need."

"They must be on his desk."

Hadn't Isabelle said Zabrina had to work this morning? Paula wouldn't bring Isabelle into this by asking. She followed Zabrina to the office. The stacks of boxes were gone. Evidently Josh had been busy cleaning up.

Zabrina rifled through papers. "Josh isn't the most organized person."

Those boxes would have contained bike accessories and parts with hiding places for powders. "During the past four days," Paula said, "he managed to uncrate and sort through dozens of boxes, despite the store closure."

"He had to do that with items flying off the shelves but doesn't know how he'll cope with delays in the supply chain."

"When's the next shipment?"

"That's Josh's business. Here it is." Zabrina picked up an envelope and read the writing on the front. "Paula Savard. Is that you?"

"Yes." If Herb was telling the truth, Josh had likely moved the drugs he'd uncrated quickly to dealers outside the store. A police search of the premises wouldn't turn up anything until the next supply arrived.

The door chimed someone into the store. Paula edged into the showroom, Zabrina behind her.

From the entrance, Josh stared across the showroom at Paula. "Did I leave the store open? I was sure I closed up last night." He looked past her. "Zab?"

Zabrina drew up beside Paula. "I came to talk about Olivia and let myself in."

Josh's eyebrows shot up. "Is something wrong with her? Couldn't Isabelle take her?"

"Olivia's there and it's all fine." Zabrina held up the envelope. "I found her insurance stuff. She can take it with her and contact you later with any problems." Zabrina thrust the envelope at Paula.

Josh nodded. "Everything should be there."

Paula opened the flap to check.

"I'm in a rush, Paula," Zabrina said, her tone sharp. "I have to get to work, and my daughter is more important than your insurance claim." She looked at Josh.

He cleared his throat. "Paula, if you don't mind leaving us to discuss this."

Clearly "discussing Olivia" was code for something else. They wanted Paula out of the way, which seemed the best reason not to leave.

"This will take a second." Paula pulled out some papers from the envelope. Receipts. She pretended to study them intently.

Zabrina touched her forearm. "Our problem with our daughter is highly personal. Please give us our privacy."

Paula stifled an urge to snap *Drop your phony plea.* She took a breath and looked up at Zabrina. "You can talk in the office. It will save me another trip to verify the documents here. I'll use the service counter if that's okay." Without waiting for a reply, she moved behind the counter, facing the bike accessories corner where they'd set up Olivia's table.

Paula slowly laid out the papers on the counter. Zabrina and Josh remained in place. Even with the office door closed, they'd know Paula might hear them from her current location, and if she were curious enough to eavesdrop, she'd move closer, toward the wall lined with helmets. They were waiting until she left, but she'd wait them out. Once customers arrived, their presence would protect her from whatever this pair was up to.

Josh scanned the showroom. "Where's Herb anyway? He should be here by now."

"Did you tell him the store reopened?" Zabrina said.

"Of course." Josh took out his phone. "I'll try him again."

Zabrina shoved her hands into the pockets of her pricey-looking sweater-coat. If Herb had lied to Isabelle, he'd split because he killed Kelsey. Suppose Kelsey had gone to CounterTops' basement Monday night or early Tuesday morning to check on Gabe and found him dead. Most people in that situation would either call emergency or a friend to help with the situation. Gabe's brother would have been her likely choice to call, but they had argued the evening before. It would have made sense for Kelsey to call Herb, her long-time colleague, who shared her opposition to the store being used to deal drugs.

"No answer." Josh returned his phone to his jacket pocket. His brow furrowed. "Herb was weird when we talked yesterday."

"Forget Herb," Zabrina said.

Dustin insisted he'd heard no noise downstairs the night Kelsey died. This jibed with Kelsey being there with a person she trusted, who'd bludgeoned her by surprise. Had she threatened to expose the drug dealing, prompting Herb to kill her out of loyalty to Josh? But why would Kelsey and Herb have gone to Gabe's sleeping area? To get his personal belongings?

These might include drugs that would point to the store's illegal activities.

"Weird in what way?" Paula asked Josh.

Zabrina shot her a glare. "If you're finished your insurance business, please leave."

"Something in Herb's voice," Josh said. "Like he was saying goodbye. Reminded me of Gabe's farewell message." He looked at Paula. "I told you about that yesterday."

Zabrina sniffed. "Then you don't need to repeat it now."

Paula realized she was fiddling with her scarf. They'd catch that nervous gesture. She dropped her hand and picked up a receipt. The paper shook so much she returned it to the table. The door chimed. A customer entered the store. She exhaled in relief.

"Send him away, Josh," Zabrina said. "We need to take care of this, and I have to get to work. This has dragged on long enough." She crossed her arms.

Josh went over to the customer and spoke in tones too low for Paula to hear. Zabrina tapped her boot on the floor and stared at Paula, clearly waiting for her to pack up and go. Paula resumed her pretense of checking the receipts. She longed to send a follow-up message to Novak or Mike, but it would make Zabrina suspect Paula was here for more than insurance. From the corner of her eye, Paula saw Josh guide the customer to the exit. The man left, and Josh pressed a button on the keypad beside the door. The Open light in the window went dark.

* * *

Novak's cell phone pinged. Isabelle had texted, *News on Herb?*

She'd shown remarkable restraint, for her, by waiting a whole night to follow up. She deserved a reply in thanks for her information, but Paula's ten o'clock arrival at Westwinds was approaching. Novak simply typed *No* instead of explaining that, as he and Mike had expected, they'd found no signs of life in Herb's house the previous night. His neighbours knew nothing of his plans to go away. In fact, they knew little about him except that he liked to tinker with his bike and, to the amazement of one man, he acted in amateur theatre. Most described him as a quiet loner. One joked, "Is he a serial killer?"

Later, at Westwinds, Mike's check of registries revealed that Herb's daughter owned his house. When Mike phoned her, she said Herb had transferred the home to her during the height of his gambling addiction so he wouldn't lose the place. She implied his gambling was still an issue between them and had caused the estrangement. She agreed to let them search the house and told them that her father used to hide a key under a flowerpot. Novak and Mike returned, found the key, and searched his sparsely furnished home. Their best clue to his whereabouts was a pile of books about the Klondike Gold Rush. They focused alerts to jurisdictions en route to the Yukon.

Novak looked out his window. The city skyline sparkled under blue sky, backdropped by a mountain panorama, Nose Hill off to the side. The highway overpass obstructing the scene made it less spectacular than the clear horizons viewed from his ranch, but if he had to be cooped up, this glass office was decent. He checked the time. Nine forty-five. If Paula wasn't here yet, he'd get Mike's take on her message. Novak left the fishbowl and found Mike talking on the phone in his cubicle. He waved Novak to the visitor's chair.

Mike hung up. "Good news. They picked up Herb in Red Deer."

An hour and a half north of Calgary. "He didn't get far."

"He stopped for dinner and got into an all-night poker game," Mike said. "An observant cop noticed the truck we'd described parked at the restaurant. Different licence plate, but they ran a check. Turns out, Herb swapped his current plate for one he'd kept from a previous vehicle. They're bringing him in now." His gaze strayed to his cubicle entrance.

Novak swivelled around toward Furey.

"Great work about Herb," Furey said. "Shearer's called a meeting in ten minutes."

"We'll be there," Mike said and Furey left.

Novak swivelled back. "I got a text from Paula about an hour ago. She was at Cycle Life, I presume for her insurance claim, and referred to meeting you at ten. There was no reason for her to contact me. Do you think she sent it to say that if she doesn't show up and you can't reach her, you should ride to the rescue?"

"Ten." Mike tapped his forehead. "In all this Herb mess, I forgot she was coming in."

Novak took out his cell phone. No new message from Paula. He sent a reply to her text, *Are you still on schedule?* If she didn't answer, he'd try an old-fashioned phone call.

"Herb's daughter's arranging for his lawyer," Mike said. "It will be hours before we get anything from him. Shearer's meeting will be a boring recap."

Novak nodded. "It won't hurt you to skip it and see what's up at Cycle Life. I'll note anything of interest at the meeting."

Mike stood, went to the coat rack, and got his gun holster. He turned to Novak. "You go. Paula texted you, for her own reasons." He set the holster on his desk. "On your way, keep an eye out for her driving to Westwinds. She's usually prompt."

Novak gulped. What if Paula was in trouble and he blew it? Her life was too important for him to handle this alone. "No time for me to book a cop car."

"Take mine," Mike said. "As long as you don't crash it." He put on his jacket, dug his car keys out of his pocket, and tossed the keys over his desk.

Novak stretched sideways and caught them. He looked at Mike's holster. "I'm not authorized to carry a gun."

"If you don't discharge the weapon, no one will know about this." Mike's jaw grew firm. "But if you have to shoot, do it."

Chapter Twenty-Four

Paula's phone rang in her purse. She glanced at her watch. Almost ten.

"Aren't you going to answer that?" Zabrina said.

"It's unimportant insurance business." The ringing died. Paula gathered the receipts from the counter and shuffled them into a different order, stalling. If Novak had understood her cue and the caller was him or Mike, her nonreply meant send help.

Zabrina moved farther away to check her phone while Josh tested the wheels on a couple of bikes, probably to appear cool about this waiting game. They seemed less at each other's throats than they'd been the first time Paula was here.

Paula's mind reeled with speculations. If Kelsey had found Gabe dead on Monday night, would she have called Josh for help despite her opposition to the store's drug trade? Josh was the manager, and he had a fondness for Gabe. Josh also had a motive to kill Kelsey. She was young, perhaps easily swayed. Had he convinced her they needed to confiscate the drugs in Gabe's sleeping area to protect the store's reputation—a store founded and still owned by her grandfather?

Zabrina returned her phone to the pocket of her sweater-coat, which must have cost hundreds of dollars, based on the quality. Her wardrobe and Prius seemed outside the range of a nurse and a store manager with a minority share in a modest bicycle business. But not outside the range of someone in the drug business.

"I told my boss I'd be late," Zabrina said. "The usual kid-problem excuse."

Josh took out his phone. "I'll try Herb again."

Why didn't Zabrina leave for work? Or circle the block in her Prius and come back to talk to Josh after Paula was gone? Was Zabrina worried that Josh would reveal too much? Through her hospital work, Zabrina would have access to prescription drugs. Josh might have started the store's slide into drug dealing by giving his surplus pills to customers, but if Zabrina had seen the opportunity of a ready market for drugs, she could have stolen them from her workplace. She seemed clever enough to accomplish this if she wanted.

"It's not like Herb." Josh put his phone away.

If Novak was on the verge of arriving, Paula could risk challenging Josh. She looked him in the eyes. "Herb's not as loyal as you think," she said. "Did you know he supported Kelsey's plan to eventually get rid of Cycle Life's drug-dealing business?"

Josh's mouth opened.

"Don't say anything, Josh," Zabrina snapped. "She'll twist what you say into lies."

"There's nothing to say," Josh told Paula. "I don't know what you're talking about."

Zabrina moved closer to Josh. Despite their marital separation, were they business partners? Kelsey's long-range plan had been to take over the store. She was Zabrina's friend, her confidant. Had Zabrina sussed her out under the guise of friendship—learned what Kelsey really thought about the drug business and whether she'd be willing to let it continue under Josh and Zabrina's wings?

Josh squinted at Paula. "What makes you say this about Herb?"

"Shut up, Josh," Zabrina said.

"The police told me." Paula kept her gaze on Josh, counting on his exaggerated belief in her police connections. "Herb confessed everything."

"There's nothing to confess," Zabrina said. "Josh, she's lying. Cops don't share information like that with nobodies like her. You know that from my brother."

"She's got an in with them," Josh said. "Something to do with her work." His eyes widened. "Are you wearing a wire?"

"No."

She wished she were, or that she'd set her phone to record. If she took it out now, they'd clam up. Or worse.

Zabrina scoffed. "She'd lie about that too." She pivoted toward Paula. "I'm pretty sure you're not wired, but shall I prove it by ripping off your bra?"

Paula forced herself not to turn away, but Zabrina's smirk suggested she'd guessed correctly. *No wire.*

Zabrina stepped to the counter. "Now that you've finally finished your work here, please leave so Josh and I can discuss more critical matters, like our child."

Josh shook his head. "I can't get over Herb."

"Get over him," Zabrina snapped. "Cops know confessions are false half the time. If Herb did this, he made up some story to save his hide."

"How is his hide on the line?" Josh asked.

"I don't know." Zabrina paused. Her eyebrows arched. "Maybe he killed Kelsey."

Josh's mouth dropped again. "Herb?"

"He's a big, strong man. She was a small woman."

"Yes," Josh said. "But why?"

"His gambling addiction." Zabrina shrugged. "It makes people do desperate things."

"He's off gambling," Josh said. "More or less."

"More on it than off from what I hear." Zabrina's fingers drummed the counter. "Let's say Kelsey finds Gabe dead in the basement. She calls Herb for help."

"How do you know that?" Josh asked.

"I don't," she said. "I'm thinking through the possibility."

So was Paula, but she was replacing Herb with Zabrina in the scenario. Kelsey finds Gabe and calls

Zabrina, her friend. Tells her Gabe overdosed, hours after the fight with his brother Sunday night. Zabrina knows there's strong evidence of Connor's obsession with Kelsey, who rejected his advances. She sees an opportunity to get rid of Kelsey, the opposition, and set up Connor as the killer. Zabrina says she'll come to the store. She puts on transparent hospital gloves, goes with Kelsey to CounterTops' basement, and suggests they check Gabe's sleeping area for evidence of drugs.

"Why wouldn't Herb have called 911?" Josh asked.

Because Zabrina wouldn't have wanted to call attention to the store's drug dealing.

The pieces were falling into place.

Zabrina continued tapping the table with her manicured nails. "For some reason, he didn't want to. Or Kelsey didn't want him to. He's not here and she's not alive to tell us, sadly."

Kelsey wouldn't have wanted her grandfather's store soiled by drug dealing, but why would she have gone to Zabrina for help, and not Josh or Herb? Perhaps she felt closer to Zabrina, or . . .

"Kelsey didn't want to end the drug business." Paula started at her own words.

Josh blanched. Zabrina stopped drumming.

Where was Novak?

What if Zabrina had sussed out Kelsey and discovered she dreamed of taking over both the store and the drug business? At the moment, Cycle Life's drug dealing was relatively small scale, but the opportunities for growth were enormous. Would Zabrina want to hand over control to Kelsey?

Paula braced her shoulders and turned to Josh. She couldn't back down when she'd come this far. "Zabrina drew Kelsey into a phony plan to oust you from the business. Josh, you were naïve to think the end result would be Kelsey getting this original store and you shifting the drugs to a second location. Zabrina wanted it all, the entire drug business. Gabe's death was her chance to eliminate Kelsey."

"What are you talking about?" Josh said.

Paula hoped her hunch about him was right and that he wasn't a cold-blooded killer. "Remember Gabe's message to you from beyond the grave." Paula couldn't see the relevance, but Josh might.

"She's trying to manipulate you, Josh," Zabrina said.

True, and Paula hated using Josh's beliefs against him. She retreated to the wall lined with bike helmets. If needed, she'd duck into the office and lock herself in rather than run past Zabrina and Josh to reach the front door. But did the office door have a lock? If it didn't, she was screwed. Josh strode toward Zabrina, who backed up and stopped beside Paula. The two of them faced Josh. Paula planted her shaking legs apart. Her elbow grazed Zabrina's.

"She's making this up," Zabrina said. "To get her friend Connor off the hook. I warned Kelsey he was dangerous, but she wouldn't listen. The obvious person she'd call when she found Gabe dead was his brother. When Connor saw him lying there, dead from an overdose, he went wild again, like the night before, and blamed Kelsey for his brother's death."

Paula looked at her. "How did you know about Connor and Gabe's fight?"

Zabrina's eyelashes flickered. She'd slipped.

"Kelsey told you when she called you for help Monday night," Paula said. "Did she also mention the candlestick?"

"Candlestick?" Josh's brow knit.

"In the basement." Paula's legs grew steadier, to her surprise. "Don't you see? Zabrina and Kelsey check Gabe's sleeping area for drugs, Zabrina sneaks up behind Kelsey, grabs a candlestick, knowing this will cast blame on Connor. She bashes Kelsey on the head." No noise for Dustin to hear. Zabrina cleans up all the drug evidence implicating Cycle Life and leaves.

"No," Josh said.

Zabrina stared at Paula. "What's that about a candlestick? It wasn't on the news. The cops definitely wouldn't share that detail with you. Josh, she got that from her friend Connor. That proves he did it."

Paula cursed herself for giving that away, and then remembered. "I found the body. I saw the weapon beside her."

Josh's eyes widened. "She's right. I was stupid not to see." He glared at Zabrina and lurched forward. "You killed Kelsey."

Zabrina yanked Paula's scarf, toppling her sideways and into Josh's path. Paula reeled backward as he tackled her, smashing her into the wall. Helmets crashed around Paula.

* * *

At the team meeting, Mike sat in his usual place these days at the far end of the room. Shearer pointed to the suspects' faces, pinned to the bulletin board, and explained what they already knew about each one. Herb had moved to the prime position, above Connor. Mike would choose either one over Josh to be the bad guy, for Paula's and Novak's safety. Novak could be arriving at Cycle Life now. From the minute Novak had strode out of the Homicide office, Mike had pondered why he'd handed his friend and mentor the potential rescue role. He concluded it was to give Novak the adrenalin rush. Mike would have many more. Homicide was who he was. It would take more than his recent slump to boot him out—such as Novak screwing up and needlessly firing on Josh.

Mike brushed that possibility from his mind to focus on what he might be able to do remotely. Novak's last text had stated that Paula hadn't answered his call and that he would check his phone again before entering Cycle Life. Mike pictured his most-recent visit there, under falling snow. Herb coming out of the store, turning to make sure the door was locked. *Shit.* What if

Josh had locked Paula in the store? The door code. Had Novak recorded it in his report when he questioned the staff, or was it somewhere else in the file? Novak might find it on his phone, but not quickly enough. Mike took out his phone and scrolled through the reports on the case.

"Vincelli," Shearer said. "What's your take on that?"

Mike glanced up. "Tell you later. Got something important."

"What?"

"Move on. It's in the works—not ready yet."

There it is. Mike copied the numbers into a text message and sent it to Novak. Had any cops advised Josh to change the door codes after the break and enter and two suspicious deaths in the building? If so, Mike hoped Josh hadn't gotten around to it.

* * *

Crumpled on the floor, Paula rubbed the small of her back, which throbbed. Josh had rammed her into a helmet on the wall. He remained in his landing position on his hands and knees, his back arched.

Zabrina stood in the corner and stared down at them both. "Smart, Josh." Her voice oozed sarcasm. "Attacking Paula will really help your credibility."

Paula looked up at her. "Are you planning to pin this on him now, instead of Connor or Herb?" She was foolish to provoke her, but Zabrina would damage her own credibility if she retaliated.

The entrance door chimed, and Detective Novak burst in. Tension drained from Paula's body. She slowly rose to her feet.

Novak ran toward them. "What's going on?"

"Handcuff them both," Paula sputtered.

"That's ridiculous." Zabrina crossed her arms. "I have nothing to do with this store."

Josh rocked back to a squat and stared at the wall, which formerly held helmets lined up in neat rows. "It's over," he said. "The store, the business." He looked up at Zabrina. "What will happen to Olivia?"

A good and terrible question. Both her parents would be in jail.

Paula touched her scarf, now draped loosely over her shoulders. She lifted the longer tail to peer at the butterflies and flowers that had brought her to this unexpected place.

Novak phoned for backup and removed the handcuffs from his holster.

"See," Josh said to Zabrina. "I told you she has an in with the police."

"Shut up, Josh," Zabrina said, but she lowered her arms and placed them behind her back, perhaps to show her cooperation.

"Save your statements for police headquarters," Novak said.

They'd want Paula's statement too. The police would take hours to process them all. All she wanted was to hop on a plane to Sam's arms, but that wasn't possible.

Zabrina and Josh remained silent while they waited for the backup to arrive, him beside the service counter, her in the corner once occupied by Olivia's table. Paula asked Novak if she could drive herself to Westwinds.

"If you feel up to it," he said.

"I will in ten minutes or so." She rubbed the small of her back. "So much for avoiding adventure."

"Me too," he said. "Cold case work is supposed to be boring."

"Do you hear that?" Josh called across the room to Zabrina. "She's with them."

Zabrina glared at him.

Paula was glad she could finally ignore them. She turned to Novak. "Do you mind if I Skype with Sam before going into Westwinds? I'll keep it short."

"No problem," he said. "Police bureaucracy will wait for you."

Outside, the day had warmed up enough for her to open her car window. Fresh air boosted her mood on the drive to Westwinds' parking lot. She set her phone on the dash mount and Skyped Sam. When his face appeared, she took a moment to relish its comfort and unloaded her summary of events, her voice growing shaky. Sam's frown deepened as she neared the conclusion.

"I was more scared than I'd thought," she rasped.

"Who wouldn't be?" he said. "What's the saying?" He paused. "The brave recognize fear, but face it down and move forward. Something like that."

His words warmed her even though she was still too shaken to grasp their meaning.

"I hate that we're stuck across the ocean from each other," Sam said. "It's looking more and more likely that neither of us will be able to travel before fall."

"We'll make it work," she said, and chose to believe it. "Is there a quote about placing a little faith in the unknown?"

He smiled. "I'll search for one tonight."

* * *

In her home office, Isabelle listened as Paula detailed her experience at Cycle Life the previous day. Their boss Nils watched with equal awe on the RingCentral split screen.

Paula wrapped up. "Afterwards, at Westwinds, I talked with Novak and Mike. We agree Kelsey probably participated in the drug business as much as Josh and Herb. She looked after the accounts, which kept a record of shipments. When they check Cycle Life's computer, the police suspect they'll find codes indicating where suppliers hid drugs in bicycles and parts. Easy to do with small—but valuable—quantities of powder."

Isabelle swivelled in her chair. "Herb didn't seem to know Zabrina was involved."

Paula nodded. "Novak called her 'the brains of the operation.' Clever of her to learn about Kelsey's ambition during her big-sisterly chats—and, conveniently, about Connor's obsession with Kelsey. Novak's convinced she anticipated that Olivia would eavesdrop and tell someone what she heard. Zabrina would know about her daughter's inclination to be nosey and talkative."

"And about Olivia's hearing superpower," Isabelle said. It might actually be real.

"The police confirmed that Zabrina worked the night shift Monday," Paula continued. "Olivia would have been sleeping at Josh's. Zabrina left work shortly after eleven, claiming illness. When Kelsey called Zabrina, frantic over Gabe's overdose following his argument with his brother, Zabrina seized her chance to frame Connor. Her added touch was to use an object he'd thrown in anger as the murder weapon. At least, that's the main theory Homicide's floating now."

"The best news from all of this," Nils said, "is that Connor has been released."

Paula beamed. "I was so glad to drive him home yesterday. From our insurance perspective, Josh's receipts match the Robbery unit's complete list of items recovered in Kelsey's grandfather's garage. Cycle Life's sole damage is the broken window. I expect they'll withdraw that small claim, and we'll close the file with no payment."

"The insurance company will be happy." Nils stroked his chin. "I still doubt our little firm will survive the pandemic, but I trust you two will land on your feet."

Isabelle glanced at the time on her computer. "I have to go and pick Connor up. Since Erin and the guys have to work this morning, he's coming with me to say goodbye to Olivia. I really wanted to homeschool her, but it's right for Zabrina's brother to take her." Isabelle swallowed a lump in her throat.

"Detective Novak owns a ranch near where the brother lives," Paula explained to Nils.

"Small world," Nils said. "Paula, about that new whiplash claim . . ."

Isabelle left them to their business talk and drove to Connor's apartment. He met her at the front entrance dressed in a T-shirt and shorts. Today was sunny and warmer, but she was glad for her light sweater.

"It's weird going to Zabrina's house after what she did to Kelsey," Connor said, as they walked to the car. "My fantasy for Kelsey ended in those store basements, when she took me to see Gabe." He grimaced. "But I hate what happened to her."

"Obviously," Isabelle said. "How are Dustin and Finnegan making out?"

"They're warily becoming friends," Connor said. "Dustin moving in with me will help with rent."

"It's good to have roommates."

"He's okay company," Connor said. "Dustin tried to help me and Gabe. Plus, he's not messy and won't bring in friends to hang out. I also laid down the law with him on drugs."

Isabelle had laid down the law with Habib—no more "babe." She was serious about it this time. He'd promised to do his best to break the habit.

She and Connor got into the car and headed out of the neighbourhood.

"Dustin can also look after Finnegan and the apartment when I can travel again," Connor said. "Meanwhile, I want to get back to painting. I have lots of ideas churning."

Isabelle took that as the best sign her friend would work through his brother's death.

The GPS led them to Zabrina's two-storey home. A new-model pickup was parked in her driveway. Her brother met them at the door and introduced himself. Adam wore jeans and a western shirt, not his RCMP uniform. He gestured them to the living room, where Olivia stood at the easel. She didn't look at them.

Isabelle padded over the Oriental carpet and stopped by the easel. "Connor's an artist too. He can teach you all kinds of crafts."

Olivia swished her brush on her pie-tin paint palette. She slashed a brown streak across the paper. "I'm moving far away."

"Only an hour by car," Isabelle said. "Connor and I will drive there to see you."

"No you won't." Olivia slapped her brush on the palate so hard that droplets sprayed onto Isabelle's nose.

She didn't wipe them off. "I promise."

"We'll look after her." Adam squatted beside Olivia. "You'll have your cousins to play with, and our dog and horse, and lots of land for running around. Your cousins have tons of toys to share with you, and we'll bring all of yours in the truck. I'm also thinking we need a new puppy."

"A puppy?" Olivia's gaze darted to him and then back to her easel.

Isabelle crouched beside them both. "Can I learn to ride with you?"

"You bet," Adam said.

He was tall and dark like Zabrina, but Isabelle thought he seemed nicer than his sister, sort of like a younger Detective Novak. She hugged Olivia goodbye, and the child's stiff body softened. At the front door, Isabelle told Adam she'd be in touch about visiting his acreage next Saturday.

As she and Connor trotted down the stairs to the sidewalk, Connor asked, "Why did you promise I'd do stuff with her?"

"You've got lots of time on your hands," she said. "Maybe Detective Novak will let us stay overnight at his ranch. That would be cool to hang out. I'll message him."

* * *

337

Novak strolled with Mike across the ranch, the sky a blaze of blue overhead. Puffy clouds dotted the horizon. Most of the snow was gone, and the earth was moist. It would be time to plant grasses for hay once the risk of frost was gone. Novak would pitch in and supervise the work. A month ago, who'd have believed he'd be capable? They stopped next to Mike's car.

"Hard to leave this rural idyll for work," Mike said.

"I'll join you later." Novak would detour to Canmore to update Farida Bashar on what had happened. The resolution was overdue, but it might make a tiny difference in her life. "You'll appreciate not having me as a burden anymore."

"It was no problem."

"Yes, it was," Novak said. "You're sure you won't mind me spending a couple of nights a week in your apartment?"

"It'll be a challenge." Mike's lip twitched. "But not as much as making a case against Zabrina."

Novak nodded. "She's one cool cat." On the drive to the ranch, both had predicted Zabrina would never confess, would try to throw Josh under the bus, and, with her lawyer's help, would further muddy the waters of reasonable doubt with allegations against Connor and Herb. Homicide was in for a pile of work to make the evidence stick. Novak was eager to be part of that action for three days a week.

After Mike drove off, Novak ambled to his pickup truck, which was parked in front of the house that he and Christine had built. Before getting in, he checked his phone. There was an email from Isabelle—could she and Connor spend the night at his ranch when they visited Olivia? That was forward of Isabelle, but he rather liked forward women. Too bad Zabrina was a killer. He should be forward himself and take some steps, like plugging in to the local community. Church had been Christine's thing, but there were probably events at the local legion he'd enjoy. Or maybe he'd find a group of retired cops who got together to drink and complain about the modern world. And these hilly country roads, with beautiful views and little traffic, would be perfect for an e-bike. He might check them out at Cycle Life, if it got back in business under new ownership or management.

Novak replied to Isabelle, *Glad to have you anytime.*

Then he looked at the house he'd shared with his wife. *Not bad, Christine, an old coot like me, having all these plans.*

* * *

Mike spotted Megan and Furey at the coffee centre, absorbed in their conversation. They probably wouldn't notice Mike if he slipped passed, but sooner or later he'd have to deal with their in-his-face involvement. Might as well start now.

Furey grinned at him. "We were just talking about the super job your friend Paula did. And what a rush for me to help bring home a homicide case. To think I had doubts about transferring from traffic." He raised his mug in a salute. "I've got to run. Shearer wants me for something or other."

Mike watched him saunter down the hall. "Nice guy, if a bit chatty for me."

"Could be why he isn't my type."

Mike gaped at Megan. "Oh? He's not?"

She tucked her cropped hair behind an ear.

"Oh." Mike felt his face flush. He'd missed his first chance with her by not asking her out. It wasn't often you got a redo. But this could be awkward with Furey and a mess at work if Mike's and Megan's involvement went south. *Start with a tentative step.* "I'm planning to dust off my bike this weekend," Mike said. "Do you like cycling?" *Dust off?* She'd think he was Novak's age.

"I love it," she said.

"Have you biked the canal path to Chestermere Lake?"

"Not since January or so."

"You ride in winter?"

"When it's not miserable."

He only biked when it was warm and the streets were clear. Keeping up with her would be a challenge in many ways. He liked that.

* * *

Paula left her mother in the studio happily making masks and mulling over plans for the garden. On her way to the house, a text arrived from Mike. *Okay if I stop by your office to touch base on my way home? Case moving along but no real updates.*

She'd done enough updating of her own today during her three-hour Skype lunch with Sam. Already, the mid-afternoon sun was high in the sky.

Upstairs, she put on capris and a yellow cotton top to suit the warm afternoon. She dressed it up with the silk scarf her mother had ordered for her birthday gift, a print of a fairy-tale German town. It would be a long while before she'd wear the butterflies and flowers scarf, which the police had taken as evidence.

Paula slipped on her sandals and set off down the street, waving to Walter on his front porch. His wife was still COVID free and locked down in her residence. Paula continued under blue sky to the railroad tracks and glanced at the entrance to the Elbow River Pathway. Callie's death there had launched Paula's involvement with Homicide. She'd like to think that her new friend Connor's case had ended it, but why close the door before she knew what was coming next? As Sam and her mother had both said, "Take each case as it comes and don't worry about us."

She let herself into her office building and walked up the staircase. Footsteps thudded above her. She picked up speed and recognized Valeria's waist-length braid bobbing on the back of her orange-and-red dress.

340

Paula caught up with her at the landing. "You're here on a Saturday?"

Valeria raised her right arm. She wore a cast from her hand to her elbow. "I'm making up for two days of missed work. I stupidly fell chasing my kids around the house and broke my wrist. Spent Wednesday night in emergency."

"But you came in Thursday," Paula said. "You met my visitor on the stairs." That was the day Josh had been here, fishing for information.

"Sorry, in all the confusion, I forgot to reply to your text. No, I don't know of anyone else working in the building. And I spent Thursday vegging on the sofa, cursing myself for always being a klutz."

Paula studied her, from frizzy bangs to running shoes. Josh had described the woman he'd met as cute and sporty. Valeria might be attractive, but "klutz" didn't suggest athleticism. "Then who did my visitor meet?"

Valeria tittered. "Maybe our resident ghost?"

Paula got a chill. Josh had said the woman on the stairs reminded him of his dead sister. *People see what they want.* Had he met a spectral projection of her . . . or Kelsey?

"Come to think of it," Valeria said, "Wednesday, I crossed paths with a tall man. We didn't speak. I assumed he was on his way up to see you."

That would have been Mike. "He'll be here again any minute."

Valeria's face lit up. "That explains why you're here on this gorgeous weekend. I couldn't resist going out for a walk."

The doorbell sounded from Paula's office. She excused herself to let Mike in and returned to find Valeria still on the landing.

"They say this COVID wave has peaked," Valeria said. "When the restaurants reopen, do you want to meet for coffee or lunch on a patio?"

"Sure," Paula said. She could use another new friend, one closer to her age than Connor, and she'd like to probe Valeria more about this "resident ghost."

Valeria left as the top of Mike's head appeared above the railing. Paula ushered him into the office with a sense of déjà vu. He'd visited around this time nine days ago, although more daylight hours and today's sunny weather made the office brighter. Mike accepted her offer of coffee, and they settled at the mahogany table, across from each other, in their usual places.

Mike explained that preparations for the court hearings were going as expected. Herb was talking in exchange for reduced charges; Zabrina and Josh were silent, on their lawyers' advice. "We're glad to get this midlevel drug supplier trio, rather than people like Gabe who street-deal to support their habit." Mike sipped his coffee. "So, do I owe you my firstborn child as payback for dragging you into the case?"

"We're good." Paula smiled. "It was worth it for Connor. As for the next time . . ."

Mike peered over his mug.

"I'm in, if it's right," she said. "But don't make it too often."

"Deal." He took another sip. "I'd like to stay but also want to get home. There won't be many more chances for a family dinner while I'm still living there."

"That reminds me—Mum wants to have you and Novak over for a barbecue one day when we can sit outside."

"Sounds great. Can I bring a friend?"

Paula detected a faint blush on his cheek. "Of course." That would make the barbecue more interesting.

"So did the storm produce enough car crashes for your bread-and-butter claims?" he said, perhaps to shift the subject away from himself.

"Sadly not," she joked. "My project for the rest of this spring will be to figure out what I'll do if the company folds and decide how much time I want to spend overseas with Sam."

"You could do a lot of work remotely, including some civilian jobs for the police." Mike's lip twitched. "One I have in mind could drag you into trouble again."

That too could make life more interesting.

The End

Susan Calder books also published by BWL Publishing Inc.

Paula Savard Mysteries

A Deadly Fall - 1
Ten Days in Summer - 2
Winter's Rage - 3

To Catch a Fox

Susan Calder is a Calgary writer who grew up in Montreal. *Spring Into Danger* is her fifth novel and the fourth book in her Paula Savard Mystery series. Susan's short stories and poems have won contests and appeared in numerous magazines and anthologies. She has worked as an insurance claims examiner and served on the boards of the Alexandra Writers' Centre Society, Crime Writers of Canada, and When Words Collide Festival for Readers and Writers. Susan is a co-chair for Bouchercon World Mystery Convention, Calgary 2026.

Website: www.susancalder.com
Facebook: Susan Calder Author
Twitter: @Susan_Calder
BWL Author Page: Calder, Susan - BWL Publishing Inc. (bookswelove.net)